THE UNKNOWN DAEMON

OMNIS BOOK TWO

M.M. PARKS

Book Cover by Samantha Sanderson-Marshall

Edited by Jessica McKelden

CONTENTS

AUTHOR'S NOTE

This book is intended for adults only, and contains subject matter that may be difficult or disturbing for some readers. Sensitive material includes, but is not limited to: profanity, animal death in childbirth, animal stillbirth, violence, explicit sexual content (including Dom/sub dynamics), death, grief/loss, emotional abuse from a parent, drug use, and pregnancy.

Reader discretion is advised.

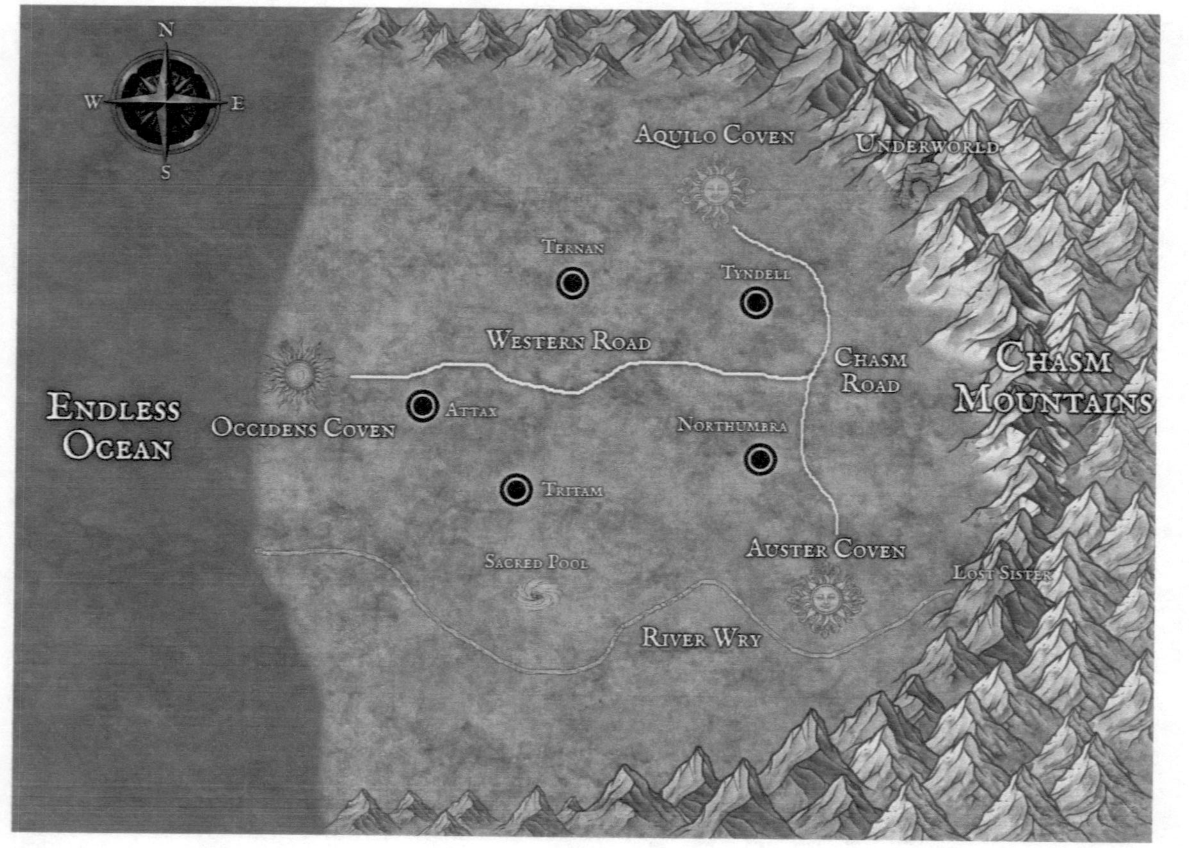

ENDLESS OCEAN
AQUILO COVEN
UNDERWORLD
CHASM MOUNTAINS
TERNAN
TYNDELL
WESTERN ROAD
CHASM ROAD
OCCIDENS COVEN
ATTAX
NORTHUMBRA
TRITAM
AUSTER COVEN
SACRED POOL
LOST SISTER
RIVER WRY
N
E
S
W

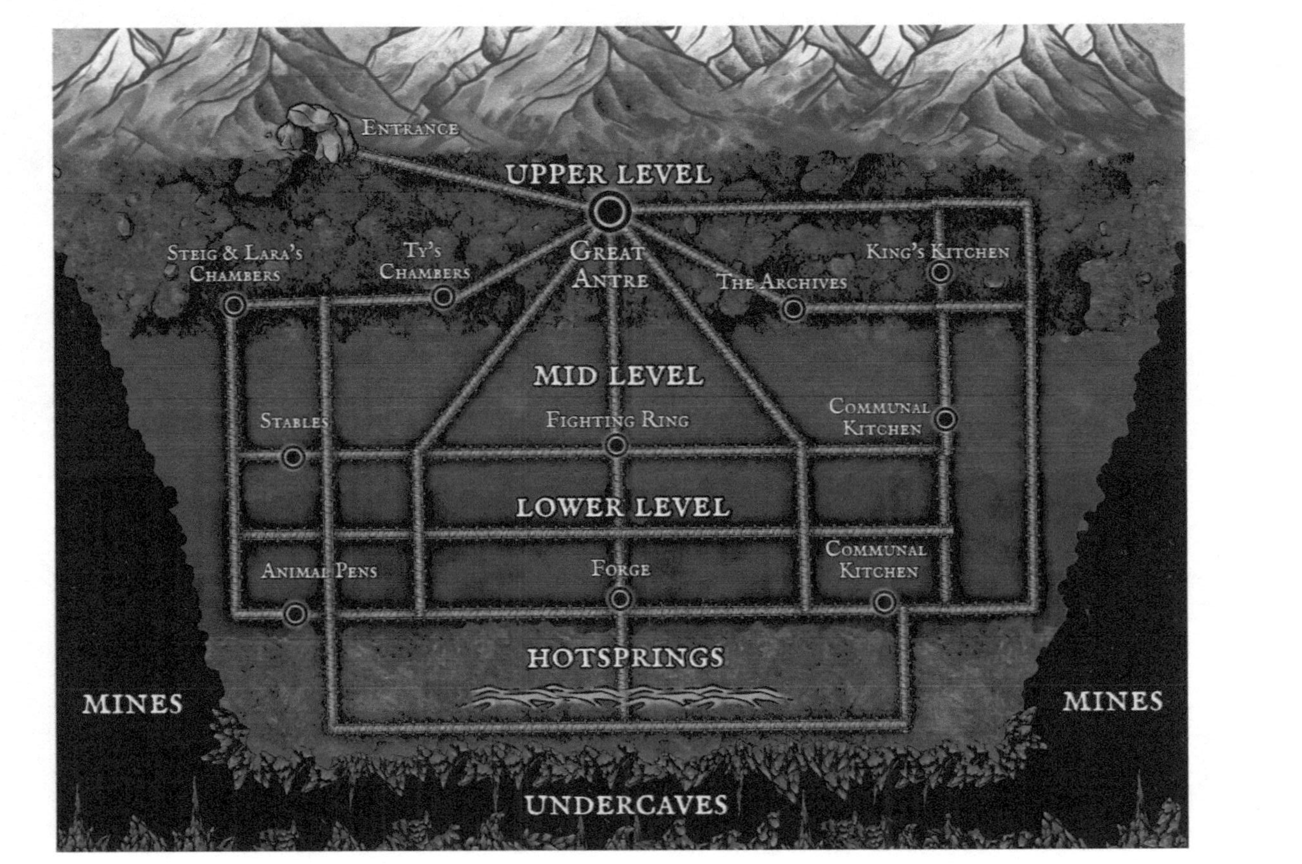

Entrance
UPPER LEVEL
Steig & Lara's Chambers
Ty's Chambers
Great Antre
The Archives
King's Kitchen
MID LEVEL
Stables
Fighting Ring
Communal Kitchen
LOWER LEVEL
Animal Pens
Forge
Communal Kitchen
HOTSPRINGS
MINES
MINES
UNDERCAVES

To all those who feel torn between their past and their future.
It is time to embrace the unknown.

PROLOGUE

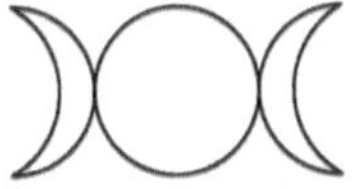

Mel

IT WAS A TRICKY thing, being in so many places and times at once. One minute, Mel was picking up a shell on the beach—it was pink with deep, rough ridges and they wanted to take it home for their collection—and the next, they were in the past, watching three people they had never seen before climb a jagged, snow-covered mountain. At least, Mel thought it was the past, but truly, they had no idea.

Mel scrambled to take in the scene as it flashed behind their eyes. The people were men—at least, Mel assumed they were, based on what features they could see under their fur-lined hoods—but they didn't look like any men Mel recognized. All three of them had strangely pale skin and eyes that were as dark as night.

Mel watched as the men struggled in the deep snow, their faces strained and pinched with concern. Why was Mel seeing this?

That was the problem with visions. They came and went with no explanation of their significance. Mel worked hard to interpret their importance to Gaia, but they swore, sometimes, the visions seemed to hold absolutely no significance at all.

Like the time Mel was sitting at the kitchen table, eating some freshly baked bread, and suddenly they were inside a pitch-black, snow-covered forest watching a woman they vaguely recognized from their childhood debating what to cook for dinner with several of the strange-looking pale people. One of the pale people, a woman, was skinning a felled deer on the ground as she spoke, and Mel remembered vividly how entranced the woman had seemed as she watched the blood spilling into the surrounding snow. Other than that, it was a seemingly innocuous vision, and Mel wasn't entirely sure why Gaia would need them to Know this.

But Mel was used to it at this point. They'd been a seer for the last eight years, since their Summoning at age twenty-seven. At first, they had been grateful when they received their Gift of *omen*. Seers were extremely rare among the three Covens, and there hadn't been one in Occidens in over a century. Thus, their position was a highly coveted and influential one, and for that they were grateful.

But they quickly learned it wasn't quite the blessing they'd thought. Due to the nature of their Gift, they didn't always have the capacity to take part in daily life, so they often found themselves outside of it. Always watching, always waiting for the next vision. Trying to figure out what came next, or what had already come—Mel often got those two confused.

They mostly spent their days by themself, trying to make it through the necessary activities of living—eating breakfast, bathing, dressing, cleaning up. But it often took them twice as long as anyone else to do those things. They were grateful Syrelle, their matriarch, and the rest of the Coven provided for them as best they could, because when Mel received four to five visions a day, the images always yanking their mind to and fro, it often became hard to keep track of their day-to-day needs.

The Coven had been on edge lately, though, ever since the escape of the daemon and the Auster witch, and Mel had become a bit neglected. Their laundry was piling up and there were dishes in the sink that needed washing. But Mel didn't blame Syrelle or the others. It was an extremely irregular time.

It was only a couple nights after the witch and daemon had fled, when Mel was sitting in their favorite green upholstered chair, knitting a new shawl and drinking some chamomile tea, that they heard a knock on the door.

"Come in," they called. It was just a formality, of course. There was only ever one person who came to visit them this time of night.

Syrelle walked in the door, her hawkish hazel eyes landing on Mel instantly as a motherly smile crossed her face. Her dark-blonde hair was piled high on her head, as usual, though her eyes looked more tired than they normally did. Though Mel supposed that was to be expected.

"Mel, how are you?" Syrelle greeted warmly.

"Oh, you know, here and there," Mel replied, mustering a smile in return.

"I'm sorry I haven't been over the last few days. I assume you've heard about the Auster witch and the daemon who escaped?"

"Yes, Cara came to do my washing yesterday and updated me," they replied. Syrelle's daughter often came to assist them when Syrelle herself didn't have the time. She was a sweet child. She always stayed to chat with Mel afterwards, and she was a pretty good conversationalist, for a teenager.

"Well, I hate to get right to the point, but I need to know if you've seen anything regarding the Auster witches, or any more about the amulet. We're holding the Auster matriarch and the escaped witch's sister here until we're confident they had nothing to do with it, but I'm not sure what else to do," she said, wringing her hands together in that anxious way she often did when she felt the pressure of her position too keenly.

"What does your Knowing tell you?" Mel asked her.

Syrelle arched her eyebrow at them. She was about ten years Mel's senior, but the two of them had developed a friendship over the years—ever since Mel received their Gift and Syrelle ascended as the Coven matriarch. Syrelle relied on Mel's counsel, and Mel, in turn, relied on Syrelle's kindness.

"My Knowing tells me they're concerned about her—the witch who escaped—and that they don't trust the daemon who took her, but beyond that, I'm not sure. They've sworn they had no knowledge of the daemons' plans for the amulet, but it's hard to Know if they're lying. Fear for the witch is overwhelming any of their other signs," Syrelle added, not unkindly.

Syrelle was a cautious woman, and Mel knew she likely did not want to escalate the enmity between the Covens unless necessary. It was bad enough that the sister of the future Auster matriarch had been captured and held prisoner. Even though that move had been more than warranted, the smart thing to do would be to choose peace, because if they didn't, they both knew it would be far too easy for the other two Covens to pull their weight once more and force Occidens' hand, pushing them from their territory...or worse.

But luckily, Mel had seen the future, and they could help Syrelle in this.

"I have seen her, the witch who escaped. She will re-unite with the amulet," Mel stated simply. They'd seen the two escapees together, actually, though it was rare for Mel to see a daemon in their visions. They supposed this was an extension of the fact that witch magic did not work on daemons, and vice versa, thus they likely only saw the daemon because of his association with a witch. Either way, Mel had seen the witch holding the amulet, surrounded by the daemon as he'd been described, as well as two others who must have been his companions. Mel remembered the way the purple amethyst had glinted in the firelight that was lighting whatever dark cave the four of them were in, and more than that, Mel Knew the witch's intentions. She wanted to break its spell.

"But I haven't seen any other Auster witches involved. Just her, the witch who was here, and the daemons," Mel finished.

"I see." Syrelle nodded, taking in this information. "And what of the amulet? Will it be returned to us?" she asked, her eyes filled with bleak hope.

Mel was silent. They hated having to be the one to deliver bad news, especially to those they loved. But Syrelle knew better than most that to resist the future was futile, so Mel simply shook their head.

Syrelle sighed. "I suppose I have little choice but to let the Auster witches go then, on the condition that they help apprehend the daemon and the witch if given the opportunity."

No argument, no demand for more details. Syrelle always took Mel's word on these types of things, and it was something Mel appreciated. Because Mel didn't exactly know how to explain *why* they thought the amulet wouldn't be returned to Occidens. They just Knew that the amulet was powerful. Too powerful. That's why Occidens had kept it hidden all these years after all—to keep it from the others. To keep it from being used again. Mel had seen all that, of course, the amulet's history, and part of its future. Enough to suggest that now that it had been discovered again, there was no going back. At least not until it was too late.

But then again, they hadn't seen everything, not yet.

Syrelle rose to leave, her eyes darting to the dishes in the sink. "Been a heavy vision day today?" she asked kindly.

"A bit," Mel answered. They hated being a burden, and sometimes, they hated how different they were. But they knew their visions were important to Gaia...somehow. Even if they didn't always understand them.

"I'll send Cara tomorrow," Syrelle said, moving towards the door. "Sleep well, Mel. Thank you as always for your counsel."

As Syrelle closed the door gently behind her, Mel returned to their knitting. They listened as Syrelle's footsteps retreated down the street, until all of a sudden they felt their tea fall to the floor and their hands reached out to grip the arms of their chair.

A giant winged creature flew through the air. Its bat-like leathery wings cut through the misty clouds, pushing the air as if they were capable of creating the very wind itself. The creature was long and serpent-like, with terrible teeth and the curved horns of a goat. And its eyes...they were the brightest blue and slit like a cat's, yet they seemed almost human in their depth. It was absolutely terrifying and majestic all at the same time, but Mel didn't know how it was possible. They'd never seen a creature like this before. What in the Underworld did this mean?

And then everything happened so fast.

They saw a newborn baby, bundled in blankets, and sleeping soundly. It was—is? Will be?—surrounded by those strange pale faces, one of whom looked so familiar from childhood, but they couldn't quite place it. She was an older woman, in her fifties maybe, with long blonde hair and light-green eyes. All of them were huddled inside a temporary building made from animal hides and it was...cold. So, so cold.

Then the vision changed and they saw an older man sitting on an elaborate gold chair, his face half-shadowed by the blue torchlights on the walls of the dark cave he inhabited. But Mel could tell he was not happy. He was talking with someone Mel couldn't quite see. An older woman with dark-brown hair. Her back was facing Mel and they couldn't see her face, but they could hear her voice.

"He's being a fucker," the man said, his voice echoing through the cavern.

"Don't call your son a fucker," the woman chastised, a hint of amusement in her voice. "He's under a lot of pressure. And besides, if I remember correctly, you were sometimes quite the fucker yourself at his age."

The man grunted in reluctant agreement, and then the vision ended.

Mel opened their eyes, their vision swimming as their living room came back into view.

What in the Underworld was that?

The creature. The baby. The man in the cave. Usually when visions came to them in a sequence like that, it meant they were connected somehow. A series of events where one led to another led to another. But how in Gaia's name was Mel supposed to decipher which came first? And what the fuck were they supposed to do about it? What role did they have to play?

Mel glanced down, looking at where their chamomile tea had spilled onto the worn carpet at their feet, spreading like the blood in the snow they'd seen all those months ago. Mel sighed and put aside their knitting, leaning over to pick up the empty mug and walk it into the kitchen.

How should they explain this to Syrelle? She always liked updates about Mel's visions, even if they were cryptic, but Syrelle also craved a defined, clear path. She wanted to know exactly which way to lead the Coven to achieve their desired ends. A direct answer. A this or that. A yes or no. But Mel couldn't always give her that.

Because what people didn't understand about finding your path was that you didn't find it—it found you. Gaia may have her will, and Iblis, too, but there was only one way events could ever transpire. In any given set of circumstances—the only set of circumstances that could ever and would ever exist—there was only ever one choice, one reaction a person would make, and they'd make it every time.

There was no changing the future.

The future was fixed, the past was fixed, and it was only the present that was in flux. It was only trying to understand how people get from the fixed past to the fixed future that was confusing to Mel. And if Gaia was showing it to them, it was a future Gaia needed them to know. Needed them to help bring about. But why?

After returning their mug to the kitchen, Mel resumed their knitting. Their hands worked the dark threads of yarn as Mel tried to put the visions aside, at least until they received more information. They hoped whatever was required of them would become clear sooner rather than later.

But either way, they Knew: whatever was happening, whatever was *coming*, it was important. And afterward? Well, they could only see so far, but it felt like it just might remake the world as they knew it.

CHAPTER ONE

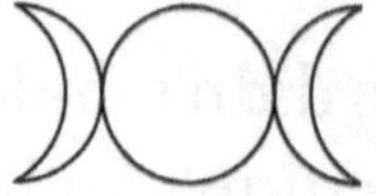

Ena

ENA WALKED THROUGH THE woods, her boots crunching through the thin layer of snow that covered the ground. She let her Knowing guide her, searching for signs of a rabbit burrow or raccoon den or squirrel's nest—anything—but it was no use. Small game had gotten more and more scarce as they'd approached the jagged peaks of the Chasm Mountains. This far northwest, it was colder, and the trees, which had thinned out as the land elevated, were shorter and scrubbier than she was used to.

The plants were strange too. There were fewer of them, and many species she didn't recognize. She struggled to attune her Knowing to the different landscape, and it made her feel extremely out of her element. She never realized how much her magic relied on her familiarity with her surroundings before, and the feeling put her ill at ease.

She walked alone through the sparse trees, wrapping her cloak tighter around her to protect from the chill. Her thighs ached from the long hours spent on horseback, but despite their soreness, it felt good to stretch them as she walked.

She and Ty had been traveling—or more accurately, fleeing—for almost a full week now. The pace they'd kept, barely stopping to eat or sleep, had been brutal. But they'd both agreed that moving as quickly as possible was the smart thing to do. They weren't sure if any Occidens witches were pursuing them after their disruptive escape from the rival Coven's village, so they'd been confined to the backcountry, avoiding roads and villages, riding well past sundown most nights, to put as much distance between them as possible. Ena Knew their horse was getting tired, and so was she.

But they were almost there. In another day's time, they'd be rendezvousing with Steig and Turner before returning to the Underworld. Apparently, the three of them had an agreement in place and the men were to wait for him at a specified location if they ever got separated, and even though it had been well over a week since Steig and Turner had fled with the amulet, Ty insisted they would still be there. Returning to the Underworld without him would only be their last resort.

But what awaited them all when they got to the Underworld...well, she knew it was well past time that she asked him about *that*. It was true that they'd been so focused on putting as much ground between them and Occidens as possible that there hadn't been much time for idle conversation, but it was also true that, deep down, part of her was afraid to ask.

After almost thirty minutes of walking to no avail, Ena noticed the sun was starting to dip below the horizon, so she decided to give up on her quest for food and head back to their camp.

She was about a quarter mile away from where they'd stopped when she sensed it—a subtle shift in the air, and the smallest depression in the snow at her feet.

There was an animal nearby. But what kind?

She began to look around slowly, and almost missed it. As white as it was, it nearly blended in with the snow-covered ground in the distance, but then she saw the silver on its ears, and the silver-tinted fur around its neck, and she had to hold in her gasp.

A Canus Elk.

This was the second time in her life that she'd seen one of the incredibly rare, supposedly immortal creatures. The first had been with Ty, nine years ago—the day they'd had their first kiss. She'd told her matriarch Heran about it afterward, and the old woman had agreed it was an auspicious sighting, since Canus Elks often portended significant or Gaia-blessed events. Though what it had indicated that day, they hadn't been entirely sure.

Ena watched the Elk as it moved slowly, stumbling. But that couldn't be right. The last time she'd seen one, its grace and beauty had been almost ethereal. Something about this one seemed off. What was it doing?

Ena hid, her body partially blocked by a tree, as the Elk lowered its front legs and lay on the ground. What a strange thing to do this close to sundown when predators were emerging, searching for a meal. Was it injured?

Ena took a cautious step closer, using her Knowing to lighten her footsteps, mimicking the rustling of the snow-dusted branches of the trees as they swayed in the wind. The Elk didn't seem to notice her, or if it did, was too distracted to care.

And then she saw it—a small pool of shimmery, silver liquid spreading out from under the Elk, spilling into the snow.

Ena's heart sped up—something was wrong. The Elk was injured. They were supposed to be immortal—she'd never heard of a dead or dying Elk being found, ever—but maybe that was just a myth.

What should she do? Should she leave it alone? It was a wild animal after all, and intervening when it was hurt or scared could be dangerous for her.

As she watched it, she could tell its breathing was becoming labored. Its skin sucked in around its ribs as it huffed and puffed, struggling to get enough air.

She couldn't just stand here and do nothing, but she didn't want to act alone.

"Ty," she spoke, her voice quiet as if he were right in front of her. She knew he was nearby and would be listening for her with his *venator*. "I need you," she said.

The Elk didn't even seem to flinch at her voice, and Ena Knew it was in pain. Hoping Ty was on his way, she threw caution to the wind and approached it slowly.

Its eyes were closed where it lay curled on the ground. It was clearly a female, lacking the gigantic silver-tipped antlers she and Ty had seen on the buck last time, but it was no less large. Twice as big as the largest deer, its fur looked soft enough to curl up in, the thick, silver-tinted mane around its neck shining in the low light of sunset.

Ena lowered to her knees in front of it and cautiously reached out to touch it. Its fur was unimaginably soft, like the fur inside a kitten's ear, and this close, she could see its belly was noticeably swollen—it was pregnant. It must have been in labor, but she knew from experience with the animals they cared for in her village, that this was not progressing normally. The Elk seemed highly distressed, and the spreading silver liquid was clearly its blood. Stroking her hand gently over the Elk's abdomen, she felt the unborn calf inside—only it was still as a stone. No movement, no squirming. It could just be resting, she told herself, but deep down, Ena Knew. The calf was no longer living.

Just then, she heard Ty approach from behind her, and she couldn't help the tiny flip her stomach did at the sight of him.

He stood in the low light of the evening, his broad shoulders backlit by the setting sun. His hand flexed at his side where he gripped the sole knife they'd escaped with in readiness, as if prepared to fight whatever obstacle stood before them.

Even though they'd been reunited for a week already, her heart still skipped a beat every time she saw him, like part of her still couldn't believe he was here. That she was here, with him. That she'd chosen to be here.

Ty's dark brows lowered in concern as he approached. "You called for me?" he asked. Then his green eyes widened as they landed on the Canus Elk before her. "Is that what I think it is?"

"Yes," Ena said, relieved by his sturdy presence. She'd always felt safer with him. "It's a Canus Elk, the same as we saw nine years ago. But it's a female in labor, and it's not doing well. I think the calf is stillborn."

Ty looked from her to the Elk, his face a mix of concern and awe. "What do you need from me?" he asked, sheathing the knife and lowering to his knees beside her in the snow.

"I—I don't know," Ena said, suddenly unsure. She wasn't the one who normally attended the animal births back home, though she'd witnessed a couple. She'd usually chosen to assist Heran with human healing instead.

Cautiously, she reached out to touch the shimmering liquid that was spreading around the Elk, drenching the snow and its fur in a dark, iridescent gray. The liquid was sticky on her fingers, and she was met with an intense sense of foreboding at the feel of it on her hands.

"I don't see the calf emerging from the birth canal," she said, looking under the Elk's tail at the swollen area that was the source of the oozing silver blood. "It should be coming out by now, even if it is a stillbirth, so I don't know what's wrong." She knew from her limited experience that animal births tended to be much quicker and more straightforward than human ones, and the rare times that they did not go as planned, there often wasn't much to be done to help, especially with a wild animal, and certainly not without her Coven's stash of potions and herbs.

The Canus Elk shuddered before them, its breathing turned to gasping, coming even faster and shorter than before. Ena felt helpless, and sadness engulfed her for the beautiful creature before her and its unborn calf.

She didn't know what else to do, so she reached down into her Knowing, hoping Gaia might guide her with her will, and she felt her Gift there—her *visanis*. The Gift she'd once been so enthralled with yet hesitant to use, now seemed like second nature to her after their escape from Occidens, and she knew what she had to do.

She gave over to it, letting it grow inside her, drenching her from the crown of her head to her fingertips, like rainfall soaking the earth, until she felt the thread form between her and the Elk.

{*Rest.*}

She spoke, her voice coming out in that eerie echo she was now accustomed to.

{*Feel no more pain.*}

The Canus Elk's breathing immediately slowed as the pain left its body. It appeared now to be in a deep sleep, and she Knew it was close to death. She placed her hand against the Elk's swollen belly one more time as she stroked her hand down its fur, soothing it as best she could, even in sleep.

Several minutes passed as they knelt there beside the creature, and eventually, the Elk's breathing stopped. Its body went still, and she Knew it was dead.

Tears filled her eyes. She wasn't normally one to cry at the natural death of animals—they were a part of Gaia's balance after all. But something about this death felt...wrong.

"Ena," Ty said, his voice grave. Ena looked at him, meeting his light-green eyes as they glowed in the sunset. "What is this? What does this mean?"

Ena swallowed. "I'm not sure," she began, shaking her head. "But I don't think it's good."

She ran her fingers across the snow on the ground, wiping the Canus Elk's blood off her fingers as best she could before standing up.

"Do you want to leave it here?" Ty asked softly, rising to stand next to her. "I'm not sure of your customs, but we could bury it. Or burn it," he added gently.

"No, we'll leave it," Ena said firmly. "Its body will nourish the animals and bugs that find it, and its life will return to the soil, propagating new growth in due time. It will serve Gaia's balance in the end."

She spoke the words that were routine to her, but inside, she wasn't entirely sure if it had been Gaia's will that this creature should die. She got the same sense of wrongness she'd felt when she received the vision of the amulet being used. The same gut instinct that assured her what the witches had done, forcing the daemons into the bond with Iblis, was wrong. She Knew something here was terribly off, too, but she didn't know what, if anything, to do about it.

Ty nodded, watching the Elk reverently along with her as he reached out and grasped her hand. His heat and strength were a balm to her emotions, and she gripped his hand back firmly, until together, they turned to head back to camp, leaving the Canus Elk and its unborn calf behind them.

The sun had fully set now and the air was filled with the still coldness that came with approaching winter. They returned to their small campfire to find their overworked horse safely grazing nearby on the scrubby plants that littered the snowy, pine needle-covered ground.

"Are you okay?" Ty asked as she released his hand, moving to stoke up the fire to keep herself busy.

"Yeah, I'm okay," Ena answered truthfully. "Just...confused." Though a part of her was shaken up by the event, she was no stranger to death. She just hoped that whatever meaning she was meant to discern from it would become apparent soon. She didn't like not knowing. "Thanks for coming when I called," she added, giving him a small smile.

"Always," Ty said, looking her over appraisingly. Her heart skipped a beat when their eyes connected. In the dim light, she could just make out the dark *onata* tattoos that marked the shaved sides of his head—the ones that had once made her feel such resentment towards him, now filled her heart with sadness, knowing he'd been forced into serving Iblis to acquire them. Butterflies squirmed in her stomach at the look he gave her. They were only a few feet apart now. Was he going to kiss her?

They hadn't talked at all about what had happened between them in Occidens, nor what her coming with him had meant for *them*. Yes, they'd slept together, and admitted their feelings, but they'd both thought they were saying goodbye. What were they now that she'd chosen to come with him? Were they together? She wasn't sure they even knew *how* to be together. They'd gone from a temporary summer fling, to nine years of separation, to captor and captive, to...whatever they were now. Not to mention, there were still many reasons why they couldn't—shouldn't—be together long term, but Ena wasn't sure those reasons mattered to her anymore. Did they matter to Ty?

He looked away from her then, breaking their eye contact as he turned to rummage through their dwindling supplies. "Here," he said, offering her one of their remaining hunks of cheese. "Once you've eaten, you can rest if you want. I'll take the first watch tonight."

Ena smiled wryly at him. He always took the first watch, letting her sleep well over half of the night, to his detriment. The man looked almost as exhausted as she felt.

"Are you sure?" she asked skeptically. "That's the third night in a row you've taken first watch."

"I'm sure," was all he said, giving her an arch look as if he dared her to argue. He'd probably love it if she did.

"Okay, fine," she said with a put-upon sigh that made the corners of his mouth tip up.

Gaia, he was beautiful.

Forcing herself to focus on her food, she finished quickly, then laid down by the fire, her body and mind absolutely spent.

She thought she would fall asleep quickly, but her mind kept turning to the ominous events with the Canus Elk. The unknown of it all...and for the first time since she'd fled Occidens with Ty, she let her mind turn to her sister. She wished Greya was here to ask about it, and Heran, and her heart wrenched at the thought.

Because she'd left them.

What were they thinking now? Were they worried about her? Looking for her?

Guilt swept through her, especially for how she'd left things with Greya. The last conversation they'd had was in anger. Ena hadn't had a chance to fully explain everything. To tell her all the details she'd learned about Ty and the other daemons, about the amulet and the ritual the witches had completed binding them to Iblis against their will. She knew without a doubt that she'd made the right decision to come with Ty, she just hoped that when all this was over, when they figured out how to break the bond, she'd be able to explain, and that Greya would understand.

Heran, on the other hand...she didn't know how her matriarch would react to her abandoning the Coven to work with daemons. And part of her was still incredibly angry that she'd kept such secrets from everyone—that all the matriarchs had. But the woman had been like a grandmother to her—had raised her—and she knew she could be stubborn, but she cared deeply for the Coven. If only there was a way to help her see the error in her thinking, maybe she would come around too. Ena was hopeful, but still...she had a sinking feeling that explaining everything to Heran, and getting her acceptance, would be a much harder task.

She listened to the fire crackle and spit, trying to calm her mind of all the questions and emotions that filled her after everything that had happened, and everything that lay ahead.

She found her eyes drawn to Ty as he sat stoically across the fire, and part of her wondered...did he know why she'd really done it? Why she'd chosen to leave with him? Because yes, part of her had done it to restore Gaia's balance, and to right the wrongs of the past by breaking the bond. But another large part of her had done it for him. Just to be with him. Did he know that?

As she finally drifted off to sleep, she was filled with the certainty that no matter what came next, no matter what she had to endure in the Underworld, or with her own Coven, that if she could just be with him, then it would all be worth it in the end.

Chapter Two

Ty

THE NEXT DAY, TY awoke with the dawn. It was later than he intended, and he groaned as he opened his eyes to see the sunlight filtering through the trees. His entire body felt stiff and rigid, including his...

Memory flooded him. He'd been having a dream that Ena was riding him, her tits bouncing in his hands as she rocked into him, and now his cock was hard as stone.

Looking around, he turned to find the woman of his dreams peacefully sitting by the fire, stoking it with a long branch.

She was certainly a sight to wake up to. Her dark-brown hair glowed in the early-morning light, and the cold, crisp air made the pale, creamy skin on her cheeks and the tip of her nose slightly pink.

"Morning, sleepyhead," Ena greeted as she looked towards him, seeing that he was awake.

He grunted in response, it being the only sound he could muster as the blood flowed back into his brain.

Ena laughed. A sensual, delicate thing that made his heart race.

"What?" he asked, sitting up and giving her a small smile in return. Did he amuse her somehow? He hoped so. He wanted to hear that sound again.

"Nothing. You're just extremely grumpy when you wake up," she said, teasing.

He grunted in acknowledgment, on purpose this time. She laughed again, and he felt like he'd won a prize.

Standing up, he scratched at his unruly beard. It was getting too long and he needed to trim it, but it'd been weeks since he'd been in a position to do so. Just one more thing he was eager to do when they finally arrived at their destination.

Seeing that Ena had turned her attention back to the fire, Ty strode off into the woods to take a piss behind a tree, his body finally starting to wake up.

He'd spent most of last night thinking about what had happened with the Canus Elk, and what it meant for them. Only in the wee hours of the morning had he finally, reluctantly, woken up Ena to take over on watch so he could sleep. He would've let her sleep the whole night if he could've, but he knew he needed to be alert as they rode today, given how close they were to the entrance to the Underworld.

Clearly, he'd been more tired than he'd thought, because it seemed like no time at all had passed before the sun woke him up. He wasn't mad about it, though—waking up to see Ena by the fire was... Well, for the first time in nine years, he actually felt like his reality might be better.

Or at least, he hoped it would be soon. They'd been traveling so hard and fast the last week—his only focus on getting them both as far away from Occidens as possible—that there'd been zero time for anything else.

He was pretty sure they'd done it, though—he'd been using his *venator* constantly, watching and listening for any signs of pursuit, but all had been quiet. He hoped that by the time the witches had figured out they were gone, they'd gotten enough of a head start to make catching up to them impossible.

But still, he couldn't let his guard down—not yet. And especially not with whatever new threats on the horizon the Canus Elk portended.

Returning to their fire, Ty watched as Ena began her now-familiar morning routine. After building up the fire with the logs and branches Ty had broken for her last night, she shook out her cloak, picking off large hunks of moss and sticks, before finger-combing her hair and re-braiding it.

He'd never admit it, but he often found himself mes-merized just watching her move. Like she was some elusive, rare animal he still couldn't believe was his, and it was completely new territory for him.

He'd never been this...familiar with anyone besides Steig and Turner before. Certainly not a woman. He couldn't even recall the amount of times he'd watched Steig and his wife Lara over the years and yearned to have that kind of intimacy with someone. But he'd assumed he would never be able to, and so after a while, it had gotten so painful to think about that he squashed the idea of ever having that with anyone entirely from his head.

But now here they were, living in a sort of unspoken harmony.

Averting his eyes before she could catch him watching her, Ty rummaged through his pack and pulled out their last hunk of stale bread and an extremely beat-up apple. Breaking the former in two, he handed one half to Ena, along with the apple.

"Don't you want to split this too?" she asked as she took the apple from his hand.

"No, I'll be alright," he said.

"Are you sure? You're bigger than me. You should probably have it," she said, trying to hand it back to him.

"Just be a good girl and eat your apple before I give it to the horse, okay?" he said, giving her a wink.

Her cheeks turned pink, and this time he knew it wasn't the cold. "Suit yourself," she said, taking a bite. He watched as some juice dribbled down her chin, and she proceeded to wipe it off with the back of her hand.

Fuck, now was so not the time for all the dirty thoughts that image just gave him.

Turning away once more, he took a bite out of his bread as he went to ready their horse.

After finishing her food and kicking out their fire, Ena came over just as he finished securing the last of the saddlebags. He got her mounted up first before climbing up behind her, his body snug against hers, and wrapped his arms around her waist to grab the reins.

As always, it was the most exquisite torture. The smell of her surrounded him, and he could feel the curves of her body tucked up against his. He could touch her in a million small ways all day but in none of the ways he wanted to—the definition of teasing. He loved it and he absolutely fucking hated it at the same time.

But he knew their cozy little torturous routine wouldn't last. If they made good time, they'd be meeting up with Turner and Steig at the rendezvous point later today, and then...he'd have to finally tell her what was coming.

He'd already put it off way too long, but they'd been focused on moving as quickly as possible, dodging villages and taking back routes to throw any would-be pursuers off their trail. Or at least that's what he told himself. In all honesty, he was just being a coward.

Because there was that voice...that nagging worry in the back of his head. What if she changed her mind once she knew? What if she decided to leave?

But he couldn't hold off any longer—she needed to be prepared, even if it...changed things. So he'd break the news to her, tonight, once they reunited with Steig and Turner.

And if she accepted it, which he hoped to fucking Iblis that she did, then maybe it would be time for a different conversation—one that scared him nearly as much.

Did she want to be with him now?

He'd tried for so many years to forget her, to push her away with his anger...but now she was here. She'd come with him. She knew everything—well, almost everything—and she'd still chosen to come.

Yes, it was first and foremost to help with the amulet and breaking the bond, but...she'd said she was *his*. And as Iblis was his Master, as much as it scared him, he wanted to have her, in all the ways he'd always dreamed. Would she let him?

"You alright back there?" Ena asked, giving him an arch look over her shoulder.

"Yeah, of course. Why?" he said, clearing his throat and trying to clear his mess of thoughts.

"You're just squirming like a worm. Do you need to pee or something?" she asked, and he could hear the teasing smile in her voice.

He couldn't help but smile back. "No, viper," he said drolly. "Just trying to get comfortable."

"Here," she said, wiggling forward slightly in the saddle. "Is that better?"

"No, it's worse," he said, pulling her back into him so her ass was cradled between his thighs as it had been. "I'm done squirming, I promise. We're almost there."

They'd been riding most of the morning, their horse weaving easily through the sparse, short evergreens. Long gone were the oaks and maples that dotted the landscape further west—the climate here was drier and harsher this close to the Chasm Mountains. Luckily, the snow had melted with the morning sun as the temperature crested above freezing, but with the brisk pace their horse was keeping, it was still fairly cold.

"Where exactly is 'there'?" Ena asked cautiously, glancing over her shoulder at him again. "Where are we meeting them?"

"It's a cave hidden behind a waterfall—a small one. Steig, Turner, and I used to play there as kids when we were given permission to leave the Underworld."

"Permission from who?" Ena asked, her brow wrinkling.

Did she really not know? It didn't sound like she'd been taught much of anything about daemons and the Underworld, but still, for the witches to not teach her even the basics...it seemed downright insulting.

"Cole, my uncle. He's the king."

Ena paused at that, and Ty could see her delicate brow furrowing in confusion. "What's a 'king'?" she asked, sounding out the word like it was foreign, which apparently it was.

Ty tried to suppress his smile. He supposed it made sense. She'd been raised by the witches, who chose matriarchs to lead their Covens—witches with strong Gifts, to be sure, but also women who were adept at leading and uniting others. She'd clearly never been exposed to another way of doing things.

"A king is...like a leader. Kind of like your matriarchs, only...their opinion is unilateral. They don't need to consult others; their word alone is law."

"So Cole, your uncle, he makes all the rules for the daemons by himself?" Ena asked cautiously, seeming surprised by this development.

"Yes. He divines Iblis's will, then communicates it to us, letting us know which missions Iblis wants us to undertake. But he alone decides who goes and when, as well as oversees all the other inner workings of the Underworld."

"Oh," Ena said, as she contemplated this.

His body tensed slightly, wondering if she was about to ask any follow-up questions. The whole topic could lead to another, which he didn't really want to discuss right now, but then, thank Iblis, he heard it—the delicate spilling of water.

He redirected their horse to follow the sound. The mountains loomed above them as they tucked themselves even closer to them, following their baseline, until finally, across the scrubby plain, Ty spotted it.

It was just as he remembered—a delicate stream of water falling off the mountainside as if pouring from a never-ending pitcher. The waterfall was small, only about a foot or two across, but it fell gracefully into a shallow, rocky streambed that meandered across the landscape. And behind the waterfall was a narrow cave entrance. It looked unassuming and barely penetrable, but Ty knew that it widened inside, its tall walls damp and slightly moldy from the humidity of the waterfall. Memories of himself, Turner, and Steig splashing and playing in the water in the summer and staying up all night laughing and joking in the cave flooded his mind as he looked for signs of his friends.

He couldn't see any movement coming from the darkness within. Were they here? He'd be lying if he said he wasn't a little apprehensive about seeing Steig and Turner. He knew in all likelihood that they would still be here—there was no way they'd go back to the Underworld to deal with the absolute shit storm Cole would rain down on them without him, except as a last resort. But he didn't know how they would feel about Ena being here.

Stopping their horse in front of the stream, Ty dismounted and helped Ena do the same. Leaving their horse to drink from the stream and graze freely on the sage that surrounded it, Ty approached the cave entrance.

"It's beautiful," Ena said, speaking up slightly to be heard over the sound of the waterfall.

Ty smiled at her over his shoulder. "I know," he replied. They did always have a similar appreciation for nature's beauty.

"Where are their horses? If they're here, shouldn't we see signs of them?" she asked astutely.

"They might've tied them up farther away to avoid attention. That's what I would do," Ty said. "I'm gonna go check for them inside. I'll be right back."

Ena nodded at him, seeming somewhat distracted by the waterfall and all the new plants that grew along the streambed as she bent down to touch one.

Ty ducked to the side of the waterfall, following the thin strip of ground that bordered the stream on either side at the entrance to the cave. The mist sprayed his coat as he passed, leaving him feeling slightly damp as he entered the darkness.

Walking through the narrow opening, he had to lower his head slightly lest he hit it until the passageway opened up on the inside. Once his eyes adjusted to the darkness, he saw the tiniest glimmer of light at the end of the tunnel, and he couldn't help the wide smile that grew on his face.

They were here.

He picked up his pace, walking quickly until the cave opened into a wider chamber, and there, standing next to a small fire, were the only friends he had in the world.

"Took you long enough, asshole," Steig said, smiling in return as he removed his hand from where he'd held it in readiness on his dagger. He moved to Ty, pulling him into a tight hug.

Ty hugged him back, relief flooding him at being reunited with his best friend. There was a minute there, back in Occidens, where he wasn't sure if he'd see them again, and the emotions of that near-loss hit him in force now as he gripped his friend tightly.

He patted Steig's back a few times for good measure before they broke apart, then he turned to Turner.

His younger cousin's eyes were bright with unshed tears as he, too, pulled Ty in for a hug. "It's good to see you, brother," Turner said, thumping him on the back and holding the base of his neck gently.

"You too," Ty replied, before pulling away to take stock of him. "You two look well," he said, noting their rested appearance.

"Well, we've been twiddling our thumbs here for over a week. You want to tell us what the fuck happened to you?" Steig asked in that surly way of his, though Ty knew from experience that it belied his concern underneath.

"It's a long story," Ty said, waving him off. "But there's something important I have to tell you first."

He never got the chance, though, because at that moment, Turner and Steig looked past him as the sound of delicate footsteps echoed into the chamber.

"What the fuck is she doing here?" Steig asked venomously, his hand going back to his dagger.

Ty turned around to see Ena. The darkness of the cave and the firelight suited her as they played across the gorgeous planes of her face, and her blue eyes seemed to glow in the dim light, reflecting and amplifying what was there like a beacon as she stared back at Steig with equal venom.

"*She* is here to help you, Steig, or did you think you'd be able to break the witch-made bond to Iblis all on your own?" she responded, before turning her gaze on Ty. "Sorry I came in unannounced. I just got tired of waiting out there," she explained.

"That's fine. I was just about to tell them about you, and...everything," he responded, wondering exactly how much he should tell them. While Turner would support him either way, he knew Steig was uncomfortable with the idea of him and Ena being together, not without good reason. He was a protective friend and, given all the trials he'd had to go through to be with Lara, he knew Steig didn't want him to have to go through anything even remotely like that.

"You're here to help us?" Turner asked, some confusion in his voice. "Did Ty tell you everything, then?"

"Yes," Ena said calmly. "He did. And not only that, but... I had a vision when I put on the amulet." Ty remembered what she'd looked like when she'd put it on—her eyes going white and ethereal as if she was seeing something that wasn't there, the way she'd screamed and writhed in pain as she witnessed the ritual. "I saw it being used to create the bond to Iblis, and then my matriarch confirmed everything, and well... I can't explain it, but I Know it's not Gaia's will. It needs to be rectified to restore the balance. So that's why I'm here."

"And we're just supposed to trust you?" Steig asked suspiciously. "What if you're lying and you're just here to steal the amulet back the minute our backs are turned?"

Ty felt his ire rise at the way Steig spoke to her and he had to actively work to keep himself calm. "She helped me escape the Occidens Coven, Steig," Ty said, anger creeping into his voice despite his best efforts. "She used her Gift to get me out, at great personal risk. And she came here with me, leaving her Coven and family behind to help us, so, yes, you will trust her," Ty said with authority, his voice echoing around the dark cave.

Steig didn't look away, and Ty saw him clenching his jaw. The man clearly didn't like it, and in all likelihood, he wouldn't trust her—at least not right away. The bastard was extremely suspicious and private, to a fault. But he would accept her, if only because Ty asked for it. And not just because of who Ty was, but because he trusted Ty. They'd been friends since childhood, and their bond had been forged through years of having each other's backs.

"Fine," he gritted out, just as Ty expected. "But you better have a plan for this, because you know as well as I do, having her there will be extremely complicated."

Ty released his breath, relieved to at least have Steig's tepid acceptance. "I do," he said. "But first things first, I want to see it."

There was no question what he was talking about. He needed to set eyes on it, to assure himself that they really *had* gotten it—that it was here, and all their efforts had been worth it. That everything they still needed to do would be possible.

Steig looked over at Turner, who nodded and turned away from them to dig around in one of the packs that sat on the cave floor. After several seconds, he pulled out an object wrapped in an old, dirty piece of someone's shirt and handed it to Ty.

Ty unwrapped it reverently as all three of them gathered around. As soon as he folded away the layers of fabric, the amethyst in the amulet's center caught the light of the fire. It glowed in the dark, seeming to refract all the light in the room in its crystalline structure.

There was an undeniable power about it, even Ty could recognize that. He wondered if Steig and Turner could, too, or if it was just his witch half making him sensitive to it. Either way, the necklace seemed to throb with energy, humming with whatever magic was inside it.

Ty looked over at Ena to see her watching it intently, too, her brow slightly furrowed, until she looked up and caught his eye.

"Can I?" she asked, holding out her hand.

Ty hesitated. He trusted Ena with his life at this point, since she'd literally saved it, and she had every right to hold the amulet, given what she'd sacrificed to be here. But still, his stomach clenched remembering the last time she'd touched it.

"Are you sure you want to? After what happened last time?" he asked her cautiously, memories of her scream ringing through his head.

"Yes," she said, her voice steady, as one corner of her mouth tilted up into a small smile. "Let's call it an experiment."

Ty nodded, reluctantly acquiescing to her wishes as he passed her the amulet. His heart rose up his throat as he gently released his hold on the necklace, placing it in her slender hand.

Silently, she stared into the crystal, as if willing the vision to come, but nothing happened. Her eyes didn't turn white, she didn't succumb to any visions. She seemed fine.

Everyone seemed to collectively let out a breath. The amulet still pulsed with power, but at least they weren't at risk of Ena having a vision every time she touched it. A good thing, given it'd be necessary for her to handle it if they were to figure out the elements to breaking the spell.

"I guess it was just a one-time blessing from Gaia," Ena mused as she turned the amulet over in her hand. She traced the symbols etched into it with her finger, as if trying to feel out their secrets through touch. "These symbols...I'm not sure what they all mean. That will have to be one of the first things we look into once we..." Her voice trailed off.

"I suppose we should talk about that. What's to come, what you need to expect. What we all need to expect," Ty said, looking around at them all in turn, feeling the weight of what he was about to ask of her.

Because even though he didn't know exactly *what* Ena was to him, she was his to protect. There was no doubt about that. And he'd do his best to do just that.

"Let's tie up the horse and get settled, then I'll tell you the plan."

CHAPTER THREE

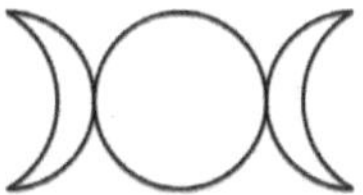

TY LEFT HER AS he went outside to fetch their horse and tie it up where Steig and Turner had brought theirs. This, unfortunately, left Ena standing in a dark cave with two daemons who did not trust her all that much.

"I'll take that back now, if you don't mind," Steig said as he approached her, holding out his hand for the amulet.

Ena begrudgingly wrapped it back up in the old, dirty piece of cloth and handed it to Steig who went to hide it deep inside one of their bags again. A large part of her resented his sense of ownership over it. It was a witch's amulet, after all, and it was *she* who had been granted the vision when she touched it.

But even though she was annoyed with his surly attitude, a part of her understood it. After hearing everything the witches had done to force daemons out of society and into the Underworld—and the way the matriarchs had hidden it from everyone—she wasn't sure she fully trusted them anymore either.

Besides, she also knew Steig was extremely protective of Ty, especially when it came to her. She hadn't forgotten their conversation in Attax when he'd warned her to stay away from Ty. She respected him for it; she just hadn't listened.

"You hungry?" Turner asked as he approached, interrupting her thoughts.

"Yeah, thanks," Ena said, smiling kindly at him. They'd eaten the last of their provisions before setting out that morning, so Turner's offer warmed her. And she was glad that at least one of Ty's friends didn't hate her.

He rummaged around in one of their packs before pulling out a hunk of jerky—turkey this time, different than the bricks of beef they'd had before, thank Gaia. They must've been able to make some trades at a village along the way here.

"So what happened to you two? In Occidens?" Turner asked in that curious, open way of his.

"Well," Ena said, wondering where to begin. "We were captured by the witches there, and they held us for a few days. Then my sister and the matriarch of my Coven came to get me and negotiated my release. That's when Heran told me everything, about the amulet and what it was for. But Ty..." Ena paused, her throat tightening at the memory. "They were going to put him to death. Drown him in the Endless Ocean. And I...I couldn't let that happen, so I used my magic to break him out."

She decided to leave it at that for now. They didn't need to know the entire mess of feelings and history that went into that decision. All that mattered was she'd helped him escape and was here to help them now.

"Thank you," Turner said quietly. "For helping him. Even after everything we put you through. He's like a brother to me and I..." He trailed off, seemingly at a loss for words. "Just thank you," he ended sincerely.

"You're welcome," Ena said, emotion clogging her throat at how much Turner clearly cared. Part of her wanted to reassure him that she hadn't just done it out of a sense of responsibility. That something drew her to Ty too. That she was *his*, and there was no way she could let him be killed, but she didn't know how or whether she should admit that to him, especially after everything Steig had said to her, so she kept her feelings to herself.

Ena and Turner sat down by the small campfire and ate in silence as they waited for Ty to return. Blessedly, the cavern was large enough that the smoke from it was able to disperse, but it still gave off enough heat to take the chill off when sitting next to it.

She knew the instant Ty walked in a few minutes later. It never ceased to amaze her the way his presence affected her—his body seemed to alter the drab, damp feeling of the cave, filling it with energy and life once more as Ena's eyes instinctively landed on him, like a moth drawn to a flame.

She stood as he approached the fire, Steig coming to join them.

"Well?" Steig asked, making space next to him for Ty.

Ty hesitated, stroking his full beard several times before speaking, as if contemplating how to begin.

Ena felt her stomach twist. Whatever he had to say, it was clearly making him nervous.

"Okay, I've given a lot of thought to how we should play this," Ty began. "Obviously, we need Ena to have access to the Archives and the books I got from Petyr if she's going to help us figure out how to break the bond, but I'll have to keep the amulet close to me, so she'll need access to my chambers too. There's not an easy way of sneaking her in and keeping her hidden, so...she'll have to pose as our prisoner."

The daemons went quiet, tension filling the air.

"You don't mean..." Turner began, concern on his face.

"Mean what?" Ena asked. Why did they all look concerned? Was posing as their prisoner going to be that horrible?

"He means you'll have to pretend to be his witch-slave," Steig said bluntly.

Ena whipped her head to Ty, who looked at her with a hint of guilt in his eyes. "What does *that* mean?" Ena asked tensely.

Ty sighed, as if reticent to tell her more, but he spoke anyway. "Daemons have a history of...keeping witches, and mortals," he said, his voice gentle, but firm. "It's not something I'm supportive of, and it doesn't happen very often, but ever since the bond was created, some daemons have taken witches as a form of punishment and forced them into servitude in the Underworld."

Ena had heard rumors of witches and mortals being taken by daemons to the Underworld, never to be seen or heard from again, but just like Canus Elks, she'd thought it was a myth. A rumor that was spread about the Underworld to scare witch children, but that no one could ever prove. But now that it had been confirmed, her mind spun in horror. How many witches had been taken over the years and forced into servitude?

Then the most horrible thought of all occurred to her.

"Wait, your mother. Was she...?" she asked, unable to complete the thought.

"No, she wasn't," Ty answered. "In fact, from what I know, she refused to be seen and treated as one. That was part of why she was not welcome there."

"I see," Ena said as she tried to wrap her mind around all this.

"I swear, Ena, if there was another way to bring you there, and keep you safe, I would do it," Ty said confidently. "I know it's not ideal, but you'll be under my protection. You'll...belong to me. So no one else is allowed to touch you, let alone hurt you." His eyes were filled with sincerity, like he was beseeching her to see it this way too. He'd clearly given this a lot of thought. "Yes, you'll have to pretend to be completely subservient to me, and the other daemons, but it's the only way."

Ena paused as she contemplated this. It definitely did not seem ideal. Having to bow and scrape to a bunch of daemons? What would she be required to do for them? For Ty? She didn't love the idea, but she didn't know what else she had expected. That they'd just let her live there as an honored guest? This did seem like a good solution to keep her there safely, but she wasn't one for accepting a less-than-ideal solution without fully thinking it through.

"But wait, won't we tell everyone that I'm there to help break the bond? Shouldn't that garner me some good will on its own without me having to be a witch-slave?"

Her tongue tripped over the word like it was dirty. It felt offensive to even say it.

Ty looked at Steig and Turner, some unspoken understanding passing between them.

"It's not that simple," Ty replied. "We are the only ones who know about the amulet and the true history of the bond to Iblis. There are those, we hope, who will also be supportive of breaking it, but for now, it has to be kept secret. There are too many others, my uncles Cole and Zak especially, who will not be supportive."

"Why wouldn't they want to break the bond? Don't they want access to Gaia and to rejoin mortal and witch society too?" She was admittedly naïve about the inner workings of the Underworld, but this felt obvious to her.

Ty shook his head. "Not necessarily. My uncle's power comes from his direct connection to Iblis, and the hierarchy that he maintains in the Underworld. Breaking the bond would disrupt that, even in the best of circumstances. He would never willingly give that up."

"So we have to hide it from him. From everyone," Ena said, seeking confirmation.

"Yes, at least for now," Ty answered.

Ena nodded slowly, but she felt Ty's eyes linger on her, watching her reaction to all this.

"So how are we gonna say we captured her?" Turner asked. "Can't exactly tell Cole about everything that happened since we took her."

"I've thought about that too," Ty said, redirecting his attention back towards the group. "Our original mission was for Steig to pose as a bard in a series of southern villages and destabilize the populations by using his *cupido* to increase birth rates."

"What the fuck?" Ena said, staring open-mouthed at them. "Are you serious? That's horrible."

"Well, lucky for you we didn't actually do it," Steig said, seeming annoyed by her negative reaction. "We were too busy kidnapping you and finding the amulet."

That didn't make her feel better.

Sensing this, Ty jumped in. "Look, I know you think it's bad, Ena, but it does give us the perfect cover story. We'll say we stopped by the Auster Coven around Samhain to affect the mortals who were there, too, but that you inadvertently discovered what we were, and so we had no choice but to take you."

"So not too far from the truth then?" Turner asked, his blond eyebrows raising in realization.

"Yes, that's the point. We have to be careful around my uncle Zak," Ty explained to Ena. "He has the Power of *mendacium*, which means he's flawless at lying, and he can sense when others are lying too."

"Alright." Turner nodded. "What do you think?" he asked, looking to Steig.

"I think that could work," Steig mused, nodding in agreement. "Cole will love the fact that Turner burned down the matriarch's house in the process. The sick bastard will see that alone as a job well done."

Ena put her face in her hands. This was a lot. Not only was she about to go into the wolves' den, pretending to be their witch-slave, but she'd have to avoid lying in front of Zak, and keep her cool around Cole, which would likely be tough given that he seemed like such a cruel, vindictive asshole.

She felt Ty reach out and place his hand on her shoulder.

"Ena," he said gently. He spoke quietly, as if just to her, ignoring Steig and Turner who could, without a doubt, still hear them. "What are you thinking? Tell me."

She'd be lying if she said she wasn't apprehensive about all this—terrified even. But, she'd already come this far. And wasn't this exactly why she'd chosen this path? Didn't she want to take the risk? Not just to right the wrongs of the past, but for Ty. To be with him. Yes, it would be chaotic as fuck, and not at all balanced and controlled like her life had been for the past twenty-seven years, so that felt overwhelming. But if she were being honest, if she put aside the fear and apprehension...it also felt thrilling. And it was high time she leaned into that.

"I'm thinking it sounds complicated, and dangerous, but...I can do it," Ena said firmly, coming to her decision. She lifted her head up to look at the daemons as they watched her, assessing. "I will do it, if that's what it takes."

Turner smiled at her then, big and unguarded, and even Steig gave her a curt nod of appreciation.

But Ty paused, searching her eyes for any form of hesitation. She let him look, showing him that she meant it, and she was steady as a rock.

A brief flash of pride filled his eyes before a slow, wolfish grin broke out on his face. "Good. Then tomorrow, we go to the Underworld."

Chapter Four

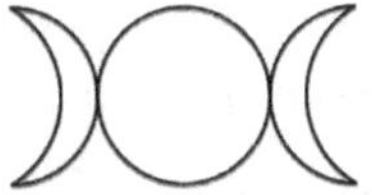

Ena

THE SUN WAS ALREADY setting outside the cave, so Steig volunteered to take watch. Ty was confident that the threat of Occidens witches pursuing them had passed, but apparently this close to the Underworld, there could be other daemons passing by, and it would complicate things if the four of them were caught here before speaking with Cole.

Turner had curled up on the far side of the cave, his snores already echoing off the damp walls, and Ena found herself sitting alone, her mind trying to process all she had learned. She felt good about her decision to pose as Ty's witch-slave, but she couldn't help but wonder where that left *them*—the two of them, together, or not together, as it were. She was just wondering if she should go and find Ty to talk about it all, when he approached her.

"Did you get enough to eat?" Ty asked quietly as he sat down next to her.

"Yeah, I did," Ena said, touched at his care.

"Good," he said, staring at her in that intense way of his. "You should get some sleep too. Steig and Turner agreed to take turns on watch so we can rest."

"Okay," Ena said, but she didn't move a muscle. She stared back at Ty, their eyes locking in the firelight, so much unspoken between them.

Why wasn't he kissing her? Was he giving her space? He'd said he would always be hers, but that didn't necessarily mean he wanted to be together. Should she be brave and tell him what she was thinking?

She looked away to fidget with her hands, not knowing how to begin the conversation they needed to have.

"Ena, I—" Ty began, seeming unsure too. She looked back up at him, drawn to the uncharacteristic vulnerability in his voice. "I don't know where we stand, or what's going on in your head after...everything. I know you came to help with the amulet, and I'm so grateful for that. But I need you to know..."

Ena's heart lodged in her throat. Was he about to say he didn't want to be with her? That they couldn't be, that it was too complicated? Was this him letting her down gently?

And then he reached out and took her hand in his. His palms were warm and steady, and the feel of them enveloped her.

"I know things are complicated, and they're about to get even more so. So, if you want to just make this about breaking the bond, and not about us, I'll understand. But I don't want to push you away anymore. I can't. Every second we're not together, every second I'm not touching you, or kissing you, is like torture. I meant what I said in Occidens. I'm yours, and I always will be. If you'll have me."

Ena's heart ached at his words, and she felt tears prickle in her eyes. How on earth was she meant to respond to that? She had no words, so she did the only thing she could think to do—the only thing she felt like doing.

She leaned forward and kissed him.

He smelled like woodsmoke and honey, cedar and stone, and she breathed him in like he was the only air she would ever need. Ty inhaled sharply as their lips came together, breathing her in too, before bringing his hand up and cradling the side of her face.

Ena felt herself falling into it, wanting to get lost in his kiss, but she had something to say too, so she stopped herself and pulled away, looking deep into his eyes.

"I meant what I said also. I'm yours, Ty, and I want to be with you. In every way," Ena said quietly, her heart feeling lighter than air at finally being able to speak the feeling out loud.

Ty smiled widely, the joy and relief evident in his eyes, before pulling her into him and kissing her again, fiercer this time. His tongue parted her lips, entering her mouth as his warm taste filled her. Ena had been waiting for this every day since the last time they'd kissed, and she gave herself over to it completely.

Their kiss deepened as his tongue swirled and teased around hers, driving her absolutely mad as he wrung her body tighter and tighter. Ena whimpered a little, leaning further into Ty's body until her breasts were pressed against him. He hummed low in his throat at the contact, then reached out to grab one of her breasts, stroking his thumb over her nipple in a way that made her clit throb.

"Wait," Ena said breathlessly, suddenly realizing where they were and pulling back again. "Are you sure we should do this...here? Turner's right there," she whispered, looking pointedly in the man's direction.

Ty never took his eyes off her, his gaze dark and commanding. "Turner sleeps like the dead. He won't wake for anything," he said, his voice low.

"And Steig?" Ena asked shyly. "Won't he sense us? You know, with his Power?" She knew his *cupido* could amplify lust, and that meant he had a heightened sense for it as well.

Ty gave her a wicked look, the corner of his full mouth tipping up in such a way that made her want to bite his lip until she drew blood.

"So let him sense us," Ty said, raising his eyebrow in challenge.

Gaia, this man. He knew her too well. She could never back down from his challenges.

Besides, it wasn't like she hadn't engaged in her share of public displays of affection before—her tryst with Cris at Samhain last year was a fairly recent example of that—but this...with the others so close. For some reason, the thought made her heart beat faster with excitement, and only added to that throbbing ache between her legs.

She met Ty's eyes and nodded slowly at him. *Yes.*

"Lay down on your side, viper," he told her without hesitation.

She did as commanded, laying down so her back was to the wall and she could see the whole cavern, with the small fire, their packs and supplies scattered about, and Turner asleep on the other side.

Ena swallowed as she felt Ty lay down behind her, his hard chest at her back, before slipping his muscular arm under her head as a cushion. Then she felt his other hand slowly pull her dress up, exposing her pussy to the cold air of the cave.

"Just tell me if you want me to stop," Ty whispered in her ear, but there was no way she wanted to stop. She felt her clit throb as wetness filled her. "Nod if you understand me," he said. She'd never heard his voice sound quite like that before. So in control. Every word a promise and a challenge.

She nodded her understanding.

He brought his hand around to her front, drawing circles with his finger just above where she so desperately wanted to be touched.

Then he moved his finger lower, right over her clit, grazing over it gently, before dipping his finger ever so slightly inside her. He brought the tip of his wet finger back to her clit, swirling it around in tight circles that drove her mad.

She had to stop herself from moaning loudly at the feeling, instead grunting in a choked-sounding way as her hips bucked involuntarily into his hand.

"I bet you're so fucking wet for me, aren't you, Ena?" he said, his voice low and tight with desire.

"Yes," she replied in a whisper. It was all she could manage.

He dipped his finger inside her again, deeper this time, hitting her clit with the heel of his hand as he moved it slowly in and out.

"Fucking Iblis, Ena," he groaned. "You're wetter than the River Wry. Have you been like this all day?"

Ena laughed breathlessly. "Yes," she said again truthfully. "I'm always wet around you."

He growled low at that, a rumbling, almost animalistic noise that made her cunt clench.

"Tell me what you want," he said, his voice calm and demanding.

"I—I want you to fuck me," she said in a whisper, her voice almost pleading, as she tried to focus on making words and not everything he was doing to her.

Ty chuckled at her tone, sounding so pleased with her. "Then spread your legs for me, viper."

Ena did as commanded, opening her legs as Ty removed his finger. She felt him unbutton his pants behind her and heard the shuffle of clothing being lowered before she felt the hot length of his cock pressed up against her.

He dragged his smooth cock over her bare ass in a teasing motion that made her moan. She arched back into him in invitation, reaching back with her hand to pull his head closer to hers.

"Do it," she said darkly.

"Not until you ask nicely," he said, rubbing himself against her again.

"Please," she gasped, surprised at how desperate she sounded.

He didn't need to be asked twice. Lining up his cock at her entrance, he pushed in in one smooth, wet motion, her slick pussy parting for him as he sank in to the hilt.

They both had to quiet their groans. Gaia, it felt so fucking good to have him inside her. She didn't think anything compared to this. The euphoria of his closeness. The wholeness of him filling her, and the feral pleasure when he began to move.

He rocked his hips slowly at first, stretching her out, then moved faster. Reaching up with his free hand to pull down her bodice, he removed one of her breasts and fondled it gently, stroking his thumb over her nipple as he moved inside her.

"You have no idea how many ways I've dreamed of fucking you, Ena. How many things I want to do to you."

Ena whimpered at his words. She wanted him to do those things. Whatever he wanted. She wanted him to do everything to her.

"Will you let me do whatever I want once we're alone again?" he whispered low in her ear.

Ena looked over her shoulder at him, biting her lip to keep from shouting as he drove into her. "Only if you let me do whatever I want too," she said seductively, her words punctuated by the slam of his hips into her.

"Fuck," he groaned. "Ena." He grabbed her face, tilting it towards his to stick his tongue down her throat. He kissed her until she was breathless, picking up his pace as she got closer to her orgasm.

"What is it you want most? Tell me," he commanded, looking into her eyes, his pupils blown wide.

She wanted so many things. How could she even answer that question? But there was one thing she hadn't been able to stop thinking about since their time in Attax.

"You in my mouth," she answered honestly, all shame lost to the wind as he moved his hand down to her clit once more. She groaned. "Coming on my tongue."

Her words seemed to break him, as he moved frantically inside her, the sounds of their bodies slapping together echoing off the cave walls, and Ena broke.

She bit down on her lip so hard she drew blood as her orgasm tore through her. Her pussy throbbed and clenched around Ty's cock as she felt his release spill inside her, mixing with her wetness to create an intoxicating slickness that had her arching her hips back against him for more.

"Damn, viper," Ty said breathlessly. "You are so fucking stunning when you take what you want from me."

He pulled his cock out of her slowly, and she mourned his loss as her body went limp. Lazily, she flipped around so they were facing each other. He looked at her with desire still swimming in his eyes. What they'd done had been fucking amazing, but after so long without one another, it was never enough. All that talk of what they wanted to do had left her wanting more.

And he clearly felt this too, because he moved his free arm lower between them, and then she felt his fingers at her entrance, two of them this time, as he slowly, gently dipped them inside her. She gasped at the feeling, her body still so sensitive after her orgasm. Then, meeting her gaze, he raised them to her mouth, showing her the slick mixture of their pleasure on his fingers. He arched his eyebrow in silent question. Did she mean what she'd said?

But there was no question. She locked eyes with him before reaching out and drawing his fingers into her mouth, sucking with hollowed cheeks until they were clean. His jaw clenched as she swirled her tongue over his fingertips, the taste of the two of them together combined with his salty skin hitting her tongue.

A wide seductive grin spread over her face as she released his fingers. She'd never done anything like that before, but she'd fucking loved it.

An absolutely stunned and entranced look came over his face as he watched her, but it was quickly replaced by a devious glint when he saw her smile.

"You're so fucking evil," he said, one corner of his mouth tipping up as he lowered his head to whisper into her ear. "And I love it."

CHAPTER FIVE

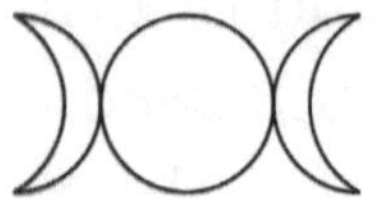

Ena

ENA AWOKE TANGLED UP with Ty the next morning, and despite what lay ahead of them, she couldn't help the contented hum that left her throat as she nuzzled into his warmth. This was the first time they'd gotten to sleep next to one another since everything had changed, and she relished it.

"Rise and shine, lovebirds!" Steig shouted at them from across the cave, a hint of bitterness in his voice. "The sun's almost up."

She felt Ty stir awake beside her, placing a chaste kiss on her forehead before extricating himself from their cozy nest of cloaks and standing up. He reached out a hand to help her up too before heading to the cave entrance, giving Steig a look of challenge on the way out, as if daring him to say what he thought.

She didn't even realize she was staring longingly after Ty until Turner came over, holding another piece of jerky out to her as he chuckled to himself.

"What?" she asked defensively, suddenly feeling self-conscious.

"Me? Oh, nothing," Turner said, failing to hide his grin. "It's just...you two are really going for it, huh?"

"Yeah..." Ena said, suddenly feeling shy about it. They hadn't discussed what they would say to Turner and Steig, but seemed like their secret was out now.

"I'm happy for you two. Should put a stop to the crackling sexual tension we had to endure all those weeks of traveling," Turner said, giving her a teasing shoulder bump.

Ena rolled her eyes, even though deep down she was enjoying Turner's playfulness, until she caught Steig staring daggers at them as he packed up one of his saddlebags.

"You got something to add, grumpy?" Ena asked him, daring him to say what he thought. If Ty wasn't scared of him, then neither was she.

Steig just shook his head. "Nope, just... Good luck, I guess." He said it in that usual curt way of his, but underneath, Ena could have sworn there was a hint of sincerity.

Ty strode back in a few minutes later, having fetched their horse and filled Ena's waterskin for her. She drank greedily from it before leaving the cave to relieve herself in the woods.

She still couldn't get over how different the landscape was here. It was so much rockier and more barren than she was used to, and she honestly couldn't imagine how the daemons had survived here for so long. The soil wasn't suited for agriculture, and there wasn't much game. How were they surviving under the mountains?

The morning air was crisp, and Ena wrapped her cloak tighter around her. Bless Greya for bringing Ena's own dark-green cloak from home when she'd come for her in Occidens, so at least she was no longer forced to use the one Steig had "borrowed" for her from the small village of Tritam.

The thought of Greya brought a small flash of guilt to her mind, though. Yule was coming in a few weeks, and she wondered if she and Perse would be hand-fasted on it as they'd planned. The thought of missing it wrenched at Ena's heart, as did any thought of her sister.

After relieving herself, Ena wandered back to the cave opening, where she saw Steig and Ty readying the horses. They were deep in conversation, but something about the tone of their voices made her stop where she stood, hidden by the thick trunk of a pine tree.

"Well, don't hold your tongue on my account. Spit it out, motherfucker," Ty was saying to Steig. His voice was low so as not to carry, but she could feel his anger.

"I'm not holding my tongue, asshole. You already know where I stand. Even if you do trust her, how can you think this is a good idea?"

"It'll be expected of us anyway, given what she'll be pretending to be, so it's not like we'll have to hide it. Why can't you just be happy for me?" Ty asked through gritted teeth.

"I *am* happy for you," Steig said, his voice hushed and angry now too. "I know what you feel for her, and that may be all well and good for right now, but what about after?"

"After what?"

"After we break the bond? What then? What kind of future will you two have? You know what's expected of you."

Ty ran his fingers through his hair before bringing them down to stroke his beard in that nervous way of his. "I don't know, Steig, but I do know I feel hopeful about us for the first time in a long time, and I'm not willing to give that up. Not anymore."

Steig sighed, an extremely exasperated, put-upon sound. "I can understand that, but Ty...just be careful. Okay?" the man said beseechingly. "I'd hate to see this end badly for you, or her."

"It won't," Ty said. "I have it under control, I promise."

Steig nodded, though Ena could still sense his reluctance.

"Now, are you with me?" Ty asked.

"I'm with you," Steig said, his anger simmering down.

"Really?" Ty asked, sounding skeptical.

"Really. If you're all in, then I'll try to be too," he said, reaching out to grip Ty on the shoulder.

Ty nodded at him, and gripped him back, and Ena felt the tension dissipate between them as she emerged from behind the tree, walking again towards Ty.

His face lit up as he saw her, a smile breaking apart the harshness of his features. "Are you ready to go?" he asked her.

"Yep," she said, giving him a warm smile in return. She was glad that Ty seemed to have worked things out with Steig—it would be much nicer for them if he was supportive—but some of the things he had said, some of the difficulties he'd hinted at, left her feeling a bit apprehensive.

She chose to push those from her mind as Ty helped her mount up and settled in behind her. Turner, who had finally made his way out of the cave, and Steig followed suit on their own horses. Ena was pleased to see that Turner's horse, Mahnin, was healthy and well cared for. She'd developed a soft spot for the beautiful creature when they'd met in Attax after Ty had traded one of his best daggers to purchase her. For some reason, Ena felt a strong affinity for the black, glossy mare, and she was secretly jealous that she didn't get to ride her herself.

The four of them rode for most of the morning, weaving back and forth across the elevating landscape, nestling themselves deeper into the foothills. They rode at a good pace, stopping just once for a brief break, but everyone seemed in good spirits as they joked and shared about their recent experiences. Ty finally had a chance to share in detail what it had been like with the Occidens Coven, and Turner had been thoroughly impressed hearing the details about their escape.

But sometime around noon, Ena felt the air around her companions shift. They fell silent, almost as if they were under a spell, as they entered a shadowed pass between two of the peaks. Ena had never been this deep into the Chasm Mountain range before. She'd been to the edge of them south of here where they neared the Auster Coven, but the witches never ventured beyond the edge of the foothills. There was never any reason to.

The four of them moved deeper into the pass as it got narrower and colder, the only sound the clip-clop of their horses' hooves on the rocky soil. Ena wanted to ask how close they were, but she didn't dare speak. Something about their eerie silence told her not to—like they were concentrating, and she shouldn't disturb them.

After about an hour, they turned the corner and stopped as Ena found herself facing a huge, gaping hole in the side of the mountain—the entrance to the Underworld.

It was clearly not natural. It was jagged and uneven, and looked like it had been made by hand, whether by pickax or...something else. Wide enough to fit at least two horses side by side, and tall enough for someone twice her height, it was pitch black and intimidating in and of itself, but that wasn't even the strangest part. Etched all around the edges of the opening were symbols—they looked like complex markings made of lines and angles, kind of like the letters she knew, but different. There was no doubt that they were significant, but what they meant, Ena had no idea.

"What are those?" Ena asked in a whisper as the men dismounted.

"Runes," Ty answered, as he wrapped his hands around her waist to help her off the horse.

"What are runes?" she asked, realizing that she probably sounded like a child with her constant questions, but she couldn't help herself.

"Runes are a form of magic used by daemons to infuse their Powers into objects. We call it Imbuing. These ones, for example, are Imbued with a daemon's Power of *ambago*, meant to confuse mortals if they were ever to stumble upon the entrance."

"What would happen if they did?"

"They wouldn't know what they were looking at, and they'd feel confused enough to think they were lost and turn around."

"That's fascinating," Ena said, contemplating this form of magic that was entirely novel to her. "And does it impact daemons too?"

"Not if you already know where the entrance is," Ty said. "That's why we were all concentrating so hard as we entered the pass. It takes focus to overcome the magic."

"Huh," Ena said, feeling grateful that daemonic magic had no impact on her. Though Ty had said that had been an unintended consequence of the witches' spell binding daemons to Iblis, and suddenly she wondered...would that change when they broke it?

Gripping her hand, Ty guided her and their horse towards the entrance and stepped inside.

It was pure darkness. She couldn't see more than a few feet in front of her, and her heart pounded as they entered it.

After taking several steps into the dark, her eyes began to adjust, and she saw why. The entrance immediately lowered into a wide set of stairs carved into the cave floor. Now that she was directly above it, she could see lanterns placed strategically along it, illuminating the staircase, but as they moved to walk down them, their horse balked.

"Shh, shh," Ty said, attempting to soothe the animal, who clearly had no interest in going down the deep, dark stairs into the unknown.

"This one's freaking out too," Turner said, wrestling with Mahnin, who was trying to flee out of the cave.

"Iblis, this always happens with the unfamiliar ones. Let's leave them here for now and we can send Myka up to get them later," Ty said, leading their horse back towards the entrance and tying it to a metal bar drilled into the cave wall that looked like it was made especially for this purpose.

Steig and Turner did the same, even though Steig's horse seemed to be having no trouble—Ena supposed that one must have been with them since they'd left the Underworld—and then the four of them continued, now horseless, down the stairs.

Ena was surprised to find that the air was damp in the cave, but not stale, and as they got progressively deeper, instead of getting colder, the air seemed to get warmer and more humid. How was that possible?

The metal lanterns that lined the staircase were strange too. The flames inside them were blue, and they didn't flicker like candlelight. There was no wax to be seen, either, only a dark black substance that filled the bottom and which seemed to create an unwavering flame.

The staircase continued to wind down and around until it flattened and widened at the bottom, opening into a wide hallway lined with the same lanterns. Branching off the hallway were archways that led to other hallways, dozens of them which seemed to form an elaborate network under the mountain.

Ena was speechless already, taking in all of this, but as the hallway ended and opened into a huge cavern, she was in utter awe.

The chamber was enormous, the ceiling easily twice as high as the tallest tree she'd ever seen, with thousands of spiked stalactites, some as large as Ty, hanging menacingly down from it. Her footsteps echoed as she walked, the sound of them small and foreign to her ears as they became lost in the cavernous space. All around her, the dark-gray rock walls of the chamber were carved with giant pillars that almost seemed to blend into the stone, but upon closer examination were decorated elaborately with swirls, circles, and dots in patterns that resembled Ty's *onata* tattoos. The pillars were complimented by more pointed archways that dotted the space, leading into countless alcoves along the floor of the cave, each alight with the strange blue glow of the lanterns she'd seen walking in.

A carved staircase wove around the edges of the cavern, leading to landings every few stories up with archways branching off into more passageways into the darkness. And to top it all off, a raised platform was carved into the wall at the far side of the cavern. It was empty right now, and Ena couldn't help but feel like something important was meant to go there.

Together, the carved walls and lights all around the chamber, though slightly intimidating, were incredibly beautiful and she couldn't help but admire the artistry. To think that these walls had been carved by hand by daemons over the course of centuries was mind-boggling. The skill and time that would take alone left her with a feeling of intense awe for these people she knew so little about. How was it possible witches had been ignorant of this for centuries? Was it willful? All to keep the secret of the amulet and what they'd done? Because staring at the wonder of what daemons were capable of...a part of her understood witches' fear of them, and yet she found herself utterly fascinated.

She was so overcome by the vastness of the space and the artistry of its architecture that it took her a surprisingly long time to notice that they were not alone.

At the rear of the chamber, seated around a long, wooden table braced on metal legs, there were about half a dozen daemons, and all of their eyes were on the four of them as they made their way across the floor.

At the head of the table, facing them as they approached, was a large man. He was leaning back in an elaborate, gold chair, one of his elbows laid on the armrest as his fist propped up his rigid jaw. He was attractive, with short dark hair and slightly golden, hazel eyes. He looked to be somewhere in his fifties, with a similar build to Ty.

And he looked unhappy.

This must have been Ty's uncle Cole, the King of the Underworld.

Directly to his right sat a similarly sized man with dirty-blond hair and brown eyes, who looked undeniably like Turner. This must be his other uncle, Zak. She'd never made the connection before, but there was no doubt he was Turner's father.

The four other daemons were a mix of ages and genders. There was a large, bulky wall of a man with even more *onata* tattoos than Ty; a skinnier one with greasy hair who reminded Ena of a rat; and two women—one seated next to Zak who was brown-haired with bright-blue eyes, and an older woman with black hair who looked to be the senior of the group. All of them had *onata* tattoos, like Ty, Steig, and Turner, but some more than others, and they were all dressed similarly in the warm cave, with even the women wearing long-sleeve shirts and light, cotton pants, not unlike what mortal and witch men would wear in the summertime. The only thing that distinguished the women were the leather bodices they wore over top of their shirts.

Everyone was quiet as the four of them approached, and Ena's stomach tightened. If this room was any indication of the power the king wielded, it was intimidating to say the least.

Ty casually placed his large hand on the small of her back, leading her forward until they stopped at the opposite end of the table from where Cole sat, watching them like a hawk eyeing its prey.

"Ty," he greeted coldly. "You've returned." The man spoke quietly, but there was no need for more volume. The sound of his deep voice echoed around the cavernous space, making it loom larger. "I was beginning to think you were never coming back."

"My apologies, Uncle Cole," Ty responded, his voice steady and practiced. "We ran into some complications."

"I can see that," Cole responded, a feline smile spreading across his face. "What's this you've brought?" he asked, looking directly at Ena with a mixture of curiosity and disdain.

"We've taken a witch," Ty said stoically.

"Taken a witch, you say...and a very pretty one at that," Cole said, seeming entertained by the idea.

Ena's skin prickled under his focused attention, and she felt Ty stiffen beside her.

"It's been decades since we've had a witch-slave in the Underworld. What a...*gift*," he continued, over-enunciating the last word. Something about the way he said it told Ena he wasn't entirely pleased by this development.

"Yes, Uncle. I know she'll be most useful to us. I have big plans for her," Ty said, unwavering in the face of his uncle's double-talk.

"Undoubtedly," Cole said, the feline smile returning to his face. "I'd love to hear more of these plans you have, but I'm sure you're all very tired and need time to settle in, and as you can see, we were in the middle of a Convening." He gestured with an open hand to the table filled with daemons before him.

"Of course, Uncle. I can come back to debrief you on the mission and my plans at your convenience," Ty said, inclining his head slightly in deference.

Cole nodded once, as if in dismissal.

Ty placed his hand on Ena's back to lead her away, but Cole stopped them.

"One more thing, before you go." The way he spoke sent shivers down her spine, almost like there was a hidden threat to every word. "I know I would feel a lot more comfortable having a witch around if she were properly attired." He said the word "witch" like a curse, spitting it out between his teeth.

Ty froze and slowly turned back to face his uncle. "You know it won't work on her," he said tightly.

"Of course, but just for appearance's sake," Cole said, seeming delighted by Ty's hesitant reaction. He turned to the daemon on his left, the brick wall of a man who looked like his nose had been broken several times. "Gunnar, fetch an *imperae* collar for our new arrival."

Gunnar rose from the table, heading for one of the alcoves. It held several trunks, storing Gaia only knew what, and he lifted the lid off one, revealing a variety of metal objects. He grabbed something large and circular, and returned to their end of the table, handing it to Ty.

Up close, it looked to be a necklace of sorts, but not like the ones Ena had seen before. It was made entirely out of a thick band of metal, iron most likely, and was open on one side to presumably slip onto her neck. Carved into it were runes like the ones that had been on the entrance to the Underworld.

She looked up at Ty, who raised his eyebrow slightly at her. *Trust me?* he seemed to ask.

She gave an imperceptible nod. *With my life*, she thought.

He raised the *imperae* collar to her throat, pulling apart the metal slightly to slip it around the middle of her neck. The metal felt cold against her skin, and she was keenly aware of the feeling of Ty's fingers against her throat as he pushed it closed at the back. The necklace fit snugly, warming quickly against her skin. It wasn't uncomfortable by any means—she still had plenty of room to breathe and swallow—but something about the way they were all looking at her made her feel like there was much more to it than she knew.

"Good," Cole said, eyeing them closely. "Now you're dismissed," he added, with a flick of his hand. "Oh, and Steig," he added as they turned to go.

Gaia, this man certainly loved to elongate goodbyes.

"I'm sure my daughter is most excited to see you, but I do expect a visit from you soon too," he added pointedly, before turning his attention back to the daemons at his table.

Steig nodded in understanding, and turned to join her, Ty, and Turner as they all but fled the room.

CHAPTER SIX

Ty

TY WAS TENSE WITH unspent rage. His body vibrated with it as they retreated back down the passageway, and he had to resist the urge to rip the *imperae* collar off Ena's neck immediately.

He should have expected Cole would do this, but somehow, he hadn't thought the man would demand something that was purely symbolic and just...petty. But he should have known better, and he would never make that mistake again.

Once they were far enough from any prying ears, he turned to Ena as she walked beside him. "Are you alright?" he asked in a hushed tone, trying to dispel the simmering anger by checking in with her.

"Yes," Ena said soothingly, as if she could sense how upset he was. "But I do have a lot of questions."

Ty smiled ruefully, relieved that she was simply her curious self and not as disturbed as he was. "I'm sure you do. Don't worry, we're almost there," he said.

The four of them walked tightly as a group as they weaved through the seemingly endless and identical passageways that made up the Underworld, until they stopped at a familiar set of large, wooden double doors.

"We'll be good from here. Thank you both," he said, turning to look at Steig and Turner.

"Of course, brother," Turner said, patting Ty on the shoulder. "I'll give you both a chance to settle in, but I'll come find you later." He gave Ena a warm smile before nodding at Ty and continuing down the hallway past Ty's room.

Steig, however, hesitated.

"Go on, I know you're eager to see Lara and the kids," Ty said to him.

"You don't know the half of it," Steig said, running his hand through his hair. "But I just wanted to see if you wanted me with you, when you talk to Cole later. You know, for moral support."

Ty placed his hand on Steig's shoulder. "I appreciate the offer, but I can handle it."

"Are you sure?" the man asked, giving Ty that look he always gave when Ty was about to do something reckless. "You know that bastard can twist minds with his words just as easily as he can spread disease with his hands."

"Trust me," Ty said, giving his friend a reassuring look. "I can handle him."

He really could. He wasn't afraid of Cole. He knew to tread lightly around him, and not to provoke him, but he'd been handling his uncle for years. He knew what to say, and how to say it, to avoid any negative repercussions for himself or the people he cared about.

Even if it was increasingly hard to keep his anger in check.

"Alright, if you say so," Steig replied, seeming convinced for now. "Then do me a favor, and don't bother me for at least two hours," he said, raising his eyebrow in a meaningful way before he took off like a man on a mission down the hallway.

Ty chuckled after him. He knew Steig was super hard-up after several weeks away from his wife, especially because he and Lara were practically attached at the groin when they were together—hence their many children. He was happy for them, as he always had been—but it stung just a little less to think about that now that he finally had...

He turned back to face Ena, and the rage that had lingered in his body was quickly replaced with anticipation.

"What was that about?" she asked, clearly sensing there was some joke she'd missed.

"Nothing. Just Steig being a horny motherfucker," Ty said, reaching down to turn the iron handle on his door, and ushering them inside.

The chamber was just as he'd left it. He watched as Ena's eyes roamed over the space, starting with his large bed that took up most of the room. It was covered in furs from some of his more impressive hunts, and at its foot sat the trunk filled with countless trinkets and mementos from his childhood, including his prized hunting knife—the first thing he ever made in the forge.

Her eyes slowly left the bed and landed on his armoire—filled with the clothes he hadn't touched in over a month—and his bookshelf, which was littered with his favorite histories and tomes on Underworld geology and metallurgy, before finally landing on the round wooden table set with two fur-covered chairs in the corner.

Yes, everything was the same as when he left it, and yet having her here made it seem so incredibly different.

He'd never felt this way before—this mix of apprehension and excitement at having a woman in his private space. He'd had women in his room before, obviously, but he'd never cared what they thought of it—he barely cared if they stayed the night afterwards or not. He'd never truly wanted to show it to anyone before, and he'd been pretty private about his things.

But now...some strange part of him wanted her to see everything. What would she make of him?

He walked over to the table in the corner of the room where one of the *imperi* had already left a fresh pitcher of water with two cups.

Iblis, that was fast. They must've been notified of his arrival while he was talking to Cole...or maybe even before. He wouldn't be surprised if the whole "you caught me during a Convening thing" was just a power move. Cole was notorious for them.

He poured a glass of water for Ena and handed it to her. She took it wordlessly, her eyes drawn to one of the darkrock lanterns on the wall.

"So...this is your room," Ena said, seeming fascinated by it all as her eyes flitted again from detail to detail.

"Yes," Ty said simply, watching her reactions like a hawk. But she didn't say anything else.

"You said you had a lot of questions," he offered, pouring himself a glass next. "So go ahead. I'm here for you."

Her eyes landed back on him, and he instantly felt the blood rush to his cock.

Fuck, how did she do that with just one simple look?

He resisted the urge to adjust himself noticeably, knowing that this was not the time for that. He needed to go see Cole soon, but first, he wanted to make sure she was truly alright, and quell any of her concerns as much as possible.

"Okay, so what's that?" she asked, pointing to the lantern on the wall that glowed with a constant blue flame.

"It's a darkrock lantern," Ty said.

"What's...darkrock?" she asked, her brow furrowing as she watched it.

Iblis, how did she look so fucking adorable saying new words? There was something about that little line of uncertainty that formed between her brows, and the way her lips moved slowly around the letters like they were some new and delicious food. Fuck, it made him want to stick his tongue down her throat while she said it just to feel what it was like to be inside that perfect mouth.

He dragged his eyes up from her mouth and cleared his throat, remembering that she'd asked him a question.

"It's a black, rock-like substance that's found deep underground, far beneath the Underworld. It's a fuel of sorts. We mine it here, and burn it in our stoves for cooking, but when its crushed and mixed with animal fat, it also creates a long-lasting and bright flame that we use in the lanterns you've seen."

"There's a mine under here?" Ena asked, her eyes lighting up in curiosity.

Something fluttered in his chest at her reaction. The mine was one of his favorite things about the Underworld.

"Yes. There's several, in fact. Some for darkrock, some for other metals. There are significant deposits of almost every metal known to this side of the Chasm Mountains in the areas underneath and surrounding the Underworld. That's part of why this area was chosen when daemons sought refuge here."

"That's fascinating," Ena said, musing over this as she took a step toward the darkrock lantern, watching its solid blue flame before turning to look at him. "Is that why it's so warm down here? From burning the darkrock?"

"No," Ty said, moving to stand next to her in front of the lantern. "That's from the hot springs that run underneath us. They're closer to us than the mines, and there are aqueducts that run the warm water from there throughout the Underworld. It helps keep it livable down here, year-round."

"Really?" Ena said, her eyes widening. "That's amazing."

Ty smiled at her, and he was struck suddenly by a profound sense of disbelief.

Ena, a witch—*his* witch—was here in the Underworld.

"What?" Ena asked, her cheeks reddening slightly, catching him staring.

"Nothing," Ty began, reaching out to gently grab her face, stroking his thumb gently across the beautiful blush on her cheek to assure himself that she was real. "It's just, part of me can't believe you're actually here. I spent so many years dreaming of you in this very room, and now...here you are. It almost doesn't feel real."

Ena smiled up at him, and his chest felt tight. Did she know she had that effect on him?

"I know the feeling," she said, stepping closer into him.

He took the movement as permission and leaned down to press his lips to hers. Her lips were so incredibly soft, like two warm rose petals, and he parted them gently with his own. She opened for him, leaning into his body automatically like she was drawn there, and Ty pressed her lower back into him, feeling her breasts squish up against his chest.

His heart beat faster, and his cock hardened as everything they'd done last night came rushing back to him. The way she'd obeyed him and practically begged for it, the things she'd admitted, and the feral enjoyment in her eyes when she'd sucked his fingers clean.

Iblis, she was so fucking perfect for him, and it drove him absolutely wild.

His fingers dragged down the side of her neck as he deepened the kiss, only to snag on the cold iron of the *imperae* collar.

He pulled back, guilt flooding him as he looked down at it. Ena inhaled sharply, as if missing his kiss, before reaching her hand up to touch it herself.

"Shit, Ena," he said, stroking it with his thumb. "I'm so sorry about this. I should have warned you."

Ena looked down, watching his hand as he touched the collar. "What is it exactly?" she asked.

"We call it an *imperae* collar. It's Imbued using runes, like the ones you saw on the entrance to the Underworld, only instead of causing confusion, the collars are Imbued with the Power of *docili*. They make the mortal, or daemon, who wears it docile and compliant to commands."

"Like my *visanis*?" Ena asked, seeming concerned by this association.

"Sort of, but it doesn't compel them to do the command, like your Gift. It just increases their susceptibility to suggestion, and makes them more willing to do things without resistance."

"Others have worn them before?" she asked, her brow furrowed.

"Yes, the mortals that have been taken and forced to serve here in the Underworld, they wear them. And some daemons, too, are forced to wear them as punishment. Those who do are called *imperi*, and they are made to serve the upper- and mid-level daemons."

"There are different *levels* of daemons?" Ena asked, this idea seeming distasteful to her.

"Unfortunately, yes," Ty answered, steeling himself to reveal one of the more shameful aspects of his home. "It's part of the hierarchy I told you about, the one

Cole insists on. Not all daemons are afforded the same privileges as Steig, Turner, and I."

"I see," Ena said, contemplating this.

He knew these ideas were foreign to her, and he was worried how she might react. There were many things about the Underworld that were complicated, and he didn't want her to judge them all on the ways they'd been forced to be.

"But why did he make me wear it?" she asked. "The collar, I mean. The magic in the runes won't work on me because I'm a witch."

"Exactly," Ty said, raising an eyebrow. "Cole made you wear it anyway, as a symbolic gesture. Just to illustrate your status as a witch-slave. To make sure everyone, including me, knows your place in the hierarchy."

Ena scoffed at that and turned away from him, taking a seat in the chair. She seemed...not upset, exactly, but annoyed.

"I know this is a lot to take in," he said sympathetically. Would it be too much?

She sighed, then looked up at him. "It is, but I'm fine, I promise. It's just that your uncle seems like a fucking piece of work," she said.

Ty couldn't help but laugh. That was one relatively mild way of putting it. He would go with "manipulative piece of shit," but that was just him.

"Believe me, I know," he said. "That's part of why I want to break the bond. To break his hold on this place. If daemons had more of a choice...they might not all follow him."

Ena nodded. "I get it," she said. "I'm okay, really."

Ty's chest swelled with pride to see how well she was taking everything in stride, and part of him relaxed slightly. "You're doing so well with all of this, Ena," he said gently. "I'm impressed. But let me know if that changes, okay? I don't ever want you to feel scared. You know I'll protect you, right?"

"Yes, Ty, I know," she said, giving him a small, sweet smile. "I trust you."

Something about the way she said those words made him feel so...powerful. It was absolutely intoxicating.

"But you know...it is strange," she continued, staring up at the low cave ceiling.

"What is?" he asked, following her gaze.

"Being underground," she said. "At first, it felt off-putting. I'm so used to the sky, and the trees, and all the signs of the animals and plants. But here, my Knowing is so...quiet. I can't read any of the daemons, and there's no animals, and yet..." Her eyes turned toward the stone wall beside her, and she reached out, stroking it gently with her fingertips. "I think I Know the stone," she said, her voice quiet as if she were concentrating.

"What's it feel like?" he asked gently, always fascinated by her magic and what her Knowing revealed.

"It feels...old. Older than anything I've felt before. Its age is...almost unfathomable. And it's so steady—unchanging in a way nothing else back home is," she said, shaking her head as if trying to understand. "And I Know it wants to remain that way, but even still...it *has* changed. It's changing now, as the water rushes through it, and we walk across its floors. This mountain is still moving. Just very, very slowly," Ena finished, a small look of awe on her face.

Ty watched her, enraptured. How she Knew all that after only being here for such a short time was undeniably impressive. It'd taken daemons centuries of study and experimentation to learn about stone, its histories, and how it changes. It was one of the things he loved about his home, and he couldn't wait to show her more of it.

But not now. Now, he had other unfortunate business to attend to.

"I should get going," he sighed. "Cole will want that debrief, and I still need to get Myka to attend to our horses."

Ena nodded solemnly, dragging her attention away from the stone.

"But while I'm gone, I thought you might like a bath," he added.

Her eyes lit up at the word "bath." "You have a bathtub in here?" she asked, looking around excitedly.

"Yes," he said, smiling at her excitement. He loved pleasing her. "Come on."

He led her through the archway next to his bed, hidden behind some hanging deer hides, that led into the bathing chamber, and heard her small gasp as she followed behind him.

"What in the Underworld is that?" she asked, pointing to the metal seat set above a hole in the cave floor.

"It's a toilet, like an outhouse. It's set above an aqueduct of the spring water I told you about, so it carries away the waste."

Then her eyes turned to the sink and the bathtub. "And how do you get water for those?" she asked. "Does someone bring them?"

"No, those come from the pipes too." He demonstrated, walking over to the bathtub and turning the metal knob on one side of the cave wall, opening the valve that let water flow out of the aqueduct and into the tub.

She stuck her hand in the stream of warm water as it flowed out of the cave wall. "Ty, this is amazing," she said in awe. "Every room here has this?" she asked, disbelieving.

"No, not every room. Mostly just the upper-level daemons," Ty said, some shame creeping into his enjoyment of her fascination. "It's meant to be a privilege, for those of us who fulfill Iblis's missions with our Powers. The mid- and lower-level daemons, who work in the forge and the mines, have communal bathhouses that they share."

She nodded, but Ty could tell the hierarchy felt strange to her. Witches, and even mortals, didn't have one that was so strict and determined by something out of one's control. Yes, some villages and Covens had more resources and more influence, but the differences were not so stark, and not enforced so intentionally.

Once the bath was filled, Ty turned off the knob, stopping the flow of water. "Take as long as you want," he said to Ena, gesturing for her to get in. "You'll be safe here, and I'll be back as soon as I can."

Ena nodded as he turned to leave, but then she grabbed him, stopping him. Standing up on the tips of her toes, she kissed him gently, in a way that set his blood boiling, before pulling back and looking up into his eyes with certainty and understanding. "I just want you to know I'm alright with all this, Ty, really. I know you want to change things here, and that's why I'm here. I'm with you," she said.

He smiled down at her, a sense of relief flooding him. He'd spent so long keeping secrets from her, it felt so good to not have to hide anymore.

Because even after everything, she was still here. Nothing had scared her away yet. And Iblis, it made him feel so...whole.

Holding her face in both hands, he gently kissed her one more time, before pulling back reluctantly to leave. "I'll be back soon, Ena. Enjoy your bath."

CHAPTER SEVEN

Ty

LEAVING ENA ALONE AS she prepared to bathe in *his* bath was definitely one of the hardest things he'd done in a while, and that included fighting off a dozen bandits and getting stabbed in the gut a few weeks ago.

Trying to shake her from his mind, he moved quickly through the passageways of the Underworld, heading for the stables on the mid-level where Myka maintained their horses. But it was almost impossible to do, so he gave in and let himself imagine that he was watching Ena undress, and appreciating the way the water would hit right at the level of her breasts when she sank into the water, hiding them just a little bit, but if the water were clear enough he could still see her nipples through it.

Iblis, the thought made his mouth salivate as he walked. Maybe he should go back and...

No, fuck. He really shouldn't go back. There'd be time for all that later—hopefully. He really needed to go talk to Cole—the sooner the better.

Pushing out the dirty thoughts, he entered the stables to find Myka brushing down a large chestnut horse with a black mane. The chamber was spacious, containing a decent-sized training pen and a row of individual stalls for the other five horses they kept here. A specialized aqueduct ran along the perimeter to carry away the horse waste that Myka swept into it, and another ran through their stalls to provide them with fresh water. Ty knew that if he peeked inside the stalls, he would see that each one was also filled with straw that had seen significantly better days.

Ty didn't blame Myka for that, though. He knew the daemon loved the horses he cared for like they were his own children, but getting a regular supply of straw and horse feed had always been difficult in the Underworld.

"Myka," Ty greeted, giving the quiet, middle-aged man a broad smile as he approached.

"Ty!" Myka responded gleefully, turning to look at him. "I'd heard you were back."

"News travels fast," Ty said as he reached out to shake the man's dirty hand.

"It always does around here," Myka said, his gray-blue eyes shining as he smiled. "It's good to have you back. Did you have a successful mission?"

"Yes," Ty said, slipping into the lie as easy as breathing. "Iblis will be pleased."

He felt a twinge of shame for lying to Myka about everything he had planned with the amulet. He was one of the daemons who Ty knew, in all likelihood, would be supportive. The man struggled to care for the horses underground year-round, and being welcomed back into the villages above would appeal to him greatly. But he couldn't risk word spreading to Cole, so for now, his plans had to remain secret.

"Ahh, I don't know why I even asked!" Myka said jovially, waving Ty off. "You always do well. Your father would be so proud."

The mention of his dad left a sinking feeling in Ty's stomach. It wasn't every day that someone mentioned him, and the feeling almost took him by surprise.

"Thank you," he said quickly, trying to brush it off. "How goes everything with the horses?"

"Well enough," Myka said, though his smile fell a bit. "I do wish we had more hay. You know how tough it gets for the horses to forage aboveground this time of year."

"I hear that," Ty said. "I'll talk to Cole about sending a group out on a mission soon to bring some back, and see what we can do."

"I'd appreciate that," Myka replied gratefully. The man was well-suited to caring for horses, due to his Power of *lenio*, which allowed him to soothe both people and animals, but it was not highly valued by Cole for missions in service of Iblis, hence Myka's status as a mid-level daemon. He knew that left Myka in a tough position when it came to advocating for himself and the horses under his care, so Ty often tried to step in when he could.

"Unfortunately, I've got three new arrivals for you," Ty explained, feeling a bit bad for dumping the new horses on him so suddenly. "They're waiting at the entrance. I hope it won't be too much trouble."

"No trouble, no trouble," Myka said, putting down the horse brush and closing the stall he was in. "I'll go fetch them right away. Spooked, were they?"

"Yes, exactly," Ty said. "Two of them we acquired while out on the mission."

"Ah, I see, poor dears. Won't be a problem," Myka said, walking back towards the main passageway with Ty. "Glad to have you home!" he added as he turned right to head towards the main stairwell that led up to the entrance.

Ty smiled at him warmly before heading the opposite direction, preparing himself to speak with his uncle. It was always a process to do so, but it was necessary to arrive calm and focused so the man couldn't take advantage of any unchecked emotions.

Ty cleared his mind as much as possible of all thoughts of Ena. It wasn't exactly easy, because pretty much every thirty fucking seconds he was imagining what she was doing by herself in the bath, but he knew it was critical if he was going to convince Cole with his story—especially if his uncle Zak was there too. He'd have to stick as closely to the truth as humanly possible and let nothing show.

Making his way upward, he once again entered the Great Antre.

Ty's footsteps echoed around the vast cavern as he approached where Cole sat on his throne at the head of his table. The king was alone now, praise Iblis, and reading the divination rune stones scattered in front of him across the tabletop. He didn't look up at Ty's approach.

"Uncle," Ty announced, stopping at the far end of the table. "I wonder if now is a good time to debrief you on the mission."

Cole looked up reluctantly, his eyes assessing. Ty hated that he insisted on having meetings in the Great Antre and not in his private chambers, the way his dad used to. But Cole loved the spectacle of it all. The Great Antre was the most central chamber in all the Underworld, connecting all the other levels and passageways in some way. Cole's presence in the center of it all sent a message and kept everyone on their toes.

"Nephew," he began, a predatory smile on his face. "I'm glad you could finally spare the time to speak with me. I'm sure you have many things demanding your attention now that you've returned. Not to mention all the new...distractions."

"I came as soon as I was able," Ty said, squashing his anger at the outright ridiculous insinuation that he'd taken too long to return. It had barely been an hour since they'd last spoke. But this was what Cole did, especially to him, knowing he was prone to rage.

Like Steig said, Cole didn't just spread disease with his hands, he loved to throw people's mental state off with his words too—finding those subtle weak spots in someone's mind that he could make fester.

Cole gave him a knowing smile. "So tell me...how were you able to serve Iblis on this mission?"

Ty lowered his head in deference before beginning his practiced response. "Steig was successful in using his Power in several different villages along the Western

Road, according to Iblis's will, and I was able to use my *furor* in a small village in the area as well."

"All that took so long?" Cole asked pointedly, his eyebrows raising.

"We ran into some bandits on the way and lost a horse. And, of course, we ran into some issues with the witch."

"Ahh, yes," Cole began, looking far too eager to discuss the topic. "I'm dying to hear how you came to acquire our new witch-slave. It's a very exciting development... We haven't had one in decades, not since your mother, if I recall."

"My mother was never a witch-slave," Ty responded shortly, feeling tension creep in. He needed to keep calm, though—he couldn't take the bait.

"I guess we'll have to agree to disagree on that," Cole said deliberately, his eyes lighting with devious glee.

Ty willed his body to relax before clearing his throat to explain. "On our way west, we stopped at the Auster Coven during their Samhain celebration. The plan was for Steig to use his *cupido* on the mortals visiting there, but we were discovered when the witch caught Turner using his Power. We worried that killing her outright, so close to the rest of her Coven, would garner too much suspicion, so we took her instead, and Turner burned down her house as a cover."

Ty paused, waiting to see if he bought this bastardized version of the truth. But Cole simply steepled his fingers in front of him, resting his elbows on the table, so Ty continued.

"The farther we got from the Coven, the more it became apparent that the witch was willing to cooperate with us in exchange for her life, so instead of killing her, we decided to bring her with us to add to our cover while we completed the mission, and ultimately, brought her back here."

"So you spared her life?" Cole asked, as if this wasn't obvious.

"Spared isn't the word I would use," Ty said, letting an edge enter his voice. "We simply... found a better use for her."

"Hmm," Cole said, contemplating. "And how exactly will she be used?"

Here came the tricky part. He needed an excuse for the research Ena would be doing about the amulet and breaking the bond to Iblis. Something that made the books she'd need seem less suspicious, but still, he hated to reveal what he had to.

"She's extremely knowledgeable about the Covens and witch magic. She can provide information on how best to destabilize them. And," Ty continued hesitantly, as if this were truly a secret he'd been keeping. "I have a theory. I think there may be some way to Imbue her Gift into an object using daemonic runes. Some way to combine witch and daemon magic, so the object will work on witches. And then use it to impact the Covens."

Cole's eyes lit up. Ty knew the vengeful fuck would love this idea.

"And what exactly is her Gift?" Cole asked, intrigued.

Ty paused. This was the part he'd been waiting for. There was no way Cole wouldn't go for it after this.

"*Visanis*," he said, raising one eyebrow in invitation.

Cole threw his head back and laughed with dark glee. "*Visanis*, you say?" he asked, grinning from ear to ear. "My, my, this is an interesting development. *Visanis* is a rare Power, even among daemons... What do you think of this, Zak?"

Fuck.

Ty whirled behind him to see his uncle Zak emerging from a nearby alcove. The bastard must've been waiting there the whole time, listening to their conversation. He hoped he'd been careful enough with his words to avoid any outright lying.

"Sounds like an interesting theory, Ty," Zak said as he approached them. He was a bit smaller than Cole, and a couple years younger, but he was just as shrewd. He may not have had the outright power that Cole had in the Underworld, but he was undoubtedly Cole's right-hand man, always there to jump when his big brother told him to. Although he hadn't always been that way. In fact, Ty remembered a time when he and his uncle Zak had been fairly close—before his dad died.

Zak's deep-brown eyes studied Ty as he moved to stand next to Cole's throne.

"I will commune with Iblis and see what the rune stones can tell us of his will in this regard," Cole said. "In the meantime, follow this theory of yours. I'll expect an update in time for your *onata* celebration."

Ty nodded. The *onata* celebration... That reminded him.

"Thank you, Uncle," he said, bowing his head slightly in deference. "I wonder, will you be sending a group out on a mission to trade for supplies for the celebration?"

"Yes," he said. "To trade and fulfill other services to Iblis, of course. Why?"

Ty was no stranger to the kind of "trade" that was encouraged on missions—where supplies were acquired as much through theft as the actual exchange of goods. Cole was always going on about how Iblis wanted them to take what they were owed from witches and mortals by using their Powers. They were encouraged to do this, even though the forge usually produced more than enough metal goods to trade in good faith for whatever daemons needed. But meeting the needs of the Underworld was never Cole's priority—it was serving Iblis and fulfilling his many vendettas, so Ty had learned to frame any request with this in mind.

"I've heard from Myka that the horses could use more hay to make it through the winter. And I know how vital the horses are to being able to complete missions for Iblis, so I wondered if you'd want them to get some on their way," Ty finished pointedly.

Ty hated his uncle for many things, and his hyperfocus on serving Iblis was definitely one of them, because it wasn't a goal Ty shared. But still, sometimes he wasn't sure if that intense focus made him a horrible King of the Underworld, or a great one.

"Fine, yes. I'll make sure they bring a large enough cart with them," Cole said dismissively.

Taking that tone as his cue to leave, Ty nodded in appreciation and turned to walk out.

"Oh, but Ty," Cole said, stopping him as he left with a warning tone. "I'm worried this is becoming somewhat of a pattern, and I would caution you to not let it become a habit."

"Let what become a habit?" Ty asked, knowing he was walking right into whatever trap Cole had laid for him with that comment.

"This...softness for *witches*," Cole replied, spitting out the word "witches." "I know your mother was one, but you're a daemon, Ty, through and through. Don't forget that."

"I haven't forgotten," Ty said truthfully. "I never will."

CHAPTER EIGHT

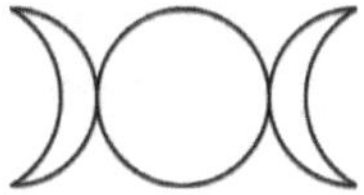

Ena

ENA STEPPED OUT OF the bathtub, her skin shriveled like a prune after being in the water for so long. Her dark hair dripped on the floor as she searched for a towel, eventually finding one tucked on an open wooden shelf in the corner of the small stone chamber.

Wrapping herself in it, she went to the mirror and wiped away the steam to take a look at her appearance. Her hair was longer than when she'd left home, and her eyes were sunken with dark circles. She'd definitely lost some weight with all the traveling and scarce food, but hopefully she'd be eating more regularly now, and that would remedy itself. She was grateful to be done moving around for the time being, and hopefully get some better rest.

She was about to look away, but her eyes caught on the *imperae* collar around her neck.

She hadn't lied to Ty; she really was okay with wearing it if it kept their true mission a secret. But the iron still felt strange around her neck. She knew the magic didn't work on her, but knowing what it did to others, and what it represented, left her unsettled.

It was harsh in appearance, almost crude. She could tell already that daemons were expert blacksmiths and metallurgists, but they had not put the same artistry into this collar. It was basic—almost ugly. But she supposed that made sense. Why waste your people's talents on an artifact that was meant to enslave those deemed less worthy?

Dragging her eyes from it, she looked around the bathing chamber instead. It was interesting, seeing all of Ty's little belongings scattered around. There were metal scissors, and a bone-handled toothbrush made with pig bristles. She saw a sewing kit, too, not unlike the one she'd stitched him up with a few weeks ago, and a large pumice stone next to the bath.

She never thought they'd have a chance to be so...domestic, and she found herself endlessly fascinated by all the small things that made him, him.

Wandering out of the bathroom, she took in the rest of Ty's room. It was cozier than she'd imagined, with all the rugs and the warmth from the hot springs flowing throughout the Underworld. Not that she'd imagined anything like this at all, really. She'd thought he was mortal for so long. Part of her felt like it was still trying to catch up to everything that had changed in such a short time.

Walking over to the bed where she'd left her dirt-covered dress, she debated putting it back on for a minute, but she couldn't bring herself to do it. After weeks of travel in the same outfit, and all the horse-riding and ground-sleeping she'd done, it was filthy and worn, so she walked to Ty's armoire instead. He had to have something in there that she could wear until her clothes could be cleaned.

She opened the creaky piece of furniture to find a few clean shirts hanging inside next to several wool coats. She pulled one of the shirts out and let her towel fall to the floor before pulling it over her head. Since no one was around, she indulged herself in giving it a deep sniff.

It smelled like Ty—the cedar and honey scents most notable in the fresh clothing, and the feeling of his presence wrapped around her, comforting her, despite his physical absence.

Gaia, she was glad no one had been around to see that. There was no denying—she had it bad.

At least she knew she wasn't alone in that fact now. Her stomach fluttered slightly, thinking of last night and everything that Ty had said...and what they'd done.

Her thoughts were interrupted when there was a decisive knock on the door.

Ena whipped her head towards it. Glancing down at her attire, she hesitated. Should she answer the door? This was Ty's room. Was she technically allowed here, as a witch-slave? Would their cover be blown already? They hadn't discussed any of that before he'd left.

She flitted around nervously for a second, before deciding that, no, Ty would have warned her if she needed to stay hidden, and he'd said that she'd be safe here, so she cautiously went to the door and cracked it slightly.

A woman stood in the hallway. She was tall, with dark-auburn hair and brown eyes. She had a few freckles scattered across her cheeks, and they moved as she smiled friendlily at Ena.

"You must be Ena. I'm Steig's wife, Lara. I was sent to bring you some clothes," she said, holding up an armful of said clothing.

"Oh," Ena said, opening the door a bit more. Wait—should she trust this person? She'd heard a decent amount about Steig's wife, but she had no idea whether this person was actually her. She could be lying...

Ty hadn't said how cautious to be with the other daemons yet, and she hadn't thought to ask. But he *had* said that being his witch-slave afforded her some protection from the other daemons, who weren't allowed to touch her without his permission, and this woman did seem to genuinely be here to bring her clothes.

She opened the door the rest of the way and stepped aside as Lara entered the room.

The woman looked Ena up and down, noting her strange choice in attire. "Looks like I came just in time," Lara said jokingly.

She seemed to note Ena's hesitation, because she walked over slowly to the bed to place the clothes down, like she didn't want to spook her.

"I've heard a lot about you. It's nice to finally meet you," she said, her warm smile returning.

"Ty told you about me?" Ena asked cautiously. What exactly had she heard?

"No, not Ty. He didn't like to talk much about you, understandably. But Steig told me," Lara began. "The infamous witch who broke Ty's heart."

Ena didn't quite know how to respond to that. Should she defend herself? It hadn't been her fault, after all. Lara never gave her the chance, though.

"I must admit, I've never met a witch before," the woman continued.

Ena was shocked to hear this. "Not even on missions?" Ena asked, failing to keep her surprised tone to a minimum. But now that she mentioned it, Ena noticed she didn't have any visible *onata* tattoos like Ty, Steig, and Turner did. Did that mean she was one of the mid-level daemons that Ty mentioned who worked in the forge and mines instead?

"I don't go on missions. My Power is not fit for it, according to my father," Lara said, giving her a tight-lipped smile.

"Your father is Cole?!" Ena asked, her eyebrows jumping up. She had no idea Steig was Cole's son-in-law, although now all that talk earlier about him needing to report to Cole made a lot more sense.

"Don't hold it against me," Lara said. "I know he's a bastard. But we can't choose who our parents are."

Ena smiled a little at that. At least she agreed he was a bastard. "Well, I won't hold it against you, as long as you don't hold my being a witch against me. We're not all you've been told," Ena replied.

"Likewise, though I'm betting you already knew that or you wouldn't be here," Lara said, sizing her up. "Here—" She reached down into the pile of clothes on the bed, picking out a pair of the same light cotton pants that she was wearing, a dark-blue man's-style shirt, and a leather bodice vest that laced in the front. "Try these on," she said, handing them to Ena. "I'm a bit taller than you, but it's the best we can do until we can get more for you. Trysh is about to finish another batch of fabric and can make you a few things soon."

"Thanks," Ena said sincerely. Even though she wasn't used to wearing pants, this was infinitely better than putting her dirty dress back on. "How did you know I needed clothes? Did Steig send you?"

"Iblis, no," Lara said, shaking her head and smiling widely. "He's still recovering from our reunion and spending some time with the kids. Ty came to see me on his way to the mines, asked me if I could help you out."

"Oh," Ena said, trying to sound okay. Ty was at the mines? She knew he likely had many responsibilities here, and things to catch up on now that he was back, but her heart sank a bit to hear that he wasn't coming back right away.

"Iblis, you two got it bad for each other, huh?" Lara laughed, a beautiful, lilting thing that lifted Ena's spirits just by hearing it. "He gave me the same forlorn look when he stopped by and asked me to come to you on his behalf. But don't worry, he said to bring you over for dinner too. He'll meet us there soon enough."

Dinner? With Lara and her family? That sounded...strangely nice. Ena didn't realize how off-putting it would be to only know three people in the entire Underworld, and two of them only cursorily. Lara didn't seem too bad, and if Ena was going to be here for a while researching the amulet and posing as a witch-slave, it might be nice to make some more connections beyond Ty, especially if he was going to be busy a lot.

"Thanks, that sounds nice," Ena replied, giving her a warm smile. "I'll go get dressed."

Ena dipped back into the bathroom, quickly taking off Ty's shirt and stepping into the clothes Lara had given her. The pants were form-fitting and very comfortable, but definitely too long. She had to roll them up several times at the bottom. The shirt was also a bit long, so she tucked it in and rolled up the sleeves, but the vest-style bodice fit well, and accentuated her figure nicely. Ty didn't have a full-length mirror in his bathroom, but from what she could see in the small vanity one, she thought she looked pretty good. Different, but good.

She emerged from the bathroom to find Lara hanging up the rest of the clothes she'd brought in Ty's armoire. She supposed that meant she would be staying here. She hadn't asked Ty explicitly about that, but she was relieved. She didn't want to be anywhere else but with him.

Lara turned around to look at her, taking in her new outfit. "It suits you," she said, smiling warmly.

"Thanks," Ena replied, smiling back.

"Come on, I'll take you to our chambers. Fair warning—I don't know what Steig told you about us, but we have four kids, ages two, four, six, and eight, so it definitely will be chaotic. I hope you're okay with that." Lara looked at her, gauging her reaction as she went to open the door.

"Not a problem," Ena replied sincerely. She didn't have a vast amount of experience with children—she was the youngest sibling in her home, so she didn't have any extended up close and personal knowledge of them. But there were always kids running around her Coven's village. All adults usually had a hand in keeping an eye on them and helping them if need be, so she was at least aware of the madness that often ensued when multiple children were around.

"Good. Besides, if they get too crazy for you, I can always use my Power on them," she said, smiling widely. Was that a joke?

She found herself intensely curious about what Lara's Power was, but before she had a chance to ask, Lara ushered her into the passageway outside Ty's door, and she found herself following this new daemon deeper into the Underworld.

CHAPTER NINE

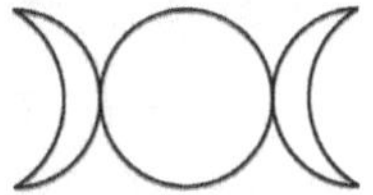

Ena

ENA FOLLOWED LARA THROUGH the dimly lit, twisting passageways of the Underworld. They took a right, then a left, then another right, and by the time they reached another large set of double doors, Ena's head was spinning trying to keep track of how they'd gotten there. It all looked the same—the same blue darkrock lanterns, the same dark-gray stone walls. She hoped she'd be mostly escorted around by one of the daemons she knew, because there was a very good chance she would get lost on her own.

Lara pushed open the double doors they'd stopped at, leading them into a large, homely chamber that was even more spacious than Ty's.

A sizeable wooden table was centered to their left, with low benches on either side for seating, and to their right, several comfortable-looking wooden chairs covered in furs were clustered around a series of wooden children's toys, including a couple long toy daggers and carvings of animals: a bird, a deer, and a wolf. There was a large blanket strewn halfway across the chairs, creating a dark hidden space underneath.

"Apologies about that," Lara said, gesturing to the mess of furniture. "The kids were playing 'Iblis in the Cave' earlier so you might have to move some stuff if you want to sit down."

Ena smiled at that. "No problem," she said, wondering how exactly one played "Iblis in the Cave."

Just then, Steig and Turner emerged from the open archway to the left. There was another archway leading off to the right, too, but this one was hidden by a wooden door. The bathing chamber, maybe?

"Ena," Turner greeted, his blue eyes warming with a smile. He'd clearly bathed too and was dressed in similar garb as herself. "Are you settling in okay?"

"Yeah, I am, thanks," she said, touched by his concern. Then she turned to Steig, who looked unhappy to see her as always, his dark eyes suspicious and cold.

Then the screaming started.

Two boys who must've been the six- and four-year-olds came dashing out of the room Steig and Turner had come from, yelling "Attack!" as they jumped on their father.

Steig put on a fake air of viciousness, grabbing them both at the same time and roaring as he flung each of them in turn onto a fur-covered chair. The boys erupted into fits of giggles as they landed on the chairs, instantly getting in position to attack again.

"Get the wolf!" the bigger one yelled, picking up his wooden toy weapon and holding it up to his father.

Steig snarled like a wolf at them, pretending to be distracted by the long dagger while the younger one jumped on his back.

"Arrgghhh!" Steig cried, feigning a wound and collapsing on the floor.

The two boys fell into fits of giggles as they pretended to triumph over the vicious wolf.

Lara laughed beside her, watching the show. Again, Ena was surprised by how captivating her laugh was—it seemed so lighthearted and free, so full of joy.

Ena turned back to see Steig laughing now, too, and it caught her off guard. She didn't think she'd ever seen him laugh before.

She found herself staring at the playful domestic scene, somewhat in awe, and smiling to herself, when she heard the door open behind them.

Ty walked in, and her gravity shifted. His presence seemed to fill the room, like he was larger than it, and all eyes turned to him.

She noticed he was wearing the same clothes as when he'd left, and Ena realized that out of all of them, he still hadn't had the chance to bathe and change his clothes since returning. She instantly felt annoyed on his behalf. Who in the Underworld was keeping him so busy that they couldn't give him a few minutes to wash up after such a long journey?

But then he smiled at her, and her annoyance vanished.

"I see I'm the last to arrive," he said, looking her over and taking in her new clothing and clean appearance. He came over to stand next to her, placing a hand on her lower back in greeting before leaning in to whisper in her ear. "I missed you," he said, his voice low and rough.

"Sorry I was gone so long. Everything go okay getting here?"

Ena nodded, finding herself rather tongue-tied all the sudden at his closeness.

He pulled back a bit, but she didn't miss the way he briefly looked down at her leather bodice where her cleavage was on prime display.

"Like my new outfit?" she asked, teasing him.

"I like everything you wear, but yes, I am enjoying this particular view immensely. Will you turn around for me later so I can see all of it when there aren't children present?"

Ena giggled—actually *giggled*—at that. She didn't remember the last time she'd giggled.

Ty seemed to like it, because he smiled wickedly at her response.

"You know we also exist, right?" Turner asked pointedly from beside them, grinning at Ty.

"Of course, but you don't look like *that* in a leather vest, so excuse me for ignoring you," Ty said jovially before clapping Turner on the shoulder in greeting.

Steig didn't seem to mind as much, as he had descended into another wrestling match with his children. Meanwhile, Lara had disappeared into one of the rooms through the archway, from which Ena could smell the delicious scent of roasting meat wafting out.

"Is there a kitchen back there?" Ena asked, suddenly curious about the rest of their chambers. The kitchen was always the central part of a witch's home. Ena practically grew up in the kitchen, grinding herbs for potions to help Heran and watching her sister cook.

There were many times she could recall spending the entire day there, as other witches and visitors came and went, bringing potions and food in trade, laughing and talking.

The thought sent a pang to her heart. As much as it felt right to be here, she still missed her Coven.

"Yes," Ty said. "You want to see it? I'm sure Lara won't mind."

Ena nodded enthusiastically, so Ty placed his hand on her lower back, leading her through the archway. There was another small passageway with several rooms that must have been bedrooms branching off of it, but at the back was another open archway leading into a small, unusual kitchen.

Darkrock lanterns lit the space, which was filled with a wooden island, and two large stone countertops, carved right into the wall of the cave. They were hollowed out underneath, with two large metal boxes installed in the empty space.

The metal boxes looked almost like square cauldrons, but they had a door on the front, and they seemed to be putting off heat, because it was warmer in here than the other rooms.

Lara was standing in front of one, stirring a pot that was placed on top of it. It looked to be the source of the delectable smell, and Ena found herself fascinated yet again.

"What are those?" she asked, pointing at the metal boxes that seemed to emanate heat.

"Stoves," Ty explained. "They're forged out of metal, and then we burn darkrock inside to create heat to cook on. That one's for pots and pans," Ty said, gesturing towards where Lara was stirring. "And that one's like an oven," Ty added, pointing at the other one that had several doors on it, presumably to place goods for baking.

"Wow. Does everyone's chambers have those?" Ena asked. That seemed like a significant feat of engineering to create the stoves and carve the counters right into the wall.

"No," Lara said, chiming in from where she stood cooking dinner. "The upper level daemons, including my father, are usually served by the king's kitchen, and the mid-level and *imperi* each have a communal kitchen they use. We had a special one installed here because of my position."

"Lara is the overseer of the kitchens. She handles the rationing for each one, and the planning for celebrations," Ty explained.

"But don't think I'm too domestic," Lara said, smiling at his description of her. "I can still kick your ass in the fighting ring."

Ty laughed at that, but Ena was confused.

"Fighting ring?" she asked.

But before anyone could respond, they were interrupted by a huge dog that came from behind them, barreling right into Ty's legs.

"Cerberus!" Ty cried, bending down to scratch the dog's ear.

Ena took it back. "Huge" was an understatement. The dog could've been a small deer. It was black, with a sleek coat, and large flopping ears. Ena had to dodge its whip-like tail as it wagged ceaselessly at Ty.

That's when Ena realized—this was no ordinary dog, not like the ones the mortal villagers kept to scare away predators from their chicken coops.

It was a hellhound.

"He's missed you, you know," Lara said, coming over to pat the hound on the head. "But he does get an enormous amount of attention from the children, especially Leela, who likes to try and ride him," Lara said, smiling fondly.

Having gotten his fill of Ty for the time being, the large dog fixated his black nose on Ena, sniffing her up and down, likely confused by her new scent mixing with that of Lara's clothing. She cautiously reached out to pet his head, and he leaned into her, nearly knocking her over with his weight. She couldn't help but laugh. All the horrifying things she'd been told about hellhounds—that they were vicious creatures who did daemons' bidding and hunted small children in the night—well, they certainly did not add up to this picture of an oversized puppy that just wanted pets.

"Cerberus is your hellhound?" Ena asked Ty, trying to satiate the dog's need for scratches.

"Yeah, he's been mine since my father passed, but Lara and Steig take care of him for me now, since I'm gone so often," he explained.

It struck Ena then how much she still had to learn about Ty. He had such a full life here. A history she would never fully understand. What else didn't she know?

"Okay, time for dinner," Lara announced, dragging Ena from her thoughts. "Cerberus, you get," she said, shooing the hound away with her free hand. "You already got your dinner, you big monster." In the other hand, she carried a large metal pot.

Ena and Ty followed her out to the table. While they'd been in the kitchen, someone had set it with metal plates, cups, and spoons.

Steig and Turner already sat at the table, wrangling the younger ones into their seats. Meanwhile, an older child, about eight years old, appeared from down the hallway carrying their youngest, a toddler with the same dark-red hair as Lara.

"Dada!" the littlest one shouted, running over to Steig and climbing into his lap. He obliged her, smiling softly as she perched on his knee.

As everyone sat around the table, Lara dished out what looked like a venison stew into each of the children's bowls before serving herself. Then each of the adults served themselves in turn.

It smelled delicious, filled with carrots, onions, and potatoes, and a slightly different combination of herbs than Ena was used to.

Looking around at the children as they chatted with their parents, and Ty and Turner as they ate, she was struck yet again by how domestic and normal the scene was. These children could have easily been mortal or witch children, not at all the picture of daemonic depravity they'd been told about. And while she was thoroughly impressed by the way daemons had adapted to their circumstances—the innovations they'd developed were astounding—she knew there were things about living in the Underworld that were not ideal.

How often did they have to go out and pretend to be mortal in order to trade for the food they needed? Did the children ever go to the surface? Did they see real versions of the animals they had wooden carvings of? How often did they get to play in the woods and explore the beauty of Gaia's balance? They deserved that too.

Not for the first time, she was struck with a profound sense of guilt for the role witches had played in forcing daemons into the Underworld, and it made her feel all the more motivated to figure out how to break the bond for them.

Ena ate her stew in silence, watching the cheerful scene before her. Once the children had finished—which happened surprisingly quickly as they got distracted—they went off to play in their makeshift chair-cave once more, with the eldest pretending to be Iblis, scaring the other three until they screamed and ran out. Even Cerberus seemed content as he lay down and guarded them peacefully from a fur rug in the corner.

"How did everything go with Cole?" Turner asked Ty in a hushed tone from where he sat across the table. "Did he buy it?"

Ty nodded as he finished a mouthful of stew. "I think so, but your dad was there."

Turner looked down, picking at his food.

"Don't think we missed the way the bastard completely ignored your presence during our arrival," Steig said, drawing Turner's attention to him. "You'd think he would spare at least a glance or a greeting for his sole heir."

"Heir"? That was a new word. Ena was about to interrupt and ask what that meant, but the conversation continued before she could.

"I'm used to it," Turner said, trying to seem unbothered, but Ena could tell he was. "I just hope your skills at deception circumvented his Power."

"They always do," Ty said cockily, leaning back in his chair. "But that's not all I need to tell you." He looked at them each in turn, including Lara. Did she know about the amulet? She must, being Steig's wife, and they didn't seem to hesitate talking about it in front of her. "I convinced Cole that Ena would be useful in researching ways to Imbue her Gift into an object using daemonic runes so we can use it to disrupt the Covens. He's obviously on board with that, but he wants an update by the *onata* celebration in two weeks' time."

"He wants me to do what?" Ena asked, her stomach clenching with nerves. Would she really be expected to do that?

"Don't worry, you won't actually do it. It's just a cover so he's not suspicious when we start researching magical objects, and witch and daemonic history for the amulet."

Ena felt relieved, slightly. The cover story made sense. It was ingenious, really, but it still felt icky to even pretend to be doing something like that to the Covens. Despite what a few witches did in the past, she knew they deserved none of that.

"So what will you start with?" Steig asked from where he sat next to Lara. His hand wandered idly around to the back of her neck, brushing her hair away as he drew lazy circles on it. She saw Lara lean slightly into him, closing the gap between them on the bench.

"I'll take Ena to the Archives tomorrow," Ty said, looking over at her. "There's a bunch of books there we can look through, including the ones I got from Petyr."

Petyr... Ena remembered what Ty had told her when they were in Occidens—about the mortal bookbinder friend he'd made while out on a mission. The one who'd told him about the amulet in the first place. She still had so many questions about him and how he knew what he knew, but maybe looking through his books would give her some answers.

"Okay," Ena said, feeling eager to get started. "Where are we keeping the amulet?" she asked. She didn't know why, but ever since Gaia had granted her the vision when she put it on, she had felt possessive of it. It was a witch's amulet, after all.

"Turner has it, for now," Ty said. "Why?"

"Well, I think I should keep it, or Ty, I mean," she said, looking hesitantly towards Turner and Steig.

Lara was silent as she watched them all, and part of her was curious to know what the woman thought about all this. She was Cole's daughter, after all, even if it was clear she did not hold allegiance to him.

Steig and Turner exchanged a look across the table, and it annoyed her.

"What, you still don't trust me? I'm here, aren't I? I'm risking my life to be here. I left my family. You think I'll run off with the amulet the first chance I get and leave you all behind?" she challenged.

Steig looked at her coldly. So much for what he said to Ty about being all in.

Then Lara spoke up.

"She's right, you know. I may not have Zak's Power but I can tell she's being sincere. Besides, no one can fake all the longing looks these two have been shooting at each other," she said, giving Ty a wry smile. "I wouldn't be surprised if her being here to help break the bond is just an afterthought to riding Ty's dick."

Turner instantly burst out laughing, and Ena's jaw nearly hit the floor. Steig just shook his head, like he was used to these antics, but Ty leaned back again, smiling way too cockily as he put his arm over the back of Ena's chair. Ena smiled despite herself, hiding her face in her hand. Gaia, what had she gotten herself into with this group?

"I am here to help break the bond," Ena said, trying to suppress her smile at the teasing around her. "And sure, I won't hide the fact that I also like his dick," she added, gesturing at Ty beside her, who was smiling like he'd won some sort of prize. "But that's beside the point. If this is going to work, the rest of you need to extend a little bit of trust my way."

"It's not that we don't trust you," Turner said, sighing as he wiped tears of laughter from his eyes.

"Speak for yourself," Steig grunted, and Lara elbowed him slightly in the side, giving him a shut-the-fuck-up look.

"It's just that, it's only been us. The four of us, for a long time. We're the only ones who knew about the amulet and wanted to do something about it, and now we have the amulet, and it feels strange to give it up somehow, after all the effort and planning we put into getting it. To let you just have it," Turner finished, looking apologetically at Ty.

Ty had been suspiciously quiet during this whole interaction, but she wouldn't be surprised if it was tactical. He'd clearly done all he could to convince them of her trustworthiness, and she knew it was time for her to stand on her own two feet and defend herself. To show them who she was.

"I get that, I do," she said. "But I don't know how else to convince you that we want the same thing. That I want to break the bond and restore the balance just as much as you do. So you're just going to have to take a leap of faith and trust me," she finished. It wasn't much of a speech, but it was really all she could say.

Turner nodded in understanding. "You're right," he said, standing up to pull something from his pocket. It was the amulet, wrapped in the same dirty cloth they'd kept it in on the journey here. He handed it out to her confidently, like that was all it took for him to trust her. Just her word, and the word of his friend.

Steig, on the other hand, avoided eye contact completely, but Lara seemed to speak for both of them as she gave her a small, trustworthy smile as Ena stood up to take the amulet from Turner's hand.

Ty looked over at her as she sat back down, a slow smile spreading across his face. "Let's make a toast then," he said, standing up to grab the green-tinted bottle that sat in the center of the table.

Ena had wondered what it was, but no one had seemed to touch it yet. He popped the cork on top and gestured to them to finish the water in their cups. Then, one by one, he poured some liquid out of the bottle into their glasses. It was light brown, and strong-smelling. She recognized it instantly—it was woodwater. The same highly alcoholic substance she'd used to disinfect Ty's wound after they were attacked by bandits.

Ena brought the cup to her nose, smelling suspiciously. The aroma was spicy, but slightly sweet, and highly alcoholic.

Ty raised his cup in the air, and the rest of them followed suit, holding their drinks up before them.

"To witches and daemons, working together. May we restore the balance, and cause a little chaos along the way," he said, winking at Ena as he finished. Then he downed his drink in one big gulp.

Not wanting to be outdone, Ena brought her cup to her lips and did the same.

Gaia, it burned!

She sputtered, wondering if she was about to throw up as her mouth flooded with saliva. But then the warmth spread, deep in her belly, and the spicy, aromatic flavor of the woodwater hit her tongue and she found that, actually, she quite liked it.

Looking up at Ty where he stood beside her, she realized she liked a lot of things she never thought she would, and the feeling was incredibly freeing.

Chapter Ten

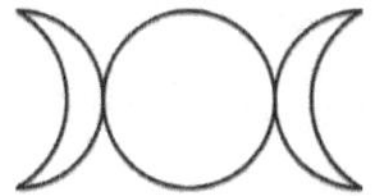

Ena

ENA WOKE UP TO a pitch-black room.

She could hear Ty breathing deeply next to her and feel his body heat, so she knew she wasn't alone, but when she'd fallen asleep last night, the lanterns had still been lit, and now it was disorienting waking up to the endless dark of the cave.

Then she heard a small click as the door to Ty's room opened, and she stiffened.

Was someone coming in?

She rolled towards Ty. "Ty," she whispered as quietly as she could, fear creeping into her voice. "Ty, wake up! Someone's in the room."

Her Knowing could sense them. It wasn't a malicious presence, but it was a strange one, and she didn't know what to make of it.

She felt Ty stir beside her as blue light suddenly filled the room. Someone had lit one of the lanterns.

Ty whipped his head towards her, checking to see that she was okay, before his eyes landed on the stranger lighting the lanterns, and his body language relaxed.

"It's okay," he said gently, running his hand through his unkempt hair. "It's just a timekeeper."

"A what?" she asked, pulling the covers up to her chin as the figure moved throughout the room. They were wearing a black robe with the hood up, making it hard to discern anything about them, but she saw the light from the lanterns glint off an *imperae* collar around the person's neck.

"A timekeeper," Ty explained, his voice rough with sleep. "They light the lanterns in the morning when the sun comes up so we can maintain our sense of day and night underground."

"Oh," Ena said, keeping her voice low. "Is it okay that I'm in your bed?" she whispered, suddenly self-conscious about it.

Ty chuckled as he turned towards her, wrapping his arm around her waist and pulling her into his body. "Yes," he said, his voice low and soothing. "It's expected, given that you're my..." His words trailed off, as if he was reluctant to say them.

"Witch-slave?" she asked, her eyebrow arching. She, at least, wasn't afraid to say it. She knew Ty felt guilty for the position he'd had to put her in, but truly, she understood, and she was here willingly.

"Yes...that," he said somewhat bitterly. "Witch-slaves are often taken for servitude of all kinds, and that includes...sexual arrangements."

"Hm," Ena said shortly. She certainly did not like the idea of witches being forced into sexual servitude, but given that it was the only recourse for a witch to be in the Underworld, she couldn't help but wonder...were all witches who came here forced into it? Or had there been others, like her, who came here willingly for...personal reasons? Somehow, the idea that she might not be the only witch who chose to endure this for someone they had feelings for was comforting.

The timekeeper finished lighting the last lantern in the room and quietly slipped out, leaving them alone again.

"That timekeeper was wearing an *imperae* collar too. Are they...?"

"No, they're not a witch. There are no other witches here besides you. They're a mortal."

That explained why her Knowing had sensed the person when they first entered the room, but it was uncomfortable to think of mortals being forced into servitude here too.

"How many mortals are being kept here as *imperi*?"

"I think about a dozen, last I checked. Most of them were taken by Cole or some of the other upper-level daemons as punishment. Usually for uncovering their identities while out on a mission, or sometimes for more...nefarious reasons."

Ena swallowed. She didn't like thinking about what these poor mortals had been put through, all in the name of keeping daemonic activity a secret.

"That's horrible," Ena said, her brow wrinkling in concern.

Ty looked away, as if ashamed. "I know," he said. "It wasn't always that way, though. Cole has been ramping up the practice over the last fifteen years since my father died. He thinks it's what mortals deserve for shunning us and choosing witches."

"Do others think that too? Or just him?"

"Others do...but not everyone. Not the majority, I don't think."

Ena nodded, still feeling troubled by the information.

"I promise we'll change things, Ena," Ty said earnestly, sensing her discomfort. "It all starts with breaking the bond. If we do that, it will pave the way for other changes. Do you understand?"

Ena nodded again. "I do," she said assuredly. "I'm glad you want to change things, and I'm glad to help you."

Ty smiled at her then, that one corner of his mouth lifting in that charming way it did as he brushed some hair away from her brow, tucking it behind her ear.

He leaned in slowly and kissed her. The kiss was gentle and sweet, but still, Ena felt that spot between her legs ache instantly at the contact. Heat spread throughout her body as she opened her mouth wider, inviting him in. The smell of cedar, stone, and honey surrounded her, and she found herself scooching further into him, lining up their bodies as they lay on their sides so they were touching from toes to chests.

It reminded her of all those mornings traveling that they'd awoken next to each other. She could never admit it then, but she had wished fervently to do exactly this. To wake next to him, peacefully, feeling content, and kiss him. Have him hold her in his big, strong arms and make her feel safe and loved. She could admit it now, though, and she thought if she could wake this way every day of her life, she'd die happy.

The kiss escalated as Ty slipped his tongue into her mouth. His hand dragged down her front to land on her breast, where he stroked her nipple through her thin shift. Wetness instantly pooled between her legs as she reached between them, fumbling with the hem of his shirt. She moved to lift it up, wanting desperately to stroke his increasingly hard cock where she could feel it against her stomach, but he stopped her.

"Uh-uh, viper," he tsked. "You first."

"What do you mean?" she asked breathlessly, feeling a little indignant that he had stopped her from her explorations.

He leaned forward to whisper, his lips grazing over the shell of her ear. "I bet your cunt tastes so fucking sweet in the morning. Be a good girl and spread those legs for me so I can find out."

Fuck. She had no idea why, but the way he said that had possibly made her more turned on than she'd ever been in her entire life.

"Yes, Master," she whispered seductively in reply, remembering how much he'd liked it when she called him that.

Her heart was pounding as he threw the furs and blankets off her and pulled her to the edge of the bed, lowering himself between her legs.

As she pulled up her shift, bunching it around her waist, and let her knees fall apart for him, she realized what it was about this feeling that mesmerized her.

Doing what she was told, letting him take command, letting go of her control—it made her feel so *free*. Anything could happen, and while that thought normally scared her, when she was with Ty, where she felt safe, it felt...addictive. She knew without a doubt that she'd do anything he told her to, and that she'd be happier for it.

Ty pulled his own shirt over his head, tossing it to the side, revealing his muscled chest and arms, covered in *onata* tattoos. Then he stared down at her sex and breathed in deeply. "Fucking Iblis," he said, and with no hesitation, he lowered his head and licked her from entrance to clit.

"Shit," Ena said involuntarily, her whole body lighting up with the exquisite feel of his tongue against her.

"Did you like that?" he asked, looking up at her, his piercing green eyes alight with glee and lust.

"Yeah," Ena said, almost incapable of forming words.

"Good," he said, lowering his lips and kissing her gently right on her clit. Ena's body twitched in response. "Keep being a good girl and tell me what else you like."

He swirled his tongue around her clit once, twice, then placed his mouth over it and sucked—hard. Ena gasped as Ty pulled back and chuckled darkly.

He was enjoying this. Enjoying toying with her, making her react.

And as much fun as it was losing herself to pleasure and letting him take control, she couldn't let him have all the power.

She snaked her hand down her front and used her finger to swirl around her bud, which was still wet from Ty's ministrations. Ty watched her, enraptured, as she stuck the finger inside herself, moving it in and out slowly.

"I like this too," she said as he looked at her, unblinking.

She pulled the finger out, and Ty grabbed her hand as she did, bringing it to his mouth and sucking the taste of her off her fingers. The feeling of his warm, wet mouth around her finger drove her wild, and she watched as his eyes darkened.

"As sweet as you thought it would be?" she asked, her voice coming out sultry and breathless.

"Sweeter. You're the most delicious breakfast I've ever had."

Ena smiled, a small giggle escaping her at his words.

"Now stop talking while I make you come so hard you forget your own name," he said, then he full-on stuck his tongue inside her. He moved it in and out before licking up her center, swirling around her clit again and again until he stuck his own finger inside her. It was so much bigger than her own, she couldn't help but gasp again.

He pumped it in and out in a perfect rhythm, and her hips started chasing his movements as he licked her. She couldn't help herself—she reached down and grabbed his hair with both hands, pushing him harder into her as she ground against his tongue, moaning loudly.

He growled in pleasure at her enthusiasm, licking her faster in time with his finger as he added a second one to join the first.

He pumped them in and out hard, and when he curled them slightly, stroking her from the inside, Ena lost it—her orgasm tore through her as she cried out, her legs shaking as the waves of pleasure ebbed and flowed through her. Involuntarily, her knees fell apart further, as she slumped back on the bed.

Ty pulled back. She could see her wetness glistening on his lips and in his beard. Part of her wanted to feel embarrassed about it, about how wet he now was because of her, but Ty looked so pleased as he smiled at her, she knew there was nothing to be embarrassed about.

She looked down and could see his thick cock, erect and ready between his legs. Pushing herself up onto her elbows to see him better, she looked him in the eye. "Come here," she said, her voice desperate and seductive.

Ty leaned over her as she reached for his cock, stroking her hand up and down it, pumping it teasingly, but then a loud knock on the door rang through the room.

Ty turned to look at the door. "Shit," he said, sounding frustrated. "Coming!" he yelled at the door.

He picked up his discarded shirt and threw it on before striding to the door. Ena pulled her own shift down and sat on the edge of the bed as he opened it, revealing another *imperi* standing in the doorway.

This one, a man, was dressed in regular attire, but still wore the collar, and if Ena had to guess, she'd say he was a daemon, because her Knowing couldn't sense a thing.

"Sorry to disturb you, sir. Here's the breakfast you requested."

"Thank you," Ty said, as the man handed Ty a tray of food.

"And I've been sent with a message from Dev. He wishes to speak with you as soon as possible."

"Alright," Ty said with a sigh, stroking his beard as he thought. "Tell him I'll meet him in an hour."

The man nodded briefly before turning to leave, and Ty closed the door behind him, bringing the tray over to the table.

"What was that?" Ena asked.

"I forgot I requested breakfast be brought to us at this time," he said.

Ena recalled what Lara had told her last night, about the upper-level daemons being served by the king's kitchen. She'd never had breakfast brought to her like this before, and although she felt slightly guilty that the *imperi* were the ones forced to work in the kitchens, she had to admit, it was surprisingly nice.

"I see," Ena said, moving to join Ty at the table. "And who's Dev?"

"Dev is the overseer of the mines," he said, running his hand through his hair as though he were stressed about something. "It makes sense that he wants to meet. I really should go talk to him as soon as I can, but I want to get you settled in the Archives first."

"What are the Archives exactly?"

"It's where we keep all the books in the Underworld, except those in peoples' private collections, of course. And that's where I keep the books I took from Petyr."

"Why do you keep them there and not here? Shouldn't they be kept hidden?" she asked.

"I keep them there so if they're ever found, they can't be associated with me or Steig or Turner. But they are still hidden—you'll see."

"Oh," Ena said. That seemed smart, but it dawned on her how difficult it must have been for Ty to live like this for so long—in such a hostile world where he'd constantly had to watch his back from his uncles, living in fear. No wonder he was filled with rage. And now, on top of that, he had to keep the amulet hidden, too, and—

"Wait—the amulet!" Ena said, suddenly remembering and turning to look at the nightstand. "When I fell asleep last night, I had it wrapped in a cloth here, but now it's gone."

"Don't worry, viper," Ty said calmly. "After you fell asleep, I moved it." He went to the trunk at the foot of the bed, digging through it before pulling out a small wooden lockbox. "I figured, now that I've locked it, I'll melt down the key in the forge so you'll be the only one who can open it using your spellword."

Ena's heart warmed. Not only was that a great idea, but it showed how much he really, truly trusted her with all of this, and it meant everything.

"Okay," Ena said, feeling the smile spread across her face.

"Now, come on," Ty said, gesturing to the plate of hard-boiled eggs, bread, and cheese he'd spread out on the table. "After we eat, I'll take you to the Archives before I meet with Dev."

"Okay, if you say so," Ena said, her tone playfully skeptical as she stood up and walked over to where he stood by the table.

"What?" Ty asked, his brow furrowing in confusion.

"It's just... I don't know how you could possibly be hungry after that extremely filling breakfast you just had" Ena smiled widely at him, very pleased with herself for the joke she'd made.

Ty laughed, that contagious sound that lifted her, making her feel lighter than air. Then he grabbed the back of her head, pulling her in closer to him, kissing her soundly. "Don't remind me," he whispered in her ear as he pulled back. "I can't wait for seconds."

CHAPTER ELEVEN

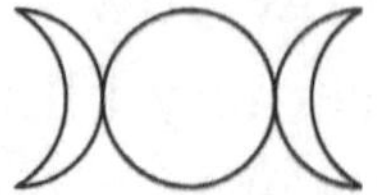

Ena

AFTER THEY FINISHED EATING and dressing, Ena followed Ty out the door and into the labyrinth of passageways. Unfortunately, in order to reach the Archives, they had to cross through the Great Antre—which was apparently what the gigantic central cavern she'd initially met Cole in was called—and she understood now why Cole liked to make his presence known there.

It felt as if she and Ty were on display as they walked across the intimidating space to the staircase that was carved into the walls around it. The other daemons eyed them, and Ena did her best to appear as an obedient witch-slave, walking a step behind Ty, with her head slightly lowered as he'd instructed, but she didn't miss the smug looks of satisfaction many threw her way when they noticed her collar. Although she thought she caught a few pitying looks too.

She saw others wearing them, as well—the *imperi*—carrying things to and fro, in and out of rooms, and down the many passageways, and it was strange. In her Coven, all witches shared the work. A witch's Gift determined what path they were best suited for,

for serving Gaia, but no one was relegated to work that did not suit them, nor were they forced to serve others. Everyone chose to help one another, taking turns with the most undesirable tasks. But to see an entire group of people forced into certain tasks by virtue of perceived slights against daemons, or more specifically, Cole, made her feel incredibly uncomfortable.

After ten minutes of winding down endless passageways, Ty stopped and led her through a set of large, double-arched doors with golden doorknobs. They opened into a large chamber—not as large as the Great Antre, but still impressive. The most astounding part, though, was the shelves and shelves of books that lined the walls, stretching up to the ceiling of the cavern.

Ena had never seen so many books in her life. She'd thought that Heran had had an impressive stash of spellbooks, journals, and histories, but this was way, way more than that.

In the center of the room sat several large wooden tables with dimly lit darkrock lanterns placed atop them. Hard-looking wooden chairs were placed around them for seating but scattered around the room were several cozier-looking chairs, too, decked with furs like the ones in Lara and Steig's chambers. The whole area was so incredibly inviting, which surprised her.

Branching off the far end of the chamber was a dark passageway, and out of it came an older man. He had gray hair, receding at the top, but long on the sides, that was tied back into a short ponytail. He wore similar black robes to the timekeeper but had no *imperae* collar.

He shuffled closer to Ena and Ty, a smile gracing his wrinkled face, causing his kind brown eyes to crinkle at the corners. "Ty, my boy," the man greeted warmly. "I'd heard you'd returned. Safe and sound, looks like?"

"Yes, Nial," Ty greeted, smiling in return.

"Good, good. It's wonderful to see you," Nial said, placing his hand in a fatherly way on Ty's shoulder, and it warmed Ena's heart to see it. She had been starting to think all daemons besides Ty, Turner, and Lara—and maybe sometimes Steig—were assholes.

"What can I do for you both today?" Nial asked, his eyes darting towards Ena in a curious way.

"Ena is our new…guest," Ty replied, pointedly avoiding her degrading title, which was interesting. "And she'll be working on a project for me and the king, so she'll be needing access to the Archives on a regular basis."

"I see, I see," Nial mumbled. "And what kind of resources will she be needing?" he asked Ty, his eyebrow arching as if communicating something unspoken.

"She'll need volumes on Wiccan and daemonic history, runes and Imbuing, and…I'd like her to have full access to my private reserves," Ty said.

Nial nodded in understanding.

Ty's private reserves…that must be the books he got from Petyr. Did Nial know about them? Did he know about the amulet?

Ena looked over at Ty, hoping for more explanation. He looked back at her, giving her a small reassuring nod.

He knew what he was doing, and he'd explain later.

"Certainly. Give me a few minutes and I can have her set up in your usual alcove," Nial said before glancing at her curiously again, then shuffling off to get a large wooden cart with metal wheels. He immediately began filling it with books that he pulled off the shelves, not even bothering to look at the titles as he stacked them on the cart.

"Your usual alcove?" Ena inquired with a smile, as Ty guided her with a hand on the small of her back towards one of several recesses carved into the chamber. Inside was a small table and two cozy, fur-laden chairs. It was more sequestered from the rest of the Archives than any of the other alcoves—whomever sat in here could avoid being seen by anyone who entered through the front doors, and she knew that was a purposeful choice.

"Yes, I found myself visiting the Archives quite a lot before my most recent mission. For...my own curiosity." Ty gave her a small smile, and a glint entered his eye.

The way he was still talking in code told her that Nial most likely did not know about the amulet, which made sense, since they'd said only Steig, Turner, and Lara knew about it.

As Ena and Ty sat down at the table beside one another, she turned to him to confirm.

"He doesn't know?" she asked in a hushed tone.

"No," Ty replied, equally quiet. "But he's loyal to me and was to my father. That's why he's helping me, keeping those books for me, even though he doesn't know what's in them."

"What does he think you're working on?" Ena asked.

"I don't know. He's never asked. I'm sure he suspects it's something Cole wouldn't like but...I can't tell him. Not without risking the work we're doing."

"Because of your uncle Zak?"

"Yes, exactly," Ty replied, his tone going steely.

"But where does he keep the books? And what if he's found with them?" Ena looked around but couldn't see the old man taking books off the shelves anymore. Had he gone down that dark passageway again?

"In his private chambers, through there," Ty said, gesturing at the passageway in question. "Cole isn't suspicious of him, not like he is of me, so I don't think he'd go looking. But if he did, well, the old man specializes in keeping rare manuscripts and tomes. My hope is he'd be able to play them off as being of strictly academic interest."

"And why is Cole so suspicious of you? You're his nephew. Shouldn't that garner some goodwill?" Ena asked.

"It's...because of my father. They didn't get along. Cole didn't agree with the way he ran things."

Ena put two and two together. "Your father was the king before Cole? Before he died?"

"Yes," Ty said, looking at Ena, assessing her reaction to that information.

That was certainly interesting, and made sense for Cole to mistrust Ty if he didn't get along with his father. From everything that Ty had told her, his father seemed like a good man and likely had different ideals than Cole. She wondered vaguely how daemons chose who was king anyway, given that Ty's father and his brother seemed so different from one another.

Just then, Nial came shuffling over, pushing the cart full of books.

"Okay then, here we have the most comprehensive tomes on runes, Imbuing, and daemonic history. Don't have much on Wiccan history, for obvious reasons, but there's a few mentions in some of these," he said, gesturing to a smaller, distinct stack of books. "And of course," he said, picking up a discreet burlap sack filled with books at the bottom of the cart. "Your private reserves."

"Thank you, Nial," Ty said kindly. "This is a great start."

"Of course, of course," he responded, waving them off. "Just shout if you need more."

Ty nodded, and Ena gave the man a small smile before he left them.

Looking through the cart of books, she felt almost giddy. All this new knowledge at her fingertips...she couldn't wait to dive in.

Back home, she'd read almost every book in Heran's possession—multiple times. She had fond memories of sitting in Heran's altar room late at night, sounding out words with the matriarch's help so she could practice new spellwords and potions. She'd wanted to learn everything she could, and Heran had encouraged her to.

Except, of course, for the knowledge that had been hidden from her. A wave of resentment trickled through her, souring the fond memory, but the feeling was lost when Ty opened the sack that contained the books he'd gotten from Petyr, and her eyes landed on a book she recognized.

It was a large book with a dark-green leather cover, and it looked old, just like the other copy she'd seen a few months ago. She picked it up, placing it on the table and flipping to the title page, where her suspicions were confirmed.

The Evolution of Magic, it read. The same book Heran had showed her after she received her Gift.

"I don't believe it," Ena mused in awe. "This is the same book Heran showed me months ago, explaining how witch and daemon magic come from the same source. I'd never seen it before then, because she'd hidden it. I can't believe Petyr had a copy of it too. I wonder where he got it from."

"I don't know how he got these particular books, but Petyr was…industrious," Ty said with a melancholy smile. "He was known to procure books that fascinated him through whatever means necessary."

"No wonder you two got along," Ena said wryly.

"Yeah, we really did," he said, a regretful tone in his voice.

Ena didn't know what to do. Should she encourage him to talk more about their relationship? Maybe it would help Ty to open up about it. But then again, prying too much could cause him to shut down. He clearly didn't like to talk about Petyr, and for good reason—he had been unintentionally responsible for his death.

This was new territory for her, but she decided to let her natural curiosity guide her.

"How did you two meet?" she asked gently.

Ty sighed, and she thought at first that maybe he wouldn't answer, but then he did.

"At the guesthouse in Ternan. I was there trading, and using my *furor* in small amounts, as was my mission, when he joined in on a card game I was involved in. We got to talking about our common interests. He was well-read on many topics, but knew a lot about metallurgy specifically, so he offered to show me his private collection back at his shop, and it was there he told me about his theory about the amulet. One he'd developed after reading these journals," he said, gesturing to the other, smaller books in the sack.

Ena was quiet for a second, letting his story sink in. "It's not your fault, you know," she said gently. "You didn't start that fire. You didn't intend for him to die."

Ty's eyes lifted to hers. They were filled with guilt and regret. "I may not have started it, but I was the ultimate cause. It was my fault, and I've accepted that. But...it's also part of what drives me. To do all this," he said, gesturing at the books. "To change things so I'm never forced to do something like that again. So I have a choice."

Ena reached out and touched him gently on the shoulder. They were close enough, part of her wanted to hug and kiss him—comfort him. But she didn't know if that kind of affection would be appropriate in public.

He placed his hand over top of hers and gave it a squeeze. The look in his eyes told her he appreciated her presence, her understanding, but that she shouldn't pry anymore. The guilt was clearly still something he was working through.

"I should go," he said, clearing his throat and breaking the moment. "I promised I'd go see Dev about the mines. Will you be alright here?"

"Mmhmm," Ena said. If she were being honest, she couldn't wait to dive into these books and see what she could find.

"Okay, good. I'll be back later to get you. Don't go wandering on your own," he said cautiously.

Ena needed no explanation as to why. She knew there were many here who held contempt for her, and plus, she had no desire to get absolutely lost in the passageways.

"I won't...Master," she said, giving him a little smirk.

He smiled and shook his head at the teasing, before looking down at her mouth, like he wanted to kiss her, but clearly thought better of it, before turning to leave.

Feeling glad that she'd been able to lift his spirits slightly before he left, Ena sat down in the cozy fur-covered chair and started to flip through *The Evolution of Magic*.

She and Ty had decided that her initial goal should be to figure out more about the amulet, especially what the unknown symbol on it meant. If she was going to break the bond, she'd first need to understand the elements that went into the spell the witches used to bind daemons to Iblis in the first place. Only by understanding it could she hope to reverse it.

She already knew they'd need one witch from each Coven, and daemonic blood, to complete the spell—those things she had seen in her vision. But how the amulet worked, and what the spellwords they'd chanted meant, was what she still needed to figure out.

This book seemed like a good place to start since it was written by witches, but as she read, she was disappointed to find that there wasn't much relevant to the spell.

It began by explaining how, at first, there were only mortals. Then, a chosen few were granted magic through a union of Iblis and Gaia. A union...what did that mean? Ena didn't know what to make of that, but it didn't seem relevant to the spell, so she kept reading.

The book was dense, and next explained how the two races of magic operated, the most common types of Gifts and Powers each had, and then delved into the inner workings of a witch's Knowing, including numerous examples of how it was used, as well as the speed, strength, and healing magic of daemons.

She got so caught up reading she didn't even register the time or the rumbling of her stomach until a young woman wearing an *imperae* collar appeared before her carrying a tray of food.

The woman explained that Ty had had the food sent for her, with the message that things were taking longer than he thought and he wouldn't be back for another hour or so.

Ena thanked the woman, who lingered a little too long, looking at her like a curiosity, before she left.

Ena absentmindedly ate the slices of pork and slightly-past-its-prime apple that she'd been given while next reading about the split.

It was written exactly as Heran had described, where daemons, whose Powers were suited to chaos, disruption, and discord, chose to serve Iblis and move to the Underworld for secrecy, and witches, with Gifts of earth magic, chose to serve Gaia and maintain the balance. No mention of the amulet. No mention of the bond to Iblis, and no mention of the way witches had essentially forced daemons into the Underworld by ostracizing them.

She was starting to feel a bit frustrated by this—by the lies, intentionally or unintentionally written in this book—until she caught something. The vaguest passage, which mentioned something she'd never heard of before.

And thus, no longer able to live in harmony with one another, the two races severed ties forevermore, just as the third race, the worshippers of Omnis, had done eons ago.

Omnis? She'd never heard that word before, nor had she ever heard of a third race of magic.

She was still puzzling over this when Ty finally returned, a smiling Turner at his side.

"How'd it go?" Ty asked, looking her up and down as if assessing for injuries and seeming relieved to find her in one piece.

"It went fine," Ena said, unable to hide her frustration.

"Did you find anything useful?" Turner asked quietly, looking around to make sure no one was listening, which they weren't.

"Not really," Ena said. "But I'm just getting started. Although...have either of you heard of Omnis?"

"Omnis?" Ty asked, his dark brows furrowing. "No, what's that?"

"I'm not sure," Ena said. "I just found some vague reference to it in this book on the history of magic. It mentioned 'worshippers of Omnis.'"

Ty looked over at Turner, who shook his head. He hadn't heard of it either.

"Come on," Ty said, gently grabbing her hand. "You've been sitting in here most of the morning. Maybe a break will do you some good, and there's somewhere else I want to show you."

"Really? Will I like it?" she asked, her eyebrows jumping up as a smile spread across her face.

"You will. I promise," Ty responded with a wolfish grin. "Follow me."

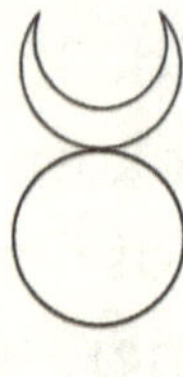

Ty

AFTER ENSURING NIAL HAD safely returned the books from Petyr to their hiding spot in his own chambers, Ty led Ena back through the Great Antre to the passageway that led to the fighting ring on the mid-level.

He was itching to get his hands on an ax and hit some shit, especially after dealing with the clusterfuck that was the mines all morning.

Dev was great—he had a wealth of knowledge and good instincts—but he had trouble dealing with Cole. Ty seemed to be the only one who could get the bastard to budge and provide more resources to the miners, or convince him that exploring new areas of the under-caves was a good idea.

Cole had never had a mind for the mines or forge; his exclusive focus was on serving Iblis through missions. And while Ty knew those missions were important for ensuring their Powers were granted by Iblis, he also knew that it came at a detriment to the innerworkings of the Underworld and all the other important aspects of running an entire community underground.

Lara had told him about the food shortages beginning in the mid-levels already, so they needed to keep up their production of metal goods in the forge so they'd have plenty to trade this winter when Cole sent daemons out on missions. This was, of course, the way Ty preferred to do things, as opposed to Cole, who encouraged stealing from mortals instead. But they couldn't steal everything, and they couldn't produce more goods without expanding the mines—certain areas were already depleted.

But the thing Ty resented the most was how necessary he was here, how much of a burden everything already felt, and he knew it would only get worse.

But he wanted to release that burden, at least for a little while, so he led Ena and Turner into the training facility.

It'd been a few months since he'd been here—not only because of the mission he'd been on, but also because before then, he'd been so consumed with research on the amulet he'd barely had the time. He couldn't describe the relief he felt at having Ena's help with the research side of things.

Besides, he knew she'd be infinitely better at it than him anyway.

As they entered the sparse space lit by darkrock lanterns, he was pleased to see that it hadn't changed in his time away. Rows of every kind of weapon imaginable lined the wall—axes, long swords, short swords, daggers, maces, war hammers. Beautiful weapons, made by some of their most talented blacksmiths.

Ty usually brought his own weapons, but hadn't had a chance to make a new axe for himself since his old one had been taken by the Occidens witches. It would take a while to make a new one anyway, since that axe had been Imbued with runes that triggered his *furor* in any daemon or mortal who used it. He absentmindedly hoped the witches never traded it to a mortal, or they'd be in for a rude awakening.

Beside him, he watched Ena as she took in the space. What would she make of this? He knew she wasn't a fighter—not in a physical way, at least, and probably had never seen many of these weapons before. But he thought maybe she'd like to try.

Fighting hand-to-hand was a core part of daemonic culture. All daemons were trained to fight from a young age—partially in preparation for future missions in which it might be necessary, but also because it was a great source of exercise underground, and a good outlet for daemons' natural tendencies towards discord. For what was violence if not chaos incarnate?

"What is this place?" Ena asked, eyeing the weapons on the wall with caution.

"A training facility," Ty explained, walking over to them.

"So...a place for fighting?" Ena asked, raising her eyebrow in skepticism.

"Yes," he replied, one corner of his mouth quirking up despite himself.

One day, he should maybe examine his compulsive need to challenge her and push her into new things, but she seemed to like it, or at least tolerate it, and he certainly liked it. He liked seeing what she could do, and he liked seeing how she would react, because she always surprised him.

Ena watched as Turner walked over and grabbed two short swords from the wall, testing the grips in his hand. Ty, of course, grabbed an axe and dagger. His preferred fighting style. They had long swords, of course, which could lend an advantage against an opponent with shorter weapons, but Ty's training was practical. Mortals and witches didn't have weapons like that, and to carry around swords in polite company would be to draw too much attention, so he opted for axes and daggers, which were multi-use, and easier to pass off as tools, not weapons.

"Why?" she asked, her nose crinkling up a bit, as if the idea of fighting was foreign to her, which, he supposed, it was. She'd told him that their encounter with the bandits a few weeks ago had been the first time she'd ever had to fight or use her magic against anyone else.

"For fun, exercise…mental stimulation," Turner answered for him, giving a shrug and smiling devilishly.

"You two are going to fight then?" Ena asked, seeming intrigued by the idea.

"What do you think, Shadow? Should we fight?" Ty asked Turner, teasing him with his old nickname.

Even though Turner was only about a year younger than Ty, they'd been inseparable as kids, with Turner following him around wherever he went. He'd earned the nickname "Shadow" from some of the other boys their age, and he knew the man hated it, so there was no better way to get his goat.

"You fucker." Turner grinned at him, his blue eyes glinting in the light.

Ty laughed as he removed his shirt, tossing it to the side as he gripped his axe and entered the center of the large, intricately decorated circle carved into the floor of the cave. "Watch and learn, viper. You're next," he said with a wink before turning back to Turner.

The two of them circled each other, watching for who would move first. Ty reached out with his *furor*, just a touch, just to see where his cousin was at. The man didn't usually tend towards anger, but Ty would exploit what he could, just to give himself an edge in the fight. The man might seem nice and well-mannered compared to other daemons, but he was ruthless in the ring, so he needed to take whatever advantage he could get.

Instead of the minor annoyance he was used to sensing in his cousin, he was surprised to sense a significant amount of untapped rage. What had happened? Ty furrowed his brow at his friend, who knew his tactics by now.

Turner shook his head slightly in response. He didn't want to talk about it.

Alright, that made sense. It must have had something to do with Zak—when the utter prick wasn't ignoring his son, he was constantly putting him down for his kindhearted nature and using him for his own ends. Something must have happened between them.

Ty backed off with his *furor*. He had no desire to get his ass kicked by his angry friend, and he didn't want to exploit a real sore spot unless Turner asked him to—he knew from firsthand experience that it could be extremely cathartic to let that rage out from time to time, but he wouldn't do it without Turner's consent.

As if sensing his decision, Turner struck first. He whipped out with his short sword, swinging for Ty's head, and Ty met his blow with his axe, the sound of metal on metal echoing through the cave.

Turner spun around and swung with his other sword, this time aiming for Ty's middle, and Ty dodged it, again deflecting Turner's strike away with the handle of his axe.

Seizing Turner's momentary distraction, Ty pivoted and swiped out with his dagger—a beautiful sixteen-inch, decorated blade that he envied—but Turner caught his wrist, just inches from his neck.

But the man had been forced to drop one of his swords to do so, so now he only had one. Ty felt a feline grin spread across his face.

That was just a warm-up. Now came the fun shit.

He launched forward with his axe, forcing Turner to take a step back as he met Ty's blow with his sword, which he now held with two hands.

"Want to yield, Shadow?" Ty taunted.

"Never, asshole," Turner said, glee filling his voice.

Ty swiped out with his dagger again, but Turner dodged it. His heart pounded now, and his body felt alive with adrenaline.

This was what he fucking lived for.

Turner stabbed forward with the sword, low—a much harder move to block with his axe—but he managed to swipe it to the side. If this were a real fight, and not just a spar, he would've thrown his axe right into the man's skull and been done with it, but obviously that was not the goal here, so instead he swung his dagger at Turner's throat, but the man was quick as a cat and pulled backwards, as Ty suspected he would.

Then Turner swung up with his sword, hitting the hilt of Ty's dagger and knocking it from his hand, so only his axe remained.

A feral laugh bubbled up in Ty's throat, and he saw an answering smile on Turner's face. This was way too much fucking fun.

Then a delicate sound from outside the ring caught his attention, and he couldn't help but look.

Ena was smiling widely at him, a gentle laugh having escaped her as she watched them. He could see the enjoyment written on her face, and as he breathed in deeply, his *venator* caught a whiff of—oh, fuck.

Was she turned on watching this? Her scent was different—deeper and muskier than normal, and as he breathed in again involuntarily, he could swear he caught the wet scent of her pussy in the air.

Capitalizing on Ty's distraction, Turner swept forward, knocking Ty's remaining weapon out of his hand, and the axe clanged to the floor.

"Fuck," Ty lamented. "You got me."

"I wouldn't have if she wasn't here," Turner said, breathing just heavily as he was. "You should come every time. You're quite the helpful distraction," he said to Ena with a grin.

"I was just standing here minding my own business," Ena said, feigning innocence.

Ty walked up to her, wiping the sweat from his brow before leaning over her. "You forget I can smell you, viper, and yes, it's very distracting."

Ena's face went slightly pink at that. "Smell, like...?"

"Like I can tell you enjoyed watching us. Am I right?"

Ena looked away, her face going even redder. "Fine," she said, meeting his gaze once more. "I won't deny it. It was sexy as hell. You're really..." Her gaze dragged over Ty's bare torso before coming back up to his eyes. "Fast."

Ty smiled at her genuinely. She was too fucking cute, and part of him wanted to drag her back to his rooms and fuck the shit out of her, but maybe they could go for the next best thing.

"Come over here, then. It's your turn to try."

"My turn?" she asked, sounding shocked. "But I don't know how to fight."

"That's the point. You should learn. You never know when it might come in handy."

"I've never had cause to fight before," she said. "Witches don't usually need to."

"Well, you're in the Underworld now..." Ty replied. "And daemons fight."

"I thought you said I was protected because I was your witch-slave. That no one could touch me."

"That's technically true, yes. No one is allowed to touch you without my permission, but daemons don't always follow the rules," he finished menacingly.

Ena rolled her eyes at him, in that way she did when he challenged her and she wanted to act annoyed, but he knew deep down she loved it. She was outspoken enough to tell him if she didn't, and he could always sense when she just needed that little extra push to do what she really wanted. That little bit of permission to say "yes."

"Okay, fine. Got a recommendation?" she asked, gesturing towards the wall of weapons.

"For you? Daggers, for sure. They're lightweight, but deadly when someone gets too close. Perfect for a viper," he said, smiling mischievously at her.

"Why do you call me that anyway?" she asked as he handed her two choice daggers, a bit smaller than the one he'd been using, but still excellent.

"Viper?" he asked.

"Yeah, you never did before. You only started on Samhain when you...took me."

She clearly wasn't mincing words, but okay, fair enough, he did *take* her.

And he was so fucking glad he did.

"I saw your mask on the floor where you dropped it, the one decorated with serpents. That was yours, wasn't it?"

He'd been upstairs, searching for the amulet, when he saw her walk down the hallway of the matriarch's house, dropping her mask on the floor. It wasn't until he'd walked into the altar room and seen her standing there, smelled her as he grabbed her waist and put his hand over her mouth, that he realized he couldn't reveal that he knew her and use her name, so "viper" had just come out.

"Yes, that was mine," she said, testing the grip of the daggers in her hands cautiously.

"Well, there you go. It suits you," Ty said, grinning at her.

Ena smiled back, a dark grin he hadn't seen before spreading over her face. It almost reminded him of the way she looked when she gave in to her *visanis*—calm, in control, and powerful. If he was a lesser man, he would be intimidated, but he just found it hot as fuck.

"Okay then," she said. "Show me what to do with these things." She held the daggers out before her, inspecting them like they were likely to bite her.

"Well, first you have to work on your stance, like this," he said, bending down and grabbing her thigh to move her leg into the proper position. He still wasn't totally used to her wearing pants all the time—he'd only ever seen her in dresses before. Her thigh was supple to his touch, but muscular underneath. He resisted the urge to stroke his hand up and down it, or Iblis-forbid, bite it. Turner was still standing on the sidelines watching, though, and he didn't necessarily want such an attentive audience for the things he wanted to do to her.

"Good," he said as he stood up and assessed her stance. "You feel how steady you are in that position?"

"Yeah, definitely," Ena said, looking down at her feet.

"Okay, now weak spots to go for, when you're close to your opponent," Ty said, stepping closer to her. She looked up at him with big blue eyes and he felt his heart stutter.

Fuck, she was pretty. She probably had no idea what those eyes did to him.

But, Iblis take him, that would have to wait until later. This was important for her.

"The throat," he said, bringing her arm up so her dagger lay across his throat. "Underneath the ribs," he said, bringing her arm down so the dagger was now pointed at his gut. "And, of course"—he guided her hand down with both of his, so the dagger was right at his balls—"the groin."

"Hmm," Ena said playfully, looking down at where her dagger was pointed. "You're a bold daemon helping a witch put a dagger right to your balls."

Ty chuckled before leaning in to whisper in her ear. "I know you wouldn't dare. You like them too much. And plus," he added, his voice dripping with lust as he ran a hand through her hair and tightened his grip on a handful of it. "If you did try something, you know I'd punish you for it."

Ena gasped, a small sound that sent a shot of blood right to his cock. Turner could definitely overhear them, but Ty couldn't help himself.

Ena was too much fun to play with.

"Okay, now," he said, releasing her hair and pulling away from her again before things escalated. "I want you to come at me with those and we'll go from there."

Ena stood for a second, assessing, clearly unsure of where to begin, but Ty saw the moment she decided to just go for it. Her weight shifted forward, and she swung out quickly with the dagger in her right hand, going for Ty's throat.

Ty, being a daemon, was naturally faster, so he dodged her easily, but then she changed hands, swinging towards his stomach with her left.

He was impressed with her natural instinct, but he dodged that one easily too.

"Not bad," he said. "Try again."

She tried a couple more times, missing him handily each time, and he could tell she was getting a little frustrated.

"Why don't you have a weapon?" she asked, huffing a little bit. "Or am I too bad to even warrant that?"

"This is about you getting more comfortable with your strikes, not about defending mine, yet. Now try again, but this time, go for the gut first, then the throat in a combination move."

She did as she was told, and she was honestly a natural. She had excellent control over her body and her movements, and her balance was impressive.

But Ty knew she was the type of person who got upset when they couldn't do things perfectly the first time. That was why she never backed down from his challenges—she hated to lose.

The next time, he told her to do the same move again, but faster, and when he dodged her easily again, Turner laughed from the sidelines.

"What's so funny?" Ena asked Turner, her voice snippy. "I didn't ask for this, you know."

"No, no, I know, it's just...reminds me of my youth. Me and Steig going after this bastard, who could easily dodge us, at least at the beginning. It wasn't until I got older that I could kick his ass." Turner smiled at him, crossing his arms where he stood watching. "So don't worry. It takes time, but you'll get there."

"Hm, time, yeah," Ena said, her mood becoming surly.

"Do you want to stop?" Ty asked. He didn't want her becoming too cranky. That wasn't the point.

"No, let's go again," Ena said, getting back in her stance. "I want to."

"Okay," he said. "Try and surprise me this time."

Ena paused for a second, as if contemplating her move. Then, quick as a snake, she struck out with her right hand, going for his throat as he heard her whisper.

{*Ignis*}

The darkrock lantern on the wall a few feet away exploded with fire. It startled Ty, who leapt back from the flames, right to where Ena had her dagger waiting, pointing directly at his balls.

He looked down slowly at it, feeling it before he saw it, then up at the feral grin on her face.

"Surprising enough for you?" she asked, feigning innocence, but he could tell she was incredibly proud of herself.

Ty felt an answering wolfish grin spread across his face. "There's my viper," he said.

Ena laughed as she pulled her knife back, looking far too pleased with herself. Maybe he should punish her later anyway...

His thoughts were interrupted by the sound of heavy footsteps coming down the passageway outside of the fighting ring, and he tensed.

He felt Ena turn towards the sound and take a step backwards into Ty as the door opened.

She was right to be cautious as Gunnar and Chans, two of Cole's currently favored upper-level daemons, entered the room.

Ty looked to Turner and saw concern written on his cousin's face. This was about to be fucking annoying.

"Ty," Gunnar said, his grin displaying several of his missing teeth. The man was about a decade Ty's senior and had always been an asshole as long as Ty could remember. The last several years, he'd been rising in the ranks. Cole frequently chose him for missions because of his Power—the ability to incite panic, or *metus*, was obviously useful for serving Iblis. "Good to see you again," the man said, rubbing a hand through his closely cropped brown hair.

"Gunnar," Ty said simply, not bothering to hide his annoyance with the man's presence.

"We just came to train a bit, if you don't mind sharing the space," he said, his eyes darting to Ena.

Ty fucking hated it and had to physically stop himself from lashing out at the man. "We were just finishing actually," he said calmly. "The space is all yours."

"Shame," Gunnar said darkly. "I would have loved to play with your witch-slave a little bit. That is, if you're willing to share her?"

His companion, Chans, snickered next to him, eyeing Ena in a murderous way.

Ty felt rage boil up inside him. It yearned to escape, to break upon Gunnar for the mere suggestion that he share. He'd *shared* her for the last nine fucking years and he was absolutely done with that shit. She was his, and he'd never share her again with anyone if he had his way, let alone these absolute dickbags.

"Not in the mood for sharing," he managed to grit out. He had to keep his cool. He couldn't let them know how strongly he felt for Ena. They would almost certainly relay that information to Cole, and that would only spell trouble for her.

"Are you sure?" Gunnar asked, moving closer to Ena and pulling a dagger from the sheath on his waist. "I'm sure we'd all appreciate the chance to make the witch scream." His eyes filled with malice as he dragged it down Ena's jawline—not hard enough to make her bleed, but Ty saw her flinch back a bit in confusion and fear.

Ty whipped out, grasping Gunnar's wrist before his dagger could complete its perusal of Ena's jaw. "Don't worry, Gunnar," he said, feigning nonchalance and taking a step closer to the man so he stood between him and Ena. "I'm making her scream enough for the both of us."

Gunnar looked at him and grinned, his crooked nose spreading out as he did. "If you say so," he said, his dark eyes staring lecherously at Ena, filled with both hatred for her kind and lust for her beauty.

Gunnar turned away, heading for the wall of weapons, but Chans lingered.

"Filthy witch," he said, spitting on the floor at Ena's feet.

Ty snapped, and he knew there was now no fucking way they were leaving this room without blood on them. "You know what," he said, much too calm. "I changed my mind. I will share her with you two...if you can beat me."

Gunnar turned around where he stood at the weapons wall. "You want to spar with me and Chans?" he said, looking pleased.

"Yeah, why not?" Ty said. "I could use the practice." He smiled at the men menacingly.

Turner cleared his throat. "Ty, can I speak to you for a second?"

Ty turned to look at his cousin. He didn't look concerned, per se, but was definitely annoyed. He walked over to him, grabbing Ena's wrist and gently leading her over with him.

"Are you sure you want to do this?" Turner whispered under his breath as he stared daggers at Ty. "Take them both on at once? They're not mortals, Ty."

Ty shrugged. "Fine, I'll tell them fists only. Happy?"

"Ty," Ena said, her voice tense. "Why are you doing this? They were gonna let me go."

Ty turned to look at her, and his heart stuttered again. How could he explain to her the guilt he felt for bringing her here? He'd known how some of the daemons were likely to treat her. He knew the things they'd say. They'd said them all about his mother.

How could he explain that he needed to do this, to show her, to show them, to show *himself* that she was his and that he could protect her?

"Trust me," he said. "This needs to happen. They need to see that you can't be taken from me."

Ena looked concerned, but she nodded.

Turner gave a put-upon sigh. "Alright, you crazy bastard, but if they fuck you up, I'm not carrying you back to your room all by myself. We'll have to get Steig."

Ty laughed at that. "Don't worry. It won't come to that."

Turner hadn't truly experienced what he could do. Unbeknownst to them, he'd always held back, just a little, when sparring with his friends, but he had no intention of doing that now.

Ty walked into the center of the fighting ring, placing his axe and dagger on the floor outside it. "No weapons," he announced. "You two are due on a mission soon, aren't you?"

Gunnar nodded slowly, placing the sword he'd selected back on the wall. "Good point," the man said. "Wouldn't want to disrupt Iblis's plans. Doesn't mean I'll go easy on you, though, boy."

Ty didn't even respond to that. He'd let his fists do the talking.

Gunnar and Chans entered the ring with Ty. Both men had stripped off their shirts, as was custom, and he could see their *onata* across their chests and arms. Gunnar had the most, given he'd been at this longer than Ty, and he was a jacked as a fucking boulder, but Ty wasn't afraid.

Chans, on the other hand, was smaller, lither, with greasy black hair tied back into a low ponytail. His Power was *maeror*—not quite as viable in a fight, because he couldn't imagine himself having any sadness for the man to exploit, but either way, Ty would have to make sure to keep his emotions under control, lest Gunnar capitalize on any fear and turn it into panic.

The two of them circled Ty as he raised his fists in readiness, guarding his face. He didn't usually fight without weapons, but it was the safer bet with two daemons who were not as likely to pull deathly blows.

Gunnar struck first, his meaty fist arching towards Ty's face. Ty ducked low, avoiding it easily, and then he felt it—the first little slip of anger.

Did this fucker not know he lived for this?

He felt the channel between him and Gunnar, and pushed it wider, feeding it with his own anger.

The way Chans had spit at Ena's feet.

The insinuation that Gunnar wanted to hurt and fuck what was his.

Cole and his manipulations. The way he was fucking up the Underworld with his vendettas.

The way he'd kept Ena from him for nine fucking years.

The way Ty himself had let Cole win. Let her be kept from him.

The fact that his mother had left him.

The fact that his father had left him.

He was so fucking angry, and he gave it all to Gunnar.

The man's face turned red, and he let out an animalistic scream. He came barreling towards Ty with no plan. Ty saw Chans balk and back up a step, realization dawning as Gunnar started throwing his fists wantonly, using all his strength and none of his speed to try and hit Ty. Ty dodged him easily, and as the man slowed down further with exhaustion, Ty struck.

He slammed his fist into the man's face, watching as another one of his teeth went flying from his mouth, blood and spittle spraying through the air. The man stumbled back, dazed, and Ty struck again, nailing him in the gut.

As he doubled over, Ty brought his knee to the man's face and crushed it into him.

Gunnar collapsed onto the ground, unconscious.

A knockout with just a few hits? What a fucking loser.

Ty grinned maliciously, turning his attention to Chans, whose face paled with the tiniest bit of fear. He might not be such an easy target for Ty's Power.

Chans darted for him, striking at his middle.

Damn, the fucker was fast. He nailed Ty in the abdomen, making Ty suck in a breath as the air was knocked out of him. He struggled to breathe, but gave in to the pain, pulling the man's arm closer to him before he could move away.

Holding on to him with all his might, he rammed his knee up into Chans's balls. The man doubled over in pain, and Ty struck him in the face, feeling bone crunch beneath his fists, but the man didn't go down. He staggered back up, clearly still working through the pain in his groin, as he swung and landed a blow on Ty's face.

Ty felt his lip split, filling his mouth with blood, which he spat onto the ground.

He heard Ena gasp in fear from the sidelines, but he didn't dare look at her.

He went right back to assessing for an opening, when Ty sensed it.

Chans's anger—not at him, but at Ena. At the witch, just because of what she was.

Ty capitalized on it and fed him.

Anger at the daemons for treating Ena so poorly, for making her wear that fucking collar.

Anger at the witches for binding them to Iblis and damning them forever.

Anger at the matriarchs for keeping it all a secret.

Anger at the daemons for accepting their fate.

Anger at Iblis for always, always being his Master.

Round and around his anger went, a never-ending cycle of torment within him that he yearned to be free of, that he yearned for peace from, but he knew that he would never have it, and that fact made him the angriest of all.

Chans's reaction was different from Gunnar's. The man stopped, clutching his chest—right over his heart. Ty could hear it beating faster, harder. It was almost beating *too* hard as all of Ty's anger hit the man.

Fuck, he was having a heart attack.

Chans collapsed on the ground, struggling for breath and clutching his left arm in pain.

Dammit. He couldn't let him die. Cole wouldn't like that.

Ty let him go, relieving him of the channel of anger between them. He saw the man's color return, and his breath even out, but as he looked up at Ty, Ty kicked him square in the face, knocking him the fuck out.

Both men lay unconscious in the circle now, unmoving on the ground. Ty made sure they were well and truly done before he allowed himself a deep, calming breath, and turned toward Ena and Turner.

Turner's face was filled with respect and glee. "Fuck yeah, brother," he said, coming over to clap Ty on the shoulder. "Don't know why I ever doubted you. That was epic."

Ty accepted Turner's congratulations with a smile as he caught his breath.

Then Ena approached him, too, concern etched on her features. "Are you okay?" she asked him, her voice grave. She moved to touch his lip where it was split, but something told him the split lip was not the only wound she meant.

"I'll be fine, now you're safe," he said, the anger in him beginning to dissipate at her touch.

And he meant it—he really would be fine. Because despite all his anger, despite all the rage and regret he had about his life and the world, she was here now. They had a chance now, to fix everything, to be together—and he would never let her go again.

And if beating up a couple of daemons to send a message was what it took to keep her safe, and *his*, then he'd do it again, and again, and again.

But as he moved to pick up his shirt, and the three of them readied to leave, he suddenly remembered the feeling of Chans's anger—the dark rot of hatred that he'd had for Ena, just because she was a witch—and he worried that maybe the message would not be enough.

CHAPTER THIRTEEN

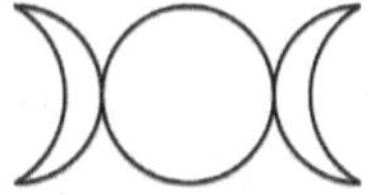

Ena

ENA FELL INTO A routine over the next several days. She spent her mornings looking through books in the Archives, while Ty was busy tending to the mine, or the forge, or one of the many other things that seemed to require his attention. Then, in the afternoon, she exercised with her daggers with Ty, or sometimes just Turner, in the fighting ring.

She found she actually liked the act of letting go and being present that fighting entailed. She needed to maintain concentration, yes, but it was also freeing to shut off all other thoughts and focus only on the task at hand, losing herself in the flow and chaos of the fight.

And she certainly needed it as an outlet for her frustration.

It wasn't like she thought she'd figure out the entire binding spell in one week, but she would have liked to have made more progress by now. She'd already read all of *The Evolution of Magic* and started on some of the other books from Petyr—which turned out to be a witch's journals, though she couldn't quite figure out whose—but had discovered nothing concrete. She planned on expanding her search into some of the daemonic books in the Archives soon, especially those focusing on runes, because she knew she also needed something to sell their cover to Cole at the *onata* celebration next week.

She'd planned to give Ty an update on her research this morning before he left, but he'd been summoned by Cole before the timekeeper arrived. She was starting to realize how critical he was to the functioning of the Underworld, how much people here relied on him, and while she fully admired him for that, she resented the way those duties kept him from her.

They'd barely had time for anything but passing kisses and quick fucks in the morning before he was called away, or sometimes in the dark and quiet middle of the night, both of them half-asleep. He often didn't come back to his rooms until Ena was asleep, but he always sent Turner to escort her to and from the Archives, and he always had food sent for her. And the nights when he wasn't available to join her for dinner, she'd been invited to Lara and Steig's, which was always a good time, but still...she missed him.

One morning, after a few days of this routine, Ena was dressed and waiting for Turner to arrive when she heard a knock on the door. Assuming it was the daemon in question come to escort her to the Archives, she opened it to instead find Lara standing there, her auburn hair braided over one shoulder.

"Hiya, sunshine," she said, grinning at Ena's appearance.

Ena felt a slight pang go through her at the greeting. Greya used to call her that sometimes, and the memory of it hurt to recollect.

Brushing the feeling aside, she mustered a smile for her new friend. "Hey," Ena said, surprise in her voice. "What are you doing here? I was expecting Turner."

"I asked him to relinquish his witch-slave duty to me for the day. I wanted to show you around a bit more, if that's okay with you?"

"Absolutely," Ena said. She was a bit disappointed that she wouldn't get to enact her research plan, but that could wait a day. She *was* curious to see some of the other areas of the Underworld. "Where did you have in mind?"

"I thought we could stop by the mid-level kitchens first, since you had such a fascination with mine, and then we could go see Ty in the forge."

Her heart leaped. They were going to visit Ty?

Lara rolled her eyes. "Well, we can skip the kitchens if you're that excited to see the guy," she teased.

"No, no," Ena said, laughing at her offer. "Let's see the kitchens first."

Ena joined Lara in the passageway, where they headed toward the Great Antre. Ena was starting to figure her way around a *little* bit. She at least knew what direction the Great Antre was and how to get to the Archives from there, but everywhere else was mostly a blur.

"So my reaction was that obvious, huh?" Ena asked Lara as they walked.

Lara looked over at her, one eyebrow raised. "Oh yeah," she said. "Your face lit up like a darkrock lantern."

Ena buried her face in her hand, but couldn't help but smile underneath.

Lara laughed. "Don't be embarrassed. I think it's sweet," she said. "Ty's been...well, he's been grumpy for a long time. I can tell you make him happy in a way I've never seen before."

Ena blushed. "He makes me happy too."

She changed the topic then, asking about Steig, who was apparently also off doing Cole-mandated duties while an older daemon woman watched the kids, until they reached the Great Antre.

Taking one of the ground-level passageways, they went down a stairwell to the mid-levels. Ena had yet to see much of the mid-level yet, aside from the fighting ring, since the Archives and Ty's and Lara's rooms were all on the upper level.

As Lara led her through the mid-level passageways, she could tell a difference almost instantly. The rooms were clearly smaller, with more doorways lining the halls, and the passageways were narrower, too, the ceilings not as high.

They passed several daemons as they moved about—no *onata* tattoos to be seen—which made sense, given that none of them were eligible to receive them. These daemons seemed different too—their attitudes were humbler, almost like the witches and mortals she knew.

Ena could tell they were making their way towards the center of the level, and eventually, they walked through a large open archway, entering into a spacious cavern filled with the same metal stoves Ena had seen in Lara's kitchen. There were about a dozen of them lined along the walls, and the air was filled with the conflicting aromas of several different foods cooking. About half a dozen people moved around the space—chopping and stirring and chatting casually with one another.

Lara greeted several of the daemons as they entered, and they greeted her warmly in return, but the same couldn't be said about the way they greeted Ena. Their eyes darted to her *imperae* collar, and they looked at her with a mixture of pity and suspicion. But Ena found that she was, unfortunately, getting used to that reaction, and it didn't stop her from enjoying the unique atmosphere.

It was friendly, cozy, but for some reason, watching the daemons interact with one another, especially in the kitchen, made Ena's heart ache for home. Despite choosing to be here, she missed her Coven, and she missed Greya.

"Are you alright?" Lara asked, pulling her aside next to an unused stove. She had clearly noticed the conflicting emotions on Ena's face, and her brow was furrowed in concern.

"Yeah," Ena said, trying to wipe the forlorn look off her face. "It's just..."

She paused, wondering if they had advanced to the part in their friendship where Ena could share some of these things. She didn't want Lara to think that missing her Coven meant she excused what witches had done in the past, or that her loyalty was to them over Ty and the daemons, but Lara had been nothing but kind to her, so...maybe it would be safe to open up.

"It's my sister," Ena explained. "Being here reminds me of her. She loves to cook. She makes the absolute best biscuits this side of the Chasm Mountains," Ena said, smiling sadly. "I try not to think about it, but I miss her. A lot. She's like my other half, and we didn't part on very good terms."

Lara looked at her sympathetically. "Did those terms maybe have something to do with Ty?" she guessed, raising her brows.

Ena nodded. "I just hope she forgives me for coming here. I hope I get the chance to explain better about everything, and that she'll believe me." Ena offered a watery smile, trying to act as if she wasn't distraught at the thought, but Lara wasn't falling for it.

"She'll believe you," Lara said simply. "If she's anything like you, she'll come around."

Ena laughed slightly at her confidence. "How can you be so sure? You don't even know her. You barely know me."

"I know you're brave as fuck for coming here. And loyal to Ty, for choosing to help him after all these years. If you're as close as you say, when the time comes, I know she'll believe you. And I bet she's already forgiven you."

Ena felt the knot in her heart loosen slightly, and she stared gratefully at Lara.

Should they hug? Ena felt like maybe they should hug, but she didn't know if Lara was a hugger. Gaia, new friendships were awkward sometimes.

Luckily, Lara spared her any more fretting. "Come on," she said simply, nodding towards the back of the kitchens.

Ena followed her friend as they resumed their tour of the kitchens. Lara showed her the food pantries, which were communal for the entire mid-level. She explained how they rationed the food, giving each family an equal portion, but that since they hadn't yet built kitchens in every home, thanks to Cole and his refusal to sanction the labor required, they often came together to cook and share what they made.

Ena found herself in awe of the cold storage room, which had been Imbued with runes from a daemon's Power of *algus*, which was similar to the witches' Gift of *glacio*, lowering the temperature of the room, making it cold. In it, Ena saw slabs of meat, from venison they'd hunted in the surrounding area, or the chickens, pigs, and goats they kept on the lower levels.

In the other, smaller room, Ena saw sacks of grain, potatoes, garlic, onions, and sparse bunches of herbs. She could tell instantly by their aroma that many of them were too old to be of much use in cooking. She wondered how often they were able to get new supplies. Without the ability to grow their own food underground, Ena realized how difficult it must be to keep the entire population fed.

"Where does all this food come from?" Ena asked Lara.

Lara led her back out of the dark pantry into the well-lit cooking space. "Some of it we trade for. When upper-levels go out on missions, they're often tasked with retrieving supplies as well. It serves two purposes—helping aid them in the cover, and allowing us to get what we need to survive. But..." She hesitated, as if she were nervous to admit what she was about to say.

"Some of it is stolen?" Ena asked, eyeing her friend.

"Yeah," Lara responded matter-of-factly. "I hope you won't go getting all witch-judgy on me. We only do what we need to, and with my father in charge...well, it's not always up to us."

"I'm not judging," Ena said sincerely. "Just...wishing it were different."

Lara sighed, watching the families cooking and laughing together. "Me too," she said sadly.

"So, what level of daemon are you, then?" Ena asked her as they made their way back out into the passageway. "You said your Power isn't suited for missions and that you manage the kitchens instead, but you live on the upper levels."

"I'd live on the mid-levels if it wasn't for my father and my husband. Steig is upper-level because of his Power, so I live there, too, but yes, technically my Power makes me a mid-level daemon."

"So...what is your Power anyway?" Ena asked. She'd been extremely curious, but had been hesitant to ask. Witches' Gifts were often a sign of their status in the Coven, especially for matriarchs since their Gifts tended to be rarer, and clearly, daemons' had even stricter ideas about Powers and status, so she didn't want to make Lara feel like she was judging her.

"It's *gaudium*," Lara said without shame. "I can bring people joy—cause a euphoria so intense you break into a fit of giggles," she added, smiling widely at Ena. "It's extremely useful as a mother, I'll give it that, even though I try not to use it too often. But...not as suitable for missions," she said with a shrug. "Making mortals and witches happy is not quite fitting with Iblis's desire for discord."

She said that last part ruefully, and Ena was again struck by the utter bullshit of this arrangement—both that daemons were separated based on what Iblis wanted, and that they were all forced to serve him at all.

"How does Cole interpret Iblis's will anyway? How is it that he can say so definitively Iblis doesn't want that? In my experience, intense happiness, at the expense of everything else, can be just as destructive as other emotions." She remembered that drunk-on-life feeling she'd gotten from Ty nine years ago when they'd first met, and she recognized it welling up in her frequently when they were together now too. Who was to say that feeling wasn't chaos incarnate, given the way it had made her uproot her very life?

"Mostly divination with rune stones, and sometimes Iblis comes to him in dreams, but a lot of times, I think he just follows his instincts," Lara replied, sounding bored by the idea.

"Hmm," Ena said, pondering that.

"What? You're suspicious of that?" Lara asked, misinterpreting her reaction. "How do witches interpret the will of Gaia, anyway?"

"No, not suspicious, just...that's similar—very similar—to the ways witches commune with Gaia. Our matriarch will also use divination, but with bones, and Gaia visits her in dreams as well. But it's also often just...her natural instincts that guide her, like you said."

"Hm, yeah," Lara said, seeming intrigued by the similarities as well. "Seems like maybe witches and daemons have more in common than we thought," she replied, smiling widely at Ena.

"Absolutely," Ena said, returning the smile to her new friend in kind.

CHAPTER FOURTEEN

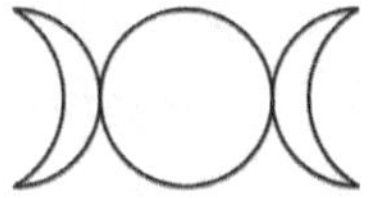

Ena

ENA FOLLOWED LARA AWAY from the communal kitchen down a new passageway until they came to a steep, dark staircase that wound deeper into the depths of the Underworld. After about ten minutes of descending, Ena began to feel a bit dizzy and disoriented. This was deeper than she'd ever gone before, and she realized they must be going to the lower levels.

The air began to get staler the lower they went—more dank and cave-like than above—and eventually, when the staircase bottomed out, instead of being pleasantly warm as it had been above, it was *hot*. Like sweat-dripping-down-your-back hot.

Ena fidgeted with the leather corset she was wearing over her shirt, pulling it away from her body to get some air on her skin as Lara led her down a passageway towards an open archway beyond which Ena could see the blue glow of a blazing darkrock fire.

The sounds of clanking metal and rushing air from the bellows echoed down the passageway, and as they walked through the doorway into the forge beyond,

Ena was floored. If she thought the ingenuity of the kitchens was impressive, this was…otherworldly.

Dozens of hearths carved right into the stone walls of the cave lined the giant cavern. The glow from them lit the room so brightly, Ena had to squint her eyes.

She'd never seen this large of a forge before. Usually, in the villages along the Chasm Road, there was one blacksmith, maybe two, each with their own hearth, but this was ten times that.

Steam filled the air from where the blacksmiths rapidly cooled their metals to harden them, but unlike other forges she'd seen, there was hardly any smoke at all—she supposed that was from the darkrock, which burned cleaner than wood.

Almost every hearth was occupied by a daemon, some pounding daggers on their anvils, others shaping more delicate objects like chalices and utensils. Most of the blacksmiths were men—large and muscular, like most daemons—but Ena was surprised to see there were female daemons here, too, looking equally strong as they moved their metal in and out of the fires.

Then her eyes landed on Ty, and her mouth went dry.

He was standing at a hearth near the back of the room, shirtless. His muscles and tattoos, covered in a delicious sheen of sweat, were on exquisite display as he pounded the object he was working on. They rippled and moved as he worked, his leather-gloved hands gripping tightly to the hammer and tongs he held.

Ena moved towards him like a moth drawn to a flame. She vaguely sensed that Lara was following her, and she was glad about that, but at this moment, she only had eyes for Ty.

Ty looked up as she approached. It was loud in the forge, all the overlapping sounds of metal being shaped and the air flowing through the tuyeres, so she didn't know if he heard her or smelled her, but either way, the look on his face made her heart pound.

His green eyes, already aglow from the light of the fire next to him, lit up, and a wide smile broke across his face. "Ena," he said, speaking loudly to be heard over the noises. "Just give me one sec."

He turned back to his work for a second, which she could now see was a large axe-head, like the one he used to carry before it was taken from him at Occidens, glowing orange with heat. He pounded it a few more times, flattening the blade into a thinner, more flared shape, before dunking the head into a barrel of water next to him. Removing it from the water after a few seconds, he laid the axe-head back on his anvil before putting down his tools and taking off his gloves.

"It's good to see you," he said, approaching her. "What are you doing here?"

"Lara offered to show me around a bit, so I've been getting a tour of the other levels."

"I see," he said, his eyes roaming from her legs to her chest to her face in assessment. She didn't know quite what he was assessing, or appreciating, but she was suddenly aware of the feeling of her nipples on the inside of her shirt, and Ena tried hard not to look down at his sweaty chest and think about how badly she wanted to run her fingers over his incredibly defined muscles.

Lara cleared her throat loudly, breaking the tension between them.

"It's good to see you too," Ty added, turning to Lara and nodding in greeting.

"Thanks, cousin," she said, giving him a teasing smile. "Look, I'll be right back. I want to go talk to Ferra about some stoves for the lower-level kitchen." She gestured towards one of the female blacksmiths working a few stations away from Ty before giving Ena a sly smile and walking off, leaving the two of them alone.

"So, how's your tour been?" Ty asked, taking a step closer until she could feel his body heat, even above the heat of the forge.

"Good," she said, smiling sweetly at him. "Even better now," she added.

Were they flirting in the middle of the forge? Yes. Could everyone around them see? Yes. Did she give a fuck? Absolutely not.

Somehow, despite sleeping next to him every night, she missed him. She wanted more of him. She wished she could follow him around all day, like a friendly cat in the shadows, just watching him move and talk and...

"Hey, Ty!" They were broken again from their reverie as one of the other blacksmiths, a large, burly male daemon with a shock of red hair, approached them. "Can you come be the striker for me?"

Ty reluctantly dragged his eyes away from Ena to look at the man. "Sure, just give me a minute here," he said, gesturing at Ena.

The man looked down at her, realization dawning on his face as he took in her *imperae* collar. He nodded quickly before walking away.

"You seem busy," Ena said once they were alone again.

"Yeah, kinda," Ty said, rubbing the back of his neck. "I'm sorry I've been so absent lately, it's just..."

"You don't have to explain," Ena said. "You're in high demand, I can see that," she said. In all honesty, she found it admirable how much he seemed to care about his duties in the Underworld, how much everyone relied on him. He clearly was well-respected among the other daemons. And while that meant she didn't get to see him as much as she wanted, she understood. He was doing his best for his people.

"I'd love to come help you with your research tomorrow, if you could use a second set of eyes," he offered. "Assuming I don't get called away for some emergency."

Ena smiled at that, knowing there was a very good chance he would, but appreciating that he wanted to try. "Yeah, I could definitely use help. I know we're getting closer to the *onata* celebration and I have yet to find anything to appease Cole."

"Don't worry too much about that, okay? I can handle Cole," Ty said reassuringly, running his hand down her arm.

"Ty!" another daemon called to them as she approached, holding out two blacksmithing tools that Ena had never seen. "Can I ask your opinion on something? I'm not sure which tool to use for this flask. It's delicate work."

"Sure. I'll be there in a minute, okay?" Ty responded kindly.

The woman called her thanks before turning to walk back to her station.

"I'm starting to feel like a distraction," Ena said, arching her brow at him.

"Oh, absolutely you are," he said, grinning in that infectious way of his. "But the best kind of distraction." He leaned down to whisper low in her ear. "I can tell how sweaty you're getting under that shirt of yours. Fuck—you make me want to rip it off with my teeth."

Ena giggled—just straight-up giggled like a little girl at that comment. Gaia, if she had any self-composure, it was dead and gone by now. She was so lost for this man.

"Mmhmm. What else about me distracts you?" she asked coyly, reaching out her hand to stroke the bulge of his bicep.

He sighed, pulling back so he was looking at her face once more. He locked eyes with her, staring into her with every ounce of his attention. "Your eyes..." he said.

"My eyes?" She wasn't expecting that. She thought he'd wax poetic about her cleavage in this vest or something, but...her eyes?

He gripped her chin gently, as if afraid she might look away. "I could drown in them, viper. I love it when you look at me."

Ena swallowed, and she could swear her heart skipped a beat. How could she even respond to that? She just stared at him, her mouth hanging open like a lovestruck fool, when Lara returned to their side.

Ty released her chin, and Ena cleared her throat, trying to regain her composure after the absolute putty
he'd just turned her into with that comment.

"Cool with you if we head back, Ena? I've got to go
check in on the kids."

"Yeah, sure," Ena said. "I should stop being such a
distraction anyway." She smiled shyly up at Ty again as
he chuckled slightly.

"Anytime, viper," he said, trailing his hand down her
arm once more and squeezing her hand slightly before
releasing her.

She wished fervently that she could kiss him goodbye,
like she'd seen Greya and Perse do a hundred times,
but she knew that while sexual exploits were expected
between them as a witch-slave and her master, anything
that made them appear like they were in a relationship
would be a red flag, so they had to keep public displays
of affection to a minimum.

Ena watched Ty walk away, off to help the redheaded
man who'd come up to them a few minutes ago, before
turning towards Lara and following her out of the forge.

She was silent as they walked, deep in thought, because she couldn't shake the feeling that there was this
new...feeling inside her when it came to Ty. She already
knew she was his, that she'd been so hung up him for
nine years that she hadn't even tried giving herself to
anyone else, but now...

She knew in her bones that there was absolutely no
coming back from *this* feeling. This mix of admiration
and respect, reliance and safety, desire and lust. All

these things swirled inside her, making her feel light as air in his presence.

She didn't dare admit it to herself. Their future was still so uncertain. They had a million other things to focus on, and while she was immeasurably happy that they got to finally be together, she knew they couldn't promise each other a future—not yet. She certainly hoped that breaking the bond would change things, but they had a long way to go before then, so no.

She wouldn't admit it to herself, not yet, but deep down, she knew exactly what the feeling growing inside her was.

CHAPTER FIFTEEN

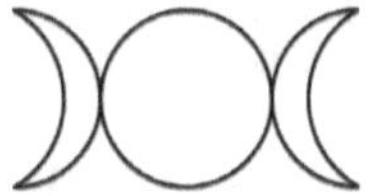

Ena

TY WAS, UNFORTUNATELY, NOT able to join her for research the next day, or the next. Almost an entire week went by in the blink of an eye, and Ena was starting to feel increasingly anxious and frustrated that she hadn't found any of the additional information they needed about the amulet or the binding spell.

On the day before the *onata* celebration, Ena spent the entire morning poring over the witch's journals that Ty had gotten from Petyr for the third time. Mostly, the journals were just records of potions made and spells conducted, including who those services were traded to and what was received in exchange, with an occasional brief description of the negotiation that led up to the trade. So far, the only information of value she'd found was a vague description of the amulet—the same one that Ty had already identified before he'd come to Auster to look for it.

It was located on an inventory list—a dry categorization of all the sacred objects in the Coven's possession and their estimated value. One line mentioned an amulet of great power that was being kept with "the

Coven matriarch," but there had been no way to tell which Coven it was referring to, hence why Ty had come to Auster first. Now, obviously, they knew it had been referencing Occidens, but that was old information, and Ena hadn't been able to find anything else helpful to their cause.

She made a mental note to ask Ty more about Petyr, and how in the world the man had deduced so much about the amulet from such little information, because there was no way he could have known what the amulet was for or what the witches had done from the little Ena had read.

In the end, though, Ena decided to put aside her futile efforts researching the amulet and instead focus on their other dilemma—what to tell Cole tomorrow at the *onata* celebration about their mission to figure out some way to Imbue her Gift into an object. She'd put her efforts on that issue on hold after Ty had told her not to worry about it, but still found herself wanting to contribute *something*, if only to make things easier on him with Cole, so she sought Nial for some books on runes and Imbuing.

She found the old daemon puttering around the Archives, pulling books off shelves and then putting them back with seemingly no rhyme or reason.

"Excuse me, Nial?" Ena asked cautiously.

"Yes, my dear," he said, turning towards her with a kindly smile. "What can I do for you?"

"I'm looking for more books on daemonic runes and Imbuing. Do you know where I can find some?"

"Yes, certainly, my dear," he said. His black robes swished at his heels as he turned and shuffled to the far side of the Archives. Ena followed him as he began haphazardly pulling books off the shelves and loading them onto a cart for her. He didn't even seem to check the titles or reference any sort of system to know where the books were; it was as if he already knew what every book contained and where it was.

After loading a dozen books on the cart for her, he pushed it over to her worktable.

"Thank you," she said, picking up the first tome and flipping it open to find depictions of runes inside. "I have to say, I'm so impressed. How is it that you know exactly where all the books are?"

He smiled kindly at her again. "It's my Power, my dear. My *memoria*. I remember everything I've ever seen or heard my entire life. Absolutely everything I've done lives in my memory, from the time of my birth."

Ena's jaw nearly hit the floor. "Wow, really?" she asked in awe. "That's amazing."

"It can be...yes," he said, smiling sadly. "But I won't sugarcoat it, my dear. It can also be a burden too. Sometimes, the past is meant to be forgotten."

Ena returned his sad smile as he turned to leave, but she was struck by how true his words were. There had certainly been times in her past where she'd wished to forget everything that had happened with Ty, but now...now she was endlessly grateful that she remembered, even if those memories did sometimes still feel painful. Those experiences had made them both who they were and, in the end, brought them back together.

Ena sat down at her table in the hidden alcove and began flipping through the books. She first wanted to understand the basics of Imbuing, so she could maybe come up with a plausible way of extrapolating its techniques for use with Wiccan Gifts. Something that would satisfy Cole without actually working—because the idea of Imbuing her Gift into an object to be used on a witch was rather horrifying.

After a few minutes of reading, she found herself struck by how complex this magic was. The runes seemed to act as a receptacle, she discovered, one that held the daemonic Power indefinitely within the object they were carved into. Different runes were required to hold different Powers, and so it was always an experiment to determine the correct combination and sequence of runes for any given Power and object.

It was similar to spellwords in that the correct phrasing and word had to be used in combination with one's Knowing to create the type of result one wanted. And, not for the first time, she was struck by how disappointing it was that witches and daemons did not share this knowledge with one another. There was so much more to daemonic culture than Ena had ever dreamed.

Ena continued poring over the books, but soon became stumped by continued references to the "binding rune." This was apparently a cornerstone rune in Imbuing, and a variation of it was supposed to be included on every Imbued object to bind the Power in place.

Bind the Power...could it be?

Ena flipped frantically through a rune dictionary which cataloged every rune that had been developed and successfully used to Imbue something, looking for an image of the binding rune.

Then she gasped when she saw it.

Her suspicions were confirmed; it was the symbol on the amulet she'd been looking for! The only one she didn't know, the one she'd never seen before.

It wasn't a one-to-one. The daemonic version was more angled, with straight, harsh lines instead of the more elegant, curved ones on the amulet, but it was undeniably, conceptually the same thing.

That meant...

Ena's head spun with the implications of this discovery.

Had witches learned this symbol from daemons? Or was this something that they'd developed together prior to the split? And more importantly, what was it doing on the amulet? How did the amulet have anything to do with binding or Imbuing?

Ena knew that amulets worked by enhancing magic and spells, so the symbols on it likely indicated the intention of the enhancing magic. She ran through each symbol in her mind...

The triquetra, the magic of the three Covens. Ena knew one witch from each Coven was involved in the spell—it required their combined magic, and would enhance it.

The goddess symbol, representing Gaia. The amulet drew upon and enhanced her magic. And Iblis's, too, since the horned god symbol was also on there.

And then the binding rune was used to...what? Bind the spell in place? She knew the magic of the spell wasn't simply Imbued into the amulet, otherwise how was it keeping all daemons from accessing Gaia's magic without them being near it?

So in all likelihood, the enhancing properties of the amulet were creating a much farther-reaching binding effect than was normal with simple Imbuing. The amulet was enhancing the binding effect, so rather than binding the spell into just one daemon who touched the object, it was binding it within each daemon in existence, using the enhanced magic of the three Covens, Gaia, and Iblis to do so.

Gaia, the power of that was...mind-boggling. No wonder she got such an eerie feeling when she held the amulet.

Ena looked around, finding the Archives mostly empty. She desperately wanted to discuss all this with Ty, but by her estimation, Turner wouldn't be coming to escort her to the fighting ring for at least another hour.

Ena flitted around the Archives, flipping absentmindedly through books she'd read a dozen times already, and drawing sketches of the binding rune to bring back with her until finally, Gaia be blessed, Turner arrived.

He noticed her agitation right away. "You alright?" he asked, his fair brows crinkled in concern.

"Yes, fine," she said. "I just... I think I found something, but I need to talk to Ty about it."

Turner's brows shot up in excitement. Gaia, the man really had no game face. The excitement exuded off him. "Really?" he asked. "What is it?"

"Not here…" she said. A few other daemons had come in since she'd made the discovery, and she didn't want to risk talking about it in a public area.

The two of them packed up the books, surreptitiously returning Ty's private reserves to Nial, before making their way back to Ty's room.

Turner dropped her off, then left immediately to go find Ty. Ena paced the room a few times before settling in front of the trunk at the base of Ty's bed. She opened it and rummaged around until she pulled out the small, unassuming wooden box that could only be unlocked with her magic.

Using her Knowing, she felt for the delicate metal mechanism within, and spoke.

{*Clavis*}

The small lock clicked, and Ena carefully opened the box to reveal the amulet.

The look of it always took her breath away—it was beautiful and terrifying at the same time, the feeling of it sending chills down her spine. And while part of her yearned to wear it—to touch it—another, wiser part didn't want to touch it with a ten-foot pole.

Just then, she heard male voices and the door swung open. She stood swiftly, blocking the view of the amulet, but luckily it was just Ty, Turner, and as a bonus, Steig had come too.

"I found him," Turner said joyfully. "And we figured Steig should be here to hear this as well."

"What about Lara?" Ena asked. She didn't want to leave her newfound friend out of the mix.

"I'll relay the information later. She's got her hands full right now," Steig said, in perhaps the least gruff response she'd ever heard from him. Maybe talking about Lara brought that out in him.

The three of them gathered around her expectantly, and it suddenly overwhelmed her with a sense of déjà vu as she remembered them doing the exact same thing weeks ago after she'd done the locator spell to find the amulet. How far they'd come now...

"Well, viper," Ty said, breaking their silence and looking down to where she held the amulet. "What did you find?"

She lifted the box, holding it in front of her so they could all see. "The symbol, this one here," she said, pointing to the intricate knot at the base of the amulet. "I think it has daemonic origins. It's similar to the binding rune used in Imbuing. Do you all recognize it?" She pulled out the paper in her pants pocket where she'd drawn the angular binding rune.

"Yes," Ty said confidently. "I've seen versions of this binding rune a hundred times. It's even on your collar," he said, reaching out to touch one of the runes at the edge of her collar, tucked behind her hair. "But how can you be sure it's the same?"

"Well, I'm not a hundred percent sure, but I know this symbol isn't used in Wiccan culture today, but before the split, witches and daemons intermingled a lot more, so it makes sense that their magical cultures did too. And besides, amulets enhance magic. If this one is drawing on the magic of Gaia, Iblis, *and* the three Covens to enhance the binding rune, that would explain its ability to bind the spell within all daemons. And it explains all of the symbols, and that...that makes sense, right?" Ena asked, suddenly feeling unsure.

She waited a few seconds as their brows furrowed, processing what she said, then Ty stroked his beard a few times before nodding slowly.

"Absolutely that makes sense. Ena..." he said, meeting her gaze, a handsome smile breaking across his face. "That's brilliant."

Ena couldn't help but smile at his praise. "This is a huge step forward," she continued, blabbering out of excitement now. "Now that I know the components of the amulet, I can narrow down what kind of spellwords I need to look for to explain the spell I heard in my vision, and that's the last piece we need to understand."

"Nice job, Ena," Turner said, clapping her on the shoulder. "I knew Ty wasn't lying about you being smart."

Ena rolled her eyes at his friendly teasing.

"Impressive," Steig said, giving her a nod of recognition.

She'd take it. At least it wasn't outright contempt. She was making progress all over the place!

"And I thought," she continued, "this will give you something to tell Cole tomorrow. You can tell him we found evidence that Wiccan and daemonic magics have been combined in the past, so it bodes well for Imbuing objects with Wiccan Gifts."

"Fuck yeah," Turner said, smiling widely. "He'll eat that right up."

Ty smiled at his friend, before looking at Ena again. "That is surprising—that daemonic and Wiccan magic can be used together, or at least borrowed from one another. I never thought that was possible," he said, his own excitement now palpable.

"Me neither," Ena agreed.

But it got her thinking...if witches used daemonic rune magic to power the amulet, what had that been like for daemons? What had it felt like for every daemon in existence to suddenly lose their connection to Gaia, and how was it possible that they didn't know about the amulet that had caused it? And the one daemon whose blood had been used as a part of the spell...what was her fate?

Ena was still pondering all this as Steig thanked her again briefly before hurrying off to help Lara, and Turner bid them good night, leaving to do whatever it was he did when he wasn't with her or helping Ty.

Ty went to the bathing chamber to clean up from his time in the mines and the forge, but Ena followed him, her eyes casually roaming over him as he filled up the bathtub and got in.

Ty sighed as he sank down into the water, his arms spread on either side of the tub.

He looked over at Ena where she watched him. "What is it?" he asked. "I can tell there's something else on your mind."

"You mean besides the obvious," she said, looking pointedly down at where his cock was under the water.

"Yeah, besides that," he said, winking at her.

Ena laughed, feeling warmth fill her at their light teasing. "I was just wondering...what did daemons think happened, when the witches bound them to Iblis? I know they were shunned and forced to move to the Underworld, but how did they not know about the amulet and what witches did? I would have thought the daemon woman...the one who survived, would have told others."

Ty shrugged, the movement drawing her eye to his large, cut shoulders. They were beautiful to look at, yes, but she never realized how much they carried too.

"I'm not sure what happened to her, or why we were never told what happened. We were always taught that Gaia abandoned us. That at some point, around the time we were demonized by witches and mortals and forced into the Underworld, that Gaia deemed us unworthy of her magic and unfit to carry out her will, so she removed our ability to interpret it, and so we turned towards Iblis, and embraced him instead. He became our one true Master."

"That's tragic," Ena said, her sadness at the thought entering her voice.

"I agree," Ty said sincerely. "But, I think you'd be the first to admit that witches have in many ways swung too far to the other side. As much as they embrace Gaia, they've shunned and demonized Iblis more than necessary."

Ena paused, thinking about the many chaotic, but necessary, things she'd done over the last month, especially with her Gift—fighting the bandits who'd attacked, breaking Ty out of Occidens, learning to fight with daggers. "Yes, I will admit that," she said, feeling that truth in her bones.

"So maybe," Ty began, looking at her seriously, "when this is all said and done, we can forge a new path...one that doesn't just worship Gaia or Iblis, but both—the way it was meant to be."

Ty looked up at her questioningly as he spoke, as if judging her reaction. Did he think the idea would scare her off? Daemons and witches coming together, worshipping Iblis and Gaia in equal measure?

She pondered the idea... What would that look like? She wasn't quite sure yet but...the idea of forging a new, unknown path with this man—this daemon who was hers—was quite possibly the best dream for her future that she'd ever had.

"Yes," she admitted, smiling at him. "I think I'd like that."

CHAPTER SIXTEEN

Ty

TY STOOD IN HIS bathing chamber, looking at his face in the mirror.

He turned his head to the side, assessing the *onata* that traced down the sides of his head onto his neck. He'd spent the last hour re-shaving the sides of his head and trimming his beard so his tattoos would be on complete display for the ceremony, as was tradition.

He was bare-chested still and took this time to examine his shoulders and arms, too, deciding where his new *onata* might fit. He'd only had his Power for a little over a year—though he'd been accompanying other daemons on missions since he was nineteen, a privilege granted to him because of his upper-level parentage—but he already had more tattoos than many other upper-level daemons. Most people saw this as a sign of Cole's favoritism, since he was frequently chosen for important missions, but Ty knew it for what it was—a way of controlling him.

Truth be told, he had conflicting feelings about his tattoos, as he did about so many things having to do with being a daemon. He loved the culture they represented, his people, and their lifestyle, but too often when he looked at them, he felt...shame.

Not every mission had been as disastrous as the one in Ternan—the one that had led to Petyr's death, and was still hard to think about, even this many months later. But even when they didn't result in death, he *had* caused chaos in hundreds of more subtle ways—ways that were not always his choice. And sometimes he wondered...

What would he choose when he finally *was* given a choice? When they broke the bond and he was free to interpret Gaia's will?

He didn't know, but he knew that at least it would be *his* choice, and not just Iblis's, or Cole's.

Deeming his appearance acceptable, he grabbed his black dress tunic off the vanity and pulled it over his head. It was sleeveless and trimmed in gold, with a deep V at the neckline to show off as many of his *onata* as possible. Looping his gold-adorned black leather belt around his waist, he exited the bathing chamber to check on Ena, who was busy getting ready in the bedroom.

He'd asked Trysh to make Ena a dress for the occasion, something that would help her fit in but also stand out—she wasn't a wallflower, and Ty wanted her to command respect among the other daemons as much as he did, for her own safety.

But when he walked into the bedroom, he realized his expectations did not meet the incredible reality of what he saw.

Ena's hair was mostly down—the dark-brown, wavy locks falling to the middle of her back, with just the sides pulled up into a twist with two golden hair pins laced into it, holding it in place. With her back to him, Ty's eyes roamed down her dress. It, too, was black and sleeveless, like his tunic, but with a full-length flowing skirt and a top framed by a black leather corset, cinched so tight around Ena's waist he could see every curve of her body. The shoulders of the dress were stiff and flared out, creating a powerful silhouette, and when Ena turned around to face him, he audibly swallowed.

The neckline plunged into a deep V across which the laces of the corset were tied. He could see the sides of her breasts where they squished together and all he could think about was running his tongue up between them.

"Ahem," Ena said, clearing her throat pointedly, and Ty realized he'd been staring directly at her cleavage for longer than was strictly polite.

He might've felt embarrassed about it, but fucking Iblis, she was an absolute sight to behold in this dress.

He dragged his eyes from her chest up to her face, and didn't regret that decision either. She'd darkened her eyes with crushed darkrock, as was tradition for the women during *onata* celebrations—Lara must've shown her how to do that, since it wasn't a practice among witches—and it made their bright-blue color stand out even more than normal.

Looking down, he saw the iron *imperae* collar where it contrasted starkly against the pale, milky skin of her neck. And he didn't know if it was the dress, or just her, but he'd never seen someone wearing the collar look so...powerful.

"I'll take your extended silence as a compliment," Ena said, a wry smile raising the corner of her mouth.

"Please do," Ty said, but he couldn't bring himself to return the smile. Nothing about the way she looked made him want to smile—it made him want to rip her dress the fuck off and pound into her so hard until neither of them could think straight.

But he swallowed that feeling, and opted for something slightly more appropriate, given that they needed to head down to the ceremony soon.

"It's not the first time I've been absolutely dumbstruck by you, and I'm sure it won't be the last, viper," he said, letting his eyes roam over her again. "The way you look...is pure fucking evil. How am I supposed to walk next to you all night and focus on anything else?"

Ena blushed. He loved it when she did that. It was his little prize for making her feel good.

"Good," she said, a little shyly. "That's what I was going for. You said I should command respect so people don't fuck with me, so people know I'm powerful and...yours."

"I have no doubt in my mind you'll do just that. Are you ready?" he asked, extending his arm to her.

She nodded before looping hers through it, and together they walked into the passageway.

As they got closer to the Great Antre, his nerves hit, filling his stomach with a tight dread. Yes, Ena had seen other daemons in passing, and met some of the friendlier ones, but this would be the first time she'd be on display to the entire Underworld—and at Cole's mercy. He was grateful that he'd been able to keep her off Cole's radar the past couple of weeks, by running around constantly and tending to whatever Cole requested so he'd have no reason to doubt him, no reason to come sniffing around Ena.

But now he was nervous, because there was no way to know how Cole would act tonight. In all likelihood, he had some power move up his sleeve that Ty would never see coming. He just hoped, whatever it was, that it wouldn't endanger Ena—he didn't think he'd be able to keep his cool if it did.

He felt Ena's arm stiffen slightly in his as they entered the Great Antre. The enormous cavern echoed with the voices of the Underworld as they talked and mingled and laughed. Low, chaotic drum music beat in the background, thrumming like a heartbeat through the stone walls.

Almost the entire Underworld was in attendance, dressed in their ceremonial best for the occasion. Ty spotted several friendly faces right away, including Myka, who he made a mental note to go talk to about the hay, but there were several unfriendly faces too. Those ones he cataloged closely, wanting to strategically avoid them and keep them from coming too close to Ena. Included in this category, unfortunately, were the many daemon women he had slept with over the last nine years.

Most of them were perfectly nice women, and he didn't think they would harbor any ill will towards him or Ena necessarily—he'd never promised any of them a future, and if anything, he was sure he'd been so emotionally unavailable, most of them were glad to be done with him when the time came. But he didn't want to rub Ena's face in any of it. She knew that he hadn't...abstained from sex the same way she had, but still, he couldn't even imagine being faced with anyone that she had been in a relationship with. He'd absolutely lose his shit with jealousy, so just in case, he hoped to spare her any of those feelings.

Ty led Ena over to the food tables, and more specifically, towards the abundant barrels of woodwater placed on one end, and filled them both a cup.

Heads turned towards them constantly, watching their every move. Whether it was because of him—his status in the Underworld always garnered him a bit of extra attention—or her—because she was a novelty and because she looked so fucking stunning in that dress—he didn't know.

Either way, he found it unsettling, and he wanted to tuck her back into him for protection—but he didn't. He knew he couldn't appear too fond of her. He couldn't let on that basically every waking thought he had revolved around her and that the only time he truly felt whole and peaceful was in her presence.

No, they couldn't know that he was hers. But he *could* show them she was his.

He reached over possessively, grabbing her around the waist and tilting the cup of woodwater to her lips.

She arched a brow up at him in question. *What was he doing?*

He let a wolfish grin spread across his face. *Just play along*, he communicated.

She parted her rose petal lips just a tad, and he poured the woodwater past them into her mouth. She swallowed it, licking the remnants off her lips, and his eyes tracked the movement.

Fuck, maybe that had been a bad idea. He felt all the blood in his body rush to his dick, and now all he could think about was filling that sweet, sweet mouth of hers with other things.

"Already causing a scene, I see," Steig said, breaking Ty's trance as he and Lara approached them.

"You look stunning," Lara said to Ena, smiling widely as she went to her. "Trysh really outdid herself with that one. It suits you."

"Thank you," Ena replied. "You look amazing too," she said, her eyes roving over Lara's blood-red ensemble. Ty would admit, it did bring out the color of her auburn hair well. A beautiful woman, his cousin. Inside and out.

He turned to Steig. "Bet you'll be having fun tonight," he said, winking at the man. He knew the two of them ordinarily had trouble keeping their hands off one another, let alone when they were all dressed up and surrounded by everyone's lust at a big gathering like this.

Steig grabbed his shoulder, turning them so they faced slightly away from where Ena and Lara were chatting. "You have no fucking idea how hard it is dealing with my own lust right now. Please do your best to keep yours in check, hm? For me," he said through gritted teeth, a pleading look on his face.

Ty laughed, deep and full. "No promises, brother," he said, clapping the man on the shoulder.

Just then, Turner approached them, a slight furrow on his fair brows. "Apologies in advance, Ty," he said quickly, giving him a wide-eyed look, before revealing who trailed after him.

His parents, Ty's aunt and uncle. Zak and Jyn.

"Ty," Zak greeted simply as he approached them.

"Uncle Zak, Aunt Jyn," he replied politely, bending to give his aunt a brief kiss on the cheek, her perfectly manicured brown hair brushing his forehead in the process.

"This must be the new witch-slave I've heard so much about," Jyn said, giving Ena a once-over with her ice-blue eyes. It was true that Turner mostly took after Zak, but his eyes, those were all Jyn. Except where Turner's were innocent and kind, hers were shrewd and calculating, and she turned their full force on Ena. "It's been a while since I've been in the presence of a witch," she said, not unkindly. "Tell me, what do you think of the Underworld?"

Ena glanced sideways at Ty, as if checking to see if responding was a good idea—a smart move, both to illustrate her subservience, but also because she was still learning the rules here, and she clearly didn't want to offend. He nodded gently at her, indicating it was alright to speak.

"It's…impressive," she answered, holding the woman's stare confidently, their blue eyes locked on one another.

"Hm," Jyn responded, sounding intrigued by Ena's response. "And what about it impresses you?"

"The ingenuity," Ena replied, not skipping a beat now. "Especially the aqueducts. I've never seen anything like them before."

Jyn's face lit up.

Damn, what a genius response. Did Ena know that Jyn's *diluvi* was Imbued into the aqueducts? That it was her Power to create and manipulate water that was currently being used to circulate the hot springs water throughout the Underworld? Or was that a happy accident?

"Yes, that is most impressive, isn't it?" Jyn replied, a pleased smile on her face. Flattery would get you everywhere with Jyn.

Zak, who wasn't much of a talker and generally preferred to listen and judge silently with his *mendacium*, cleared his throat and drew the group's attention back to him. "I simply came to remind you, Ty, that Cole has requested your presence. He requires an update on your progress."

"Of course," Ty said, forcing a congenial smile to his face. "We'll make our way over."

Zak nodded at him before turning to his son. "Turner," he said, "I trust your...responsibilities have been keeping you busy, but I need to speak to you soon about a new addition."

"Yes, Father," Turner responded, sounding resigned as Zak and Jyn walked away, making their way towards the dais where Cole awaited on his throne.

"Responsibilities?" Ena asked quietly, looking curiously between himself and Turner.

Turner shook his head at her. Now was not the time to discuss it.

Ty bent down to put his mouth next to her ear. "I'll explain later," he whispered, and she nodded in understanding. "Come on," he said, tipping back the rest of the woodwater in his glass. It burned on the way down, but helped to relieve the tight ball of anxiety in his stomach. "We should go get the check-in with Cole over with."

He held out his arm once more for Ena to join him, and she took it without hesitation. If she was nervous, she didn't show it, and Iblis take him, it was impressive.

They weaved in and out of daemons clustered in groups around the Great Antre, making their way to the far end, where the king's throne was situated on a raised dais, overlooking the group. He felt his uncle Cole's eyes on them the entire time.

Ty paused at the base of the dais, waiting for Cole to invite them up the brief stone staircase in front of him, which he did.

"Ty," he said, his voice somehow suspicious before Ty had even said a thing. "Thank you for taking the time to come see me."

Ty resisted the urge to roll his eyes. The man spoke as if he had taken his sweet time in coming here, rather than coming immediately after being summoned. He always pulled that shit, and it was getting old.

"Well?" he said, clearly waiting for Ty to begin. "I'm very curious to hear about the progress on your mission. Have you found anything useful?"

Ty cleared his throat, giving himself a second to get his ever-present rage under control. "We have, something very useful indeed."

"Please, do go on," Cole said, his eyes lighting up at the prospect. He was clearly curious, but Ty didn't miss the way his uncle Zak hovered at the base of the dais, listening to everything he said. He had to be very careful about his word choice.

"My witch-slave has discovered evidence that Wiccan and daemonic magic have been combined in the past, which bodes well for our mission."

"I see..." said Cole. "That is heartening news. And what, pray tell, is this evidence you speak of?"

"It's—"

Cole cut him off with a small tutting sound. "I think I'd prefer to hear it from her, actually." He gestured at Ena where she stood obediently at Ty's side.

Ty's whole body tightened at the fact that Cole's attention was on her—the most sacred thing in his life—but he swallowed the fear down, and trusted her. They'd warned her about Zak and how she would have to speak around him if called upon; she could handle this.

Ena bowed her head slightly in deference, as she'd no doubt seen others do, before raising her eyes to Cole. "Of course, King," she began, her voice coming out steady. She seemed wary, but impressively calm.

Ty moved imperceptibly closer to her anyway, trying to say with his body that he was here for her, to protect her.

"When I was going through a book on Imbuing runes," she continued, "I recognized the binding rune. Witches have utilized a similar symbol before, albeit slightly modified. So we take this to mean that some forms of magic can potentially be shared between the two races, and that bodes well for using the binding rune in combination with my Gift."

Ena finished, waiting for Cole to respond to this revelation. The silence seemed to stretch for far too long as he pondered it.

"Interesting," he finally spoke, relieving them of their tension. "That's not as definitive an answer as I would have hoped for, but I guess it's a start. What's your next step?"

"We've discussed experimenting with different runes in combination with the witch's version of the binding rune, to see if any of them work with my *visanis*," Ena replied without skipping a beat. She'd cleverly lied by saying that they'd "discussed" doing it, not that they would do it, so as not to alert Zak. Ty would've been surprised, but honestly, he was just proud, and endlessly impressed by her.

"Good...good," Cole mused. "This is exciting work from you and your witch-slave, Ty. You are serving Iblis well. Both of you." Cole's eyes flicked to Ena again before roaming down her dress. "I daresay she fits in well in the Underworld, Ty. Wouldn't you agree?"

Trap. This was a trap. Ty knew it instantly.

If he said yes, it could be interpreted as a sign that Ty wanted her to stay, and held her in higher esteem than he should, giving Cole all the more reason to banish her, or have her killed. If he said no, he'd be disagreeing with the king in public, something which would also not bode well for their relations.

Fuck the conniving fucking bastard.

Ty shrugged, feigning nonchalance. "She certainly is good at fitting things in." Ty raised one corner of his mouth in a sly smile, but inwardly, he tried not to wince at the crass words that rolled off his tongue.

A feline smile spread across Cole's face as he let out a dark chuckle. "Good answer, my boy," he said, sounding entertained. "Now, go fetch Steig and Turner so they can take their positions on the dais with you. It's time for the ceremony."

Ty nodded his head in deference before leading Ena back down the stairs into the gathering.

"Did...did that go okay?" Ena asked in a hushed tone as they walked.

"You did brilliantly," Ty said, the awe he felt for her filling his voice. "You were flawless."

Ena blushed, and he reveled in his prize.

"I'm sorry about what I said, though," Ty said. "That crude joke about you."

He didn't want to look at her too long, not here where everyone could see, but he hoped she could tell by the tone of his voice that he felt like a piece of shit for saying something like that about her.

"No, no, that was smart," Ena said confidently. "He looks like the type of guy who enjoys dick jokes."

Ty had to hold in his laughter but gave her a wide smile instead. "He absolutely is, viper."

After they located Steig and Turner, he left Ena with Lara as the three of them made their way back up onto the dais.

Three wooden chairs had been set on the landing, just a step down in front of the throne. As the three of them took their places of honor, Cole stood, rising to preside over the ceremony.

The room hushed as the drum music stopped and everyone quieted in anticipation before Cole began to speak.

"We of the Underworld bear witness to these followers of our one true God and Master, Iblis, Grantor of Power and Sower of Chaos, as they receive their markings. May the sacred *onata* brand them forever as his servants, ones who have carried out the brave tradition of enacting Iblis's will, our one true purpose, and the most necessary of evils.

"Through their actions of disruption, our Master originates.

"Through their actions of discord, our Master thrives.

"Through their actions of vengeance, our Master is sated."

With these final words, the room responded in unison, with everyone except Ena speaking the sacred response.

"By his will, do we live. By his will, do we die."

Ty had heard these ceremonial words many times in the past, and yet it was the first time since learning more about the amulet, and the binding spell, that he had spoken them.

He used to believe, as many others did, that Iblis was their benefactor—granting them Powers in exchange for a purpose. One that was necessary for the functioning of the world.

But when he heard these words now, they felt more like shackles. Lies that were told to explain the status quo. He was becoming increasingly certain that none of this was Iblis's will, or Gaia's, but witches, like Heran, who maintained the lie, and daemons, like Cole, who fed it.

Nykol, the skilled artist who'd been giving *onata* tattoos since before Ty had begun receiving them, approached Steig first where he sat in the chair farthest to the left. He stripped out of his shirt, bearing his olive skin and the myriad of tattoos that already adorned his forearms and shoulders.

Nykol placed a small metal dish on the ground, filled with powdered darkrock mixed with water, and dipped a fine needle into it. Using the mallet in her other hand, Nykol began to tap the design into Steig's skin, continuing from where his previous tattoos ended on his shoulder, moving onto his back.

Nykol's tattoos were always unique, but they told a similar story each time—different combinations of whirls and dots to represent locations and missions, the Powers that were used, and the level of success of the mission.

After completing Steig's *onata*, Nykol moved onto Ty. He removed his shirt as well, opting to have the *onata* continue from his shoulder onto his chest, right over his heart. As each tap of the needle entered into his skin, Ty felt the weight of what he'd done. Not just burning Ena's house, but the fight he'd started in Tritam, the Occidens witches he'd injured, the bandits he'd killed.

But he couldn't bring himself to regret any of it. Not when it had led him back to Ena and brought them together again. His eyes connected with hers where she stood across the room with Lara. She stared at him, unblinking as the darkrock burned into his skin. He was well-used to the pain. He barely felt it now. Instead, all he could feel was his heartbeat aching in his chest as she stared at him with those beautiful eyes.

Fuck, what was this feeling? This overwhelming, chest-crushing need for her? He'd yearned for her for years, he was no stranger to that, but this...this felt new.

Thankfully, Nykol finished his tattoo swiftly, and moved on to Turner. Ty tried hard not to stare at Ena too much. He needed to appear aloof when it came to her. But fucking Iblis, that was hard to do when all he wanted to do was be near her and stare at her in that dress.

The room started to grow restless by the time Turner's tattoos, which he'd opted to receive on his chest, too, were complete. Usually, by this time, everyone was ready to get drunk as fuck and give in to the chaos of the all-night celebration, but Cole stood again, silencing the room with a wave of his hand.

"I know we're all eager to resume the festivities, but I'd like to do one more thing. Something...special, to mark the occasion and celebrate the most surprising outcome of this most recent mission."

Cole's gaze landed on Ena, and Ty tensed.

"Lara, my dear, will you please escort the witch-slave to the dais?"

Lara looked briefly at Ena, giving her an almost apologetic glance, before doing as her father told her.

Ty could see the trepidation on Ena's face, and she wasn't alone. He felt it tightening his own. What the fuck was Cole up to?

There was no doubt in his mind that if Cole tried to harm her in any way, that would be it. He wouldn't be able to hold himself back from protecting her, and he knew that would come with dire consequences, but it didn't fucking matter.

His fists tightened where he sat on the edge of his seat, watching Ena with his heart in his throat as she came to a stop at the foot of the dais.

Cole addressed the group, smiling in that superior way of his that made Ty want to smash the man's head against the cave wall. "This witch-slave, as many of you know, was captured by these three faithful servants of Iblis on their most recent mission, and she is a prize indeed. A powerful addition to our efforts in the Underworld, as she has been Gifted *visanis*."

Several shocked gasps and murmurs whispered through the crowd at that revelation, but they fell silent at Cole's next words.

"And I think, given how unique and rare that Power is, even amongst daemons, it would be in the spirit of the celebration to receive a...demonstration."

A demonstration? What was this asshole up to? Ena's Gift wouldn't work on anyone here, except for the...

Ty's train of thought was cut off as Zak led one of the mortal *imperi* to the dais next to Ena. Her eyes darted to Ty. There was fear and helplessness in them, and it cut Ty to the bone.

What should he do? Should he stop this? Stopping it might put Ena in more danger, if Cole saw his response as a threat. But he knew Ena was still coming to terms with her Gift and didn't like using it against others unless absolutely necessary. How would she react to this? Having to use it on an innocent mortal?

"Ty," Cole began, directing his dark, malicious eyes onto him. "Would you please order your witch-slave to show us the promise of what you've brought?"

Ty held his tongue. Cole had him backed into a corner here, and he knew it. Averting his gaze from his uncle, he looked at Ena and nodded once. "You heard him, witch," he said, his voice coming out harshly as he intended.

He spoke without emotion, but with his eyes, he tried desperately to reassure her.

You need to play along with this. It's the safest choice.

Ena's chin lifted as she looked at the *imperi* that Zak had brought. The man was older, in his late sixties. He'd been brought here almost fifteen years ago after discovering a daemon using his Power. He'd bargained for his life and agreed to come to the Underworld and serve willingly in exchange for being allowed to live. But Ty remembered Turner mentioning that the man had left his entire family behind, and he thought of them often.

"W-what do you want him to do?" Ena asked Ty, her voice trembling slightly.

Ty looked to Cole, raising an eyebrow. This was his command; he should be the one to get whatever it was he wanted out of it.

"Have him fetch me a drink," Cole said, as he sat back down in his throne, looking far too pleased with himself.

Ena refocused on the man wearing the *imperae* collar, whose eyes were lowered to the floor. Ty could see the war in her eyes as she felt pressured to use her Gift on an innocent man for no good reason. But she was brave. He knew that already, and soon Ty felt the hairs on his arm stand up as the eerie voice of her *visanis* echoed around the room.

{*Fill a cup with woodwater and deliver it to the king.*}

The man didn't even look at Ena, he just moved as if in a trance, walking back down the stairs from the dais over to where the barrels of woodwater were kept. The entire room watched as he took a single cup and filled it to the brim with woodwater, then walked calmly back to the dais with it.

He walked up the stairs, and that's when Ty noticed his hand trembling slightly. Woodwater sloshed out of the cup in small amounts, leaving dark drip marks on the stone steps.

Ena's Gift might take away someone's will, but it didn't take away their fear over what was happening beyond their control.

Ena's shoulders dipped slightly in relief as the *imperi* walked directly to Cole's throne, holding out the cup in offering.

But Ty saw that feline smile spread across Cole's face, and he knew that this wasn't over.

"Most impressive," Cole said, a pleased look in his eye. "Now tell him to drink it."

Ena looked to Ty, confusion on her face. What the fuck was Cole playing at?

Ty wasn't sure, but nodded to her. *Keep playing along.* That was the safest thing for everyone.

{*Drink the woodwater.*}

The *imperi* did as he was told and brought the woodwater to his lips, draining the cup in several gulps.

The man coughed and sputtered afterward. Ty wasn't sure if the *imperi* were used to drinking woodwater, as they were usually given the most basic of provisions on the lower level.

Ty looked over at Turner where he sat next to him. The man was tense as a bowstring, and Ty could feel the simmering rage coming off him waves.

"Again," Cole said, his enjoyment at the spectacle exuding out of him. "This is a celebration, after all…"

Ena again used her *visanis* to make the man fetch a drink and bring it to the dais, where he was again forced to drink it. This continued two more times before the man started to stumble and wobble slightly as he walked, spilling more woodwater with each pass.

Cole laughed, a dark chuckle echoing throughout the room. People were starting to shift uncomfortably where they stood watching. Not only was this painful to watch, but it was fucking boring too. Cole seemed to be the only one getting anything out of this.

When the *imperi* returned with a full cup of woodwater for the fourth time, Cole paused, holding up a hand to stop Ena from speaking.

"This time, tell him to get on his knees and dump it on his head," he said, barely keeping his mirth in check.

Ty could feel Ena's indignation from where he stood. The look in her eyes was murder, and he could tell that not only was the repeated use of her magic draining on her, but she was pissed as fuck. He hadn't seen that look since they'd been by the Sacred Pool and she found out Ty remembered who she was.

Ty realized they were trapped. They were stuck inside Cole's twisted game, and Ty wracked his brain trying to think of a way to safely get them out and end this torture. Maybe he should stand up and claim to be bored, and encourage Cole to move on, but would the man listen? Or would there be backlash on him, or Ena? He didn't know, but he needed to do *something* to get them out of this, before it got worse.

He watched Ena take a deep breath, as if resigning herself to Cole's command, but then he caught a glint in her eye before she spoke.

{*Fall to your knees.*}

The *imperi* dropped roughly to his knees, letting all his body weight crush onto the stone floor, but because he fell so quickly, he lost his balance. The woodwater in his hands sloshed forward, spilling all over Cole's leg where he sat on the throne.

Cole's satisfaction vanished, and in its place was a look of disgust and anger.

The *imperi*, noticing what he had done, slurred hurriedly. "I'm so sorry, m-my king. I—I didn't mean to," he said, voice trembling and thick with inebriation.

Cole's eyes raised to Ena.

Had she done that on purpose? There was no way to prove it, but she easily could have told the man to lower to his knees, or get on his knees, and it might have had a different effect. But she had said, very specifically, "*Fall* to your knees." Had she intended for that to happen?

"You're dismissed," Cole said, switching his gaze to the *imperi* in front of him and waving the man away like a gross bug.

Cole stood up, and Ty could tell he was furious, and embarrassed, but he couldn't openly punish the *imperi* or Ena for something like this. They were still valued resources of the Underworld, so it was only socially acceptable to punish them if they disobeyed a direct order. And neither this man nor Ena had done that.

He looked over at Ty with a quiet menace. "I look forward to much more from your witch-slave soon, nephew," he said, before walking down off the dais.

The room seemed to breathe a collective sigh of relief as the drum music kicked back up and everyone started talking and drinking again.

Ty pulled his shirt back on, feeling it brush over the tender spot where his new *onata* decorated his skin, as he walked over to Ena. "Are you alright?" he muttered under his breath, bringing his mouth close to her ear as he grabbed her arm and led her off the dais.

"Yes," she said, sounding tired, but no longer so afraid.

Ty led her out of the fray of people, off to the side of the room to an unused alcove. Once he was certain they were out of earshot, he leaned one arm against the wall, caging her in with his body.

"Did you do that on purpose?" he asked her. "Make him spill the drink?"

Ena looked up at him with those big blue eyes, and the corner of her mouth tipped up in mischief. "Yes," she said. And he felt the blood go straight to his dick. It swelled under his pants, pushing up against the buttons.

Fuck. That was quite possibly the hottest, most badass thing she'd ever fucking done.

And they needed to leave this celebration. Right now.

"Come with me," he said roughly, tugging her arm, and leading her out of the Great Antre.

Chapter Seventeen

Ty

"Where are we going?" Ena asked, sounding confused.

How could she be confused? He wasn't confused at all. He knew exactly what he wanted.

"Back to my room," he said, walking so fast that he realized Ena was having trouble keeping up. He had to force himself to slow down.

"Oh, okay," Ena said, sounding relieved to be leaving. "Will Cole be mad, you think? Was it that obvious what I did?" she asked, wariness creeping into her tone.

"No, I don't think so. I mean, it was obvious to me, but I know you better than he does. Maybe he suspects, but he has no evidence."

"Okay, good," Ena said, sounding satisfied as she jogged along to keep up with him as they moved through the empty passageways away towards Ty's room. "And what was up with Turner?" she asked. "He seemed really upset when they brought that *imperi* out, and it was unlike him. Does that have something to do with the 'responsibilities' his father mentioned?"

"Yes," Ty said, trying to calm his single-minded focus to answer her very justified question. "He helps

Zak…manage them, for lack of a better word. But you know Turner. It's really tough on him when they're not treated well. He cares for them."

"Oh," Ena said, her voice soft with sympathy.

Thank fuck they made it outside his door in record time, and Ty grabbed the handle, pushing the door open like the passageway was on fire.

"What's going on?" Ena asked. "Why are you in such a rush?"

How was he supposed to explain that he literally just felt the most intense primal urge to bury his cock inside her? How was one supposed to communicate that?

"You're sure you're okay?" he settled on, trying to calm his pounding heart as he turned to face her.

"Yes, Ty, I'm sure," she said calmly.

He felt himself relax a bit, hearing her tone. She was here, safe, and they were finally alone.

"You did so well," he said, approaching her and cupping the back of her neck with his hand. Her skin was smooth, and the contact sent shivers through his body. "So incredibly, impressively well."

"Thanks," she said, her mouth tipping up into a smile. She always seemed so pleased when he praised her, and Iblis fucking damn him, he wanted to praise her all night long.

"You know," she continued, pressing her body a bit closer now. Was she catching on to his desire? "It wasn't as bad as I thought it would be. None of this is, actually. I feel like…I can handle way more than I ever knew."

"Of course you can. And just so you know, for better or for worse, I do think what Cole said was true. You do fit here."

"You think?" Ena asked, bringing her hands around his waist. Her breasts squished against his chest now, and it was all he could think about.

"Yeah, don't you?" His voice was getting low, and he was about two seconds away from not being able to hold this conversation anymore.

"Maybe. I don't know," she said, running her hands across his shoulders. "I don't know if it's the place so much as...you. When I'm with you, I just feel so..." She brought her eyes up, looking at him from under her lashes. "Free."

"Free from what?" he asked quietly, tracing her lower lip with his thumb. The plump flesh moved underneath the pad of his finger, and he was filled with the sudden urge to bite it.

Ena sighed, as if struggling to put into words what she felt. "Free of the thoughts that usually make me doubt myself or second-guess my decisions. Free to be myself, fully and unabashedly. With you...I'm just free," she whispered.

His thumb stopped its perusing, and instead, he gently dipped the tip into Ena's mouth. She opened for him, just slightly, allowing it in, and he watched as it parted her lips.

He couldn't take his eyes off it. His thumb in her mouth. The way her lips looked around it, and how warm and wet it was inside.

He looked up to her eyes then, wanting her to know what he said was true. "You know I feel the same way, right? When I'm with you...I'm free in my own way."

Free from the anger and the resentment. Free to be himself.

Ena closed her lips around his thumb and sucked, her cheeks hollowing with the motion as she slowly slid her lips off his thumb. "Show me," she said in challenge, holding his gaze.

He hauled her mouth to his, delving his tongue inside her instantly. This was no coaxing or seduction. It was pure, unadulterated need. Their lips and tongues tangled, teeth clashing as they clawed at each other.

Ty moved his hands down her front, ripping at her bodice. The laces were too slow so he just pulled, hearing the fabric tear as it exposed her breasts. He grabbed each one, full and pliant in his hands, stroking his thumbs over her nipples. She moaned into his mouth and, fucking Iblis, the sound turned him feral.

He kneaded her breasts harder before tearing her dress further off her body so her torso was exposed. His hands began to roam down to her ass where he planned to scoop her up and throw her on the bed, when she pulled away from his kiss and dropped to her knees.

Ty stood stunned, watching as she stroked his cock through his pants, which was now perfectly at her eye level. He was so hard it almost hurt, and every stroke of her hand drove him wild. She slowly undid the top two buttons on his pants, exposing the tip of his dick. Seductively, she leaned forward and kissed it—just the tip—and he felt the surge of precum leak from it as she did.

He brought his hands to his face and groaned. "Fucking Iblis, Ena," he said, drawing out the words.

She looked up at him, pure mischief and desire in her eyes, her chest still bare and nipples peaked. He didn't know what he wanted to fuck more—her mouth or her tits.

"I've been waiting for this," she said. "To feel you in my mouth."

She unbuttoned him the rest of the way, taking his cock in her hand. He'd always been well-endowed, but this was quite possibly the hardest he'd ever been, and the size of it compared to her hand was so intoxicating to watch.

Ty chuckled darkly at her words, her unabashed desire. He was so pleased with her, and he knew what she needed to really enjoy this: to let go of her control. That's what she always wanted, wasn't it? So as she moved to put the tip into her wet, open, waiting mouth, Ty reached out and grabbed her hair, pulling her back gently and stopping her.

"Then ask me nicely, viper," he said. "And maybe I'll let you choke on me."

Her eyes flashed, and he could smell the rush of wetness and musk that filled her pussy at his words. "Please, Master, can I suck your cock?" she asked, her voice breathy and almost trembling.

"That's my good girl," Ty said, smiling down at her. "Open that pretty mouth for me."

Ena did as she was told, parting her rose lips as they both moved, her guiding the tip of his dick into her, and him guiding her gently from the back of her head.

Ty's eyes rolled back as she moved her hot, wet mouth up and down him. She sucked lightly at first, getting him wet, and moving her hand slowly. Then she pulled back, looking at him as she swirled her tongue around his tip, once, twice, then laid her tongue flat and licked him from base to tip.

"Fuck," he groaned. She was teasing him so hard, he had to focus all his energy into not coming instantly. He thought he'd gotten the upper hand by making her beg, but Iblis fucking damn him, she'd gotten it back instantly the way she was looking at him with those big blue eyes. He was surprised his balls weren't just as blue at this point.

She continued teasing for another minute before taking him back into her mouth, and this time, she went deep. When his cock hit the back of her throat, he swore he stopped breathing for a second. Then somehow, she went deeper, taking almost his full length into her throat, before pulling back out, gasping.

She liked it like that, huh? Thank fucking Iblis. She was so perfect for him.

He gripped the back of her head harder this time, thrusting forward as she took him into her mouth again, and he fucked her face. Not too hard, not at first. He didn't want to hurt her. He wanted her to be able to pull away if she needed to...but she didn't. She took him deep and opened her throat as he shoved his cock inside her. He held her there for a minute before pulling her back, looking down into her eyes which were filled with tears, checking that she was okay.

She just gripped his dick harder, and he growled, barely able to hold himself back as it was.

"Touch yourself," he said in command. He wanted to hear how wet she was, wanted to dream about her sweet wet cunt while he was deep inside her mouth. And he wanted both of them to reach their pleasure together.

Ena reached down with her free hand, slipping her dress down over her hips so it fell to the floor around her. She reached her fingers between her legs and Ty watched, entranced, as she sank them inside herself. He felt her shudder as she opened her mouth to take him inside again.

She stroked him and took him deep as he thrusted into her, keeping the movement in time with her hand as she thrust two of her fingers inside her cunt, the heel of her hand hitting her clit with every pass.

She gripped his dick hard. He could tell she was getting close. So was he. Fucking Iblis, so was he.

He pulled out abruptly, taking his dick in his hand. "Stick out your tongue," he said, his voice so tight and deep it sounded foreign.

She did as he told her, her tongue flattening as she stuck it out of her mouth, ready to receive what he gave her. She watched with open, feral eyes as he jerked himself into her mouth. Just as he spilled thick ropes of cum onto her tongue, he felt her tighten as her orgasm ripped through her, a cry of pleasure escaping her as her eyes rolled back.

Ty saw stars. He swore he blacked out for a second before coming to and watching as Ena brought her tongue back into her mouth, swallowing what he'd given her.

All except a small dot of cum that had landed on her cheek underneath her eye. He watched as she brought her finger up, clearly feeling it there, and swiping it away before bringing it into her mouth and sucking it off like it was honey.

"Shit," he said, standing there in awe. That was by far the best head he'd ever gotten, and quite possibly the hottest sexual encounter he'd ever had in his life.

He could smell how turned on Ena still was, could tell she was still dripping from all they'd done. After weeks of rushed orgasms and not enough of her at all, there was no way they were done yet.

He grasped her chin and tilted it up so she met his gaze. "Turn around," he said.

She looked down at his dick, seeing it already hardening again. "Wow," she said, a seductive smile forming on her lips. "That was fast."

"Turn. Around," he gritted out.

She did as she was told, turning around so she was on all fours in front of him on the fur rug.

"That's my good girl," he said, stroking her fleshy, round ass that was now so beautifully on display for him.

Ty finally shed his shirt and took his pants the rest of the way off so he was nude behind her. Grabbing her hair and pulling her up gently so her back was flush with his front, he whispered in her ear as he notched his hard cock at her entrance. "You're my dark goddess," he said, slipping it inside her. "I fucking worship you."

She cried out as he entered her, and then he started fucking her—hard. Again, again, again. Her pussy was so slick and wet already, he barely felt any friction, just smooth glides of pleasure.

He gripped the base of her throat, gently, not squeezing, as he whispered again. "I will fuck every hole you have one day. Would you like that, my dark goddess?" he asked, his breath coming out staccato from his efforts.

"Yes," she breathed, almost pleading. "Yes, Ty, fuck yes."

"Good girl," he said, feeling his balls tighten in response to her pleading. "Now scream for me, Ena," he said. "I want everyone in the Underworld to know you're mine."

He reached around with his other hand, stroking her clit, swirling and tugging on it as he felt her rachet up higher and higher, getting closer to another orgasm, and as she finally broke, she screamed—a sound bordering on pain, but Ty knew it was pleasure. He felt his own orgasm build as he spilled into her, pumping himself with her hot, wet cunt until he was spent.

As he came down, he wanted to collapse into her—fall onto the bed and never move again—but he needed to make sure she was taken care of first.

He removed his hand from her throat, gently stroking her hair back where it stuck to her face with sweat, and probably also some of his cum. He pulled his length out of her as they both breathed heavily. He planted a kiss to her cheek, reaching with his hand to turn her face towards him. She was trembling.

"Are you okay? Was that...?"

She stopped him with a kiss, tender and gentle, her lips expressing something they both knew was happening. "I..." she began. "Yes. I'm wonderful. And I'm yours, Ty," she said, her voice full of emotion. "I'm all yours."

"I'm yours too," he said, leaning his forehead to hers and breathing her in.

He'd never felt this close to anyone in his life. This content, this calm, this...happy.

He scooped her up, tucking his arm under her legs, and brought her to the bed. After fetching her a wet cloth to clean up with, and one for himself, he laid down beside her.

She tucked into him, her head on his shoulder, right where she fit so perfectly, as he covered them up with a fur. Eventually, hearing her breathing slow down, he began to drift off to sleep, but before he did, he realized without a doubt—there was no coming back from this feeling. Ever.

CHAPTER EIGHTEEN

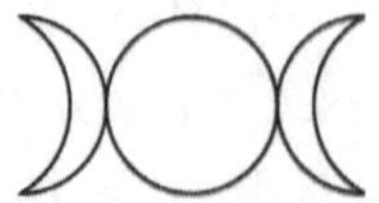

Ena

THE NEXT DAY, ENA felt an undeniable glow. She'd woken up with a smile on her face, even though Ty had had to leave early to go tend to some things. She caught herself dreamily smiling while in the bath, and she dressed in a daze.

When Turner came to the door to take her to the Archives, he took one look at her and laughed. "Good night, huh?" he asked, a shit-eating grin on his face.

"What do you mean?" she asked, her face going hot.

"Well," he began, as they walked down the hall. "You guys left pretty quickly after everything that happened with Cole, and then I distinctly remember hearing some...screaming come from this part of the upper level."

Ena covered her mouth with her hand. "Oh Gaia, are you serious?" she asked, mortification seeping in.

Turner laughed again, the sound lighthearted and mirthful.

"Fuck, that's embarrassing," Ena said. "I thought Ty was kidding when he said he wanted everyone to hear, not that they actually would."

"It's fine, Ena. Don't be embarrassed. It's good, actually."

"How is it good?" she asked incredulously. "Everyone in the Underworld heard me have a screaming orgasm."

Turner grinned, the bastard. "It's good because it's expected. Everyone knows you're Ty's witch-slave. If he wasn't...staking his claim, so to speak, it might invite others to."

"That's fucked up," Ena said.

"It definitely is," Turner agreed. "But I don't make the rules. Neither does Ty."

Ena sighed in frustration, but she knew that, unfortunately, he spoke the truth.

"Speaking of fucked up..." she began, feeling the need to change the topic. "I'm sorry about everything that happened with the *imperi* last night."

Looking sideways at Turner, she saw his smile fall, a look of guilt passing over his face.

"Is...is the man okay?" she asked gently. "Ty told me that you're...responsible for them."

"Yeah," Turner said, as if grateful that she'd asked. "He's okay. But just for the record, *none* of that was your fault."

"I know," Ena said, nodding to herself. Didn't mean she felt great about it, though. She knew she'd done the safest thing for everyone by playing along with Cole's fucked-up game, but she still hated that she'd been a part of it. "So what is it you do for the *imperi*?" she asked. "Just like...look after them?"

"Something like that," Turner said, looking away again and turning quiet.

They walked the rest of the way to the Archives in silence, so many follow-up questions on her tongue, but she got the sense that whatever Turner did for his father and the *imperi*, he didn't like talking about it, so she held it.

Once they arrived, Turner escorted her to her usual alcove before leaving to attend to his duties, and Ena turned her focus to figuring out the final piece to the binding ritual.

Now that they knew what all the symbols on the amulet represented and how they worked, Ena needed to understand the mysterious spellwords that she'd heard in her vision.

Spells had so much to do with intention, and if she didn't know what the words meant, she wouldn't be able to get the intention right to reverse it, and then the spell would fail.

So, for what felt like the hundredth time, she decided to look through the best resource they had—the witch's journals Ty had gotten from Petyr. But as she flipped through one of them, seeing the same old references, she found herself wondering yet again who the witch who wrote them was. The journals gave no indication about their age, gender, Gift, or even which Coven they were from.

But that got Ena thinking...how would this witch, whoever they were, know about the amulet's existence at all unless they were from Occidens? It made sense for them to be, but she hated to accept that as fact without evidence. Besides, the journal looked old, and there was always a chance that the amulet had at one time been with one of the other Covens.

Maybe it would be helpful if Ena could determine the witch's Coven of origin for sure, so she started to flip through the journal looking for clues about that instead.

It was extremely dry stuff, and Ena's eyes were starting to glaze over when she found an obscure trade reference near the end of the journal:

A man from Tyndell requested two vials of a pest resistance potion for his orchard, however since the fallout with the other Covens after the dark spell, trade with Tyndell is no longer allowed by the treaty, so his request was rejected.

The passage was short, and the mention of the "dark spell" so innocuous that Ena almost didn't catch it. Could it be referencing the binding ritual? She wasn't sure, but the "fallout with the other Covens" had to be referencing the rivalry between Occidens and the other two Covens.

This told Ena several things, because if this witch had been no longer allowed to trade with Tyndell, she must've been from Occidens—Tyndell was located near Aquilo, and on their side of the treaty line.

Ena felt relieved—that was at least one mystery solved—but now there was a new one too. Because if the "dark spell" was indeed referencing the binding ritual, and she described the fallout as being due to that spell...was the binding ritual what originally caused the rivalry between the Covens?

That would be huge, if so. None of the witches truly knew what had caused the rivalry between the Covens—it had simply always been that way, for as long as they all remembered. Of course, now she wondered if the matriarchs had known all along, and if it was just another thing that had been kept from her. But, either way, it being the cause of the rivalry would only make sense if the Coven matriarchs disagreed about the spell somehow.

Ena wracked her brain trying to remember what she could about the three witches in her vision—what they looked like, what they felt.

One witch, the one with brown hair and blue eyes, had seemed to take satisfaction from the daemon woman's pain and punishment. She'd clearly been the ringleader of it all.

But the other, the one with pale-blonde hair and hazel eyes, had seemed...concerned—trepidatious almost. Was it possible she didn't fully agree with what was done? And if she were from Occidens, that could explain why there was a falling out between the Covens afterwards. If their matriarch didn't completely agree with what was done to the daemons, or came to regret it afterwards, that would explain the discord between them, and the subsequent treaty keeping them in separate territories.

It was a good theory, but there were still so many unanswered questions—like how the amulet ended up in Occidens anyway, and she still wasn't any closer to deducing what the spellwords meant, but still, she felt pleased to have made some progress.

She was still flipping through the journals, looking for further confirmation of her theory, when a voice greeted her.

"Hey, beautiful," Ty said as he approached her table.

"Ty," she greeted, her face instantly lighting with a smile that felt beyond her control. "What are you doing here? It's only midday."

"I know. I finished up early for once and wanted to come see you. And help with the research, if you need it," he said, sitting down at the table. His large frame seemed to take up so much space, and she couldn't help but blush as he got close to her, thinking of last night.

"I'm glad you're here, for several reasons," she said, scooching a bit closer to him. "But mostly because I think I figured out something important."

Ty looked around the Archives, making sure they were alone before he nodded at her to continue.

"I think a disagreement over the binding spell is what caused the rivalry between the three Covens," she said.

Ty's brows jumped up in intrigue. "Really? What makes you think that?" he asked, keeping his voice low just in case.

Ena explained about what she remembered from the spell, how one of the witches seemed less enthusiastic than the others, and the brief mention of the "dark spell" in the journal being the cause of the severing of ties between the Covens.

"That makes a lot of sense," Ty said, his brows creasing as he pondered the new information. "So you think the Occidens matriarch was against it, even though she participated?"

"Yes," Ena said. "Either she was forced into it, or maybe changed her mind after the fact, I don't know, but either way, I think somehow the Occidens witches ended up taking the amulet, and maybe the other Covens didn't like that."

Ty nodded, going quiet. He seemed troubled by all this talk about Occidens, and she thought she maybe knew why.

"Ty..." she began, feeling a bit awkward. "There's something else we haven't really had a chance to discuss after...everything happened at Occidens."

He looked up at her, his green eyes piercing as he waited for her to continue. Had it really only been last night he'd had her on her knees, so commanding and dominating? Because right now, he seemed different—vulnerable and unsure, as if he was on the edge of something she didn't quite understand.

"When we were held captive there, the Occidens matriarch—Syrelle, her name was—she came to see me. And some of the things she said, well, it made me think that maybe your mother was an Occidens witch."

Ty looked away, huffing out a rueful laugh. "Yeah, I figured that out myself when they kept asking me questions about her," he said bitterly.

"What kinds of questions?" Ena asked.

"Mostly they wanted to know if I knew where she was."

"How do you think they even knew who you were?" Ena asked gently. They hadn't talked much about his mother. Ena knew it was a sore subject for him, so she wanted to proceed with caution.

"My eyes. Apparently, they look like hers," he replied, keeping his attention on the books in front of him, as if this conversation didn't matter to him at all. "But clearly, it wasn't enough of an association to spare my life," he said, anger creeping into his tone.

He got quiet then and started flipping through one of the books on the table mindlessly. Ena could tell he wasn't actually reading, just deflecting.

"Ty," she said gently. "It's okay to be upset about that."

"About what?" he said testily. "About the fact that my mother abandoned me and my father told me almost nothing about her? That her people loathe me just because of what I am?" He shook his head. "I don't want to dwell on any of that. I can't change it, so it makes no difference. I'd rather focus on the things I can change." He started flipping vigorously through the book again.

"Okay," Ena said. "But you know...we're going to need one witch from each Coven again to recreate the spell, since the amulet draws on the magic of the three Covens. That means..." She trailed off, wondering if he'd realized that yet.

"We'll have to return to Occidens to get one," he said. "I figured that. But does it have to be matriarchs, just like before? Because if so, that will be tough."

"No," Ena said, allowing the change of topic. "I don't think it has to be matriarchs. Matriarchs are chosen for their rare Gifts and leadership abilities, but it doesn't make them more suited for the spell necessarily."

"Okay...that's still going to be a tough ask for a witch from Occidens after everything that went down, though."

"I know. I'm worried about that too, unless..."

"Unless what?"

"Unless you *do* have any idea where your mother is?" she asked innocently.

"Ena," he said, giving her a side-eye coupled with a half-smile. "I really don't. And even if I did, what makes you think it would be any easier to get her to help than any other Occidens witch?"

"Well, I've been thinking..." Ena said, wondering how to explain her next theory. It was something she'd been pondering in the back of her mind on and off for days, but hadn't yet given voice to.

"I love it when you think," Ty said, tucking a strand of hair that had fallen out of her braid behind her ear. "Tell me."

Ena could tell he was flirting to pivot them away from his confused emotions, but she didn't call him out on it. Besides, she couldn't help the blush that rose to her face at his touch.

"How is it that Petyr was able to figure everything out about the amulet from these books?" she asked, gesturing at where they lay strewn across the table. "Because there's really not much in them, just a few hints as to its existence and some clues that the history of witches and daemons is not as we've been told, but no details. Did he ever say exactly how he knew about the binding spell?"

Ty shook his head. "No, he told me his theory about the amulet and the binding spell, and implied that he'd learned it from these books, but I see what you're saying. How do you think he learned about it then, if it wasn't from these books?"

"I think the books may have helped, but where did he get them? *The Evolution of Magic* is a witch's book. The journals are from an Occidens witch. I know you said he was industrious, but it would have been ballsy as fuck for a mortal to steal them."

"How else would he have gotten them?" Ty asked.

"I think he may have been given them."

"Given them? By a witch?" Ty asked, his brows shooting up in disbelief.

"Yes, by an Occidens witch who somehow knew about the amulet, and took them from her Coven, and told him about it. Maybe someone with a soft spot for daemons who wasn't on good terms with the rest of the Occidens witches," Ena said, hoping he would catch on to her hinting.

"Hold on... You think my *mother* gave Petyr the books when she was banished?" Ty asked in shock.

"I don't know... It's just a theory," Ena said, shrugging. "But it would make sense."

"Yeah, it would," Ty said. He seemed to agree, but he clenched his jaw as he looked away, as if that knowledge only made his feelings of resentment towards her worse.

Ena reached out to grab his hand. "Look, I'm angry, too, Ty. There's so much I wasn't told. So much that was hidden from me, just like you. Would it have been nice to be trusted with all the complexities of our world? Yes. Does it infuriate me that others have decided for me that I didn't have a right to know about these things?

That daemons didn't have a right to choose who they served, and witches didn't have a right to socialize with them? Absolutely fucking yes. But Ty, you can't let your anger guide you."

Ty sighed, rubbing his brow and releasing some of his tension, but she could tell it was hard for him to let go of it completely. "And what do you think should guide me instead? Because anger sure as shit comes easiest," he said bitterly.

"Hope," she replied.

Ty looked up, seeming surprised by that answer. "Hope?" he asked.

"Yes," she said. "Hope for a different future, like you described to me the other day. Hope that we can forge a new path where witches and daemons are free to worship Gaia and Iblis as they please and are able to live together once more."

Ty smiled then, a small one, before reaching out to cup the side of her face with his hand. She brought her hand up too and placed it atop his. It was large, and warm, and she could feel all his strength and passion right there where they touched.

"You give me hope," he said simply.

"Good," she replied, a soft smile spreading across her face. "You give me hope too."

Ty removed his hand somewhat reluctantly and closed the book in front of him. "Come on, I think we both could use a break from research and revelations, don't you agree?" he asked.

"Gaia, yes," she said, rubbing at her tired eyes.

"Good, then come with me," he said, one side of his mouth tipping up in a sly smile. "There's something you might like to try."

CHAPTER NINETEEN

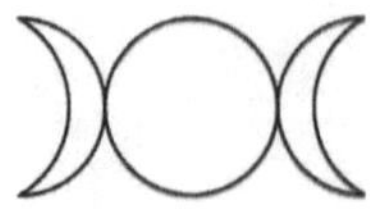

ENA FOLLOWED TY OUT of the Archives back towards the Great Antre.

"Where are we going?" she asked, when instead of veering towards his room, they headed towards a different section of the upper levels.

"You'll see," he said, winking at her mischievously.

Ena rolled her eyes at that but played along as they moved down an unknown passageway and stopped at a door. Ty knocked, and a few seconds later, Turner opened it.

"Hey," he greeted, looking slightly concerned at their appearance. "What's up?"

"You up for a trip to the undercaves?" Ty asked him, a roguish look in his eye.

Turner's smile widened. "Always," he replied. "Why? Are you thinking about...?" His eyes darted towards Ena. "Corrupting Ena with our daemonic ways?"

Ty laughed. "Unfortunately, I think that ship has sailed," he said, looking at Ena with pride.

"What?" Ena asked, barely suppressing her own smile at their obvious giddiness. "What in Gaia's name are you two talking about?"

"Oh, it has nothing to do with Gaia," Turner said, his smile somehow getting wider.

"Come on," Ty said. "Get your shoes on and let's get Steig. Maybe Lara will want to come too."

Turner disappeared into his room for a minute, before returning with his shoes on, and the three of them headed down the passageways once more towards Steig and Lara's.

Ena decided not to ask questions, and for once in her life, just be along for the ride. She trusted Ty. She trusted Turner. Whatever they had planned was clearly something fun, since they were practically skipping down the passageway like little boys getting sweets on Yule.

Once they got to Steig and Lara's door, Ty knocked, and Lara came to the door a few seconds later.

"Hey Lara, is Steig here?" Ty asked, looking behind her.

"Yeah, he's here. Steig!" She turned around and called to her husband, who came to the door, looking just as confused as Turner had.

"What the fuck is going on?" he asked, eyes darting suspiciously between each of them.

"We're going to the undercaves. Come on."

Steig laughed, dark and amused. "Are you serious? How fucking old are we? I have four kids in here," he said, gesturing behind him. "I can't be running off with you idiots doing *allucinae* in the middle of the day."

Allucinae? Now Ena was thoroughly intrigued. What in the Underworld was *allucinae*?

"Alright, suit yourself. Lara?" Ty called over his shoulder to where Ena could see Lara hovering just behind the door. "What about you? You in?"

"Fuck it, yes," she said, pushing the door open wider and popping back into view. "Just let me see if Trysh can watch the kids."

Steig turned to his wife, lifting a dark brow at her. "You're serious?"

"Yeah, why not? It's been gloomy as fuck around here. I think we could all use something fun. Don't you?" The look she gave Steig was one of pure seduction.

He grumbled something about her using that look on him before acquiescing to the peer pressure and dipping back inside to get ready. Meanwhile, Lara took off down the passageway to get Trysh, the older daemon who'd made her dress for the *onata* celebration, and, apparently, frequently watched the kids for them.

By the time she returned, Ty and Turner had gotten Steig to fetch them several darkrock lanterns to carry with them, and the five of them took off to the Great Antre.

Ena had, so far, been to the forge on the lower levels, but not any deeper into the Underworld. She knew, theoretically, that under the forge was the hot springs that powered the aqueducts throughout the Underworld, and somewhere under that were the unexplored undercaves, but she didn't know much about them.

Once they were past the busier areas closest to the Great Antre and they began the descent down the endless winding staircase that led to the lower levels and below, Ena finally had to ask.

"Okay, so are any of you going to tell me why in the Underworld we are going to the undercaves and what this *allucinae* has to do with it?" she asked the group.

Lara laughed in that intoxicating way of hers as she walked behind her on the steps. Only now did Ena realize why the joy of her laughter felt so special—it must be her *gaudium*. Even though her Power didn't work on Ena, she could still sense an abundance of joy in her, just like she could sense Ty's rage.

"The undercaves are essentially the uncharted parts of the Underworld," Lara replied. "The caves we haven't expanded into yet, and some of them are kept that way on purpose, because of the *allucinae*."

"It's those areas where the Trials are held—the rite of passage for those who turn twenty-seven to receive their Powers from Iblis. And the *allucinae* is part of what makes the Trial so...harrowing," Ty explained, picking up where Lara had left off. "It's a hallucinogenic moss that grows on the cave walls, and even though we're not purposefully given it, over time, the hallucinogens can seep into your exposed skin, and so, combined with the lack of food and water for days on end, the hallucinations usually occur during the Trials regardless."

"But, under ordinary circumstances, when you're not starved and dehydrated, it's quite an enjoyable experience," Turner chimed in from his spot at the back of the procession.

"Wait a second," Ena said, speaking to Ty ahead of her on the stairs. "Aren't the undercaves where you and Steig got lost as children?"

"Yes, we, uh...went a little too far and got lost, and, yes, the *allucinae* may have played a role in that, even though we didn't do it on purpose."

Ena laughed. "So now we're...what? Going down there to do it on purpose? Why?"

"Because it's fun," Lara called. "You remember fun, don't you, Ena? It's not all research and fucking my cousin."

"Fucking your cousin is fun for me," Ena retorted.

Lara's laugh boomed behind her. "Okay, well, this is just a different *kind* of fun. And it's supposed to bring you closer to Iblis."

"Really?" Ena asked, hesitation creeping in. Her knee-jerk reaction was that that wasn't a good thing. What if she got out of control? Or accidentally caused too much chaos or discord?

"What do you think, viper? You up for it?" Ty asked, looking over his shoulder at her.

Was she? She'd been raised to serve Gaia and the balance, so intentionally getting closer to Iblis felt sacrilegious. But, when in the company of daemons, who'd been embracing Iblis their whole lives and were still good people, she knew she needed to let that ingrained fear go. Besides, wasn't that why she was so drawn to Ty? The chaotic freedom he made her feel? And her Gift too...she couldn't deny she loved the feeling of letting go and giving in to it now that she wasn't so afraid of it.

So maybe she should keep embracing that feeling—it hadn't steered her wrong yet.

"Yes," she said. "Why not?"

Turner made a whooping noise in celebration behind her, and she shook her head, but smiled despite herself.

After another ten minutes of descent, long after they'd passed the exit into the lower levels that Lara had taken her through before, the carved staircase they'd been winding down simply ended.

It was nearly pitch black ahead of them, but with the darkrock lanterns they held, Ena could already tell that these caves were significantly more untamed than the ones above. The walls were rough, and stalactites hung low from the ceiling, so she had to duck in some places.

It was colder, too, likely because they were underneath where the hot springs bubbled. But most notably, it was dark—the dense blackness ahead of them seemed endless, and Ena could barely make out anything beyond the small rings of blue light their darkrock lanterns created.

They moved forward as a group into the darkness, and Ena found herself reaching for Ty's hand for reassurance.

He chuckled, low and deep. "Scared, viper?" he asked, turning his lantern towards her.

"No," Ena said stubbornly. "It's just...so dark. How do you even know where we're going?"

"*Venator*, remember? We're almost there," he said, squeezing her hand in reassurance.

They moved across the jagged cave floor, down several twisting passages, until they entered into a large chamber. It was nothing compared to the size of the chambers on the upper levels, which had clearly been excavated more, but it felt significantly less closed-in than the passages they'd been moving through to get here.

"Here we are," said Ty as the five of them spread out through the space.

Ena squinted, trying to make out anything about the space around her, but it looked the same as everything else. Dark, blackish-gray walls of stone. Where was the *allucinae*?

"Come look," Turner said, gesturing her over to where he stood.

He held up his lantern, illuminating the wall, and Ena watched as he ran his hand gently along it. Trailing after his fingertips, Ena saw a glowing green substance appear. It wasn't very bright, but in the glow of the lantern, she could see its color—stark against the drab walls of the cave. It was furry, like some of the mosses that grew in the forests back home, but once Turner stopped running his fingers along it, it turned back to the same blackish-gray color as the walls.

Ena's Knowing perked up in the presence of the cave-dwelling plant. There wasn't much that was alive down here in the Underworld. Yes, Ena could feel the stone, but that was different—it was a much more muted feeling than she was used to. And, since she couldn't sense daemons with her Knowing, she hadn't realized how much she'd missed using it.

Because now, she Knew this moss, and it was...so interesting. She could tell it thrived here in the dark, and it wanted to be left undisturbed. Like a silent passenger, it grew and multiplied away from predators and pests, it's eerie glow a foreboding warning of its toxicity and hallucinogenic properties.

"Okay," said Turner, distracting Ena from drinking in all she could about this strange plant. "Who's up first?"

"I'll go," Lara said, coming over next to them. "Iblis, it's been years since I've done this." She sounded giddy, and gave Ena a full, joyful smile, before turning to the wall, sticking out her tongue, and licking the moss.

Ena stared in partial disgust and confusion as a trail of luminescent green trailed after Lara's tongue.

Ty burst out laughing beside her. "You should see your face, viper," he said. "Fucking Iblis, it's priceless."

"I'm sorry," Ena said, holding out her hands as if this was suddenly all too much to comprehend. "Did she just *lick* the wall?"

Lara pulled back, her wide smile somehow even wider as she turned towards Ena. "Scraping off the moss to eat it works, too, but the moss doesn't like to be disturbed. If you scrape off a portion, it could kill the whole colony, so it's tradition to just lick it instead."

Ena pondered this for a second, and it made sense. She Knew the moss did not want to be removed from its home, but still...she shuddered in disgust.

"What's it taste like?" she asked skeptically.

"Not much," Ty answered. "Just like dirt and stone." He watched her, a light still in his eyes from his laughing outburst. Gaia, she loved seeing him so happy and un-burdened like this—it reminded her of the way he was nine years ago when they'd first met. Before he'd been kept from her and granted his Power, along with all the responsibilities that entailed.

"Here, I'll go next," he said, handing off his lantern to her.

Ty proceeded to lick the wall, too, eliciting the same eerie-green trail after his tongue as Lara had, followed by Turner, and then, reluctantly, Steig. Apparently, he wasn't much for the *allucinae* experience, so it was a big deal that they'd dragged him along and gotten him to loosen up a bit.

"Can you blame me for being scarred after what happened when we were kids?" he asked Ty after he finally succumbed to the peer pressure and licked the *allucinae*. "Besides, I never know when Cole is going to require me urgently," he added, shrugging the tension out of his shoulders as he seemed to relax slightly into whatever he was feeling.

Lara stood up on her tippy toes to kiss him on the cheek. "It's okay to live our lives, Steig. Otherwise we let him take it from us," she said quietly, clearly saying the words just for him, even though the rest of them could hear. He nodded silently and turned to his wife, tucking a strand of her hair behind her ear.

Ena turned away from their private moment as Ty came up beside her, taking the lantern back from her hand. "You're up," he said, nodding to the wall.

Ena felt absolutely ridiculous as she approached it and stuck out her tongue tentatively. Just as she was about to make contact, Ty leaned in and whispered playfully, "Just pretend it's my cock and enjoy it like you did the other night."

Ena elbowed him in the side—hard. He grunted at the impact and burst out laughing again, the sound a boon to Ena's nerves as she quickly dragged her tongue along the *allucinae*.

It was softer than she'd expected, the texture almost akin to sheep's wool, but significantly more damp and dirt-flavored.

She found it wasn't bad and turned to look at everyone as she pulled back from the wall.

"Now what?" she asked. She didn't feel any different, although her tongue felt a bit fuzzy.

"Give it a few minutes, and then you'll feel it," Ty said knowingly.

Then Lara started giggling next to her. Ena could tell, even in the dim light of the cave, that the woman's pupils were wide as saucers. She watched as Lara reached out to Steig, tugging him into her, and the two of them instantly started making out.

Ena snorted, taking a step back towards Ty and Turner. "Are they always like this?" she asked, watching as Lara and Steig started going at it like teenagers.

"Pretty much," said Turner with a sigh. "Ty and I used to always be the third wheels, but now I guess I'm just a fifth wheel," he lamented.

"You're never a fifth wheel, brother. Your presence is more than necessary," Ty said kindly, patting him on the back. "Come on, come spar with me," he said to him, walking into the center of the chamber before turning and giving Ena a wink. "My dark goddess needs to just sit back and enjoy herself."

Ena did as she was told, blushing at the use of her new nickname in front of Turner, and proceeded to sit down on the ground, leaning back against a portion of the cave wall that was free of *allucinae*.

She watched as Ty and Turner sparred half-heartedly, both of them clearly starting to feel the effects of the moss, as they laughed and dodged each other's sloppy blows.

Steig and Lara were huddled in the corner of the cave somewhere Ena couldn't see them, but she could hear their giggles and whispers in between their low moans and sounds of kissing.

She leaned her head back against the wall and tried to assess herself.

Did she feel any different yet? She didn't quite know. The effects were supposed to bring her closer to Iblis, but she didn't feel more chaotic or anything, she just felt...relaxed. She reached out to touch the floor of the cave next to her. The rough rock felt so harsh and cold against her fingers. Was it always this cold? She dragged her fingers along it until it almost tickled, and a giggle beyond her control burst from her throat.

Okay, it seemed she *was* feeling the effects now.

She continued her explorations of the stone, rubbing the rock debris on the ground between her fingers, and watched with glee as Ty and Turner sparred, both of them having removed their shirts and worked up a sweat.

Suddenly, it all felt a bit overwhelming—the noises and the movements and the feelings, so Ena closed her eyes. She could sense her Knowing and her Gift pulsing inside her—not violently, not like they did when she was scared or in danger—they were simply *there*, present and alive.

Everything was heightened—without even trying, she Knew the stone underneath her, felt it breaking slowly in infinitesimal ways, and sensed the *allucinae* growing unruly on the wall behind her. Both of them there in such an intimate way—almost as if they were an extension of herself. The feeling of it reminded her of the Summoning—the glimpses of it she remembered anyway. The way she Knew a hundred different things at once and had become one with them—but she'd been close to Gaia then, not Iblis, and she wondered vaguely how the feeling could be so similar.

She giggled again, the thought making her laugh for some reason. Her giggles escalated into full-blown laughter, and she knew she probably sounded like an insane fool, but the feeling of it lifted her, filled her chest with glee and made her cheeks ache. She realized she was happy—joyful even—not just because of the *allucinae*, but because Ty was there, shirtless, sexy as all can be, and... she had *friends*. People she trusted now, people who understood her and accepted her—all of her. And she was having fun—she was letting go and enjoying herself, not worrying so much about her path or serving her Goddess. It was freeing, and so wonderful.

Ena...

She turned to her left, looking into the dark, the smile fading from her face. Was that...?

Ena!

That voice...coming from the dark. It almost sounded like her sister. It almost sounded like Greya.

And she sounded in trouble.

Ena stood up, staring into the black void of the cave as if she could make out what was there just by staring hard enough. She took a few steps forward, bringing her lantern with her, but she didn't see anything.

"You okay?" Lara asked suddenly from behind her, startling her.

Ena whipped around to see her friend standing a few feet away, Steig no longer at her side. Apparently, he'd joined Ty and Turner in their sparring, the sounds of flesh on flesh, grunting, and taunts coming from the other side of the cave.

"Yeah, yeah, I..." Ena stared into the blank dark again. "I just thought I heard someone."

"It's the *allucinae*. It can make that happen sometimes," Lara explained gently.

"Oh, right, okay. That makes sense," Ena said, reluctantly turning away from her sister's voice.

"Usually, if you're in a good headspace, you don't see or hear anything too upsetting. The *allucinae* can turn on you, though, like what happens to most of us during the Trial."

"Right," Ena said mindlessly, still trying to shake off the strange, melancholy feeling that hearing her sister's voice had dredged up in her. The fear had sobered her, and she felt the effects of the *allucinae* start to dim.

Ena moved to join Lara where she sat watching the three men spar, a small smile on her face as her eyes tracked her husband.

"How long have you two been together?" Ena asked, desperate to change the topic from her anxiety about Greya.

"Almost nine years," Lara replied, leaning back against the wall next to Ena.

"Wow, so you got pregnant right away?" Ena asked, remembering that their eldest was eight and doing the math in her head. "That must've been...intense," she commented, hoping her shock didn't come off as rude.

"Oh, definitely. My father was not happy," Lara replied ruefully. "Our union wasn't sanctioned, because Steig's mother was a mid-level daemon. There was no way to know what Steig's Power would be, and my father didn't want me to potentially hold myself back by uniting with a mid-level daemon. Little did he know, *my* Power would be the disappointment, and Steig's would be coveted."

"Hm," Ena said, verbally expressing skepticism at their unfair system. "While I don't agree that you're a disappointment, I gotta say, I did see his *cupido* in action and it was certainly memorable. I can see why it's viewed as a powerful asset to Iblis."

"Yes, exactly. And it's quite handy in the bedroom too," Lara said, winking at Ena and laughing at her own joke.

"Seriously? He uses it on you?" Ena asked, a smile coming over her.

"Oh absolutely. With my consent, of course. But it really makes things...extra enjoyable, I'll say."

The two of them laughed together at that, but Ena had to admit, hearing Greya's voice had certainly put a damper on her spirits, and she found it tough to fully access the carefree feeling she'd had just a few minutes ago.

"You two seem like a good match then," she said. "What with the joy you can bring him with your own Power. Maybe that's why he hated me so much when we first met. Without you there, he had no joy."

Lara smiled shyly at her assessment. "Maybe, but he's also just slow to warm up to people. I wouldn't take it personally. He...he had a really lonely childhood."

Ena was surprised to hear this. She didn't know much about Steig or his history, just that he'd been best friends with Ty since childhood.

"How so?" Ena asked, her curiosity getting the better of her.

"Well, his mother wasn't united with anyone, so she raised him alone. They were very close, but she passed when he was a teenager. Ty's dad Haden took him in for a while, treated him like a son since he and Ty were so close, but then Haden died, and..."

"I see," Ena said, pondering this new information. "I'm glad they had each other at least, Ty and Steig."

"Yeah, me too," she said. "They've always been like brothers—Turner too. So he's very protective of them. I think that's why he mistrusted you so much at the beginning—because of the pain your separation caused Ty. But I can tell he's coming around."

"You think?" Ena asked, watching the dark-haired, dark-eyed daemon fighting with his friends. "He still doesn't talk to me very much."

Lara laughed again. "Yeah, trust me, that's normal. Besides, he's just under a lot of pressure, too, from my dad. Ever since we married, Cole has been...very demanding of him, so Steig does a lot to placate him. And Cole sees it as his right for giving the man his only daughter, even though I'm not the heir."

There was that word she didn't know again. *Heir.* Ena was about to ask what it meant, when she was distracted by a sweaty Ty approaching them.

"How are you feeling, viper?" he asked as he caught his breath, the corner of his mouth tipping up, as if he knew Ena had been thoroughly enjoying her high a few minutes ago.

"Good," Ena said, not wanting to ruin the mood and bring up the strangeness of hearing Greya's voice. She could tell him that later. "And you?" she asked, taking the hand he offered her to help her stand up.

"Never better, but I'm sweaty. You up for another stop before we head back? Just the two of us?" he asked. The look in his eyes was so sweet and hopeful, it warmed Ena's heart.

"Absolutely," she said. "I'll follow you anywhere, clearly," she added, gesturing around their current surroundings.

She'd said it as a joke, but it was obviously true—for better or worse. She'd left everything behind to come here—for him. And though she struggled with the sacrifices that had entailed, she reminded herself that she didn't regret it.

Besides, a part of her still hoped that she could have everything she needed in the end—Ty, her new friends, her Coven, and her sister. There was still hope for that, she told herself, if they broke the bond and helped everyone to understand.

"Good. Let's go then," he said, taking her hand, and leading her again towards the unknown.

CHAPTER TWENTY

Ty

AFTER PARTING WAYS WITH Steig, Lara, and Turner, Ty led Ena through the dark undercaves to a smaller, less-traveled staircase at the other end.

It was adorable how she clung close to him, as if the oppressive darkness both frightened and enchanted her. He'd grown up in these caves, constantly in and out of the blackness, so he didn't even think about it anymore. But seeing them now through her eyes made it feel special again—and it was just one more way that being with her made him feel so much more *alive* than he'd felt in years. For so long, he'd just been going through the motions—surviving, meeting his responsibilities, and shoving down his anger—but not really living.

Now, he felt like he was finally, truly living again. And he didn't want to stop. He wanted to show her everything wonderful about his home.

He reached for her hand as they ascended the stairs, holding the darkrock lantern in front of them. The closer they got to the top, the warmer and more humid the air became again, and he felt Ena breathe a sigh of relief next to him.

He glanced over at her to see that her face was pensive. Even in the dim light he could see that something was on her mind.

"Are you alright?" he asked, breaking the silence of their hike up the rough stone staircase. "Is the *allucinae* still affecting you?"

"No," she said, shaking her head. "I don't think so, it's just... I heard Greya when I was in the peak of it. She called to me."

"Oh," Ty said, understanding dawning. "You miss your sister."

Ena nodded, a small sad smile on her face.

"I'm sorry if you didn't enjoy it, the *allucinae*. I never would've made you do it if I thought the hallucinations would turn on you," Ty said, guilt washing over him.

"No, no," she said, squeezing his hand in reassurance. "I did enjoy it. It was fun, and different. And the hallucination wasn't all bad...it was actually *so* nice to hear her voice. I just feel so guilty about how we left things, and yes, I do miss her. I wish I could make things right again."

"Ena," Ty said, turning to her as they reached the top of the staircase. "I want you to know I'll do everything in my power to reunite you with her once we break the bond." He paused, hoping she could hear in his voice how much he meant it. "I know you made the decision to come with me, and I'm so glad you did, but I never want you to have to sacrifice what makes you who you are just to help me. I know what that feels like."

He'd spent his entire life sacrificing half of himself to make his uncle and the rest of his people happy, to fit fully as a daemon and ignore what else he could be, so he knew firsthand some of the divided feelings she must have.

Ena released his hand, bringing her own up to stroke his arm, running it down his shoulder gently. "I know you will," she said. "And I won't deny that I'm a bit sad, but lately...I feel hopeful. Hopeful that if we break the bond, she'll understand. That Heran and the rest of my Coven might come to understand, too, and that maybe...you and I could still be together. And we wouldn't have to hide."

Ty's heart swelled. He had the same hope. He wanted so badly for that to be true, his mind refused to accept any other option.

He reached out, wrapping his arm around her waist and pulling her close to him to brush a kiss against her soft, plump lips. She smelled like blackberries and it instantly made him hard, but that wasn't the point of this kiss. He wanted her to feel how deeply he wanted that too. Could she sense it? The hope that she kindled inside him?

"I want that too," he said simply, pulling back. "Now come on, beautiful. We're almost there."

As they emerged from the staircase, the sound of rushing water became unmistakable, and he heard Ena gasp in realization.

"Are we...?" Her voice trailed off as they entered the wide, intricately carved archway that led into the hot springs.

The cavern was huge, almost as big as the Great Antre, and filled with a vast lake that took up over half of the space. The water was a murky teal, and it seemed to glow in the blue light of the darkrock lanterns that illuminated the walls of the cave and the narrow rocky pathway that surrounded it.

The steam coming from the lake visibly swirled through the air as the water bubbled gently—pockets of air bursting to the surface as the groundwater flowed naturally upwards, filling the lake.

The light bubbling sound was complemented by the sound of water rushing through several strategically placed aqueducts, carrying the warm water away from the lake into the pipelines Imbued with Jyn's Power and throughout the rest of the Underworld.

He watched as Ena took in the space, her eyes roaming over the steaming lake in awe. "This is…" She trailed off, seeming at a loss for words.

"You like it?" Ty asked, feeling a smile come over him at her wonder.

"It's absolutely incredible," she said in disbelief.

Despite still being shirtless, Ty instantly began to sweat again, reminding him of the reason he didn't usually come here—it was too damn hot for him. But seeing the wonder in her reaction made it well worth it. And he wasn't done yet.

"You know, I was thinking," Ty began, leading her closer to the wide, beautifully carved staircase that led down into the lake. "I know you struggled to swim in the River Wry because of your Knowing, and the water's intentions feeling so overwhelming, but I thought, maybe, this would feel different."

Ena was quiet for a minute as she watched the water, her eyes skimming over it.

"Can you feel it with your Knowing?" he asked. There was something about her magic that had always fascinated him, from the very first day they met. Being half-witch hadn't given him a Knowing, and part of him had always been curious about it. It was always impressive what she Knew.

"I can," she said, a smile gracing her beautiful face. "And you're right, it's so different from the River Wry. It's not rushing towards the ocean, it's...already achieved its purpose, rising to the surface. It's content here. With the stone. I've never Known water this calm."

"So, what do you think?" Ty asked her, holding out his hand to her in offering. "Will you swim with me again?"

She gave him a skeptical look, but the delight in her eyes was impossible to miss. "Why are you always making me swim?" she asked teasingly.

Ty shrugged. "Because you look fucking fantastic when you're wet."

Ena laughed, her joy bursting out of her in such a carefree expression of emotion that it made Ty laugh too.

"But who knows," he added, stepping closer to her. "Learning to swim could save your life one day. Just like learning to fight with the daggers. It's a necessary skill, viper."

Ena sighed, and he knew he'd won. Her practical side always won out.

"Alright," she said, starting to untie her leather corset.

Ty found himself watching her, unable to look away as she removed her layers of clothing. She was so absolutely intoxicating she felt almost unattainable sometimes. Maybe it was because, for the last nine years, she literally had been unattainable to him, and his mind was still trying to catch up. But either way, somehow, his entire being was drawn to her, wanting to capture her like smoke on the wind.

She caught him staring as she stood only in her shirt now, which ended at mid-thigh, covering her most intimate parts, and raised a brow. "Your turn," she said, looking pointedly down at his pants.

Ty unbuttoned them slowly, maintaining eye contact as she watched him. He could feel his cock already half hard from the tension of the situation as he pulled them down over his hips, then he kicked them off to the side so he stood before her, fully nude.

"Now take it off," he said, using that tone of voice he knew made her wet, nodding at the shirt she still wore.

She pulled it off over her head, dropping it to the side so she was fully nude too.

Ty sighed as his eyes roamed over her rosy nipples and full, heavy breasts, down to her soft stomach and the curve of her hips. His eyes lingered at the apex of her thighs, covered in a dusting of dark hair that hid that delicious pussy he loved so fucking much.

"I thought you brought me here to swim," Ena said, a teasing smile on her face as she glanced pointedly down at his erect cock.

"I did, and we will, but maybe if you're a good girl for me, I'll let you come on my cock after."

Ena laughed again, low and sultry this time. "You're a cocky bastard, you know that? What makes you think I want to?"

"So you're telling me that smell I smell, that"—Ty inhaled deeply, getting a whiff of her in the air as he let out a low hum in the back of his throat—"sweet blackberry musk, is just my imagination?"

Ena blushed, and he had to actively work to calm his body and not pounce on her like a triumphant wolf claiming its prey.

"Fine," she replied, not letting him get to her. "Then maybe if *you're* good, I'll let you lick my cunt, since you seem to love the smell of it so much."

Fuck. Just when he thought he had the upper hand, she pushed him again—challenging him right back with those filthy words. Suddenly, he found it so god-damn hard to focus on swimming.

He clenched his jaw and rubbed his hand down his beard as he willed himself to calm. "Come on, viper," he said, gesturing at the water, "before you lose your chance to swim altogether."

She smiled, looking very pleased with herself, before turning and descending down the smooth, carved stair-case that led into the water as Ty followed her.

The cave floor was rocky and sloped once they entered the pool of steaming water, and Ty reached out to steady her, taking her hand as they both stepped into the warm water.

Ena let out an audible sigh of pleasure as the warmth hit her, and Ty realized that he definitely had not thought this fully through.

Fucking Iblis, this was going to be torture.

Once they were both in up to their waists and had adjusted to the almost-too-hot water, he moved closer to her, letting her wrap her arms around his neck. Their naked bodies were flush now, and Ty had to swallow and *focus*.

"Okay, now," he said, looking down at her. "We're gonna move to where I can stand, but you can't, then you can practice kicking for a bit. Okay?"

"Okay," she said, sounding determined.

He led her a little deeper into the hot spring to be sure she couldn't stand, then had her float on her stomach in the water and practice kicking her legs. He moved slowly along with her, letting the force of her movements move them both.

"How's that feel?" he asked, their faces so close together their cheeks brushed.

"Good," she said. "But I feel kind of silly."

Ty smiled. "Don't feel silly. You're doing great. Here," he said, moving around to the side of her and grabbing her waist. He tried hard, so fucking hard, to not think about how he'd love to be behind her right now, his hands on her waist while he drove into her, watching her absolutely mesmerizing ass bounce with the motion.

All things in good time, though... She needed this first.

Keeping her body elevated with his hand while he stood to the side of her, he let her kick and practice moving her arms.

She was surprisingly graceful, for someone who had never swum before, but that didn't surprise him. The woman seemed to excel at anything she put her mind to, once she got over her fears.

Next, he had her float on her back and practice kicking that way. Her dark hair swirled around her like blood spreading in the water, and the tops of her breasts and nipples just barely poked above the waterline. His mouth salivated just looking at them, but he managed to keep his tongue to himself.

She was doing so well, and he could tell this was bringing her joy. The thought filled him with such warmth—that *he* had done this for her. *He* had made her happy by bringing her here. The thought came to him then that he wouldn't even try to deny it anymore—her happiness was absolutely everything to him.

When she finished her back floats, she stood back up, clinging to him with a smile on her face. "This is so wonderful, Ty. I never thought I'd be able to do this. Thank you for bringing me here." Her words were filled with such sincerity, such gratitude, that his heart nearly burst.

Fuck, what the hell was wrong with him? Was he okay? This was...a lot. Maybe the water was making him too hot and he was getting lightheaded.

He cleared his throat as Ena looked up at him, her cheeks flushed from the warm water.

"What do you think? Ready for more or do you want to get out?" he asked, trying to hide all the overwhelming feelings swirling inside him.

"Let's get out," she said. "I think I'm starting to sweat." She laughed, the sound sending sparks of joy through him once more.

The two of them made their way back to the staircase, Ty reluctantly letting Ena walk on her own once the water was shallow enough, content to walk beside her, when suddenly she doubled over.

"Ouch!" she exclaimed. "Dammit."

Ty whipped his head towards her, his body springing into action at her sound of pain.

She was bent over, looking at her foot where she'd scraped it on one of the jagged rocks underneath the water, tiny droplets of blood forming along the cut.

"Here, let me see." Ty scooped her up into his arms, carrying her to where they'd left their clothes on the smooth landing at the top of the staircase.

"You don't have to carry me," she said, protesting mildly. "It's not that bad."

"I know, just let me see," he said, placing her down next to his discarded pants.

He knelt in front of her, holding her foot with both hands to examine it. She'd stubbed her toe pretty good, and the scrape was bleeding a little, but she was right, it wasn't bad.

Ty placed a gentle kiss on the inside of her foot, the way his father used to do when he'd been hurt as a child.

"I didn't know you had a thing for feet," Ena teased, the corner of her mouth tipping up as she glanced pointedly down at his half-hard cock, which was quickly becoming fully hard now that he could see all of her outside of the water again.

"I don't have a thing for feet. I have a thing for you," he said, pressing another kiss higher up on her ankle. "Every part of you."

He heard her breath hitch as her legs parted just a tiny bit, giving him a view of that spot he loved to worship between her legs, as she leaned back on her hands.

"What's this?" she asked suddenly, distracting him from his reverie as she picked something up off the ground.

She was holding up a small iron ring, woven with three strands of metal that were intertwined. In the center was a small but beautiful sapphire, the color as close as he could find to her eyes.

"Oh, that? I, uh...made that for you," Ty said, clearing his throat. It must have fallen out of his pants pocket when he'd removed them. He'd been waiting for a good time to show it to her, but then, well, she'd been insanely distracting. He'd been slowly working on it in the forge the last few days, in between his other projects, trying to make it perfect. It had taken an embarrassingly long time to find the exact right sapphire for it, and he almost hadn't given it to her, worried that she wouldn't like it.

Knowing all that, he suddenly felt...shy. He didn't think he'd ever been shy in his entire fucking life, but something about giving this thing to her made him feel exposed in a way he'd never been before.

"You'll have to keep it hidden," he explained quickly, not giving her a chance to respond. "If anyone sees you wearing it, it could cause trouble. Witch-slaves shouldn't have mementos like that, but I wanted you to have it. That is, if you want it."

Ena looked up at him with eyes so round he was almost scared for a second. Were those tears in her eyes? Fuck. Had the ring upset her somehow?

"Ty..." she whispered, shaking her head in disbelief. "It's so beautiful. Thank you, I..." Her words trailed off as she cleared her throat. "I don't think I've ever been given anything like this before."

A warm feeling spread throughout his chest and he found himself smiling. He suddenly felt lighter than air, and he realized with calm clarity how the anger that usually hounded him night and day had fully dissipated somehow. It was gone for now, and in its place was this...contentment.

A part of him was terrified of what this feeling in his chest meant for him, for them, but he knew he couldn't deny it anymore. He'd known already that he was hers, that she dominated his thoughts and commanded his desires, but this...this was so much more. This was utter devotion, and admiration. This was complete awe, excitement, and simultaneous peace.

He was in love with her. Fully, completely—endlessly.

Fuck. The realization caught him off guard, and he didn't really know what to do about it. Should he tell her?

Ena seemed oblivious to his inner turmoil as she leaned forward to kiss him. The kiss was gentle but passionate. She smelled like the hot springs and lavender and *her*. Ty pulled her in, grabbing the back of her head so she could never go anywhere ever again. So she'd never leave him, and keep kissing him forever.

She moaned into his mouth, and all other thoughts flew from his head except her—having her body, her heart, her pleasure.

He reached out, gently grazing one of her breasts with his palm. He felt her nipple peak underneath it and his balls tightened in response.

He deepened their kiss, stroking her tongue with his until both of them were panting.

Fuck, she tasted so goddamn good.

He grabbed her breast harder and felt her squirm underneath him, leaning closer to him like she couldn't keep away, like she was desperate for him too. She was so fucking eager, and he was obsessed with it.

He moved his hand down to her back, pulling her body flush with his. He felt her breath hitch as her breasts pressed against his hard chest, then he slowly grazed his hand down her leg, hooking it under her knee and pulling her leg on top of him. She took the hint and moved with him so she straddled him, wrapping her arms around his neck.

His cock was hard as a rock and he could feel her hot, wet pussy on top of him.

Iblis, part of him wanted to slip inside her right now—she was warm and waiting. But he wanted this to last. He wanted her to feel as good as she made him feel.

So he leaned back, pulling away from her soft lips to lay down on the warm, smooth stone floor of the cave.

"What are you—?" she asked, her voice already rough with need.

"Come here," he said, taking one of her legs in each hand and tugging up towards his face.

"You mean...?" she asked, looking pointedly down at her own cunt and then up at his face.

"Sit on my face, Ena. I want to drown in you," he said, commanding her, then he tugged her more roughly up to him, and she acquiesced.

She lowered herself onto him slowly, but he had no patience for that. He pulled her thighs down so they sat on either side of his head and gripped them—hard. He was probably leaving marks, maybe even bruises, with his grip, but she didn't pull away. She rolled her hips into him, pressing her clit onto his open mouth, and moaned like no one was around to hear.

The sound echoed around the chamber, sending another pulse of desire straight to his dick. The taste of her filled his tongue as he began to move it, stroking her slowly as she continued to grind on his face.

He nipped at her clit, once, twice, and instantly felt a gush of wetness soaking below his chin onto his beard.

She ground into him harder, faster now.

Looking up, he saw the underside of her tits, so round and full as they swayed with her motion. He reached up to grab them, squeezing them and stroking her nipples as he licked her.

"Fuck, Ty," she said, her pace quickening. She was getting close already. Iblis, he fucking loved it when she came.

He moved his hands back down to her thighs, shifting her ever so slightly on his face so that he could stick his tongue inside her. She was soaking wet, and he lapped up her juices like they were goddamn woodwater—making him just as drunk.

Tilting her back, he sucked on her clit—hard—and she cried out.

He squeezed her thighs in response. She was such a good girl for him. He loved the way she rode his face with abandon. He loved the way her tits bounced in the air, the way her thick ass felt in his hands as she ground into him.

Her body started shaking, so he gave her clit one more soft suck, and he felt the tension release from her body.

"Fuck!" she cried, tilting her head back as her orgasm gripped her. She continued rocking into his face as the waves passed, and when they finally receded, Ty scooted her down off his face, right onto his waiting cock.

There was no preamble—he shoved himself deep inside her, and she cried out in shocked pleasure.

He knew exactly what she needed now.

He drove up into her, guiding her hips down onto him as he did so. He fucked her hard, his own release barreling quickly towards him.

Her tits bounced faster now, and he wanted them in his mouth, he wanted her tongue in his mouth, he wanted to be inside her everywhere and to make her cry out his name again and again and again.

His hands came up to grab her ass—so perfectly fleshy and round it drove him absolutely wild. He smacked it, leaving a red mark in his wake.

The small hint of pain instantly made a fresh flood of wetness fill Ena's pussy.

"That's my good girl," Ty said in response. "My dark fucking goddess."

"Holy shit, Ty, don't stop. Just fuck me," she begged. "That feels so fucking good."

Ena rocked into his thrusts, giving just as good as she got, and Iblis fucking damn him, he was about to come. He could feel his release two seconds away from bursting.

But he wanted her to come again too.

He took his hand, feeling between her ass cheeks for that tight, tiny asshole. He stroked it gently, giving her time to pull away if she didn't want that. She'd hinted before that it was okay, but she might have changed her mind.

Instead, she moaned—loudly—and Ty slowly pressed the tip of his finger inside it.

She gasped as he stretched her, and the tight grip around him nearly did him in.

He moved the finger gently, in and out just a little bit—he knew this was new for her and didn't want to hurt her.

"You like that?" he asked darkly.

"Mmhmm," she said, her voice garbled and almost incoherent with her pleasure.

"Come for me, Ena," he commanded. "Ride my cock with my finger in your ass and take your pleasure."

Ena did as he told her, and thank fucking Iblis she did, because as her pussy clenched around him, he couldn't hold back any longer. He poured himself inside her, giving her everything he had.

Ena collapsed onto him, her head on his heaving chest. Both of them were breathless and sweaty, and he brought his clean hand up to stroke her back, her hair, brushing it away from where it stuck to her face.

Tell her, tell her, tell her, his mind whispered as they lay together.

But he was afraid still. Afraid of losing her. Afraid of what admitting that to her, out loud, would mean. He'd meant everything he'd said to her about his hope for them being together even after the bond was broken, but still...that doubting part in the back of his brain told him he was promising her, promising himself, a future he couldn't deliver on.

But he didn't want to be that guy again. He didn't want to keep denying it *again*. He'd been that guy for so fucking long. He just couldn't do it anymore. He wanted to give her all of him, and he was tired of holding back.

No matter what the future looked like, he didn't want to live in fear anymore, so he chose to live in hope.

He cleared his throat. "Ena, I—"

Footsteps echoed down the passageway. Someone was coming.

Ty sat up frantically, reaching for Ena's clothes and handing them to her. "Quick, someone's coming," he said to her, her eyes widening with understanding.

He was just pulling up his own pants as Turner rounded the corner, entering the chamber.

"Whoa, sorry," he said, putting a hand in front of his eyes. "Should've realized you guys would be fucking naked." He was smiling widely, the asshole. "My bad."

Ena laughed nervously, pulling her shirt over her head and then working on the strings of her leather corset. "It's okay, I'm almost decent."

"What is it?" Ty asked, apprehension filling him. There was only one reason Turner would come all the way here out of the blue, and Ty dreaded it before he even spoke.

"It's Cole," Turner replied apologetically. "He wants to see you right away. Something about meat stores being low."

Motherfucker.

Ty sighed. "Alright," he said, rubbing his beard and still smelling Ena's pussy in it. Oh well, the bastard would have to deal with him in his current state. "I'll go straight there. Can you take Ena back to my room?"

"Sure," Turner said.

"I'll see you back there," Ty said, turning to give Ena a quick kiss, before regretfully leaving her.

There'd be time to tell her later, he thought. But as he made his way towards the Great Antre, towards his uncle, anger surged in him anew. Because this was the exact reason he'd been afraid to say those three words to her.

He may be Ena's, may be deeply in love with her above all others, but he always had another Master.

CHAPTER TWENTY-ONE

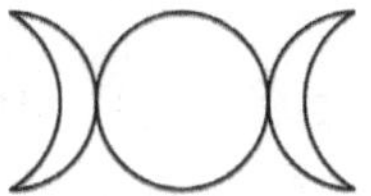

Ena

TY LEFT IN THE wee hours of the next morning. Apparently, the meat stores were getting low, and Cole had sent him and a few other mid-level daemons out on a hunting trip to harvest some game from the surrounding area. He'd explained that this was a fairly common task, and that because of his *venator,* he was often requested for these types of outings, but somehow, Ena still had a bad feeling.

The way he'd been called away had been so sudden, and she'd never admit it aloud—because she knew Turner, Steig, Lara would do their best—but she felt significantly less safe without him around. Turner had been tasked with escorting her to and from the Archives, as he did most days, but knowing that Ty wouldn't be there at night when she slept, even for a few days, well...it concerned her.

Maybe she was just being dramatic because she missed him. After their trip to the hot springs yesterday, she'd been positively glowing. Not just from the sex, which had, admittedly, been fucking fantastic, but also, there was this...feeling. This feeling had been growing between them for a while now, but she'd felt it more acutely than ever when she'd been laying on top of him. She had felt so calm, and content, like she was, for the very first time in her life, exactly where she was supposed to be.

And then he'd given her that ring... She reached into her pocket as she sat at her usual table in the Archives, twirling it gently between her fingers. It was absolutely the nicest thing she'd ever been given.

Witches didn't usually give presents; the only Gifts they received were from Gaia. She knew it was a common practice among mortals on certain occasions like one's birthday, but witches treated their belongings more communally anyway, so there was never much reason to gift someone something when they were all encouraged to share what they had.

Not to mention jewelry was rare to come by this side of the Chasm Mountains. Most of the metal that was traded was used to make more practical objects, but Ena supposed that since the daemons had such an abundance, it made sense that they could spare some for more luxury items.

But she couldn't deny that the most special part about it was that it had been made exclusively for her by Ty's own hands.

She fiddled with it now, thinking of the giddy, head-in-the-clouds way he'd made her feel, and how it somehow felt like so much *more* than before.

She'd known for a while what that feeling was, but now it was undeniable. It was practically screaming at her.

And part of her wanted to tell him what was in her heart, but another part of her was so, so scared. What if she was just being naïve again? Just like she had been nine years ago. What if she gave him everything again and it didn't work out? She had hope for their future, hope that she could have everything she wanted, but still...the thought of telling him felt like jumping off a cliff. Throwing herself into a rushing river she might drown in.

But...

That was the old Ena talking. The one who was so scared of the unknown she wouldn't even get in the water. Now she was getting in. She had faced the unknown—time and time again—and it had led her to some wonderful things. And she didn't want to go back.

So when Ty returned, she'd leap off that cliff with him. She'd tell him what was in her heart.

Smiling to herself, and feeling very proud of her brave decision, she began flipping through another daemonic book on runes. She'd again been fruitlessly trying to figure out the spellwords the witches had chanted during her vision of the binding spell, but there were only a few books on Wiccan magic here.

For some reason, she'd been feeling an increasing sense of urgency about it all. The last few nights, she'd been having dreams of the ritual—memories of what she'd seen and heard had woken her up in the dead of night—the witches' chanting echoing through her mind:

Diabolus vocare

Tellus separae

Just like the last symbol on the amulet, she wasn't familiar with any of the spellwords they'd used. It seemed, once again, that there were parts of her own magic, her own culture, that had been hidden from her.

So, feeling frustrated yet again, she decided to take a break from that and work on the mission from Cole for a bit, just in case he came around asking questions.

She'd promised Cole they would start to experiment with different runes that might work for Imbuing her Gift into an object, so she was flipping through a book on runes to see if any stood out to her as potentially being compatible with her *visanis*.

It wasn't long until she found one that she thought might work. It was one of the same runes used to control the water in the aqueducts, and was repeatedly referred to as the *imperium* rune, so she went to look it up in the rune dictionary. The dictionary contained helpful information about each recorded rune, including common uses, as well as which other runes it was incompatible with. Casually, she flipped to the *imperium* rune's entry, which read:

Imperium rune
Common uses: to control or direct certain elements (i.e. water, heat, air)
Antithetical to: diabolus rune

Ena froze. That last rune mentioned. *Diabolus*. Wasn't that one of the spellwords she'd heard in her vision?

Frantically, she flipped through the rune dictionary looking for the entry on the *diabolus* rune. The entry read:

Diabolus rune
Common Uses: to create chaos, disruption, and disorder of elements (water, heat, air, etc.)
Antithetical to: imperium rune, tellus rune

To cause chaos, disruption, and disorder? That was unexpected. Wiccan magic was usually rooted in Gaia's balance, drawing on the natural elements. Causing chaos, disruption, and disorder was Iblis's will—his domain.

But that was definitely one of the words they'd used, which meant...was it possible that the binding spell drew on Iblis's chaos magic? And if they were drawing on his magic, then...

The witches must have been channeling Iblis's will to complete it.

Ena stared at the page, her eyes blank.

It made so much sense now—why the spell had felt *wrong* from the moment she'd seen it. Why it had never felt like Gaia's will at all. And even though she knew now that channeling Iblis's will was not *always* a bad thing, in this case, it had thrown the entire magical order into chaos and had had significant negative consequences for everyone.

But also...the fact that this spellword came from a daemonic rune name meant that, again, the witches had borrowed from daemonic magical traditions to create the spellwords, just as they had with the amulet's symbols.

Was it possible the other words came from daemonic magic too?

Ena flipped frantically through the rune dictionary, looking for rune names similar to the other spellwords, and she found them each in turn:

Vocarus rune
Common Uses: to summon a mind channel with whomever touches the object, allowing the Power of the mind Imbued within to influence them.
Antithetical to: fugus rune

Separus rune
Common Uses: to sever an Imbued object's connection to the source Power, effectively removing its Imbued abilities.
Antithetical to: restoras rune

Tellus rune
Common Uses: to create equilibrium within an object Imbued with multiple Powers, balancing them and allowing them to coexist in equal measure.
Antithetical to: diabolus rune
(Note: This rune is defunct since Gaia's abandonment and is no longer effective)

Running over the spellwords in her mind, she tried to make sense of these meanings. *Diabolus vocare.* Chaos...summon. To summon chaos? Create a mind channel with chaos? Or maybe with...Iblis. That had to be it. Iblis was chaos incarnate. The witches must have summoned him, in a way, using those spellwords to directly channel his will.

A chill passed over Ena. Because that meant, in order to recreate the spell, that she would have to do that too. Summon Iblis. Not just get closer to him, as she had when she'd done the *allucinae*, but be filled with his presence, just as she had with Gaia's during her Summoning. It made sense when she thought about it—disrupting the status quo of magic had required summoning Iblis the first time, and now changing it back would be another disruption of the status quo.

The thought of summoning him lit a tiny spark of fear inside her, but there'd be time to dread that later.

She still needed to figure out the last part. *Tellus separae*. Equilibrium...sever.

Well, that one was more obvious, and it absolutely made sense. Ena already knew from what Heran had told her that the binding spell had severed the daemons from Gaia, who was equilibrium incarnate, effectively ending their ability to channel her will or access her magic.

So that was it. Summon Iblis. Sever Gaia.

The witches had summoned Iblis to sever the daemon woman's connection with Gaia, drawing on the enhancing magic of the amulet to bind the spell into place among all those who shared her daemonic blood.

Ena couldn't help herself—she laughed. She laughed big and joyfully as tears filled her eyes.

From across the Archives, Nial stared at her inquisitively, but she couldn't help herself. Waving him off with her hand, she tried to calm herself down, but her insides were galloping.

This was it. This was the remaining piece of the ritual they'd needed. The entry on *separus* said right there that the opposite was *restoras*. All they had to do was recite the spellwords, subbing out *separae* for *restorae* to match the altered style of the spellwords and that should do it. They should be able to restore daemons' connection to Gaia, again drawing on Iblis's chaos magic to do so.

Ena looked around. She had no idea what time it was. How long would it be until Turner came to get her? This was huge. She didn't want to wait until then. She needed to tell someone now. Should she go find him on her own?

Just then, Ena heard male voices. Peeking her head out of her alcove, she saw two men entering the Archives, and her stomach sank.

It was Gunnar and Chans.

What were they doing here? They didn't seem like the type to spend time reading books.

Gunnar's hulking form paused in the center of the chamber as he and Chans looked around for something.

Then their eyes landed on Ena.

Fuck. They were looking for *her*.

The two of them walked over, a sneer blanketing Chans's features, while a satisfied smile graced Gunnar's.

"Witch-slave," Gunnar called, his deep voice grating over Ena's ears. "The king wants to see you."

Fear locked up Ena's insides. Cole wanted to see her? But Ty wasn't here. Was this allowed? Wasn't she supposed to be Ty's witch-slave and only follow his commands? Should she refuse them?

She desperately wanted to, but refusing them didn't feel safe. Cole was the king, after all, and could do what he wanted, as long as he had cause.

Ena tried to keep her composure as she closed the book in front of her. Whatever this was about, she'd just have to bullshit her way through it, and hope for the best.

Tidying the books into a stack for Nial and thanking Gaia she hadn't had him get out the books from Petyr today, she glanced once at the old daemon before she made her way to the door of the Archives, Gunnar and Chans shadowing her on either side.

Nial's eyes were full of concern, and she tried to communicate to him with a look that this didn't feel right.

Get Turner. Get Steig and Lara, she wanted to say.

But what could they do anyway? Ty was gone, and no one could stop the king.

Ena was at his mercy.

CHAPTER TWENTY-TWO

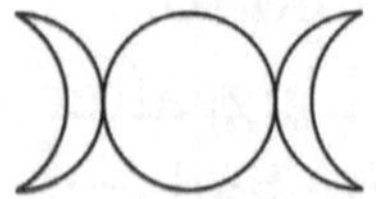

Ena

ENA FOLLOWED THE TWO daemons through the passageways of the upper levels toward the Great Antre. Neither of them touched her, but their presence made the hair on the back of her neck stand up and her stomach twist in knots. She didn't have her Knowing to truly tell her their intentions, but even without it, she could tell—they were bleeding contempt and violence.

The three of them walked in silence as Ena's mind spun. Did Cole want an update about the mission? That was the most likely scenario, but she couldn't stem the flow of dread that filled her thinking of all the other worse possibilities.

What if he'd figured out about the amulet? Or learned about her and Ty's relationship? What if he wanted her to use her Gift on someone again? Or had he figured out that she'd embarrassed him on purpose during the *onata* celebration?

Ena was sweating by the time the three of them entered the Great Antre, their footsteps the only sound echoing around the vast cavern—a chilling reminder of her isolation.

Together, they approached Cole, who was sitting at the head of the long wooden table on his throne. Ena was somehow grateful that his throne had been moved off the dais where it had sat during the *onata* celebration, but despite that, he seemed to loom over the space still, his presence pervasive.

He watched her with a look of barely contained excitement on his face, like a cat toying with a mouse, as she walked in. Ena's heart began to pound.

Nothing about this felt good. Nothing about this felt safe.

The three of them paused at the other end of the table from Cole as his face broke into a feline grin.

"So glad you could join us, witch-slave," he said, his tone gentile and charming, and so at odds with the menace in his eyes.

Ena didn't know what to say, so she remained silent. Gunnar and Chans still flanked her on either side, trapping her to the point where she felt claustrophobic.

"I require an update on my nephew's mission. Tell me, what else have you found?" Cole asked directly.

Was that all this was about? The mission, like Ena suspected? She didn't know for sure, but she began talking anyway, just to appease him.

"I, uh, did find something, actually. A lead on a rune that might work with my Gift. The *imperium* rune." Ena's voice shook slightly as she spoke, not at all like the confidence she had mustered during the *onata* celebration. But she'd had Ty at her side then, guiding her, watching her back.

Now she was alone.

She was suddenly faced with the overwhelming urge to cry. She didn't know why—she hadn't done anything wrong, but she knew she couldn't do that, so instead she plastered on a polite smile. Maybe if she just kept smiling, everything would be okay.

"Good...good," Cole mused. But he kept staring at her. He didn't seem like he was done.

Ena's hands fidgeted where they were clasped in front of her, but other than that, she tried not to move. She worried if she did, they'd take it as an excuse to hurt her. She was keenly aware that she was outnumbered here. Her use of magic was restricted, and even though she'd been training to fight with Ty and Turner, there was no way she could take these daemons on her own.

"You know..." Cole continued speaking, his voice slithering over her. "I remember you."

Ena froze.

"My nephew thinks he's so clever, bringing you here. Pretending as if you're not the same witch he tried to run to all those years ago." Cole's gaze turned hard as steel. "He's been lying to me."

Shit, shit, shit. Ena's brain was frantic. Cole knew who she was? Knew about her and Ty's history?

Her stomach dropped. What else did he know?

"But I'm no fool," Cole continued, spitting out the last word. "I remember the way he looked at you. Remember how desperately he tried to get to you." The man chuckled sadistically. "And there are those in the Underworld, myself included, who see how dangerous his feelings for you are."

Ena swallowed. Her mouth was bone dry, and she tried desperately to get her sluggish, fear-addled brain to think of a plan. She needed to do something—she could sense violence approaching, and she couldn't just stand here and let it happen. Maybe she could create a distraction with her magic and run, but the darkrock lanterns were too far away to blow up in their faces like she did to Ty while sparring.

The air, maybe? She could create a swirling vortex in the cave. But then where would she run to? They were deep underground, and they would inevitably catch her when she got lost in the passageways.

She was trapped.

Without Ty to handle this—to protect her—she had no way to protect herself. For the first time since coming to the Underworld, she truly realized what a dangerous situation she'd walked into, and regret started to creep in.

"So, as punishment for you both lying, I think an example needs to be set. To remind him, and everyone, of what you are," Cole continued, the tension in the room palpable. "But I want you to know, it's nothing personal. You've been a good little witch-slave."

Cole looked at Gunnar where he stood beside her and gave him a curt nod of permission.

Ena's head whipped to look at him just as his hand flew out, striking her across the face.

She felt the air whoosh out of her lungs as her head was knocked to the side. Her teeth cut into the side of her cheek, making her bleed, and her cheekbone throbbed with the sudden pain.

Her hand came up involuntarily to touch the spot where she'd been struck, but before she could fully register what had happened, Chans grabbed the back of her head, gripping her hair painfully and ripping out some of the strands.

She reached back, trying to dislodge his grip, but he was far stronger, and he used that strength to slam her face down onto the wooden table in front of them.

Her cheekbone exploded, the pain so overwhelming Ena couldn't breathe. She needed to do something, anything, to get away. Adrenaline rushed through her, and, remembering her training, the things Ty had taught her, she threw out her elbow with as much force as she could muster, connecting with Chans's gut.

He grunted and pulled her back up by the hair before pushing her with his full force away from him. Ena stumbled with the sudden change of momentum, and fell to the ground in a heap.

Fuck, fuck, fuck. She'd forgotten her footwork. Ty had always told her that was the most important thing and she hadn't done it. Tears filled her eyes—from the pain on her face, yes—but as she looked up at the men looming above her, all she felt was fear.

Gunnar approached her again as she reached into her Knowing.

The air in the cave was stagnant, not like the air above, but she sensed it still.

{*Aer*—}

Gunnar gripped her throat before she could get the spellword out—squeezing and choking off her words.

She could feel his death grip crushing her windpipe as she looked into his dead eyes and panic set in.

She tried futilely to pull in air, but only managed tiny sips. Black began to edge her vision and she started to feel lightheaded, when suddenly Gunnar lifted his knee, slamming it into her belly.

She felt one of her ribs crack, but she didn't fall down this time. She stumbled back a step, bent over and clutching her side. Her throat was on fire and she could barely breathe with the pain in her side.

Sensing someone approach behind her, she whipped around, hunched over in fear like a feral animal. Her eyes darted around, looking to flee, as Chans reached out to grip her wrist. He pulled it away from her body, from where she'd been protecting herself, and wrenched it to the side—not the way the bones were meant to go—and she heard it snap.

A scream echoed around the cave. She guessed it was hers but she didn't remember making it. Scalding pain flooded her wrist as she fell to her knees, and she began to lose consciousness. She vaguely felt someone kick her in the gut—again, again, until she felt blood start to trickle out of her mouth, when it suddenly stopped.

Clutching her useless wrist, shaking, she began to sob. She wanted to beg. Part of her wanted to beg them to stop.

But she didn't. She wouldn't give them the satisfaction.

She brought her eyes up to see Cole approaching her. He loomed over her shaking, sobbing body on the ground, and Ena was afraid—yes, that was for certain—but a new feeling grew in her, something she'd never felt so starkly before in her life.

Hatred. She was filled with such loathing, such utter rage as she had never felt before. And she knew then: he would fucking pay for this. She might have no recourse right now, but one day...one day she would. And he would pay in spades.

Cole stared back at her, seeming amused at the hatred in her eyes, as he reached out to grab her broken wrist, twisting it with a sadistic glee as Ena cried out in pain. "Let this be a message to you and my nephew," he said, speaking quietly so only she could hear. "We will never allow a witch to be queen."

Before she could fully comprehend what he said, he brought his knee up to her face, slamming it into her head until she fell back, her skull cracking onto the ground, and everything went dark.

CHAPTER TWENTY-THREE

Ty

TY HAD SPENT THE last several days sleeping on the cold, snow-covered ground, and feeling increasingly annoyed. It had been tough finding game, even with his *venator* and Cerberus tracking what he could.

It usually was tougher this time of year, right at the start of winter, but the lack of deer or elk seemed even starker than in years past, and that concerned him. He couldn't exactly put his thumb on it, but something felt off.

Not to mention, he was worried about Ena. He knew his skills were needed to bring back meat for the Underworld, but he didn't like leaving her alone there, even for a few days.

Although, she wasn't truly *alone*. Turner, Steig, and Lara would watch out for her, but still, he worried. He knew that as *his* witch-slave, his protection of her was the most valuable.

On the third day after he'd left, he finally found himself and his companions, two mid-level daemons with hellhounds of their own, heading back to the entrance to the Underworld with four decent-sized deer in tow.

When they arrived, he left the venison with his companions to take to the king's kitchen, where they would be processed and appropriately rationed, while he took his horse to Myka.

"Hello?" he called, as he entered the wide cavern of the stables. "Myka?"

The man in question popped his head out from a stall, where he'd evidently been re-shoeing a horse. "Ty," he said, his voice sounding on edge. "You're back."

"Yeah, I am," Ty said, handing off the reins to the man.

"Do you— I mean, how was the hunting trip?" Myka asked, seeming nervous.

"It was fine. Took significantly longer than I would have liked to track down the game, but we got it in the end."

Myka nodded at him, his eyes darting to the side.

"Myka, what's going on? Has something happened to you?"

"To me? No, no," the man rushed to say. "It's just... I heard about something, a day or two ago. About your...witch-slave, and I just wondered if you'd heard yet."

Ty's insides locked up. It took everything in him to control the chaos that descended over his mind. *Keep calm. Don't overreact.* She was just supposed to be his witch-slave—nothing to him. He needed to act accordingly and keep his composure.

"And what's that?" he asked, forming the words deliberately slowly.

"It was Cole. He..." Myka's words drifted off. The man was fearful for some reason, but Ty's patience for this was absolutely at an end.

"Myka," Ty gritted out. "Tell me now. What happened?"

"He wanted to send a message," the man finished in a rush, his voice guilty, as if he didn't know if he should be the one revealing this.

A message.

A chill went through him, and he needed no further explanation. He knew firsthand what messages from his uncle were like.

He turned on his heel immediately and left, rushing through the passageways, his mind in a blind panic.

He had to get to Ena. Had to see her. What had Cole done to her? Was she alive?

He barely even registered his own body moving as he ran through the Underworld.

Finally, he arrived at his door and threw it open.

Turner, Steig, and Lara stood in the room, surrounding his bed. They turned to him as he burst in, shock in their eyes.

Then his eyes fell to his bed, and he saw Ena.

Dark purple and yellow bruises covered the entire right side of her face, mottling her normally perfect skin, which was even paler than normal. That side of her face was so swollen, he could barely see her right eye, but he could see that the other one was closed.

Iblis, no—was she...?

As he rushed toward the bed, he saw her chest rise and fall, and he nearly collapsed with relief.

She was alive—asleep, but alive.

His eyes traced over the deep bruises that rung around her neck before landing on her arm. It lay delicately above the fur blankets, her left wrist wrapped in bandages as if the bone was broken.

Ty felt his heart shatter into pieces as he collapsed to his knees next to the bed. Her dark-brown hair was tangled and strewn across the pillow. She looked so small, so vulnerable, and he felt a grief so profound well up inside him.

He hadn't cried in years—not since his dad had died. He didn't even know if he remembered how, and maybe he should. Maybe crying would be a better reaction, but instead, his body flooded with adrenaline, blinding him in an all-consuming rage.

He looked up to his left to find Steig standing next to him. "What happened?" he asked, his voice shaking with the barely restrained emotions he was feeling.

Steig looked at him with steel and caution in his eyes. "Cole," he said simply. "He had Gunnar and Chans do most of the dirty work, but that's all I know. Turner was the one who found her." Steig looked over at the man in question, who nodded in corroboration.

"It was thanks to Nial, actually," Turner explained. "He came to get me. Told me that they'd taken her from the Archives and that something didn't feel right about it." Turner looked away from him, his eyes looking haunted as they landed on Ena instead. "They left her in an alcove in the Great Antre while they had their Convening," he said, an uncharacteristic anger in his voice. "And I'm just so—" Turner's voice broke with emotion, making him pause before he could continue. "I'm so sorry I didn't get there sooner."

Ty couldn't look at him anymore. He couldn't look at any of them. He just stared at Ena where she lay on the bed.

"Is she, has she—" Ty could barely get his voice to work. He could feel his anger and his grief spiraling out of control inside him.

"She's been in and out of consciousness for the last few days," Lara explained grimly, responding to his incomplete questions. "We gave her a potion for pain-numbing that put her to sleep, and we tended her wounds as best we could, but...she's not a daemon. She's not healing as fast as we're used to. And without access to more witch potions or their magic, I—I don't know how long until she's better."

Ty reached out cautiously to grab her uninjured hand to find that it was cold to the touch. He didn't know if he should be touching her, but he couldn't help himself. He needed to feel that she was alive.

How could they *do* this to her? How could *he* have let this happen? After all the promises he'd made her. After he told her he'd keep her safe. He should never have followed Cole's orders and gone hunting. He never should have brought her here.

"Ty." Steig's voice was tight with anger. "Watch your Power."

Watch his Power? Ty wanted to laugh, but there was no way in the Underworld he could. He didn't want to "watch his Power." He wanted to *rage*.

He looked at Steig to find the man bunching his fists already. Without meaning to, his Power was clearly bleeding out of him, affecting those around him. And he didn't give two fucks. They should be angry. They should all be as angry and devastated as him.

He felt for that channel leading to Steig, that thread connecting their minds, and he seized it roughly—pouring his emotion through it, feeding it, fueling it, as he watched Steig's breathing kick up and his chest begin to heave. The man's face got red and he screamed.

"Ty! Stop!"

But Ty didn't want to stop.

He reared back and punched the man square in the jaw, Steig's head flying backward as he was forced back several steps.

The man touched his jaw where the blow had landed, clearly feeling blood inside his mouth. "Fine," Steig said through gritted teeth, his voice dark and dangerous. "If this is how you want it, let it out. Let it out on me," he said, waving Ty towards him.

Ty screamed, his rage animalistic as he threw himself at Steig. The two of them became a flurry of fists and blood, rolling together on the fur-covered floor.

But Steig was no easy target—he gave as good as he got, and Ty reveled in it. Every hit he landed, every blow he absorbed, felt like absolution. He wanted it to hurt, he wanted to *be* hurt. The physical manifestation of his anger felt good—it felt so good because while he was in it, he couldn't feel or think about anything else. He didn't have to think about Ena and the way she looked lying on the bed. He didn't have to think about how monumentally he had fucked up by leaving her alone here. He didn't have to think about Cole and how he could possibly let the motherfucker live after this.

So instead, he threw punches like his life depended on it. Blow after blow he landed on Steig, sloppy and uncontrolled. Steig kicked him in the gut as he fell back into a chair, breaking it instantly. But he got back up, and launched Steig back into the table, knocking it over with their combined weight.

"Enough!" he heard Lara yell. Then he felt a wave of…something wash over him. Not joy, exactly, but contentment. It wedged itself in between the cracks of the rage in his mind, and it dulled it. It lessened it just enough that he let go of the channel to Steig, breaking the flow of anger between them, and the two of them rolled off one another, collapsing on the ground out of breath.

Lara approached Steig and leaned over him, touching his face in concern. Then she looked at Ty. "That's enough," she said, her voice stern but gentle.

The furrow between Steig's brows softened as he brought his hand up to stroke through her hair, and the look of care the two of them exchanged made Ty's chest ache.

His eyes were drawn to where his whole heart lay, unmoving on the bed. All his hope and his greatest fears inside one person. One beautiful, fragile witch.

His mind began to calm more now, Lara's magic having broken his rage spiral, and he began to think logically again.

Would Ena be alright? Her injuries looked bad, but if she'd survived them so far, she would likely live. They just needed to wait for her to wake up and give her time. But even then...

There was another question that haunted him, one that made his heart seize in his chest: Would she forgive him? He couldn't imagine a world in which she would. Not after he'd broken another promise. Not after he'd let this happen. She would have every right to hate him.

And that thought utterly destroyed him, because he couldn't imagine a world without her—without them together—not anymore. Before he'd left, he'd been so full of hope, ready to admit his love, and now he knew without a doubt—he was an absolute fool. How had he not learned this lesson by now? Why did he have to learn it again and again and again before it would sink in?

He could never hold on to happiness, to contentment—his Master would never let him.

He dragged his eyes away from where Ena lay to the door, as he rose. He knew what he needed to do. He was filled with such resolve as he moved to leave, but Turner blocked his path.

"Where do you think you're going, brother?" he asked in that calm, friendly way of his.

"I'm going to fucking kill him. I've waited long enough," Ty replied, his voice calm with the clarity he now felt.

Turner placed his hand on Ty's chest, stopping him from approaching the door. "I can't let you do that," he said, his voice serious.

"Why the fuck not?" Ty asked, but he controlled his rage this time. He needed to save it.

"You know why. You really want to precipitate what happens when he dies?"

"It doesn't matter. At least she'll be safe."

"Will she?" Steig asked from where he sat at the table, Lara dabbing a cloth on his split lip. "If anyone suspects foul play, especially those who support Cole, they'll come for you. For us. For her," he added, nodding at the bed where Ena lay.

Ty rubbed his face with his hands, smearing the blood from a cut on his cheek all over, but he didn't care. The only thing he cared about was there in that bed. And she wouldn't fucking *wake up*.

But Steig and Turner were right. Deep down, he knew they were.

If he attacked Cole now, in front of everyone, chaos would ensue. There were those who would follow him, yes, and consent to the change of power, but there were those who would riot. Those loyal to Cole. And he couldn't take them all—not by himself.

He needed to lay the groundwork first. Needed to release the daemons from the bond so they were open to Gaia. Maybe then he could convince more people that Cole's way wasn't the way. Maybe then he could take him out.

But not now.

Fuck.

His eyes landed on the bed again. On the pale skin and dark hair of the woman resting in it. "Okay, you're right," he said, his voice sounding small and far away, even to his own ears. "I won't go after him."

Turner removed his arm and seemed satisfied with that response.

Lara came up to him then and placed her hand on his shoulder. "She'll be okay, Ty," Lara said softly. "She's strong."

Ty tried to nod to show that he'd heard her but wasn't sure if he fully managed it. He walked over to the bed again, then kicked off his boots before climbing up beside her.

"We'll leave you two alone for a bit," Lara said, looking at Turner and Steig for affirmation. "But I'll be back soon to check on you. Okay?"

Ty grunted in acknowledgment.

He heard them shuffle around the room for a second before opening the door to leave.

Ty lay on his side, facing Ena, watching her breathe. Her chest rose steadily, but other than that, she didn't move.

Gently, he reached out with one hand, brushing some hair away from the uninjured side of her face, and she didn't even flinch.

"Ena," he whispered, his voice thick. "Please wake up. I'm so, so sorry. Please."

He didn't expect her to respond, but he still felt a sharp pain in his chest at her lack of response.

He laid there for hours, watching her chest rising and falling, but he didn't close his eyes. He couldn't. Not when his worst nightmare, the very thing he'd feared all along, had finally come to pass, and he was trapped in it. To sleep would be too easy.

No, he would stay awake until she opened her eyes and spoke to him. That was his only dream right now, and he wouldn't sleep until it became reality.

CHAPTER TWENTY-FOUR

Ty

It was several hours later, almost time for the time-keepers to come dim the darkrock lanterns, when Ty heard a gentle knock on the door.

He turned away from where Ena slept to see Lara crack it open and cautiously enter the room.

"How is she?" she asked quietly, her eyes landing on where Ena lay, unmoved from her previous position.

"No change," Ty said, sitting up slowly. He was bone-tired and sore from the fight with Steig, but he could barely spare a thought for himself. "Is it normal for her to be sleeping this long? You said she woke up for a bit before, right? Did she say anything?"

"No, she didn't. Her throat was…" Lara looked, haunted, at Ena's bruised throat. "She couldn't really talk. And then we managed to give her the potion, and she's been sleeping ever since. I—I don't know if it's normal for witches to be asleep this long after taking it."

Ty nodded. He didn't know either. They were used to the trajectory of daemon healing, which was much shorter, and they never used potions on themselves—they wouldn't work even if they did. The very few they even had in stock were given to the mortal *imperi*.

"Ty," Lara began cautiously, sitting on the edge of the bed next to him. "I didn't just come to check on you two. I was sent with a message. Cole wants to see you."

Ty's stomach dropped and his fists clenched at his sides.

Of course. The bastard clearly wanted to make sure his message was received, loud and clear.

Ty looked at Lara, letting his feelings bleed through. "I don't know if I can do it, Lara. I don't know if I can keep my cool around him anymore. Not after this."

"You have to, Ty," she replied in earnest. "You have no choice. It's what's safest for all of us right now."

Ty lowered his face into his hands. He didn't know how to deal with this. For the first time in his life, he felt completely helpless. He just wanted Ena to wake up so badly, it was all he could think about. And now he had to leave her again to go bow and scrape to the man who'd hurt her?

He felt Lara gently place a hand on his shoulder. "I promise you, Ty, he won't get away with this. With *anything* that he's done. His time will come."

Ty looked up to meet his cousin's gaze. It was pure fucking steel, and he leaned on her strength and resolve.

"I know," Ty said darkly. "I'll make fucking sure of it."

He stood slowly then and dragged himself to the bathing chamber. He still hadn't cleaned up since returning from his hunting trip, and the bastard could wait for him to take a bath first.

After he was clean and in fresh clothing, he left Lara to watch over Ena, stealing one more glance at where she lay. It hurt his heart to see her face, but he didn't dare look away. He let that hurt fuel him as he walked through the passageways of the Underworld, towards the Great Antre.

He took the time on the way to make sure his body was calm. He was unusually adept at sequestering his anger—hiding it, tucking it away where it grew and festered in the deepest parts of him. He did that now, taking several deep breaths to prepare himself for what lay ahead.

As he walked into the Great Antre, he saw Cole seated on his throne at the head of the Convening table, his uncle Zak next to him. The two of them were deep in conversation, but Cole's golden hazel eyes lit up when he saw Ty enter.

"Nephew," he said in greeting, but that fucking smile he always wore was nowhere in sight. Instead, he seemed cautious. Angry, even. "I trust the hunting trip was successful?" he asked.

"Yes, my king," Ty said, giving a deferential nod of his head. The movement and title grated on him like a blade on a whetstone, sharpening his rage where it dwelled inside him. He looked up, meeting Cole's gaze unerringly. If the bastard expected him to react, he'd give him nothing.

"Tell me...did you receive my message?" Cole asked, feigning nonchalance and leaning back in his throne as if this was the most inconsequential conversation of the day. But Ty saw through him. He was upset about something. He *was* angry. But he was also scared.

"I did," Ty responded simply.

"Good," Cole said, over-enunciating the word for emphasis. "Because I know you're up to something."

Ty's body stiffened. He'd been worried about that, but his concern over Ena had swamped everything. Now that he was in the wolf's den, fear came flooding back through him. What did Cole know? What did he suspect?

"What do you mean, my king?" Ty asked, feigning ignorance. Better to let him reveal his suspicions first.

"Don't play innocent with me, Ty. I'm no fool." The man's voice was pure venom, and he seemed ruffled in a way that Ty wasn't used to seeing. "I know you lust for my throne. I know you plan to use that witch's Gift to overthrow me, to control me with it somehow."

Ty wanted to laugh, but he kept a straight face. The man was fucking delusional—making up stories in his head like a deranged old fool. Ty had never even considered such a thing, but at least Cole didn't seem to know about the amulet.

"Uncle, I—"

Cole cut him off. "Don't lie to me, boy. The only reason you still live is because, despite your witch-blood, you are the eldest son of the eldest son, and the one true heir to the Underworld. But you and I both know it won't be yours until I'm dead."

There wasn't a day of his life when Ty didn't remember that. The fact that Cole thought he needed reminding was, again, laughable.

"So I want to give you some friendly advice, for your sake as much as mine." Cole leaned forward, placing his elbows on the sturdy table in front of him and clasping his hands together. "Witches are dangerous. They *cannot* be trusted, no matter the end you desire. You will let her go, or as Iblis is my Master, I'll take her from you."

Ty locked eyes with him and saw in the depths of his uncle's gaze that he meant it. Every fiber of his being ached to launch himself at the man, ending him and his threat against Ena forever, but he fucking *couldn't*. All he could do was nod his head deferentially to indicate his understanding.

"Good. You're dismissed," Cole said with a wave of his hand.

Ty turned on his heel and walked calmly out of the Great Antre. It wasn't until he reached the passageway that he let himself break.

He launched his fist at the hard stone walls of the Underworld, again, and again, and again, until his fist was bloodied and raw.

When he was done, he didn't feel *better*, but at least he could think more clearly. And what he thought was that it was time for them to leave.

Ena wasn't safe here anymore. *He* wasn't safe here anymore, if he'd ever truly been. They would have to flee and take whatever books they could with them to figure out the rest of the binding spell.

Because one thing was for certain: despite what Cole asked of him, unless it was *her* choice, he could never let Ena go.

CHAPTER TWENTY-FIVE

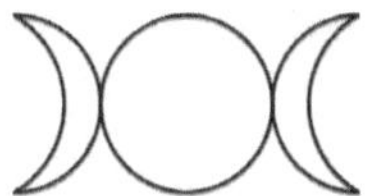

Ena

ENA WAS ASLEEP. SHE didn't know how long she'd been that way, but she could sense that it had been a while. The potion they'd given her when she had first woken up had knocked her out cold, but her consciousness had come and gone. Sometimes she'd fallen into a deep, dreamless sleep, and then other times, she'd felt herself waking up, only to be dragged under again in a seemingly never-ending cycle.

But this time felt different. Her eyes felt so heavy, but still, they began to flutter, and with effort, she was able to crack one of them open. She struggled with the other one and only got it so far open before deciding to let it close again. She could feel that that side of her face was swollen—it throbbed and was uncomfortable—but there wasn't much pain. She guessed she had the potion to thank for that.

Looking around with her one good eye, she saw that she was still in Ty's room.

"Ena!"

Movement from the other side of the room caught her eye and she tracked it. It was Lara.

"How are you feeling?" Lara asked as she approached the bed.

"I—" Ena went to answer, but her voice came out in a croak. It sounded rough and dry, and hurt to use. She moved to swallow and winced at the dull pain that accompanied the movement.

"Sorry, hold on. I'll get you some water." Lara moved to the table and poured Ena a glass of water from the pitcher there. Bringing it over to her, she leaned over the bed to tip a tiny amount into Ena's mouth.

"More?" Lara asked gently. When Ena gave a small nod, she poured a few more mouthfuls into Ena's mouth before Ena turned her head away.

"Thank you," she managed to croak out. The water had helped, but her voice was still messed up. That had to be because of the—

Ena flinched as the unwanted memory resurfaced. Gunnar's meaty hands around her throat—squeezing—as she tried desperately to drink in air.

The terror she'd felt. The helplessness.

"So how are you feeling?" Lara asked, jolting Ena's attention back towards her.

"O-okay, I think," Ena answered, fidgeting uncomfortably as the adrenaline petered out of her body once more. She was suddenly keenly aware that she hadn't moved in Gaia knew how long, and her limbs felt strange.

"Here, let me help you sit up," Lara said. Carefully, she propped another pillow behind Ena's head and then came up onto the bed next to her. Together, being careful of Ena's broken ribs, they shuffled her upward into a sitting position.

Just then, the door opened, and their attention shifted as Ty entered the room.

Sudden relief washed over Ena so intensely that her good eye began to tear up.

"You're awake," he said, rushing over to the bed in a few long strides. He knelt down beside her and grasped her uninjured hand in his. The look on his face made Ena want to cry even more. He looked relieved, too, but his stare was so intense, like he didn't want to blink for fear that she'd disappear.

"You're back," she croaked out.

She saw him wince slightly at the sound of her voice, but he hid it well, and brought his hand up to push hair away from the uninjured side of her face. "I am. I got back this morning. I'm sorry I wasn't here when you woke up. I was with…"

Ena's hand tightened unconsciously, gripping Ty's harder. She knew what he'd been about to say. She could see it in the look of fury in his eyes. He had been with Cole.

Even the thought of his name made Ena's heart rate kick up and brought a panicking tightness to her chest. She had to actively calm herself down, closing her eyes for a second and taking as deep of a breath as she could with the dull pain still echoing through her ribs.

"How—how long have I been asleep?" she managed to ask, desperate to change the topic.

"Just a day or so," Lara answered. "The pain-numbing potion was also a sleeping draft, so unfortunately now that you're awake, the pain might come back."

Ena nodded, but felt her stomach tighten at the prospect of more pain. She was familiar with the type of potion they'd used, and she knew that would likely be the case.

"I'm sorry we couldn't do more for you," Lara continued. "We only have so many potions on hand from trades with the Covens."

The mention of the Covens—of home—brought a sharp pain to Ena's heart. What she wouldn't give to be there right now—with Greya, or with Heran. The matriarch could heal her in half the time it would take on her own. Or even with Perse. Ena was sure he'd have something lighthearted to say—something that would make her smile and feel safe. In that instant, she wanted to go home so badly, she didn't know how to go on.

But she put on a brave face for her friend, who she knew was distraught at not being able to help her more. "I understand," Ena said quietly, trying to look reassuring for Lara. "I'll be fine, I promise. I just need...time."

Ty stroked her uninjured hand with his thumb. Honestly, Ena couldn't even bring herself to look down at the broken one. Would it heal properly? Would she have issues with it for the rest of her life? And her face...she knew without a doubt that her cheekbone had broken. Would she look different now too?

"Do you think you can handle drinking some broth? I can go get you some," Lara offered, concern in her eyes.

"Yeah," Ena said. "I'll try some. Thanks."

Lara gave her a watery smile before standing up and reassuring Ty she'd be right back before leaving to fetch the broth.

Ena looked at Ty, the two of them alone for the first time since he'd returned, and she knew what was coming next.

He was going to ask what happened, and the thought made the panicked feelings in her chest return.

"Ena," he said quietly, almost a whisper. His voice was full of regret and sadness, and she couldn't handle it. "I—"

"I figured out the spellwords," Ena said, interrupting him suddenly, desperately changing the subject.

"What?" he asked, clearly surprised by the sudden shift in conversation. "Really?"

Ena nodded. "The spellwords were derived from runic words summoning the chaos magic of Iblis and severing the balancing magic of Gaia. If we switch one of the words to its antithesis, I think we can reverse the spell."

Ty looked at her in awe. "Ena, that's—" He shook his head in disbelief. "That's amazing. I can't believe you did it."

Ena smiled slightly at his praise. After all this time, it still felt good to please him.

"So does that mean we'll be summoning Iblis? Like in the Trial?" he asked, his face turning wary.

"Yes, I think so. And it makes sense, because it took a great act of chaos to sever daemons from Gaia's magic in the first place, and now to restore it, we'll have to channel him again, only this time, the great act of chaos will hopefully lead to a restoration of the balance that was lost." Ena paused, thinking of how to explain the revelation she'd had before everything came crashing down. "Sometimes, I think, chaos can be necessary in the short term, to reach a new equilibrium, so if I embrace that, and channel that intention into the spell, it should work to break the bond to Iblis, and allow Gaia's magic back in."

Ty smiled at her. "Good, then we can leave right away—because I'm sorry, Ena, but I think we need to leave as soon as possible. I know you're still healing, but it's not safe here for you anymore. My conversation with Cole confirmed that. He's suspicious of us, of you, and I just—" Ty cut himself off, closing his eyes as he brought her hand to his lips and kissed it gently. "I'm so, so sorry, Ena. I'm just so sorry for everything. I never should have left you here alone."

"You didn't have a choice," Ena said, and it was the truth. She didn't blame Ty for what happened, not at all. But she did feel scared. More scared than she'd ever felt before. She knew she wasn't safe here and never would be.

We will never allow a witch to be queen.

Cole's menacing words to her before she'd been knocked unconscious flooded back to her unbidden, and she shut her eyes tight.

"Ena? Are you alright?" Ty asked, his voice full of concern as he reached up to grasp her arm.

"Yeah, I'm fine, I just...something Cole said to me."

"What did he say?" he asked, anger creeping into his voice.

"That I would never be…'queen,'" Ena said the strange word, feeling it out on her tongue. "Do you know what that means?"

Ty removed his hand from her shoulder as if she'd burned him. His brow furrowed, and he looked away from her.

"Ty?" she asked, recognizing his avoidance of a tough topic. "Tell me."

He sighed, rubbing his hands through his beard. "A queen is a coruler. Someone who rules in the Underworld alongside the king after they are united—that's our version of handfasting."

"And why…would I ever be queen? There's no way I'm uniting with Cole."

Ty sighed again, as if steeling himself for something. "It's because of me. Because I'm the heir. After Cole dies…I will be king."

Ena's heart sank to the pit of her stomach. It sank so far away she didn't know if she would ever get it back.

There was that word again. The one she'd heard but didn't know. The one that clearly had been haunting her this whole time and she felt like such a fucking idiot for missing its meaning.

Heir. Ty was the heir. It meant he was next in line to be king.

"Why didn't you tell me this before?" she asked, her voice turning hard.

"I—"

But she was too mad to hear what he was about to say. "I'm so *sick* of you hiding things from me, Ty," she said, tears filling her eyes, whether from anger or sadness, she wasn't sure. "This is huge. This changes *everything*."

"I wasn't hiding it," Ty said, his voice unwavering. "I just didn't want it to complicate things between us. I just wanted to forget about it. And it doesn't have to change anything. Ena," he said, his voice steady and convincing. "I can make you my queen. I don't care what Cole said, I'll have the power to do that. I'll be able to do whatever I want."

Ena shook her head sadly. Tears started to flow down her face, dripping through the bruises on her cheeks and falling onto her broken wrist where it lay on the bed. "I can't, Ty, don't you see? Do you not see what they did to me?"

Ty looked away as if she'd slapped him.

"There are too many here who will never accept me. Even once we break the bond, all that hate won't just instantly go away. I will always be in danger from those who mistrust witches, and I...I need to be with my family." Ena began sobbing. The homesick ache returned as she thought of her Coven. Of the safety there that she longed for.

Because, she realized, she wasn't safe here. Even with Ty back—he was only one man. And how long before he was hurt trying to protect her? How long before daemons came for him, too, for breaking the rules?

As freeing as it had been to embrace the unknown, it had also been more dangerous than she'd realized, and right now, she just desperately wanted to feel safe again.

"I—I can't be at your side here, Ty. I see that now. We...we have to stop this. Before we get in too deep."

But what he didn't know was that she already was in too deep. She was so fucking deep she was drowning. She'd wanted to be with Ty so badly she'd thrown caution to the wind. But for the first time, she saw it clearly—their relationship was not safe. It wasn't safe for her, or him. By being together, they'd been playing with fire, and soon enough, someone would get burned.

She had to be the logical one, the strong one. As much as it utterly killed her—broke her—she had to end this. For both their sakes.

"Ena, what are you saying?" he asked, his beautiful eyes filled with desperation.

"Ty." She looked at him, his face blurry because of the tears in her eyes. "It's not safe for us to be together—don't you see that? If I stay here, Cole will kill me. Even once you are king, I'll always be in danger from those who think like him. And maybe next time, they'll hurt you too."

Quiet rage filled Ty's eyes as he spoke. "I don't care if they hurt me, Ena. I've waited too long for you. I want you now. I want you every minute, of every day. I—" Ty swallowed, as if stopping himself from what he'd been about to say. "You're *mine*."

"I can't be yours, Ty," Ena said, tears sliding down her cheeks. "Not anymore."

Ty's face fell into his hands, and he held it there for several seconds.

Ena had to look away. It was too much. This was all too much. Her heart felt broken and shattered in her chest. Unfixable. Unrecoverable.

Part of her wanted to break, seeing his face like that, to turn to him, and hug him. Kiss him. Deny all of this. Take it all back. But she couldn't fucking *move*. Her wrist was broken, her face and ribs were broken. Her injuries were a visceral reminder of the consequences of their relationship, so she held her ground.

Because at least Ty would live. His people needed him as king. She saw the way they looked up to him, respected him. And if anyone could lead the daemons into a more peaceful accord with the witches and mortals, it would be Ty. He needed to live for her sake, but he needed to live for *them* most of all.

So she had to let him go.

"I'll come with you still, to break the bond, but then..." Her voice drifted off, small and quiet.

Why wasn't he saying anything? Why wasn't he arguing with her and telling her this wasn't the way? That they could figure something else out? Part of her desperately wanted that. If he fought her, if he argued and told her no, maybe she could give in. Maybe then she wouldn't have to do this.

But Ty was silent. She could just make out the sheen of tears in his eyes as he stood up, nodding his head. "Okay," was all he said.

Then he turned and walked out of the room, leaving Ena broken and alone on the bed.

CHAPTER TWENTY-SIX

Ty

TY CLOSED THE DOOR behind him, leaving his heart bloodied and still on the floor of his room. It was dead. It was gone. He'd all but felt it rip from his chest when Ena said she couldn't be *his* anymore.

But he didn't blame her. He only blamed himself.

Because he had failed to protect her. He'd listened to Cole and let himself be manipulated into leaving. He had abandoned her—again—and for that fact alone, he would never forgive himself. So why should she? There was no way he deserved to be with her after that.

And yes, he was furious at Cole and Iblis and the entire damned Underworld for dooming their relationship, but the worst part was, he understood. He understood everything she'd said to his very core. Because even if none of this had ever happened, he could never be what she needed. He couldn't keep her safe and be the heir that he needed to be for his people, to keep *them* safe, at the same time. And as much as he hated that fact—loathed it with his entire being, actually—he realized now that no matter how long he had spent denying it, it didn't change a thing.

He was the heir to the Underworld. Tiptoeing around it and pretending that it wasn't the case hadn't allowed him to keep her. He'd brought this on himself.

Ty wanted to rage. He wanted to fucking beat the absolute shit out of something, but his knuckles still throbbed from where he'd punched the cave wall earlier, and he physically couldn't handle more of that.

And besides, Ena might not be his anymore, but she still needed him. He may have failed to protect her, but he wouldn't keep putting her in danger now.

They needed to leave as soon as possible.

Ty took several long strides down the passageway when he saw Lara coming towards him, carrying the broth she had promised in her hands.

"Is everything okay?" she asked, her eyes filling with concern as they landed on him. His face must have looked just as grave as he felt inside. "Is Ena alright?"

"She's fine. I—I just need to go get Turner and Steig. Will you stay with her?" Ty's voice came out strained and thick, so he cleared his throat, but it didn't help. Lara was too quick.

"Ty, what happened?" she asked, her voice serious.

"Not now," Ty said. He couldn't talk about it right now. Iblis, he could barely even think right now, and he had things he needed to do. "Just...stay with her. Please?" His voice cracked on the last word, and he sounded pitiful even to his own ears, but Lara just nodded and didn't ask any more questions, carrying on down the passageway towards Ty's room.

First things first, he needed to get Turner and Steig, so he walked towards the king's kitchen, killing two birds with one stone, and asked an *imperi* to deliver a message to each of them, telling them to meet back at Ty's room as soon as possible.

After discussing his need for provisions with the head cook, explaining that he'd been sent on a last-minute mission from Cole, he went to Myka and did the same. He didn't like lying to them, but it was the safest thing for them if Cole were to try and blame them for aiding in his escape.

Nial would be a bit trickier, though.

Ty decided he couldn't leave Nial in possession of the books from Petyr. Iblis only knew what kind of rampage Cole would go on once he was gone, so he needed to protect those who'd helped him.

He found the old man stacking books in the far corner of the Archives. Nial's head swiveled to greet him, and a kindly smile lit up his face as Ty approached.

"Ah, Ty, what brings you here this time of night?" he asked.

"I, uh, need my private reserves," Ty replied, looking around to ensure they were alone, but the Archives were quiet as a grave.

"Of course," he said, seeming unperturbed by the late request. "I'll be right back," he added as he shuffled off to fetch the books.

When he returned, he handed the sack containing them to Ty.

"A bit late for reading, isn't it?" Nial asked, his voice solemn and pointed.

Ty gave the old man a sad smile. This was one man he couldn't fully hide the truth from. Not anymore. "I'm not planning to read them right now," Ty said seriously. "I'm going away."

The man's face fell as he nodded his understanding. He seemed saddened by the news but not surprised. It was as if he'd seen this coming. "I see," he said. "Well, I guess this is goodbye for now, then."

Ty nodded. "Thank you, Nial, for everything."

Nial shook his head. "I've done barely a thing, and it was my pleasure."

Ty gave a tight-lipped smile before turning to leave, but the man stopped him.

"Oh, and Ty?" the old man began. "You're doing the right thing. Everyone here will see that one day. There's no doubt in my mind—you're the king we need."

Ty felt all at once a relief and a crushing weight settle upon him. Did Nial somehow know what he was up to?

He stared at the man, trying to discern his meaning, but there was no time to ask those questions now. He needed to leave.

"I hope so," was all Ty said, feeling the pressure of his position more acutely than ever as he turned and left the Archives.

***

After tending to the last few necessary preparations, Ty returned to his room to find Steig and Turner already waiting inside with Lara and Ena.

They turned to him as he entered, but it was clear from the readiness in their faces that they'd already guessed why he'd summoned them.

"Thanks for coming so quickly," he said to his friends, avoiding looking at Ena where she sat on the bed. He couldn't handle that right now. "I couldn't explain in my message, but you've probably already guessed. It's time for us to leave."

"What did Cole say?" Steig asked, his dark brow furrowed as he crossed his arms.

"He's suspicious. He doesn't exactly know about the amulet, but he thinks I'm somehow using Ena to make a play for the throne."

"Paranoid bastard," Turner muttered, rolling his eyes. "Though I guess he's not *that* paranoid," he added, rubbing his chin. "We *are* trying to quietly overthrow him, just not that way."

"Exactly," Ty replied. "He's too close to the truth. That's why it's not safe for us here anymore, especially not for Ena." He'd been working hard to avoid looking at her and to keep his voice strong and steady, but he locked eyes with her now.

Her color had returned slightly, most likely thanks to the broth, but he didn't let his eyes linger on her injuries. Every second they did made him want to flay the skin from his own body just to dull the pain and regret inside him.

"Luckily, Ena figured out the remaining parts of the binding spell, so all we have to do now is recruit a witch from Aquilo and Occidens to do the spell, and we can reverse it."

"What? Really?" Lara asked, her voice turning hopeful as she looked at Ena. "You figured it out?"

Ena nodded in affirmation, a small proud smile on her face.

"I don't believe it," Lara said, smiling in relief and looking at Ty with awe. "You're actually going to break the bond."

"Yes," Ty assured her. "And that's exactly why Ena and I need to leave as soon as possible, preferably tonight if she can handle it. But I know it's sudden, and unsanctioned, so I won't ask any of you to come. Things will be complicated with Cole after this, so—"

"You can stop your little martyr speech right there, you fucker. I'm coming with you," Turner said, holding up his hand to stop Ty from speaking.

"Turner, are you sure?" Ty asked. "There will be repercussions for leaving the Underworld without his permission."

"Nope, don't care. Where else should your shadow be but by your side?" Turner asked, grinning teasingly.

Despite everything that had happened, Ty smiled, and a small warmth spread through him. He clapped his cousin on the shoulder, unable to adequately express the relief and gratitude he felt knowing he and Ena wouldn't be alone in this. That he'd have his friend by his side too.

"Thank you, brother," he said solemnly.

Then his eyes landed on Steig.

The man had been his best friend for almost twenty years; he could read him like a book. Underneath his grumpy and gruff exterior, the man was soft. He felt everything—too much sometimes—and right now, Ty could tell he felt conflicted as hell.

Steig looked over at Lara, who grabbed his hand and squeezed it before bringing it to her lips for a kiss. "It's okay, Steig," she said quietly, sadly. "We'll be fine."

He shook his head. "No, no," he said, turning to Ty. "Ty, I'm sorry. You know I wish I could go with you, but I can't leave my family. Not again. And as much as I want you to succeed, someone needs to be here. To protect those you're leaving behind."

Ty could hear the strain in his voice and see the conflict on his face. The two of them had always done everything together, for as long as he could remember. But as much as he wanted his best friend by his side, the man was right. Those they were leaving behind, like Lara and the kids, Nial, Myka—anyone who was loyal to Ty—were vulnerable to Cole, and someone needed to stay behind to protect them.

He looked his friend in the eye as he grasped his shoulder firmly. "I understand, Steig. That's the right call."

Steig looked relieved and grasped him back, pulling him into a hug. The two of them embraced, and Ty tried not to think about what this meant—that he was saying goodbye and didn't know when he'd be able to return. He clasped his friend harder to him—hoping he knew without words what he meant to him, and how hard it was to part ways.

When they finally released each other, Ty turned to Lara.

"Keep each other and the kids safe, okay?"

Lara nodded and gave him a reassuring smile before grasping her husband's hand once more. If there was anyone Ty trusted to see through Cole's manipulations and keep him in check, it was Lara. She'd been dealing with the bastard her whole life.

"I've made preparations for us to leave under the cover of night once the timekeepers come. Ena," he said, addressing her for the first time, all businesslike. There was no room for anything else right now. "Do you think you're up for it?"

She shifted slightly where she sat on the bed, pushing herself up. "I have to be," she said. "I don't want to stay here."

Her voice was firm. It was clear her decision was made, and Ty didn't fault her. Everything that had happened, everything he'd *let* happen, had clearly traumatized her, and the thought of that brought another wave of crushing grief through him.

"Okay," he said, nodding confidently, as if his heart wasn't shattered. "Then we'll pack and leave in an hour. Turner—meet us at the entrance."

The man nodded before approaching Steig and pulling him in for a hug, too, followed by Lara. "Stay safe and don't do anything I wouldn't do," he said to them, winking.

Lara snorted. "Can't promise that. You'd never fuck my husband," she said lightly.

Turner laughed, pulling her in tighter.

When they finally released each other, Turner took his leave, followed by Steig, who insisted he needed to get back to the kids. Lara stayed a bit longer to help

Ena get in the bath and wash away whatever blood still remained, before checking her bandages and helping her pack a bag.

Ty packed his own bags, fitting his weapons and books in with his clothes and travel supplies as efficiently as possible. He really didn't know how long he'd be gone, so it was hard to prepare.

But there was one final thing they couldn't forget.

Digging into the trunk at the foot of his bed, he pulled out the wooden box, locked with Ena's magic, that contained the amulet. Walking over to where Ena stood, somewhat shakily, folding her clothing, he handed it to her.

"Figured you should keep this with you," he said.

"Okay," she said, taking the box from him and slipping it into her bag. She avoided eye contact, but he couldn't tell if she was just tired, or still angry, or sad, or what. He wanted to ask her how she was feeling. Was she okay? Was she dying inside like him? Did every breath of hers hurt too? But he didn't think he should do that—she'd told him it was over, and he needed to respect that.

Just then, the door cracked open as a timekeeper walked in, their large black hood obscuring their features. Ignoring Ena and Ty, as was the custom, they one by one extinguished the darkrock lanterns that lined the walls, slowly darkening the room until only one remained.

"Not that one please," Ty requested. "I still have some things to attend to."

The timekeeper nodded their head solemnly before exiting the room.

Ty turned to Ena. "One more thing before we go," he said as he approached her cautiously. "Let's get this collar off you."

Ena looked down at her *imperae* collar, stroking it gently with her fingers as if she'd forgotten it was there.

Ty reached up behind her neck, pulling the pliant metal apart and sliding it forward off her delicate neck. Her pale skin was still mottled with bruising, and he had to swallow the rage that bubbled in him at the sight.

He put the collar down on the table and turned to her once more. "Ready?" he asked.

"Always," she said, determination filling her eyes.

There's my viper, he thought, the sentiment automatic. But with a heart-wrenching jolt, he had to remind himself that she wasn't *his* anything anymore.

CHAPTER TWENTY-SEVEN

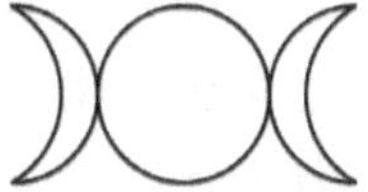

Ena

ENA FOLLOWED TY THROUGH the winding passageways of the Underworld one final time. Her whole body was sore and felt weak, so she had to go slowly, but luckily, her legs were unharmed and she had no trouble walking. Her broken wrist, however, throbbed with every step, and each breath she took made her ribs ache. At least she could crack her other eye to see out of now, though it was still difficult due to the swelling around her broken cheekbone.

Together, they made their way up the long staircase towards the Underworld's entrance. Ty carried their saddlebags and held a lone, dim lantern in front of them so they could find their way through the dark—all the lanterns on the walls had been extinguished by the timekeepers, but it had the advantage of cloaking their escape. Even without the light, Ena could tell they were going the right way, because with each step they took, the air became fresher—cooler.

She'd been underground for almost a month and hadn't realized how much she'd missed it—the smell of fresh air, the feeling of the breeze on her face. She was suddenly so eager to see the sky again that she started walking faster, but she couldn't maintain that for very long and soon had to stop and take a break.

Ty didn't say a word, just let her set the pace with a look of constant concern on his face, stopping whenever she stopped, and going again when she moved. She was glad for that. As painful as her body was, her heart was worse. She could barely stand to look at him, let alone speak, so she accepted their silence with gratitude.

Eventually, they crested the top of the staircase, and relief filled her to find Turner waiting just outside the entrance with three horses and several saddlebags of his own.

As they stepped out of the Underworld to join him, Ena's gaze instantly went to the sky. It was clear, displaying the millions of tiny stars that were scattered across it, gathered like an awestruck audience around the full moon.

She took a deep breath—the first one she'd taken in over a month, it felt like. The cold air filled her lungs so deep it almost burned, and she relished every second of it.

As if unleashing something within her, her Knowing suddenly came alive again. After weeks underground, her world was filled once more with signs of life, and she was almost overwhelmed by all the things she Knew at once.

The wind blew sharp across the landscape, rustling the scrubby plants that dotted the rocky ground. She

Knew the soil here was lacking in certain nutrients, making the plants brittle and dwarfed.

She heard a coyote yip in the distance and Knew that it was out hunting the jackrabbits whose scat she could see on the ground by her feet.

She Knew the jackrabbits must be nearby, too, because the scat was fresh and filled with half-digested remnants of the sage plants she could smell surrounding them.

She hadn't realized how much she'd missed it all, how suppressed that side of her had been these last few weeks. She wanted to just stand there and take everything in, but Ty pulled her attention from it all as he guided her to her horse.

Time was still of the essence.

She turned to look at Turner, giving him a nod in silent greeting as Ty began quickly attaching their saddlebags to the horses. It was dark, and she didn't think they'd alerted anyone to their exit, but there was no way to know for sure. She found herself glancing behind them every few seconds, watching and waiting for signs of pursuit.

When Ty was finished, he turned to her expectantly, extending his hand to assist her in mounting up. Their eyes locked, and her instinct was to smile at him, but then she remembered—how he'd hidden things from her again, how they couldn't be together, because he had responsibilities that came before her, and how their relationship wasn't *safe* for either of them, and her smile faltered.

Vaguely, she wondered how many times, how many tiny realizations like this, it would take before it stopped hurting so deeply each time.

Ty sensed her hesitation and clearly thought better of touching her, so he backed away. The sad look on his face almost broke her heart all over again.

"Turner, can you...?" he asked quietly, gesturing at Ena.

Turner's eyebrows flew up in shock at the interaction that passed between them. Had Ty not said anything to him yet?

Turner didn't ask any questions, though, he just moved swiftly to her side and picked her up gently by the waist, placing her sidesaddle on the horse, then held her steady while she swung her leg over and grabbed the reins one-handed.

She was pleasantly surprised to find herself atop Mahnin—the beautiful black mare that was a favorite of hers. She hadn't gotten to ride her solo yet, and her heart warmed a tiny bit at the thought. Had Ty given her the mare on purpose?

"You feel alright?" Turner asked in a hushed tone, drawing her attention from the horse. "You feel steady enough with one hand?"

"Yes," Ena replied. Truthfully, even if she hadn't, she wouldn't have admitted it. She needed to be on her own horse right now. She needed to be in control, and she needed to leave this place, and all the painful memories it now held.

Turner nodded and mounted up, taking her at her word, and the three of them rode single file out of the pass through the mountains, away from the Under-world.

***

They rode in silence, retracing the path they'd taken to get here all those weeks ago. Every step away from the Underworld let Ena breathe a little easier, and as the sun came up, despite starting to feel tired and pained, she found herself profoundly relieved to be away and no longer under Cole's thumb.

It was midmorning by the time they reached the waterfall cave they'd rendezvoused with Turner and Steig at. They didn't go inside, instead just making a quick stop to water the horses and eat some breakfast, and Ena was glad for that.

If she went inside, she'd have to relive the memories of her and Ty together that night by the fire. She'd have to remember how they'd touched each other secretly, and the way his beautiful confession had made her feel so incredibly hopeful.

That hope was gone now. Her only focus was breaking the bond and getting back to her Coven—to her sister and Heran, where she could be safe.

Ena was leaning back against a tree, trying to ignore the throbbing, aching pain of her still-healing arm and eating some jerky, when Ty approached her cautiously. He gestured at Turner, who was eating an apple a few feet away, to join them, and addressed them both.

"It's time we make a plan for what comes next," he said, assuming the role of leader, as he naturally did. "I've been using my *venator* to listen for any signs of pursuit, but haven't heard anything, so either Cole hasn't realized we're gone yet, or has decided not to come after us right now. Either way, we need to make moves to reverse the binding spell as quickly as possible, and that starts with recruiting witches from Aquilo and Occidens. Now, if you two are okay with it, I think we should head to Aquilo first, since we're closest to it. But after that...well, I think you'll be our best shot at making friends there, Ena, so I want to know what you think." He looked at her, a pain in his beautiful eyes that she hated to see, but knew was necessary. Still, she had to look away to hide the answering yearning in her own eyes before she responded.

"I've been thinking about that, and yes, I have a friend in Aquilo who will be a good place to start. Maybe...I can try to get a message to him, to see if he can meet with us."

She didn't miss the way Ty's eyes turned hard as ice at the use of the male pronouns.

"And who exactly is this...friend?" he asked, trying for nonchalance, but Ena saw right through him, and if her face still didn't hurt so bad, she would've rolled her eyes.

"He's just a friend," she said, trying to sound reassuring. "His name's Cris. We've known each other since childhood, and since we can't afford to be choosy about our allies, I'd say he's our best option."

Did she neglect to tell him that she and Cris had hooked up on and off for a few years and almost had sex at the Samhain celebration last year? Yes, of course. He didn't need to know that—it would only complicate things. She and Cris had never officially been in a relationship anyway; it was always casual, at least from Ena's point of view.

"Cris, as in the boy you danced with at Litha all those years ago?" Ty asked, his dark eyebrows raising.

Fuck. So much for keeping that information to herself. Did the man remember everything?

Ena cleared her throat awkwardly. "Yes, one and the same. I'm surprised you remember that."

"I told you, I never forgot." His stare was intense, filled with so much that neither of them could say, and Ena had to look away, breaking their eye contact by focusing on her jerky instead.

Thank Gaia for Turner, who chose this opportune moment to chime in.

"I'm on board with this plan, but how will you get the message to him?"

"I don't know exactly. Maybe I could use my Gift to sneak into his house and leave him a note, ask him to meet me somewhere safe to talk? He lives with his brothers, so I'll have to get around them, but that's the best I can think of right now."

"That could work," Turner replied, nodding as he contemplated her plan. "But what will you...say? You know, once we meet with him, to convince him to help us."

"I don't know," Ena said, sighing. "Witches are taught from such a young age to be mistrustful of daemons, so it won't be easy. I'm just sort of...hoping that part will work itself out."

Turner snorted. "Barely a plan in place for an absolute long shot. We certainly are a delusional bunch. What do you think, Ty?" he added, looking over at Ty where he stood, his body now backlit by the rising sun as it crested over the mountains.

"It's a good plan," Ty replied gently, nodding at Ena. "But no, I don't think we're delusional for having hope," he said, looking at Turner. "Sometimes hope is the only thing we have, and personally, I've never regretted living for it."

Ty walked away to mount up, his words still echoing through Ena's head, and together they rode on, clinging to their slivers of hope.

CHAPTER TWENTY-EIGHT

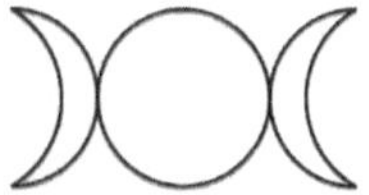

Ena

THEY KEPT THE PACE reasonable for Ena's sake and she appreciated it. She was still incredibly sore and the constant jostling from the horse was uncomfortable, but at least she was sitting down, so she counted that among her blessings from Gaia.

The greater blessing, though, was that the further they got from the Chasm Mountains—traveling inland towards the Aquilo Coven—the more the trees began to come back. Ena felt increasingly at home amongst the evergreen and deciduous mix as the landscape became more forested and familiar. There were squirrels, and birds she recognized, and it soothed her broken heart to be with them again.

Ty said they were only a few days out from Aquilo. Ena had visited their Coven many times over the years, but she'd never realized how close it was to the entrance of the Underworld—although she supposed there was no way she could have known that, given how intentionally secretive the daemons were about it.

The three of them fell into a routine over the next few days—riding during the day, setting up camp at night. She was grateful she'd packed two cloaks, because winter had deeply set in while she'd been underground, and although there wasn't currently snow on the ground, she Knew it could fall at any time.

Ena found herself mostly riding next to Turner or by herself during the day, for obvious reasons, but when they were on their last day of travel, Mahnin got distracted by some delicious ferns, and Ena found herself falling back next to Ty.

She figured it would be rude to make her horse speed up just to get away from him, so she lingered, but Gaia, just being near him was hard. Hearing his breathing, the way his body moved, the way he sat stoically upon his horse, rocking side to side with its motion. Every single thing about him made her heart ache for what she couldn't have. She was sad about it, obviously, but more than that, it made her mad—so fucking mad—and that was an emotion she wasn't really used to.

It made her want to lash out and yell at him, or entertain fantasies of riding back to the Underworld and stabbing Cole through the gut with a sword, as if it were all his fault that Ty was the heir and they couldn't be together. Which, if she were being honest, she knew it wasn't. It wasn't Ty's fault either. It was no one's, and that made it all the more hard to bear. And while she knew she should just focus on the task ahead of them, and look forward to reuniting with her Coven, being near him like this—all the fucking time—made it almost impossible to do.

The two of them had been riding in silence for a while, Turner several horse lengths ahead of them, when Ty finally spoke.

"How are you feeling?" he asked, the sound of his deep voice startling Ena.

She looked over at where he sat atop his horse, his gaze appraising her as she rode. "Everything still hurts," she said. "But it's better than it was."

"Good," he said, returning his eyes forward. "If it's ever too much and you want a longer break, just let me know, okay?"

"Okay," she replied.

"I know that you...that we..." he began awkwardly. "I just want you to know, I heard you, before we left the Underworld, and I understand."

"You understand?" she asked, confusion filling her. Part of her was glad he understood and didn't blame her for ending things between them, but another irrational part wasn't sure if she wanted him to understand. Part of her, the weaker part, wanted him to fight, to tell her this wasn't the way, and make her take it all back.

"I do," he said slowly, as if choosing his words carefully. "You were right. I can't protect you *and* serve my people. I know that I failed you. I just want you to know that I'm sorry, and I understand."

Failed her? Is that what he thought? She didn't see it that way. No one could reasonably be expected to protect her in those circumstances, with so many enemies, and so much threatening both of them.

"Ty, you didn't fail—"

Just then, a loud boom of thunder sounded, and the sky opened up as large, wet flakes of snow began to fall. Ena released her one-handed hold on the reins to pull her cloak hood up, shielding her head from the onslaught.

"I'm gonna ride ahead and scout for a good place to camp," Ty said, and without preamble, he kicked his horse into a trot, leaving Ena behind, wondering what the fuck had just happened.

Turner fell back beside her, a questioning look on his face. "What was that about?" he asked, the snow layering in his dirty-blond hair.

Ena sighed, feeling both annoyed and confused by that interaction with Ty. But she supposed it was time that someone told Turner what had happened.

"Before we left the Underworld, we sort of...broke up," she said. Ena was surprised to find that a lump immediately filled her throat at the words, as if her body rejected them, and she had to look down at her hands to hide the tears that filled her eyes.

"I deduced that," Turner said gently. "Do you want to tell me why? You guys seemed so..."

"We were," Ena said, cutting him off before she could hear him fully describe the way they'd been. "But, we realized—*I* realized—that it can't last because he's the heir. There's no way we can be together in the Underworld forever. It's not safe for either of us."

"I see," Turner said, his face grave. "You know, he didn't exactly choose it. Being the heir, I mean."

"I know," Ena said. The concept was still new to her—how someone could be born to this role, rather than chosen—but she understood. "But it doesn't matter. It's what he is, and he can't change it. I see how much the Underworld needs him, and how important it is to him to take care of them, so...I just...I have to let him go. Let *us* go. I see that now," she said, attempting to sound stoic, but her voice wobbled slightly.

"And you think you can? Just let him go?" Turner asked sincerely.

"I don't know, but I'm trying," Ena said quietly. "And I have responsibilities, too, to my family, and my Coven, that I need to uphold, so I'm trying to focus on that. Because doing this, breaking the bond, there's a good chance I'll face some negative consequences from that decision."

"You and me both," Turner said.

And Ena was glad for that window, because she was more than happy to change the topic off of her and Ty and onto Turner.

"Now that you mention it, why did you leave?" she asked. "I mean, I know you wanted to help Ty and that you believe in what we're doing. But don't you have responsibilities, too, with the *imperi*?"

"It's exactly those responsibilities that I'm running from, if I'm being honest," he said, giving her a sheepish look.

"What do you mean? Why?"

"I don't know how much Ty explained to you about what I do, and what my father does, for the *imperi*."

"Not much," she said. "Just that you were in charge of them."

"Yeah, I guess you could put it that way," he replied ruefully. "The truth is, sometimes that means keeping track of them and their health—under the magic of the *imperae* collar, they often don't take very good care of themselves. But, sometimes my father gave me other...tasks. I've had to do a lot of things I'm not proud of."

Ena paused, wondering if she should push further. But if she knew Turner—and at this point she thought she did know him at least reasonably well—he was hurting, and it seemed like maybe he wanted to open up to her.

"What kind of things?" she asked gently.

"Well," he sighed. "Cole is a suspicious bastard, as you probably already know. He would often force a daemon into an *imperae* collar for almost no reason at all. But it was our job, mine and my father's, to extract information from them. To figure out if they were plotting against him."

"You mean you..."

"Tortured them. Yes. My father would ask them questions, and if he sensed a lie—any lie at all—that was license to punish them, so it was my job to...cause pain, with my Power." Turner looked down, guilt and shame written across his face in a way she'd never seen.

"Why?" Ena was horrified to learn this. "Wouldn't the collar make them tell you anything you wanted anyway? Why did you need to cause them pain?"

Ena saw him wince at her reaction, and she felt horrible.

"Let me rephrase that. Turner, it is *not* your fault that you were forced to do those things. You didn't choose that. I saw your father, and Cole, and the way they manipulate with the power they have to get others to do things they don't want or like. It's not your fault—do you hear me?"

Turner looked at her, an immense guilt behind his eyes. "Thanks, Ena, for saying that."

She didn't miss the way he refused to agree with her, but she didn't know what else to say to convince him.

"And to answer your question, no, the *imperae* collar makes them open to suggestion and takes away their fight, but they can still lie, if they choose to, and some are better at resisting the collar's magic than others, so Cole never trusted anything they told us, unless they were consistent under physical pain and in the face of my father's magic."

"I'm so, so sorry you were forced to do that," Ena said. She wanted to reach across their horses and grab his hand, to show him she didn't judge him. She'd experienced firsthand the way Cole could manipulate situations to make someone do something they didn't want.

"Yeah, well...that's why I'm glad to be done with that place. I would've burned it down if I could, but..." He looked ahead of them to where Ty rode on his horse. "One day, Ty will be king, and I want to see what that looks like."

Ena gave him a small smile, but inside, another piece of her died hearing that. Because it was yet another reminder of how needed Ty was, and why he couldn't be *hers*—he belonged to them all.

CHAPTER TWENTY-NINE

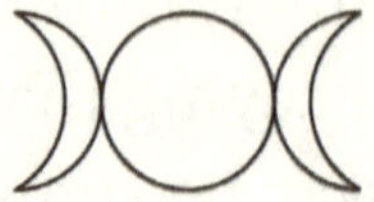

Ena

THE FOLLOWING DAY, WITH a fresh inch of snow on the ground, the three of them finally joined the Chasm Road about a mile from Aquilo.

The road was familiar to Ena, but she found herself on edge nonetheless. It was possible, now, that she could run into someone she knew—surrounding villagers that recognized her, or Aquilo witches that knew her. Though, blessedly, Yule had just passed, so without any other major celebrations in the Turning approaching, she didn't expect to see any members of her own Coven. Either way, she rode with her hood up just in case, hiding her bruised face in its shadow.

They'd decided to assume their usual cover as metal goods traders to gain access to the village, but it was tougher than visiting a mortal village, because the witches did not host visitors at guesthouses. Visitors instead had to camp in the surrounding area and then petition the matriarch to approve their trade request. And given the cold, visitors were fewer and farther between this time of year, so they really had to do their best not to stand out.

They decided that, since Ena could not show her face to Northe, the Aquilo matriarch, whom she'd met many times before, that Ty and Turner would go to petition her for a trade to maintain their cover while she snuck into Cris's house to leave the message.

When they got close to the village, they veered off the road into the woods, heading for a good camping spot Ena remembered from her childhood. While the Aquilo Coven didn't have access to a large river like the River Wry, there were plenty of smaller streams that flowed across the landscape, and Ena led Ty and Turner towards one in particular that passed by an old, gnarled oak tree that she and Cris used to climb as children.

After breaking for food, the three of them left their horses tethered and walked on foot towards the village, Ena's stomach twisting with every step.

She knew she would have to use her Gift to safely get a message to Cris without being recognized, but that didn't mean she had to like it. She didn't relish taking away someone's free will, and even though losing herself to the thrall of her Gift somehow deeply satisfied the part of her which craved losing control, she knew that afterwards she would inevitably carry some guilt.

As they approached the main pathway leading through the village, Ena left the men with a nod. She noticed a slight look of trepidation on Ty's face, but to his credit, he didn't say anything—he simply continued on with Turner towards the matriarch's house, leaving her to her own devices.

Ena veered left, down a less significant path towards a smaller house on the edge of the village, one she was intimately familiar with.

The house used to be Cris's parents, but they'd relinquished it to their three grown boys around the time they'd all received their Gifts. It was an older house, and in need of some repairs—some of the stones were crumbling and the roof had significantly more moss than was ideal—but it was cozy and welcoming regardless, just as Ena remembered it.

Walking up the garden path, she heard voices inside. Two of them, both male.

She knew that Cris's Gift of *calor* would be in high demand this time of year—he would be needed to warm the barns for animals, or assist the elderly with inadequate hearths, so he would, in all likelihood, not be home. The voices she'd heard must have been his brothers.

Attempting to look casual, she approached their weather-beaten front door and knocked.

The voices inside stopped and the door opened to reveal Cris's younger brother. He looked similar to Cris, with pale-blond hair and light-blue eyes, only he was shorter and thinner than Cris was. His brow furrowed as recognition warred with his surprise over seeing Ena, and most likely confusion over the state of her face too.

He opened his mouth, but Ena didn't give him a chance to speak.

The use of her Gift was so practiced now, she barely had to concentrate. It flowed through her, like her Knowing, always ready to be tapped into. Using it felt like second nature as she reached for the thread connecting her mind to Cris's brother's, the channel between them, and spoke.

{*Step aside and let me in. Then forget you saw me.*}

Her *visanis* compelled him, and he did as he was told, stepping aside to let her through the doorway.

Ena stepped into the warmth of their hearth room, looking around to take stock of her surroundings. The house was mostly one large room, with a sofa and two chairs clustered around the fireplace on one side, and the kitchen area occupying the other.

Ena noticed some discarded knitting on the sofa, presumably belonging to the brother she'd already seen, but where was the other one, the older one she'd heard him talking to?

She used her Knowing to assess her surroundings for signs of him.

There was a pot of something simmering on the hearth in the kitchen, and a knife laying on the counter, as if someone had been recently chopping, but no one else was in sight.

Then she heard it: a small creak of the floorboards just outside of her vision. She turned her head just as the man gripped her wrist roughly.

"What did you do to my brother?" he asked, his face a mixture of confusion and wariness. Ena almost pitied him. *Almost.* She knew what her Gift must look like from the outside, but she was done having her safety threatened in any way.

{*Let go.*}

He immediately released her.

{*You never saw me here. Continue with whatever you were doing.*}

Cris's older brother furrowed his brow, as if something had been right in front of him but suddenly disappeared. He shook off his confusion and wandered back into the kitchen, picking up his knife.

"Was someone at the door?" he looked up to ask his brother.

"No. Must've been the wind," the younger one replied as he sat back down on the sofa and picked up his knitting.

If Ena's heart hadn't been beating so hard with adrenaline, she would've taken a moment to be impressed with herself, but she didn't want to count her blessings. She needed to leave her message and get out as soon as possible.

She moved to the back of the house and down the narrow, dark hallway which led to the bedrooms on either side. Locating the familiar door at the back of the house, she opened it into Cris's room.

It was dark, with only one window, and there was no fireplace in his room, but she knew that since receiving his Gift, that probably wasn't a problem for him. He used to have to use a bedwarmer, and she remembered sitting on his bed talking late into the night, being careful not to kick it lest she burn herself.

She moved to his desk in the corner of the room, which contained some scraps of paper. Cris liked to draw, but the disorganization of his desk always shocked her—and little had changed in that regard, since it currently contained dozens of half-finished charcoal drawings and as many charcoal sticks, most of them worn down to the nub.

Her eye caught on one drawing in particular, however. It was placed at the back of his desk, leaning against the wall and held into an upright position with an empty candlestick holder. She recognized it immediately.

It was her. She remembered the day he drew it, when they'd been outside mushroom hunting and playing around. They'd practically been children then, maybe just fourteen or so. It was long before she'd met Ty, and the drawing showed her as she had been then—her hair was down her back as she crouched, reaching for a mushroom on the ground. Her face was out of view, but he'd spent an extraordinarily long time sketching her hands as they'd stretched for the mushroom.

Ena was awed that he'd kept it so long, and in such a place of honor on his desk. There were no other drawings on display except that one, and a crinkled one of a cat. She didn't quite know what to make of that, but she didn't have time to focus on it right now.

Instead, she grabbed a mostly unused scrap of paper and charcoal stick and scribbled her message.

Cris-

I need your help. Meet me tonight by the oak tree—you know the one. But please, keep this message and our meeting a secret. I'll explain everything when I see you.

Ena

She left the note in the middle of his unkempt bed, hoping he'd notice it right away when he returned, then she slipped out of his room.

She passed the two brothers, still focused on their tasks and unaware of her presence, as she quickly made her way to the front door. Cautiously stepping back out into the cold, she assessed her surroundings, assuring herself that no one had seen her come and go, before heading back to their campsite.

She hoped against all odds that Cris would believe the note—that he'd recognize her handwriting and come as she'd asked—but something about the way that drawing was displayed made her realize...maybe dragging Cris into all this would be more complicated than she originally thought.

Chapter Thirty

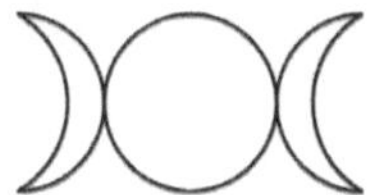

Ena

ENA MADE HER WAY back to their camp but found it unoccupied upon her return. Figuring Ty and Turner must've still been waiting to speak to the matriarch, she began collecting downed sticks and branches and used her spellword to start a fire. She sat next to it to absorb its warmth, listening to the nearby stream trickle as she ate some food and rested.

Sometime around sunset, Ty and Turner returned. Her eyes were drawn by the shuffling of their feet through the snow, and her stupid heart leaped automatically when she saw Ty.

The way he walked, so assured and in control, drew her to him—but it was painful too. Painful to see him, want him, and not be able to have him.

His gaze met hers, his light-green eyes reflecting extra light from the layer of snow around them, glowing, and she forced herself to look away, remembering what he'd said to her the last time they'd spoken alone. How he felt like he'd failed her. She didn't know how to even begin to fix that perception, or if she even should. Did it matter if they were on the same page about why exactly they couldn't be together? What was most important was that they couldn't. End of story.

Not for the first time, Ena loathed how complicated this all was. But one day, she knew, it would be over. They'd break the bond...and then go their separate ways, and the sudden thought of that wrenched Ena's heart so painfully that she almost clutched at it.

And suddenly, as much as it ached not being with him, she found herself grateful for it. Because at least, for now, she still got to be near him.

Facing the fire again, she cleared her throat before speaking to Turner as he joined her by the fire. "How did it go with the matriarch?" she asked.

"Good," he said. "She was open to looking at the goods we have to trade in exchange for some additional supplies and potions."

She looked over to see Ty checking on the horses where they were tethered several feet away, stroking one of their necks gently. Why wasn't he coming over? Didn't he want to hear about how things had gone at Cris's house?

"How did it go leaving the message?" Turner asked, drawing her attention back to him and away from what she couldn't have.

"Fine," she replied. "No issues, and I left the note, so only time will tell if he—"

A branch snapped in the distance, but Ena could tell it hadn't come from Ty or the horses—neither of whom had moved.

Ty looked over at them both with a clear warning in his eyes. He could hear with his *venator*—someone was coming.

Ena stood up as Ty moved over to join them by the fire. Was it Cris coming? Or someone else?

After a few seconds, Ena heard more movement from the dark of the woods until she could make out a figure approaching through the dim evening light. The orange flames of their fire lit upon a head of pale-blond hair, and she let out her breath.

It was Cris. He'd actually come.

"Cris!" she said, approaching him, relief and tension surging through her all at once.

"Ena!" he said, his eyes finally finding her in the dark. He rushed towards her as if to hug her, but paused, his pale-blue eyes going round as saucers as he took in her appearance. "Gaia, Ena, what happened to you? Are you alright?"

She looked up at him. He was tall—not as tall as Ty or Turner, but she still had to angle her neck to meet his gaze. He looked healthy and good, and part of her hesitated yet again. Was this the right thing? Bringing him into this? She sighed, steeling herself, because deep down, she knew there was no other option.

"I'm fine," she replied, trying for a reassuring smile. "It's good to see you."

"You too," he said, grasping her upper arms and pulling her in for a hug.

She saw Ty move closer to them out of the corner of her eye, but Turner gave them space, lingering back by the fire.

"What's going on?" Cris asked when he released her, his voice concerned. "I got your note, and I didn't tell anyone, just like you asked, but last I heard, you'd been taken by..." His voice trailed off as he looked over her shoulder to where Ty stood ominously behind her, as if truly noticing him and Turner for the first time.

Cris pulled her a few steps away, and Ena went with him willingly, knowing that Ty would still be able to hear them regardless.

"Who are these men you're with? Ena—are you safe?" Cris whispered.

"Cris, slow down," she said, trying to be reassuring. "Yes, I'm safe with them. I'm fine. I know the...bruises and everything look bad, but they're not because of these men at all. That was...someone else."

Cris nodded, seeming slightly reassured, but still thoroughly confused. "Then where have you been? Why aren't you with your Coven?" he asked, his voice still hushed.

"Cris," she began, reaching out to touch his arm in a friendly way. "Thank you so much for coming." She felt like this was an important thing to start with. It really did mean a lot that he'd come. She couldn't imagine the rumors that must be spreading about her after everything that had happened on Samhain when she was taken. "I know you have questions, and I want to explain them all to you. Can we sit by the fire?"

"With them?" he asked, eyeing them suspiciously. "Ena, please tell me they're mortals."

She sighed. She knew this would be incredibly tough for him to understand, and she didn't even know where to start, but she figured the truth was a good bet.

"They're not mortals, they're daemons. And yes, what I have to tell you concerns them, and all of us—witches, daemons, *and* mortals. I know this is...a lot. I'm so sorry to dump this on you out of the blue. But I need your help. Will you listen to me?"

Cris hesitated, looking between her and the daemons. She wanted to elbow Ty in the stomach and tell him to wipe the threatening look off his face, because it definitely wasn't helping. But Cris was clearly intrigued enough, or trusted her enough, because he gave her a small nod.

"Okay," he said. "I'll listen."

He walked with her over to the fire and the two of them sat down. Turner threw a couple more logs onto the blaze, but they didn't catch right away because of how soggy and cold everything was.

Looking up at Ena pointedly, Turner reached out, touching the fresh logs with his hands as he called upon his Power. His hands began to glow a deep red, and the logs smoked for a few seconds until they finally burst into hearty flames.

"Whoa," Cris said, watching it. He eyed Turner curiously, cautiously. "I've never seen anything like that. I guess that's your..."

"Power," Turner finished for him. "Yes."

"I see," Cris responded suspiciously, clearly trying to process all this information without freaking out. "And what can he do?" he asked, nodding towards Ty, who thus far refused to sit and was standing by the fire with his arms crossed like a hellhound guarding the entrance to the Underworld.

"You don't want to know," Ty replied, in what was quite possibly the least friendly tone she'd ever heard him use—including when he'd pretended not to know who she was and kidnapped her.

Ena had to hold back her eye roll.

"Okay..." Cris said, mistrust in his voice.

She needed to rescue this situation—fast.

"Cris, look," she began. "I'm about to tell you something that you might not believe at first, but I want you to remember that you know me. I'm not a liar, and I'm not a fool."

"Of course I know that, Ena," he said, reaching out to take her hand. "I may not trust them at all, but I'm here, I'm listening."

Ena felt comforted by her friend's presence, and his willingness to listen, so she began.

"The things we've been taught about daemons aren't true," she began. "Well, some of them are true, but not all of them."

Cris was quiet, his brow furrowed as he listened, but he didn't ask any questions, so Ena continued.

"Before I was...taken by these daemons, Heran told me that daemons and witches actually come from the same source of magic. That Gaia and Iblis came together to grant us our magic, and that some Gifts and Powers can be shared among them. Did you know that?"

"No," Cris said, shaking his head in confusion. "But I did hear about your unusual Gift. Thyla told me on

Samhain, before Heran's house caught fire and you disappeared."

"Yes, exactly. It's because of this shared source of magic that I have my Gift. But there's more... The split we've been told about, the fact that daemons chose to serve Iblis and not Gaia, is a lie. They didn't choose to serve Iblis alone, they were forced."

"Forced?" Cris asked, scoffing. "Who could possibly force them?"

"Witches," Ty said from where he stood, raising an eyebrow in challenge at her friend.

"Witches forced them to serve Iblis? You really expect me to believe that?" Cris said mockingly.

"I had a vision," Ena said, drawing his attention back to her. "From Gaia. I saw the past. The witches used a magical amulet to bind the daemons to Iblis and cut them off from Gaia's magic. And Heran confirmed it. It's the truth."

"You're serious?" Cris asked, his face turning grave. "You really received a vision from Gaia?"

Ena nodded, pleased that she seemed to be getting through to him.

"Why in the Underworld would witches even do that?"

"Because they didn't trust us," Ty chimed in again. "And they wanted to maintain their power over the mortal villages."

Ena could see that Cris's immediate reaction was to defend witches as he opened his mouth, and she didn't want this to deteriorate, so she gave Ty a shut-the-fuck-up look and drew Cris's attention back to her. "Look, I know this is hard to believe. But I saw it, and Heran confirmed it. It was witches who forced daemons into the Underworld."

"Okay... Say I believe you," Cris began. "That doesn't erase all the evil things daemons have done—disrupting the balance, killing, thieving, destroying. Maybe they do deserve to be there."

Ty chuckled, low and menacing.

"What?" Cris asked, looking up at him with hatred in his eyes. "You disagree?"

"Would it surprise you if I said no?" Ty replied, staring daggers at the man.

"Yes, actually," Cris replied matter-of-factly.

"Look, no one here would deny that daemons have done some bad things," Ena said, once again chiming in to keep the tone civil. "But there are many in the Underworld who want things to be different."

"Different how?" Cris asked, his curiosity piqued.

Ena took a deep breath. This was big—revealing their plans to someone else, to another witch who could run and tell his matriarch and spoil everything. But it needed to be done—they needed his help—so she took a leap of faith.

"Different like break the bond to Iblis and allow them to access Gaia's magic once more."

They all fell silent as they watched Cris take in this revelation.

"That's..." he began, shaking his head. "How would you even do that?"

Ena stood up and went to her saddlebag, pulling out the wooden box inside. Focusing her Knowing on the metal mechanisms, she spoke her spellword to unlock it.

{*Clavis*}

Slowly, she raised the lid, holding the open box towards Cris. "With this," she said.

Cris's eyebrows flew up as he looked at it. The deep-purple amethyst glowed in the firelight, and the silver setting seemed to shine like new, despite its age. Ena knew that, like her, Cris could sense the power rolling off it.

"Where did you...? How...?" Cris seemed floored.

"The Occidens Coven had it, but that's a story for another time." Ena closed the lid on the amulet, breaking its spell over Cris. "The point is, I've seen how much we've been lied to, Cris. And daemons...the ones I've gotten to know? They don't deserve it. Many of them are good, and decent, and the way things are now, it's just wrong, and Gaia wants me to set it right. Not just for them, but for witches too. We deserve to know the truth and decide about daemons on our own, not from lies we were fed."

And there was more, too, so much more that was pushing her to do this. Everything she'd learned about Iblis, and the freedom and necessity of being able to access his will. All the things she'd experienced in the Underworld, and the way Iblis's magic sometimes felt as natural to her as Gaia's, and how she wanted the freedom to explore that without shame. But she didn't want to scare him off, so she'd save that for another conversation. Baby steps.

Cris seemed receptive as he contemplated this. He wasn't running away. He was bouncing his knee a bit, as was his habit when nervous, but other than that, he just stared into the fire. "Say I did believe you. Why do you even need me? Why are you even telling me all this?" he asked, distress playing over his face. This was a lot to take in so quickly, and she understood his resistance to it, but she couldn't back off—they needed him.

"We need one witch from each Coven to break the spell, and I was hoping that you'd help us, help *me*, to do it."

Cris was silent. He rested both arms on his knees as he stared at the fire again for what felt like an eternity. Ena tried desperately to read him, and was tempted to use her Knowing to ascertain with more certainty his feelings, but kept it to herself out of respect.

Eventually, Cris sighed and shook his head ever so slightly. "Ena, I'm sorry, this is a lot. I—I don't know. I need to think about this," he said.

Ena's heart sank, but she understood. This *was* a lot to just dump on someone out of the blue. She'd had months to come around to the idea and still struggled to believe it sometimes.

"I understand, Cris. Really, I do," she said, making eye contact with him and reaching out to give his hand a reassuring squeeze. She could see the guilt and over-whelm warring in his eyes. "And I hate to rush you, but we need your answer soon. There are those who may be...following us, and we need to keep moving. But we'll be here for a couple more days before we move on, so just come find me once you've made your decision, okay?"

Cris stood up, holding out a hand for Ena to help her up too. "Okay," he said, nodding his head. He looked to Ty and Turner. The former was staring suspiciously at him still, his arms folded across his chest, but Turner, bless him, gave him a friendly smile and nod.

Cris looked one more time at Ena, pulling her in tight for a hug, before hesitantly turning and walking away into the forest back towards his village.

"Fuck," Turner said, once he was safely out of earshot. "That didn't go as well as I'd hoped."

"It's okay. I don't think it went too bad, actually. I understand if he needs to think things over," Ena said, trying to be optimistic. Inside, though, her heart sank. What if he didn't come around? She didn't have anyone else to really go to. No one else would trust her the way Cris would.

"What if he doesn't? Could you ask someone else?" Turner asked, voicing her inner thoughts.

"I—I don't know," Ena said truthfully.

"Don't worry," Ty spoke, breaking his silence. His voice was hard, but at least he'd uncrossed his arms. He walked over to the fire, his face glowing from its light as he spoke to Ena and Turner, his eyes serious. "He'll come either way, even if Ena has to use her Gift on him."

Ena froze.

"What?" she asked incredulously. "I didn't agree to that." There was no way she would use her Gift on a friend like that. It was one thing to use it on people trying to harm her, or in relatively harmless ways for the greater good of their goal, but to force someone against their will into this whole mess...that seemed like a step too far.

"He knows way too much now. What are the chances he's running and telling his brothers everything right now? How long until the Aquilo matriarch knows and comes after us?" Ty said.

Fuck. He was making a lot of good points. She didn't *think* Cris was telling his brothers right now. She thought she knew him better than that, but a tiny part of her now regretted not using her Knowing on him to get a better idea of his intentions before he left.

Ena sank back down onto the ground, resting her head in her one good hand.

"I know you don't like it, Ena, but it might be the only way."

Ena was silent. Yes, Ty was definitely being an asshole, and part of her wanted to smack him on his smug-ass face, but it didn't mean he was wrong.

She sighed, her lack of response indicating her implicit agreement. She really hoped it wouldn't come to that, but only time would tell, and part of her was shocked to know that if push came to shove, if Cris didn't willingly help, and she couldn't think of any other options, she might do it. And she didn't know what that said about her.

CHAPTER THIRTY-ONE

Ty

TY AWOKE BEFORE DAWN inside the small canvas tent the three of them shared. He'd had trouble sleeping, and had lain awake most of the night, staring at the tan material of the tent above him, watching it get slowly more and more sodden as the snow fell overnight.

He couldn't stop going over everything again and again in his mind. Ena had done as good a job as she could explaining it all to the Aquilo witch. It wasn't her fault he was an absolute dumbass who had no imagination whatsoever beyond what he'd been told.

But that wasn't what kept him up. It was the way the witch had looked at Ena—something about it made him want to bash the guy's face in.

What were they to each other exactly? Ena had said they were friends, but there was a comfort and familiarity there that hinted at more. And he already knew they'd danced together all those years ago... Had more happened since then?

Fucking Iblis. Just the thought of that made his blood absolutely boil and he had to sit up. He had to move and break some wood or fucking hit something.

He knew it was unjustified. She'd had nine years without him; it made sense that she'd had relationships with others—he certainly had. And if it was just that, just plain old jealousy, maybe he could deal with it. But something about seeing them together, seeing how easily they *fit*, was what hurt the most.

They were both witches, and they were from allied Covens, and there was clearly a long history of friendship between them. He could see them being together, and lasting—unlike he and Ena. It was everything he wanted, and everything he couldn't have, and that was what absolutely crushed him.

Quietly slipping out of the tent so as not to disturb Turner and Ena, who were still sleeping, he emerged into the cold morning air to build up the fire. Luckily, there were still coals, because without either of his fire-starters, he would've had to get out his flint.

The fresh inch of snow on the ground surrounding them muffled the sounds of the forest, but he could still hear animals moving about quietly nearby, and farther in the distance, the sounds of other travelers who were camped out, waking up for the morning.

Taking out his pack, he removed some provisions he'd traded for yesterday in Aquilo—some cheeses, pickled vegetables, and cured meats—and set aside a few things that he knew were Ena's favorites before eating what was left over for his breakfast.

The sun was just coming up when he heard movement from inside the tent. He looked to see Ena emerge, her dark, braided hair tousled and unkempt.

He watched as she put on her cloak and came over to sit on a log by the fire. Wordlessly, he handed her the small cheesecloth filled with things he'd set aside for her. Their hands brushed as she took them, and he felt his entire body come alive in that one simple touch.

Fuck, he missed touching her. He missed breathing her in and losing himself in her. Would he really never get to touch her like that again? The thought gutted him, and he had to look away.

At least she was here now. At least he could still talk to her. He watched out of the corner of his eye as she began eating, balancing the food on her lap and using her good right hand to break pieces off. She still wasn't moving the broken one much, and that concerned him. Was it still hurting her?

He cleared his throat, drawing her attention so she looked up at him. Fuck, he loved it when she did that, but those big blue eyes instantly turned his brain to mush and he had to force it to think.

"How's your arm?" he asked, finally getting words to come out.

"It's—"

Just then, he heard movement coming closer to them through the woods. He recognized the gait from yesterday.

There was no doubt—it was Cris.

His gaze swung to where the sound came from the woods, and Ena's eyes followed.

"Is someone coming?" she asked.

"Yes, it's your friend," he said, hoping she didn't pick up the tension in the way he said the word *friend.*

Ena stood up, placing her breakfast on the downed log behind her as she prepared to greet their guest.

"Turner," Ty called. "Wake up. We have a visitor."

He heard Turner grumble something about it being too early for fucking visitors, followed by the sounds of him moving about and getting up anyway.

Cris emerged from the woods, a pack strung across his back.

That was a good sign, and Ty felt both relieved and pissed all at once.

"Cris," Ena greeted, walking towards him. "You came back. Does this mean...?"

"Yes," the man said, smiling at Ena. Fuck him for doing that. "I thought about it all night, and I want to come with you. I want to help."

"Oh, Cris," Ena said, rushing towards him and hugging him. "I'm so glad. So, so glad. I can't tell you what it means to me to have your support."

Ena continued talking, thanking him, but all Ty could focus on was the twisting in his gut that occurred watching the two of them hug.

"I know this is huge, so huge. And a lot to take in, but I swear, this will be for the better. For everyone," she continued.

"I know. I think so too," Cris said solemnly. "But I still have a lot of questions."

"I'm sure you do," Ena was saying, nodding at him. "I promise we'll answer whatever questions you have."

"Oh, and here." Cris swung his pack to the ground and rummaged through it for a minute before pulling out two glass vials with cork stoppers. "I brought these for you. They should help expedite your healing."

"Oh Cris, thank you," Ena said, sounding immensely grateful. "You didn't have to do that. I swear I'm fine. I'm healing."

"I know, but you should take them anyway. Please."

Ena nodded, and uncorked the first vial, giving it a sniff. "Bone-stitching potion," she says, smiling at him before cautiously tipping it into her mouth and swallowing. "And this?" she asked, bringing the next one to her nose again.

"Blood elixir," Ena and Cris said at the same time. Both of them smiled at their synchronicity.

"Yes," Cris said. "It's likely not as good as yours would be, but I had some left over from a recent batch and thought it would help with your bruising."

Ena smiled and tipped the contents back into her mouth, grimacing slightly at the taste. "Thank you," she said, returning the two empty vials to Cris, who stashed them in his pack.

Finally emerging from the tent, Turner looked sluggish but awake, and Ty was grateful for the distraction. He really didn't want to keep looking at Cris and Ena—how perfect they seemed together made him both want to throttle Cris, just fucking strangle the Iblis-damned life out of him and simultaneously stab himself in the heart so he'd have a physical wound to show for this pain inside him.

"Looks like we've got a new addition," Turner said, smiling widely in that friendly way of his. "Happy to have you." He approached Cris and extended his hand out.

Cris took it cautiously and shook Turner's hand, some of the tension in the group dissipating with the action.

Ena beamed, clearly feeling immensely relieved that they had succeeded. "Alright then," she said. "One down, one to go."

***

The four of them headed west again, cutting through the backcountry. They planned to join back up with the Western Road once it got closer to Occidens, but Ty knew that would be a tricky endeavor no matter what, given how recognizable he and Ena were to Occidens witches.

They would have to figure out a plan for that once they got closer—who to contact, and how, but for now, everyone seemed to be riding the high of their most recent success.

Everyone except for Ty, of course, who was staring daggers at Cris where he sat behind Ena on her horse.

Apparently, the man had thought it was too risky for him to take one of the Coven's horses. He worried that it would've drawn too much attention, since his leaving was not sanctioned by the matriarch.

So now, Ty was watching them ride together as he shared her horse and he couldn't stop thinking about the beautiful curve of her ass, the feel of which he could so viscerally remember cupping—squeezing—in his hand the last time they'd fucked by the hot springs, nestled up against *his* thighs. The thought made him murderous.

He supposed he should be grateful that the man had come with them, and brought those potions for Ena, something Ty was incapable of doing for her, but instead, all he felt was rage. Ty spent most of the morning sitting grumpily atop his horse and barely speaking a word, until Turner rode up next to him, ostensibly to hand him an apple as a snack, and gave him a look that screamed "fucking *chill*."

After that, he tried hard to take his mind off it, focusing on the positives. They had an Auster and an Aquilo witch now. That was huge. They only needed one more from Occidens and then they'd finally be able to do it—they'd finally be able to break the spell. Everything he'd worked so hard for, everything that had happened to Petyr, everything Ena had been through, all of it would be worth it if they broke the spell, he told himself.

He loathed Cole and everything about the way he ran the Underworld. Breaking the spell would break his hold on the place and pave the way for a new era. Then, if they could find a way to get rid of him, Ty could be king and finally take care of his people the way they needed. They could emerge from the Underworld one day, and everything would be as it should. He wouldn't have to hide and downplay his witch-half; he could worship Gaia, too, if he chose.

He repeated these things in his head, and tried to force himself to focus on them, but somehow, even with their victory closer than ever, it felt increasingly hollow without the one thing he truly wanted—the one thing he could never fully have.

Up ahead, he was distracted from his thoughts when Turner struck up a conversation with Ena and the new witch. It was mostly "How's it going?" and "Do you think we should stop soon?" until Turner clearly got around to the topic he wanted to discuss in the first place.

"So, can I ask, what made you decide to join us?" he asked Cris.

Cris shrugged nonchalantly, as if the answer was obvious. "I trust Ena. I know she wouldn't lie about any of the things she told me, and neither would Gaia. When she gave Ena that vision, she gave it to her for a reason, and I'm willing to trust that too. Besides, the amulet is clearly powerful. I've never felt anything like it, and you can't fake that."

Turner nodded, seeming somewhat satisfied. "And how do you feel about working with two daemons? Think you can stomach it?" he asked jokingly, but clearly feeling the man out for any disloyalty or trickery.

Ty smiled to himself. Everyone tended to underestimate Turner, given his smiley attitude, but the man was a vicious fighter and, while he was absolutely fucking terrible at lying, he could still be cunning. Decades of working closely with his father had necessitated it.

Cris shifted on his horse a bit. "Well, I won't lie, it's definitely off-putting. I know Ena says many of the things we've been told aren't true, but I've been told a lot of bad things, so..."

"Yeah, well, don't believe everything you hear, especially not from witches," Turner said with a wink.

Cris huffed a laugh. "I guess I shouldn't now... Still trying to wrap my mind around that." He was silent for a minute, clearly falling back into his thoughts before speaking again. "Can I ask you something?" he asked Turner.

"Sure."

"How does your Power work? It's...surprising how similar it is to my Gift."

"Right, Ena said your Gift is *calor*?"

Cris nodded.

"Well, I don't know how yours works, but mine comes from my body," Turner explained. "I can create the heat, and concentrate it in my hand, and just like that, set shit on fire," he said, grinning at this description.

"Yes, you certainly love setting shit on fire," Ena replied pointedly.

"Hey, I thought I was forgiven for that whole...house incident," Turner replied defensively.

"*You* burned down the Auster matriarch's house?" Cris asked incredulously.

"Only because he told me to," Turner said, gesturing his head back at Ty.

"Don't drag me into this," Ty replied. He'd made his amends with Ena already. He didn't need to explain himself to this asshole.

Ena laughed, and he felt his grumpy mood disintegrate ever so slightly. At least she was happy.

"Anyway..." she said, suppressing her mirth and bringing the conversation back to focus. "How does your Gift work, Cris? We haven't talked much since your Summoning."

"It's similar in a way," Cris said. "But I draw on my Knowing to sense the particles in the air, or in an object, and force them to move together, to create friction and heat...sometimes light."

"Can't you do that, too, Ena? I've seen you light fires," Turner asked.

"In a way, but I need a spellword. Cris doesn't. And I can just create a spark, not warm the air to a specific temperature, or warm an object."

Turner nodded, and Ty found himself engaged in the conversation, despite himself. There was still so much he didn't know about witches and their magic.

"What about you, Ena? How does your Gift work?" Cris asked her.

Ty saw her hesitate, and it hurt his heart. She didn't need to be ashamed or embarrassed about her Gift. It was fucking amazing what she could do, but he knew she still wrestled with the idea that it was associated with daemons, and extremely unheard of for witches.

"It works a lot like daemonic Powers, actually, by allowing me to sense another's mind, only I do it using my Knowing, and then I can control them using my words, like everything I say is a spellword."

"Wow," Cris said. "That's...intense." He was quiet for a minute, but in his silence was disapproval, and something like fear, and it made Ty want to throttle him all over again. "Did you use it on my brothers when you left the note?" Cris asked.

"Yes," Ena admitted. "It was the safest thing for us. I swear I didn't harm them." There was a hint of guilt in her voice, but Ty noted that she didn't apologize for doing it—didn't even try—and he was proud of her for that.

"I know," Cris said understandingly. "I know you wouldn't do that."

He saw Ena relax a bit, and the four of them went back to riding in silence for a while. They stopped several times for brief breaks throughout the day until the sun started to set—early, unfortunately, due to the time of year—and they stopped to set up camp.

Ty found a nice spot near a small stream where the horses could drink, and a flat clearing to set up their tents. Luckily, Cris had brought his own tent, so Ty wouldn't be subjected to his presence all night. He thanked Iblis for that.

Leaving the witches to start a fire, and Turner to tend to the horses, Ty left to set a trap. This time of year, the best game available were coyotes or raccoons, given that the temperatures were too cold for much else, and so he used his *venator* to catch their scents—following their tracks to their dens.

He set a few metal traps he'd brought with him to hopefully get some fresh meat for the morning, but he wasn't very optimistic. Still, the more he could get, the easier it would be on their food stores and reduce the need for trips into villages for more supplies—something which would be increasingly dangerous the closer they got to Occidens—so it was worth a shot.

He was getting close to their camp when his *venator* picked up Cris and Ena's voices, and something about their tone made him pause.

Looking through the trees, he spotted them. The light was dim, so they couldn't see him, but with his Gift, he could make out their faces clearly.

They were sitting together on a downed log by the fire—closer than he would've liked—and Cris was staring at her. He paused for a second, knowing that he shouldn't eavesdrop, but...a larger, pettier part of him didn't give two fucks at all. He wanted—no, *needed*—to know what was going on between them, so he continued to listen.

"—was thinking you should sleep in my tent tonight," Cris was saying. "I can keep it warm for us, and it'll help with your healing. Besides, there's plenty of room."

"Oh," Ena replied, her voice hesitant and almost...disappointed. "Yeah, okay, I guess that makes sense."

Now she was gonna sleep in his tent? Ty's heart plummeted. No. No, she couldn't do that.

But she could. Of course she could. She wasn't *his* anymore. She owed him nothing.

Fuck, this was brutal. He briefly considered not listening anymore, just to spare himself any more pain, but he couldn't stop.

"You seem hesitant. Why is that?" Cris asked, not unkindly. "Are you...with one of those guys?"

"No," Ena replied. Did her voice sound sad? "Not anymore."

"But you were?" Cris prompted.

"Yes," she said simply, her voice indicating that she didn't want to talk about it.

Cris was silent for a second, and Ty was glad for it. The way Ena's voice sounded talking about all this...he felt an echoing ache in his own chest.

"You know, I lied before," Cris said when he finally spoke again.

"About what?" Ena asked, her voice confused.

"About why I decided to come," Cris said. "Part of me came along to help, and because of course I believe you, about everything you said. But...it was also because of you. To keep you safe."

"Cris..." Ena began, her voice sympathetic.

"Ena, I don't know if I trust these daemons," he said, interrupting her and lowering his voice to a whisper. "I mean, that Turner guy seems alright, but the other one? He's menacing as shit. I didn't want to leave you alone with them."

"You can trust him," Ena said, her voice imploring. "I promise you can. He just...he has his reasons for being that way."

"Okay, if you say so," Cris replied skeptically. "I'm just glad you're safe. I was so worried when you were taken at Samhain, and I haven't heard much since then."

"I'm fine, I promise. I've been fine," she said.

"Really?" Cris asked, looking down at her still-healing wrist.

"Yes," she insisted. "Aside from that, it's been...good for me. It's been an adventure," she replied, a small smile in her voice.

"You? Overly cautious Ena on an adventure?" Cris teased.

"Yes, asshole," she said, nudging him with her shoulder. "Believe it or not, I think I've...changed. Or at least, I did, for a little while," she said, seeming introspective. "Then something bad happened," she added, gesturing at her hurt arm again. "And now I'm just...feeling kind of lost again."

Cris nodded, like he was trying to understand. "Well, what about Greya and Heran? Do they know about any of this?"

Ena shook her head. "Not all of it, not yet."

Cris scooted closer to her, and reached out to put his arm around her, making her raise her gaze to his. "Well, I'm here now," he said. "And I can help protect you." Leaning forward slightly, he bent his head as if to kiss her.

Ty froze—his heart absolutely wrenched from his chest as he watched the man move towards Ena. His blood began to boil, and he involuntarily moved to run—to stop them, to grab Cris and kick the ever-loving shit out of him—but then Ena pulled back, moving away from the intended kiss.

"No, Cris." She stood up, clearly agitated at what just occurred. "I don't want that. I don't want anyone to protect me. Why does everyone keep saying that?" she asked, and he could tell she was pissed off now. "I just want... I don't know what I want anymore. I thought I did, and then everything blew up and I can't have what I want anymore, so now I just don't know."

Ena paced back and forth now, and Cris reared back, as if shocked by the sudden extreme reaction.

"You know what, that's a lie," Ena continued, some dam having broken in her. "I do know what I want. I want to be safe, *and* I want to be wild. I want to feel loved, but I want to be free. I want to keep my family and all of my friends. I want to be a witch and be with a—" Ena cut herself off. She was practically yelling now, her voice echoing through the woods, and she seemed to recognize that and quieted down. "But it doesn't matter, because I can't have everything that I want. So I have to choose," she said, her voice cracking with emotion.

Ty's heart broke hearing her words. He knew she'd felt that way, that she hadn't broken up with him because of a lack of love, but instead had done it out of fear. And while he could never forgive himself for allowing her to get hurt, he also felt her struggle so keenly, because in many ways, he had the same one.

Since she was attacked, all he'd been able to focus on was getting her to safety, and now that they were safe, relatively, he had been focused on the last few steps required to break the spell. But for the first time, he now thought, truly thought, what about after? What about when all this was over and he had to go back to the Underworld, without her? What would he do then? Because like Ena said, it was impossible to have everything he wanted, and that thought broke him, both for his own sake and hers. And in this moment, hearing her grief over it, and feeling his own so acutely, he wanted nothing more but to go to her and hold her. Soothe her.

Deny it all and fix it. But he *couldn't*. All he could do was watch from afar, and it was torture.

Ena had quieted down now, and her pacing finally stopped. Cris mumbled an apology and some reassuring words, but Ena just brushed him off and insisted on going into the tent to lie down.

Ty was frozen where he stood, though. He couldn't move; he didn't know if he even wanted to. Maybe he would just sink into the earth right here and end it all.

Out of the dark, he heard Turner approaching him.

"You alright?" Turner asked quietly. Apparently, he had overheard, too, though how much, Ty wasn't sure.

"No," Ty responded simply.

"Maybe not now," Turner replied sadly, reaching out to grasp his shoulder. "But one day, you will be. It won't be this hard forever."

He knew his friend was trying to be reassuring, but it didn't help. None of it helped. Because he'd already tried living without her for nine years and he'd been miserable, and that was before he knew without a doubt that he was in love with her.

So no, he wasn't alright, and part of him knew that once they broke the spell and she was gone from his life for good, he never would be.

CHAPTER THIRTY-TWO

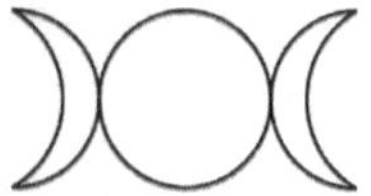

ENA AWOKE THE NEXT morning next to a snoring Cris. She'd reluctantly agreed to sleep in his tent with him, even after the failed almost-kiss, because she had no good reason to say no except that she didn't want to be that far from Ty. Which was ridiculous because they were no longer together like that—a fact that she had to painfully remind herself of almost every hour of every day. Besides, after her outburst last night, she thought maybe it would be good for her to get some space from him.

She cringed with embarrassment just thinking about what she'd said. There was no way everyone, including Ty, hadn't heard her innermost thoughts spill out after Cris had tried to kiss her. Not that any of what she'd said was necessarily a secret, but still. It was all so fresh, she just didn't want to continuously open that jar of hurt for both of them.

Sitting up and emerging from under her blanket, she began to put her boots on. She'd admit it was rather nice to have the tent warmed by Cris's *calor*, but his presence wasn't the same as Ty's. Not by a long shot.

Even though Turner had taken to sleeping in between them, she could still sense Ty, just on the other side of him. She could hear his breathing, smell his scent in the tent, and it always soothed her. Without that, this morning she had woken up agitated.

The air was cold and she could see her breath instantly upon emerging from the tent, so she went to build up the fire. Soon, everyone else began to stir, too, and she was glad that no one asked her to talk about last night.

After eating a quick breakfast from their provisions—because unfortunately, Ty hadn't had any luck with his traps last night, probably thanks to all the noise she'd made—they packed up and continued heading west.

They rode for several days, carving their way through the backcountry, and began to fall into a rhythm. Cris seemed to be on pleasant-enough terms with Turner, and coexisted with Ty, so they all chatted together companionably. When she could, Ena explained more about everything to Cris, filling him in on the binding spell and what to expect for breaking it. He was endlessly curious about her experiences in the Underworld, too, which she also shared, although she kept some of the more traumatic ones to herself so as not to scare him away. And, of course, she told him about Occidens, given how crucial that information was for their next task.

Every night, she, Ty, Turner, and Cris sat around the fire planning—trying to think through different scenarios for how they could contact an Occidens witch and sway them to their side. But every situation they envisioned seemed nearly impossible. Not only did Ena and Cris have zero contacts at Occidens, because of the rivalry, but she and Ty were most surely wanted by them because of their escape and theft of the amulet.

They agreed their best hope was to identify a witch who maybe knew Ty's mother and held sympathy for daemons like she most likely did, but how to go about finding someone like that was the tough part. They planned to send Cris and Turner in, since they wouldn't be recognized, to hopefully start some conversations with people while pretending to trade, and go from there, but Ena felt like there was a good chance that might not amount to anything.

They continued on anyway, clinging to that fool's hope, until they were only about a day or so away from Attax—the last mortal village before Occidens.

They were planning to camp one more night in the backcountry, and join up with the Western Road tomorrow, before they made their way into the village, but Ena slept fitfully that night, despite the warmth of her tent, and again awoke earlier than the others.

Putting on her boots, she emerged from her and Cris's tent, letting her eyes adjust to the dim morning light, and let out a small, startled cry at what she saw.

A small person with a slight, somewhat androgynous figure and short brown hair sat at their mostly dead fire, poking it with a stick as wisps of smoke curled into the cold air.

"Excuse me!" Ena said, shock and confusion warring in her tone. "Who are you?"

Ena Knew almost instantly that they were not threatening. Instead, they seemed almost relaxed, which was extraordinarily weird. She hadn't seen a single other person outside their group in almost a week, and yet here was this stranger sitting around their fire? How did neither she nor Cris hear them coming with their Knowing? Or Ty with his *venator*? Not to mention, having a stranger just barge into an unknown campsite and make themselves at home was unheard of.

The person looked at her. Their eyes were big, brown, and friendly, though something about them was a bit...odd. A bit unfocused.

"Oh, good morning," they said. "I'm glad you're finally awake. I'm Mel, short for Melas."

The stranger stood, approaching Ena with their hand extended as if to shake. But Ena didn't offer hers in return and didn't intend to until she knew what the fuck was going on.

"Ty!" Ena called, but she knew their voices had already awoken him. She could hear him shuffling inside the tent, likely throwing on his boots.

Seconds later, he emerged, his hand on the knife at his belt as he sized up Mel. "Who the fuck are you?" he asked, not even trying to be polite the way Ena had.

"Oh wow, you do look like her," Mel said, smiling widely and seeming extremely unconcerned about Ty's menacing attitude.

"Look like who?" he asked, confusion and caution etched on his face.

"My bad. I get things out of order sometimes. Did I already tell you my name?" they asked, looking between Ena and Ty.

"Yes, your name is Mel, short for Melas. You just told me." Now it was Ena's turn to be confused. "Would you mind telling us what you are doing here in our campsite?"

"I was looking for you," they said. "I Knew you would be here."

"What? Why? How?" Ena's mind spun with questions, she couldn't get them out fast enough.

Turner and Cris had emerged from their tents at this point, too, and were standing next to Ena and Ty, forming a wall of witches and daemons as they questioned the newcomer.

"Sorry, let me back up," Mel said, holding up their hands in apology. "My name is Mel. I'm a witch from Occidens. I came to find you because I saw that I already found you. And that you'll need me for what's to come."

They were an Occidens witch? Oh no—did this mean the Coven already knew of their approach?

"What do you mean you saw that you already found us?" Turner asked, his brow so furrowed he looked like he already had a headache from all this.

"In one of my visions. I already mentioned that, I thought...or I guess not," they said, grasping their chin in contemplation. "Either way, I'll say it again. I have the Gift of *omen*."

"*Omen*? Wow," Cris said, his brows jumping up. "So you're a seer? That makes a lot of sense now."

"Yes, good, I'm glad that makes sense to you," Mel said, smiling and nodding.

"Wait a minute," Ty interjected. "What did you mean we'll need you for what's to come? What do you know?"

Ty was right to be concerned—did this person somehow know about the amulet and what they planned? If so, did the rest of Occidens know already too?

They exchanged a look with Ty, raising their eyebrow at him. "I know a lot of things. You'll have to be more specific," they said. "But hurry up, in case another one comes."

Now Ena's eyebrows raised. What in the actual fuck was going on? In case another *what* came? A vision? She'd heard of the Gift of *omen*, but had never met a witch with it before. It was fairly rare, like Greya's *vita*, though not as rare as her own *visanis*. The last witch she'd heard of that had it was her own grandmother, her father's mother, who was an Aquilo witch.

Ty sighed, clearly feeling rather frustrated himself. "What do you know about us and what we're...doing?"

"Oh, that, okay. I know about the amulet and that you're going to break the spell binding daemons to Iblis. I've seen that I will be a part of that, so that's why I came to find you."

Ty looked over at Ena again, both of them wide-eyed and unsure of what to do with that information.

"Mel, if you could just excuse us for a second," Ena said, trying to sound kind and not completely overwhelmed like she was actually feeling.

Mel nodded and sat back down by the fire, continuing to poke it with the same stick they'd had before.

Ena turned to the others, jerking her head towards the woods, indicating they should follow her. Once they were reasonably out of earshot, the four of them stood in a circle to speak in hushed tones.

"Well, this was quite the surprise to wake up to," Turner said, rubbing his face. "I don't know whether to be relieved or suspicious."

"Me neither," said Ty, stroking his beard nervously. "Ena, can you use your Knowing on them? See if they're being sincere?"

"I already did," Ena admitted. From the second she found the person sitting there, she'd allowed her Knowing free rein to interpret their signs and intentions. "They didn't seem to be lying, or to have intentions of harm, but their signs were confusing. Like...jumbled. As if they were reacting to things that hadn't happened yet."

"That makes sense given that they're a seer. They clearly know a lot of what's to come, and that would affect the signs they're giving now," Cris corroborated.

"Well, should we believe them?" Turner asked. "I mean, it certainly makes it a hell of a lot easier if we don't have to find our own Occidens witch."

"Yes, but why would they want to help us? What do they have to gain? We don't know if it's a trap set by Occidens for us somehow," Ty asked, clearly not ready to let go of suspicion. But his concerns were valid.

"What do Ena and I have to gain?" Cris asked. "Nothing really, except that we feel like what was done was wrong. Maybe they feel the same way."

Ty barely spared Cris a look, but didn't argue.

"Maybe we should ask them that, and if their answer is satisfactory, then we can allow them to join us," Ena asked, looking at Ty. She knew he was the deciding factor in all this. It was he who had orchestrated all this from the beginning, and he who would be the daemon they performed the spell on. He had to trust those involved with his life—with all daemons' lives.

"Alright," Ty agreed, nodding at her plan. "We'll try that, but let me know if your Knowing picks up on anything suspicious."

Ena nodded in confirmation, and the four of them headed back over to the campsite where Mel was sitting by the fire with their eyes closed, unresponsive. Their hands had gone slack in their lap, and the stick they'd been carrying had dropped to the ground.

"Mel?" Ena asked as she approached. "Are you alright?"

The witch didn't respond.

Ena reached down to jostle their shoulder, when suddenly their eyes snapped open. They looked around, seeming confused for a second and taking in their surroundings, before their eyes landed on Ena.

"Oh, I'm back in the now," they said, relaxing the tension in their body somewhat.

"Were you having a vision?" Ena asked gently.

Mel nodded, waving her off with their hand. "Yes, but before you ask me what it was, I have no fucking idea yet, so you need to give me time."

"Oh, okay," Ena said. She had been curious but hadn't been planning to pry like that. She knew that a seer witch's visions were usually reserved for the matriarch's ears only. And that made her wonder...

"Mel, does Syrelle know you're here? Is she okay with you helping us?"

Mel sighed. "No, she doesn't know. I left her a note, so she doesn't worry. Hopefully she doesn't worry..." Mel said, seeming distracted by the thought.

Ty cleared his throat, nodding his head at Mel and giving Ena a look. Clearly, he wanted her to start their intended line of questioning now.

"So, Mel," Ena said, wondering how exactly to begin. "We're so grateful you've come to help us, but we're wondering...why do you *want* to help us? Aside from the fact that you saw that you would?"

"Well," Mel said matter-of-factly. "If I saw it happen then it has to happen. The future is fixed, so there's really no way around it."

"Okay..." Ena replied, her brow furrowing. That wasn't exactly the answer she was looking for, but she guessed it made sense.

"But, if you want to know, I've also seen what will come...after. Parts of it anyway, and I know it's what Gaia wants in the end. It was never meant to be this way, you know. Her intentions were not sincere."

"Whose intentions? Gaia's?" Ena asked.

"No, not Gaia's. The Auster witch. The one whose idea it was to bind the daemons to Iblis in the first place. She was just angry, and jealous. And just a petty-ass bitch if you ask me."

Turner burst out laughing from the sidelines, but Ena was still trying to keep up.

"Mel," Ena sighed, trying to not get frustrated. "I know we don't know each other very well yet, so no offense, but what in the Underworld are you talking about?"

Mel laughed. The sound was joyful and childlike, and luckily they didn't seem offended at all. "Sorry, I tend to get ahead of myself, and I forget that not everyone knows what I Know." They stood up, looking around the campsite. "Could I trouble you for something to eat? I've been sitting here for a while, and I'm starving. I'd be happy to explain what I can then."

"Sure," Ena said, looking at Turner, who went to fetch some provisions from his pack. He came back with some jerky and a hunk of cheese, handing it to Mel, who began to devour it immediately, as if they were afraid it would disappear.

"What I Know," Mel began, talking around the food in their mouth. "From what Gaia has shown me, is that the Auster witch, the brown-haired one, didn't trust the female daemon after she seduced the witch's husband with her Power, or so the Auster witch said. The daemon did have the Power of *cupido,* so who's to say if she actually used it on the man or not, but tensions were already high between witches and daemons, for many reasons, as you know, or maybe you don't, but that's a whole other story," Mel said, waving that idea off. "Anyway, it was the perceived personal slight that pushed the Auster witch to create the spell and convince the other two matriarchs to help her. That I know for sure."

Ena tried to keep up as Mel was talking, and parts of what they said still confused her, but a lot of it suddenly made sense.

The brown-haired witch she'd mentioned, Ena had seen her in her own vision. She was the one who'd seemed much too pleased with herself after conducting the spell. The one who seemed to enjoy watching the female daemon suffer.

"So, long story short, it was never Gaia's will that the spell be enacted in the first place. My Coven has always known that," Mel finished, as if that explained literally everything.

"Occidens has? Really?" Cris chimed in. He was clearly having just as much trouble absorbing all of this information as she was.

"Yes. Our ancestor, the Occidens matriarch, was pressured to do the spell, but immediately regretted it. She could tell it was wrong, and she tried to convince the other two to reverse it, but they refused. Luckily, she got away with the amulet and hid it. She was brave for doing that. But the other Covens were *not* happy," Mel said, laughing a little at whatever memory of a vision she was reliving.

"That's what caused the rivalry between the Covens, right?" Ena asked, seeking confirmation of what she'd already suspected.

Mel nodded, and satisfaction filled Ena at having at least figured that part out already. But the rest of what they'd said...

"Do you mean to say that all Occidens witches know about the amulet and the bond to Iblis? Not just the matriarch?" Ena asked, her mind spinning at that revelation.

"Mmhmm," Mel answered simply. "Of course, we don't go blabbing it around. That wouldn't be helpful for relations with the other Covens. And it's not like we trust daemons any more than everyone else anyway, especially since they're incapable of channeling Gaia. But we at least *know* that what was done is not what Gaia wanted. And at least from my perspective, I do feel quite sorry for them."

Mel looked at Ty and Turner then, their brow furrowing in pity, as the two daemons exchanged a what-the-fuck look with one another.

"I think I need to sit down," Turner said. "This is a lot to absorb first thing in the morning."

Ena felt much the same. She looked over at Cris, who had paled and was standing there just as dumbstruck as the rest of them. The poor guy had had a lot of information dumped on his plate lately. Maybe she should encourage him to sit down too.

Then she looked at Ty. He, at least, didn't look overwhelmed, just contemplative. What was he thinking?

He approached Mel. Not in a threatening way. For the first time, it seemed as if he really wanted to address them. Not suspiciously, but respectfully. "Thank you, for all this information," he said slowly, sincerely. "And for coming all this way to help us, on your own. That was an incredibly brave thing to do."

"Nah, I'm not brave," they said, waving away Ty's compliment. "I knew I'd get here okay, like I said—I've seen it."

Ty smiled at them in a friendly way, clearly warming up to them now, and Mel smiled back, staring at him intently.

"Now *she*, the one you look like, she was brave," Mel added, as if communicating something big and important to Ty. But Ena was, once again, lost.

"Who?" Ena asked, wondering how many questions she had left to ask before more stopped emerging.

"Kaya," Mel responded, looking over at Ena. "I *finally* figured out it was her I was seeing. Then a lot of it made sense," they said, sounding relieved.

"Who's Kaya?" Ena asked them, shaking her head in confusion.

"My mother," Ty responded. His voice was hard, and his expression more so.

"Yes! Exactly. I thought so," Mel said, clearly giddy at this realization. "I told you, you look like her. It's the eyes," they said, gesturing at Ty's face. Then they looked around to the rest of them, as if seeking confirmation of this, but no one could give them any.

"What?" Turner asked from where he sat. "You knew Ty's mother?"

"Well, I didn't know her. I was a child when she left Occidens, but I remember her. I mean, who wouldn't, what with her absconding with a daemon and stealing historic journals and all," Mel said. "And, of course, I've seen her," they added offhand.

"You've seen her, like, in your visions?" Turner asked.

"Yes," Mel answered simply.

Ena was floored. Not only was this another one of her theories proven correct—that Kaya, Ty's mother, *had* been the one to take the journals from Occidens and give them to Petyr—but this witch had seen Ty's mother? Maybe knew where she was or at least knew more about her? That was...huge for him.

She desperately wanted to ask more questions, ask all the things that she wanted to know about the last witch before her to visit the Underworld, but she knew that wasn't her place. It was Ty's.

Ena looked over at him to see what he was thinking, but his face was carefully blank.

Everyone was silent, waiting for him to continue, but all he did was clear his throat.

"Well, thank you, again, Mel, for joining us. We'll let you finish your food and then we can all take a second to figure out what's next."

Then Ty grabbed his ax from his tent behind him and took off into the woods without a word to any of them.

CHAPTER THIRTY-THREE

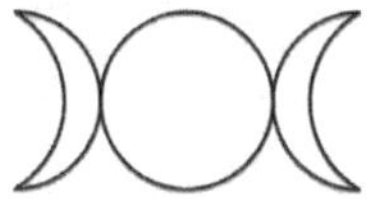

Ena

TY HAD BEEN GONE for almost an hour. After the many revelations of the morning, everyone needed a second to themselves to eat or tend to their needs, but Ena spent almost the entire time debating whether she should go after him or not.

Was he okay? She knew the topic of his mother was tough for him. He clearly felt incredibly betrayed by her abandonment, no matter the circumstances, but now to learn with absolute certainty that she was the one who'd given Petyr the books Ty had taken, and that she had had a hand in all this from the beginning? That must be a lot to swallow. Not to mention the fact that Mel, in all likelihood, knew where she was, and all Ty had to do was ask her, and he could potentially know more about his mother than he had his entire life. Would he seek that knowledge? Did he even want it?

Ena couldn't begin to imagine the conflicting feelings that would generate in him, and she desperately wanted to go comfort him. But her instincts told her that he needed some time alone. Turner, she noted, didn't go after him either, so maybe giving him space right now was for the best, but still, her heart ached for him, and she found herself waiting impatiently for his return, just to make sure that he was okay.

The sun was well up by the time he returned with a bundle of firewood under his arm, sweaty and out of breath, but seeming emotionally stable once more. Without preamble, he tossed the split wood on the ground near the fire and called everyone together.

"I've been thinking," he said, addressing them as a group as they drew towards him.

"Clearly," Turner said, gesturing at the abundance of firewood.

Ty gave him an unamused look, but Turner was unbothered—he just smiled knowingly at his friend. It was common knowledge that Ty went to his axe when stressed or overwhelmed.

"We need a plan for what's next. There's nothing stopping us from doing the spell now," Ty began. "But I worry about doing it here, so close to the Occidens Coven. With Mel having recently left, there's a chance the witches could come looking. We should move farther inland, to a more neutral location, far away from any villages. We can wait to make sure we weren't pursued, and then do the spell there."

Ena nodded. That was a good plan, a smart plan. Looking to Cris and Turner, she saw that they also seemed to be in agreement, but Mel—

"That's not where you do it," Mel said, chiming in from where they sat by the fire.

"What do you mean?" Ty asked.

"You—I mean *we*—do the spell at night in a clearing surrounded by giant evergreen trees. I've seen it."

"Do you mean the Sacred Grove?" Ena asked, her stomach bottoming out instantly at the mention of the cluster of ancient pine trees just outside the Auster Coven near the River Wry.

Mel shrugged. "I don't know if that's what it's called, but if it's as I described, then yes."

"Why would we need to do it there?" Turner asked, looking between her and Mel.

"Because that's where they did it before," Ena answered for them, the realization dawning on her. Snippets of the vision she'd had when she first put on the amulet came back to her. The dark forest surrounding the witches and the rushing sound of...the river. She couldn't believe she hadn't realized it before, but she'd been so distracted by all the other things she'd seen. They'd done the spell in the Sacred Grove.

"That makes sense," Cris chimed in. "The Sacred Grove is a powerful location—the connection to Gaia is strongest there because of the trees' longevity. They've borne witness to the Turning longer than any other living thing we know of. That's why witches love to hold our gatherings there for important events."

Ena was silently kicking herself. She'd been so focused on figuring out the elements to the spell and then getting an Aquilo and Occidens witch to join them, that she hadn't yet considered that it would matter *where* they did the spell too. But like Cris said, that did, unfortunately, make sense.

Ty turned to her, clearly sensing her distress. "Is this true?" he asked.

"Yes," she confirmed. "If my memory is correct, I think the original spell was done in the Sacred Grove, likely for the reasons Cris said, and if we want to recreate it, then...it would give us the best chance if we do it there."

Ty nodded, the weight of this hitting him in the same way it was hitting Ena.

Because if they needed to go to the Sacred Grove, that meant they'd be close to the Auster Coven—*her* Coven—and that was incredibly risky. If she were recognized, there would be no way they could do the spell in secret.

"Alright then. I guess that's where we're going," he said, giving off significantly more confidence than she felt. "But I want to be sure—are there any other elements to the spell you think we're missing? Do we need *anything* else?" Ty asked her. "Because once we go there...something tells me we're only going to get one shot at this."

He was right. They'd be blessed to get in and out of the Sacred Grove unseen, so they needed to have everything thoroughly planned out if they wanted to have the best shot at success.

She ran through the checklist in her mind. They had the amulet—she understood its symbols and the meaning and intentions behind it, and she knew the spellwords they needed to say. They had a witch from each Coven, and they had a daemon and his blood.

His blood...

Another memory from her vision flashed before her: an athame slicing into the daemon's wrist, making the daemon's blood drip into a golden chalice. The chalice and the athame used to cut the daemon's wrist—both of those were ritualistic Wiccan items. Items they didn't currently have.

"Yes, actually," Ena replied. "We'll need a ceremonial chalice and an athame. Both of those were in my vision too."

"Can't we just use a regular cup and knife? Why do they have to be ceremonial?" Turner asked.

"No, I don't think we can," Ena explained. "Ceremonial objects like that are anointed with water from the Sacred Pool and blessed by a witch. It marks them as special objects of Gaia, suited for enacting her will, and it's that intention that makes them more powerful when used in spells. If we were doing an ordinary, less-complicated spell, we might be able to get away with non-blessed objects, but with something like this...we can't risk not using them. Every piece adds to the power of the spell, and we'll need it all to do something this big."

"Well, where can we get those things then?" Turner asked, as if it were no big deal to do so.

"Any of the Covens would have one," she answered, her mind running through options. "But, of course, getting them without being noticed is the hard part."

Silently, she chastised herself for not having the forethought to ask Cris to bring them with him when he left Aquilo, but honestly, she'd been so focused on recruiting a witch from each Coven, she had to remind herself that it was a blessing from Gaia that they'd even made it this far.

"I think it goes without saying that we shouldn't go to Occidens to get one," Ty said. "That'd be far too dangerous given how recognizable Ena and I are, and it's in the opposite direction," Ty said, speaking her own thoughts aloud. "That leaves Aquilo and Auster, and since we have to go towards Auster anyway..." He looked at her meaningfully, and she knew what he was going to ask before he said it. "What do you think, Ena? Could you use your Gift to sneak in and get the objects we need?"

Ena's heart sank. Could she do that? Use her Gift on members of her own Coven—potentially on Heran or Greya if she had to? She'd considered using it on Cris, and blessedly it hadn't come to that, but even that had been borderline, so...she knew her answer almost immediately.

"No. I'm sorry, but no," she said. "I can't use my Gift on my own family like that. I know breaking the bond is important, but I don't want to do it that way."

Ty sighed, almost as if he'd been expecting that answer, but nodded in understanding.

"But that doesn't mean I still can't get them," Ena explained.

"What do you mean?" Turner asked. "How else can you get them without giving us away?"

Ena took a deep breath. She wasn't sure how the others, especially Ty and Turner would react to this, but it felt right to her.

"I want to reach out to my sister. I want to tell her what we're planning and see if she can get the chalice and athame for us."

"What?" Turner asked, shock in his voice. "You just want to walk up to your house and ask her? Is that wise? I thought she was skeptical last time you tried to explain this all to her."

"She was," Ena replied, feeling defensive of her sister all the sudden. "But I want to try again. I know so much more now, and we have Cris and Mel to back me up in case she thinks it's just Ty clouding my judgment." Not to mention, maybe it would help her cause to explain that she and Ty weren't even together anymore anyway, and she was still choosing to do this.

"And I want to tell her, but I'm not delusional," she continued. "I don't want to announce what we're doing to the entire Coven, or even Heran, and put it up for debate. I just want to tell Greya alone, and walking up to the house would not be the best way to do that. So I'm going to send her a message."

"Send her a message like...?" Cris asked, his blond brows raising in question.

"Yes, I want to go to the Sacred Pool and use the blood-to-blood spell," Ena declared.

"The blood-to-blood spell?" Ty asked. "You mean, the spell you were trying to do when I caught you there?"

"Yes, exactly," Ena confirmed.

"Caught you there?" Cris asked in horror. She had yet to fill him in on all *those* details.

"Not now, man," Turner said, clapping him on the shoulder.

Mel had been silent through all this, seeming distracted. Ena wasn't quite sure if they had entirely followed the conversation, but their blessing was important.

"Does that plan sound alright with you, Mel?" she asked them cautiously. If the witch had seen something that might make this plan implausible, Ena wanted to know now.

"Plan?" Mel said, seeming surprised at having been addressed.

"Yes, our plan to send a message to my sister before going to the Sacred Grove," Ena explained.

"Your sister, yes..." Mel's brow furrowed in thought. "What—what does she look like?"

Ena looked around cautiously at the others before answering. Why did Mel want to know that? "She's blonde, with brown eyes. About my height and body type."

"Oh," Mel said, seeming relieved. "Okay, good, yes."

"Why? What do you know?" Ena asked, feeling suddenly off-kilter. Had Mel seen Greya in a vision?

"Trust me," Mel said sadly, shaking her head. "You don't want to know."

***

After packing up their camp, they headed southeast toward the Sacred Pool. Ty led them with his *venator*, making their navigation simple, but despite this assurance, Ena could not shake the apprehensive feeling she had after what Mel had said.

It turned out, Mel had brought their own horse, thank Gaia, and Cris had volunteered to ride with them to give Mahnin a break from the extra weight.

Ena appreciated the space, especially since her wrist was feeling better and she could use two hands to guide the horse on her own now. But the downside was, it gave her brain ample time to spiral about everything that was to come.

She didn't want to pester Mel—the witch had made it clear they did not want to tell Ena any more of what they had seen. But why? Was it bad? Was it good? The unknown of it all was killing her.

And on top of that, her heart soared at the prospect of speaking to Greya soon, of seeing her face and hearing her comforting voice, but her stomach flipped every thirty seconds, thinking about what she should say, and how Greya would take it. Ena didn't know if she could handle it if Greya didn't believe her again, and if the wedge between them remained.

Around midday, Ena found herself riding next to Ty, their horses having paced themselves together of their own accord. He sat stoically on his horse, his strong hands guiding the animal around roots and bushes. His face was impassive, uncaring even, but she knew him well enough by now to know that was a mask. She wondered again how he was dealing with all of this, deep down.

Eventually, she couldn't help herself and she broke their pointed silence.

"Are you okay?" she asked quietly, even though the others were far ahead, out of earshot.

He looked over at her, giving her his full attention. The intensity of it always shocked her, and this time was no different as she felt a small shiver travel down her spine.

He chuckled darkly, not out of amusement, but irony. "I don't know," he said. "Are you?"

"I don't know either," she repeated, giving him a small, sad smile. A few seconds of silence went by before she felt compelled to ask. "Do you...want to talk about it? About your mother?"

Ty shrugged, obviously wanting to avoid the discussion. "What is there to say?" he asked.

"Well, I know we're not...*us* anymore, but I can still be here to listen, if you want."

Ty looked at her with so much emotion in his eyes. Love and anger, sadness and regret, warred inside him, just as they did inside her. She was overwhelmed for a second, seeing it all so clearly. Like a mirror into her own heart.

"I don't know what I want anymore," he said sadly. "I used to be so mad at her for leaving, but now...after everything that happened with you in the Underworld, I can understand a bit more why she left. But still...so much was hidden from me, and I—" He paused, clearly subduing his rage. "It doesn't even matter, because she can't help me now. If I had known all this a decade ago, about her and Petyr, and the amulet and everything, maybe then it would have helped, but now..." He shook his head. "Now, it means nothing. I figured everything out on my own anyway. I don't need to know any more about her."

Ena's heart ached for him, seeing him so clearly upset, but part of her understood why he didn't want to seek her out. Why seek out someone who left you? Why cling to someone who couldn't be with you? That feeling, she understood all too well.

But another part of her wanted Ty to know his mother, because at least he had that opportunity. She never would. Her own parents had both died when she was too young to remember them, and her grandparents were gone too. There was no family left for her to discover. All she had was Greya.

She was about to open her mouth to contribute this when Ty sighed. He clearly didn't want to discuss his mother anymore, and she didn't blame him, so when he changed the topic, she let him.

"What about you?" he asked. "I know you must be excited to finally speak to your sister. I know how much you've missed her."

Ena's heart melted a bit at his consideration. Even though they weren't together, it was clear he still cared.

"I am excited," she replied. "And nervous. I don't know how she is going to take it all, but I'll do my best, just like I did with Cris."

Ty watched her religiously, as if taking in her every expression. "I'm happy for you," he said quietly. "To be reunited with your Coven, your family. I know that's what you want, and I want you to have that." Ty was quiet for a beat, letting his words sink in, before he continued. "I never wanted to take you from them forever. Never wanted any of this for you. You know that, right?"

"I know," she said sincerely. She didn't blame him for anything that had happened. She knew he just wanted her to be happy. Just like she wanted him to be happy.

"I'm just glad that after all this, you'll be safe. And you'll be with people who love you," he said, his voice filled with a melancholy she'd never heard from him.

But something about the way he said it made Ena angry all the sudden. Looking down at her hands where she gripped her reins, she tightened her hold. "Why does that sound like you're saying goodbye? We're not through this all yet."

"I know, but...I can't fix any of this for us, Ena," he said. "My own mother couldn't stay in the Underworld, I don't know how I ever expected you to either. So I just...I'm trying to do what you wanted, what we agreed is best for us and everyone else."

Ena had to look away as she felt tears well in her eyes. Why was he saying this now? Her anger surged again, and she didn't know whether to yell at him or sob or both.

But the worst part was he was right—that was what they'd agreed. That was what she'd said. That was what she'd chosen, and nothing had changed. So why did having a reminder of it thrown in her face make her so upset?

Maybe she'd made a mistake opening this wound between them again. She should never have started this conversation. Part of her had wanted to be friendly, to maintain some sort of relationship with him, but it was clearly too hard to be just friends, and that realization made her hurt all over again.

Spurring her horse on, she moved ahead without a word, trying desperately to leave Ty behind her.

CHAPTER THIRTY-FOUR

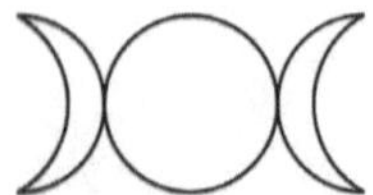

Ena

THE FIVE OF THEM traveled for several days. It was strange at first, having two new additions, but Ena found that she appreciated the company of other witches. She didn't realize how much she'd missed the ease and comfort of being with her own kind. And she felt it all the more acutely as they got closer to the Sacred Pool, and to speaking with Greya.

On their fourth day of travel, when they were only a couple miles away, memories began flooding her of the last time she was here. How frantic she'd been to speak to Greya then too, and how scared she'd been traveling alone in the freezing rain with no supplies.

This time was blessedly different in some ways—she had a horse, they had ample supplies, tents, and a witch with the Gift of *calor* to warm them despite the slushy snow that covered the ground. But she still felt just as anxious to speak to Greya—only now she was nervous about the daemons she'd brought with her, and not the ones pursuing her.

Still, the sight of the delicate, bubbling stream—so clear she could see the multicolored pebbles along the bottom—lifted her spirits. The Sacred Pool was a place of great reverence and beauty, and though she was nervous to speak to her sister, she felt empowered just being in its presence.

Just like before, they followed the crystal-clear water to its source—the murky blue pool, framed by low-hanging, moss-covered tree branches. This time of the year, its banks were covered in snow, making the water appear even bluer than last time. The sun had emerged from behind the dense gray clouds about an hour ago, and was now reflecting off the snow and water, giving the pool an ethereal glow. It was utterly breathtaking.

She heard Turner, Mel, and Cris give audible gasps and murmur words of wonder as they approached. None of them had been here before, even though Cris had certainly heard a lot about it from other witches. She could tell its beauty impacted them just as it had her, and that brought a smile to her face.

Together, they took their horses to the rocky overhang where she and Ty had dried out after their last visit. The memory of him crashing into the water after her, pulling her back into his safe, warm body, flooded through her, confusing her with conflicting emotions, but she pushed it aside.

In unspoken agreement, the others got to work starting a fire and setting up their bedrolls, allowing Ena to make her way over to the pool's edge alone. She would need silence to concentrate on the spell, especially since she'd never done it before.

She wandered over to the water, a cold breeze rippling across the surface. Butterflies swam in her stomach, both at the prospect of attempting an unknown spell, and at seeing her sister. Would this be the reconciliation she hoped for, or just add another stone in the wall between them?

She heard someone approach and turned to see Ty. He stood a few feet behind her, his large frame shading out the sun like an eclipse. All she could see was him. Their eyes met as he reached into the sheath at his side, pulling out his dagger before flipping it in his hand and holding it out to her handle first.

"You'll need this, won't you?" he asked.

Did he remember that from last time? Had he watched her try to cut her palm with a jagged stone, only stopping when the shock of his voice caused her to tumble into the pool?

"Thanks," she said, accepting the knife.

There was a heavy silence between them, as if they both wanted to speak more but neither of them knew what to say.

"You can do this, Ena," he said, breaking their quiet. But whether he was talking about the spell itself or convincing Greya to help them, she wasn't sure. "I'll be over here if you need anything." He nodded at her reassuringly, then turned and walked away, leaving her alone to face what came next.

Lowering herself down to her knees, she peered over the edge of the pool, staring deep into the water. She allowed her Knowing to come alive, sensing the intention of the pool's water, bubbling up from underground.

Not dissimilar, she realized, from the hot springs she and Ty had swum in in the Underworld.

Her heart ached at that memory, too, but, again, she pushed it aside.

She focused her thoughts on Greya instead. Her sister, her best friend. The person who knew her best in this world, and whom she missed so much. She allowed her heart to feel that yearning, to remember once more what it felt like to be in the presence of someone who was so much a part of her. The warmth in her eyes, and her laugh. The way her hands moved when she cooked, and the way her smile lit up her face. The way she smelled and the exact color of her hair—pale and golden in the sunshine.

She watched the water ebb and flow to the bank, rippling across the reflection of her face. She felt the breeze swaying in the trees around her, and looking down at her palm, she felt her blood moving—pumping—through her veins, the same blood that flowed through Greya's veins.

Taking Ty's knife in her hand, she sliced her palm. Not too deep, but just enough for the blood to well up. Holding her hand over the water, she squeezed her palm and watched as the crimson liquid dripped into it, swirling into the murky blue before disappearing. Then, she spoke her spellword.

{*Sanguis*}

The blood that continued to drip from her hand into the water began to swirl, creating a delicate whirlpool independent of the water's current, right atop her reflection.

Ena focused her thoughts. *Greya. Where was Greya? What was she doing?* She kept them regimented, kept them focused on her sister.

Several seconds went by, and Ena began to feel concern creep in. What if it didn't work? But then—

There.

Her own reflection in the water began to disappear, and another image started to replace it—blurry at first, but becoming clearer with each drop of her blood.

Squeezing her hand to increase the flow of it into the water, the image clarified.

A flash of blonde hair appeared, then the glimpse of a slightly darker-blonde eyebrow, with a brown eye beneath it.

"Greya?" Ena spoke loudly, as if her sister were far away, hardly able to keep the excitement from her voice. "Oh Gaia, it's working. Greya! Can you hear me? Can you see me?"

The spell was working! It was—

The image stopped moving, and suddenly, two brown eyes stared back at her. Right where her own reflection in the water should be, there was now Greya's face—her reflection—fully visible and rippling with the movement of the water. It was as if the two of them had swapped places, each seeing what the other normally saw when she stared into the water on her own.

Greya's brow wrinkled in confusion. "Ena?" she asked cautiously. Her voice sounded muffled, as if she herself were underwater, but Ena could still hear her clearly enough. "Ena, is that you?"

"Yes! Yes, Greya can you see me? Can you hear me?"

"Yes. Oh Gaia, Ena, how am I seeing you right now?" Her sister moved closer to whatever water she was looking at, making her reflection larger to Ena. "Where are you? Are you okay?"

The sound of her sister's voice, both overjoyed and filled with concern, brought tears to her eyes. A sudden rush of grief for all that she had been through since they parted hit her, and they overflowed instantly. Ena tried not to, but tears ran down her cheeks, choking her voice.

"Yes, Greya, I'm okay. I'm at the Sacred Pool. I did a blood-to-blood spell. I'm just—" She cut herself off, trying to get her emotions under control so Greya could understand her. "I'm so glad to see you."

Her tears dripped into the water, disappearing into her sister's reflection.

"I'm so glad to see you too," Greya said, backing her face away again. "I'm trying not to burn myself on the steam coming from this pot of boiling water. One second, let me remove it from the hearth."

Ena watched as Greya brought her pot-holder-clad hand up over the edge of her reflection, presumably moving the pot over to the kitchen counter.

"That's better," she said, smiling weepily down at Ena once more. "Ena—I don't even know where to start. Where in the Underworld have you been? I know you said you're okay, but are you really? Are you safe?"

Ena nodded her head. There was so much to answer in those questions she didn't know where to begin, so she decided to start with the most important thing.

"I am safe, yes. And as to where I've been...I actually *have* been in the Underworld."

"Gaia...are you serious? Did Ty force you there? I figured he must have escaped from Occidens somehow and kidnapped you again, even though none of the Occidens witches believed that. They all thought you'd let him go, but I told them you would never. How did you escape?" Greya's questions grew frantic and Ena had to cut her off.

"No, no, Ty didn't force me there. I went with him willingly. And as for Occidens...they were right. I was the one who let him go."

She saw her sister hesitate, her face screwed up in shock and confusion. "Ena, what? Why would you *ever* help a daemon, and willingly go to the Underworld with him? After everything they did to you, burning down Heran's house, all the harm they've caused...how could you choose that?"

Ena hated hearing the hurt in her sister's voice—the betrayal—but she took a deep breath. Somehow, this felt harder than explaining everything to Cris. She and Greya had known each other their entire lives; they had a history. Ena had always been the younger sister, deferring to Greya's knowledge and wisdom, following in her footsteps. And Greya knew all the ins and outs of her relationship with Ty and how much his abandonment had hurt her. But this was something Ena knew she was right about, and she needed to do her best to not be detracted by her sister's skepticism.

"Greya, please," she replied calmly. "I need you to listen to me with an open mind. Can you do that?"

Greya paused, closing her eyes for a second like she often did when she became overwhelmed. When she opened them, she spoke again. "Yes. Please," she said, her face still conflicted, but calm once more. "Tell me what is going on. I need to hear it from you."

"Remember that vision I told you I had, when I touched the amulet?"

Greya nodded.

"I know what it was now. It was a vision of the past, given to me by Gaia. And what I saw, what I know now, was that centuries ago, witches—one from each Coven—drew on Iblis's chaos magic to unwillingly bind the daemons to Iblis. They removed their natural ability to access Gaia's magic and interpret her will. The split—their exclusive servitude of Iblis—was not natural or chosen by them. It was forced. And not only did I see this, but Heran herself confirmed it to me before I left Occidens. This is the truth."

Greya's face scrunched in horrified disbelief, her head shaking as she tried to process what Ena had just said. "Why?" she asked, sounding sickened by the idea. "Why would witches do that?"

"Well, there are different opinions about that. According to Heran, it was because daemons couldn't be trusted with Gaia's magic. But if you ask the daemons that I know, it was because witches wanted more control and influence over the mortal villages. And, if you ask the seer from Occidens, it was because one of the witches had a personal vendetta against a daemon who she claimed seduced her husband with her Power."

"The seer from—" Greya massaged the space between her eyes with her knuckle, closing her eyes again. "Okay, I'm gonna come back to how you met the seer later. I want to believe you—I *do* believe you—but I still don't understand how you could go with them. Regardless of how they got that way, daemons are servants of Iblis and sowers of chaos. I don't see how you can trust them, even Ty. I know you have feelings for him, but Ena, you can't change what he is."

"I know it's a lot to process," Ena said, trying to sound reassuring and not annoyed that she was throwing her feelings for Ty in her face again. She knew better than anyone that she couldn't change what he was, and it hurt every blessed day. "And you're right, many daemons do use their Powers to serve Iblis in ways that are disruptive. But I think—no I *know*—that not all daemons are the same. Not all want to serve Iblis in that way, and some would like the chance to serve Gaia. And..."

She knew this part would be harder for Greya to swallow, given how much was entrusted to her as the future matriarch of the Auster Coven. How could she explain to her what she'd learned, what she'd felt, about the necessity of Iblis's chaos without sounding like she'd betrayed Gaia and descended?

"Greya, the more I've learned, the more I've realized that witches have made mistakes too. We are not without fault in this, and I think it's time we try something different—for daemons' sake and witches'. Gaia gave me that vision for a reason."

"What do you mean, try something different? You think Gaia wants you to do something about this bond?"

"Yes. We—Ty and the other two daemons who kidnapped me—figured out a way to break the bond to Iblis. To allow daemons to access Gaia's magic once more, and I believe this is what Gaia truly wants."

Greya was silent as she took all this in, hesitation and fear written across her face. "I don't know, Ena. Why didn't Heran tell me about all this? Why haven't *you* told her?"

Greya was asking some good questions, and Ena tried her best to answer them.

"This knowledge is apparently only for matriarchs. Heran only told me because Gaia revealed it to me on her own, and Heran told me not to tell you, but I had to tell you, Greya. I don't think it's right that this is being kept from us. And as for Heran...I do want her to know—eventually—but she is stubborn, and I think, to her, change and a loss of the status quo is more important than what's right in this instance. I don't want to risk her stopping us."

Greya shook her head. "Stopping you? You mean, you're going to do it?"

"Yes. We are ready to break the bond and reverse the spell. We have most of the necessary elements, including a witch from each Coven. But there's a few things we don't have, and that's why I reached out, Greya, because I need your help to get them."

"A witch from each—" Greya's brows hit her hairline. "You don't mean..."

"Yes, we have an Occidens witch. And Cris, he's helping us too. But Greya, listen to me," Ena said, her voice turning serious as she felt the flow of blood start to slow from her hand. "We are coming to the Sacred Grove to complete the spell. It has to be done there, but we still need a ceremonial chalice and an athame. We need—*I* need you to bring them to us."

"Ena..." Greya said sadly, shaking her head. "I believe everything you've said, but I don't know. About any of this. I am the future matriarch of this Coven, and if I am seen aiding daemons...that could destroy our standing with the mortal villages. Or our alliance with Aquilo. I can't just—"

"Please, Greya," Ena began, infusing her voice with as much sincerity as possible. "I know it's a lot to ask, but we're on our way now. I really want—no, I *need* you to be with me on this. I don't want to do this without you, and this is our only chance to change things. For the better."

Greya closed her eyes and was quiet, her reflection rippling even more with a new breeze that blew across the pool. "Okay," Greya said. "I hear you, and I'll do my best."

"Thank you," Ena said, relief spilling through her. "Thank you, Greya. I know once you have a chance to commune with Gaia about this, you'll know it's for the best too."

"I will," Greya said, "but that's not why I'm doing this. It's because of you, Ena. I hated how we left things, and even though I'm still trying to catch up to all of this...you know that I trust you, right?"

"I do," Ena said. "I know this is a lot, but thank you for listening to me this time." She gave her sister a small smile, an olive branch. "I love you."

"I love you too," her sister responded, smiling back at her, even though her eyes were still wary and distressed.

"Meet us in the Sacred Grove at dusk in three days' time," Ena said.

"Alright," Greya replied, nodding cautiously.

"Blessed be, sister," Ena said, and with that, she pulled her hand back, stopping the flow of blood into the pool, and the image of her sister vanished.

For the first time since she'd begun the spell, Ena sat back on her heels and took in her surroundings.

The trees were blurry, tilting. She felt incredibly dizzy all of a sudden. Maybe she should stand up? Looking up, she saw Ty and the others approaching her from their camp, just as the world went dark.

CHAPTER THIRTY-FIVE

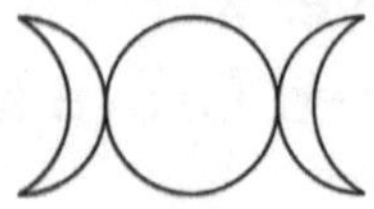

Ena

ENA FELT COLD. THE back of her head felt like it was resting on ice, and her fingertips were beginning to hurt. What was going on?

Slowly, she opened her eyes and her gaze landed on Ty—like he was the gravitational force from which she could not escape. Blinking a few times to clear her vision, she looked around to see Cris and Turner kneeling beside her as well. All of them had concerned looks on their faces. What had happened?

"Easy," Ty said, placing his warm hand on the back of her head and lifting her into a sitting position. "Are you alright?"

"I..." Ena looked around at the forest surrounding her, getting her bearings. She was still beside the Sacred Pool, laying on the snow-covered ground. "I'm fine, I think. I must've passed out."

"It was probably the blood loss from the spell," Ty said, his face screwed up in concern. "Go slow."

Turner handed her a waterskin, which she drank from greedily.

Ty reached out to help her stand up. "Think you can walk?" he asked, rising with her.

"Yeah, I think so," she said. Ty moved to hold her arm as she walked, but she pulled away from him. His closeness was confusing to her, and she didn't want it right now.

He lowered his arms, taking the hint, and with the three men flanking her, she moved slowly over to the overhang where they'd set up camp.

Mel was there, sitting by the fire alone, their eyes closed and their face impassive. Ena had learned by now that that was what they looked like when they were having a vision, and they should not be disturbed.

Ena sat down silently beside them, wrapping her hand in the strip of linen Turner handed to her, before cautiously taking another sip of her water.

After it appeared she wasn't about to imminently pass out again, Ty stalked off to set a trap in the woods, and Turner and Cris went to collect more firewood, leaving her beside the fire with Mel and a snack.

Taking a bite of her apple, Ena suddenly felt Mel's eyes on her. She turned to look at the witch, who had come out of their vision, but was staring at her strangely, as if something had just dawned on them.

"What is it?" Ena asked. "I swear, I'm feeling fine now, just a bit dizzy." Now that she mentioned it, the few bites of apple she'd taken were sitting queasily in her stomach, too, but she didn't want to mention that and have everyone continue to fuss over her.

"I figured out who it is," they said, sounding relieved.

"Who what is?" Ena asked. She was honestly getting pretty tired of Mel's cryptic musings. It wasn't like they ever fully revealed anything anyway.

"The Mother of Monsters," they said, their face breaking out into a wide grin. They laughed gently, the sound echoing around the overhang they were in.

"The what?" Ena asked, her brows shooting up.

Just then, Cris walked up, looking between her and Mel. Mel shook their head, continuing to smile and chuckle to themselves before standing up and wandering off into the woods.

Ena stared after them, wondering what in the Underworld that was about, but she didn't exactly have the energy to follow them and follow up on it right this instant.

"How are you feeling?" Cris asked, sitting down beside her.

"Fine," she said, rubbing her forehead, which was beginning to ache. "Just tired."

Cris nodded. "And how are you feeling about everything with Greya?"

Ena looked over at him, his features illuminated by the fire, and gave him a small sincere smile. "Good, actually. Hopeful. It felt so nice to talk to her and tell her everything. I know she was hesitant at first, but the fact that she trusted me this time meant so much."

"You didn't think she would?"

"I don't know. You know Greya. She's...so confident. So sure of herself and her path. I know this is a lot for her to take in. It's a big ask for a future matriarch."

"True, but I'm sure once she has a chance to commune with Gaia, she'll Know what you told her to be true. Just like I did."

Ena felt reassured and reached out to grab her friend's hand in gratitude. "Thank you, for saying that. And for coming with me. I know how big of a risk this is for you, for all of us, and I'm so grateful that you trusted me too."

Cris flipped his hand over, giving hers a squeeze in return, then sighed sadly. "You know, at first, I mostly came to keep an eye on you, because I worried about you being alone with these daemons. But now...after everything you've told me, and everything Mel has said, I really do realize how important this is, and I'm honored to be here—truly."

Ena smiled at him and felt some of her guilt at dragging him into all this dissipate, but he still seemed...sad.

"But I wanted to apologize," he said, releasing her hand and avoiding eye contact by looking at the fire. "For before, when I tried to kiss you."

"Oh," she replied, understanding dawning on her. "Cris, you don't have to—"

"Yes, I do," he said, cutting her off. "I see now, finally, that you're not in the same place I am." The regret in his voice cut her to the bone, and guilt washed over her anew.

"Cris—" she began, though she didn't really know what to say.

"No, it's okay, really," he said, stopping her again. "I'm glad to know. I've been holding out for you for so long—too long—and you've made it repeatedly clear that you're not interested in me that way, despite the fun we've had."

Ena blushed at the mention of their past trysts and looked away. She really hoped Ty wasn't somewhere overhearing this conversation.

"But I see the way you look at him—the way you look at each other—and I know that's not us. You and I, we're something different, and I just want you to know I'm grateful for what we are."

Ena was touched. She couldn't put into words how much it meant to hear him say that, to have him understand.

"I'm grateful for what we are too," she said.

Cris gave her a tight-lipped, slightly forced smile, but she could tell this closure had been good for him. He seemed to relax more as they watched the flames of the fire dance and spit in silence, and she hoped this could be a new chapter for him.

"You know," Ena said, wanting to lighten the mood. "Maybe once this is all over, you could give Thyla a chance. You know she's always had a thing for you."

Cris whipped his head towards her. "What?" he asked, his brows jumping up. "Are you serious?"

Ena laughed, and Gaia, it felt good to do so. "Yes, of course. You really never knew?"

"No," Cris said, his face still in shock.

"Wow, Cris, you are...really bad at reading others' signs without your Knowing."

"Fuck," he said, laughing slightly and covering his face in his hands. "I guess you're right."

Ena felt lighter, laughing and joking with her friend, and she clung to that feeling. Because while she was glad to be on good terms with Cris, and Greya, and to be on the path to breaking the bond, she was also hurtling towards something she dreaded.

She hadn't missed what Cris had said about her and Ty—how he could tell just by watching them that they were something else—and it hurt to hear them described in such a way. Because even though she didn't want Cris, she and Ty couldn't be *that way* either. And every day brought her closer to the moment she feared—having to say goodbye to the one person who looked at her the way she wanted, who made her *feel* the way she wanted, and she knew it would be the hardest thing she'd ever had to do.

CHAPTER THIRTY-SIX

Ty

THE FIVE OF THEM traveled as quickly as possible over the next three days. It was brutal on all of them after being on the road so long already, but time was of the essence if they were going to get to the Sacred Grove in time to meet Greya.

Ty was still skeptical that Ena's sister would show up. His ingrained mistrust of witches—and her sister, especially, after the way she and Ena had left things in Occidens—ran deep, but Ena seemed confident that she would.

Of course, there was always the chance that others would show up too and disrupt them. Ty knew what would be necessary then—for his people's sake—and he was ready, but he knew Ena and the other witches would not be okay with it, so he really fucking hoped it wouldn't come to violence.

On the evening of the new moon, three days after they'd left the Sacred Pool, they found themselves on the outskirts of the Auster Coven. Ena knew the area like the back of her hand, so she was able to navigate them through the backwoods towards the Sacred

Grove, making sure to steer them away from any heavily used paths.

They traveled in absolute silence, listening for any snap of a branch, or wisp of a scent on the wind. But there was nothing, and as they wound their way through the darkening woods, Ty began to hear the overwhelming sound of rushing water.

The River Wry.

The noise was so much louder and more powerful than he remembered. It had been almost a decade since he'd last been in the Sacred Grove—since he'd met Ena there—and as the five of them finally broke through the trees into the wide-open space, he was struck by its majesty all over again.

The clearing was large—much larger than one would expect in the middle of such a dense forest—and the ground was mostly bare dirt in the center, repeated use by the witches having destroyed the ground plants that once grew there. The remnants of past bonfires scattered the space, their ashy residues making dark smudges on the ground.

All of that was dwarfed by the towering evergreen trees that encircled the space, naturally forming a near-perfect ring. Their size was intimidating—like they guarded this space and would protect it unto death.

Ty watched as Turner's neck tilted back, straining to look at the giants that surrounded them, but Mel—the only other one among them who had yet to see them—seemed in their own world as usual, barely seeming to notice that they'd finally arrived.

Ty dismounted and tethered his horse just at the edge of the grove, the others following his lead.

Walking into the center, he could see the sky above his head. It was dusk now, but dense gray clouds obscured the emerging stars, and he was struck by an overwhelming sense of déjà vu, remembering the last time he'd been here at dusk.

It had been summer then, and he'd been just eighteen, accompanying his uncles on his first mission. He'd seen a beautiful girl with dark-brown hair on the edge of the clearing, and in his youthful bravado, had gone up to ask her to dance.

Then she'd looked at him with those eyes, and the rest was history.

He watched as Ena approached him now, her face pensive. He wondered if she, too, was being haunted by memories of this space, though which ones, he wasn't sure. Either way, a sense of melancholy hit him so deep in his bones he almost couldn't breathe—because after tonight, if they succeeded with the spell, everything would be different.

The five of them wordlessly worked together to light a fire—small enough to see by, but not so big as to attract attention—and once it was lit, they gathered around it as they awaited Greya.

The apprehension in the air was palpable. Mel drew symbols in the dirt with her finger, swirling patterns that almost resembled those used to decorate the Great Antre in the Underworld, and Cris quietly broke sticks, throwing them into the fire every few minutes. Turner refused to sit and instead paced the space, visiting and touching each giant tree in turn over and over again.

But Ty's eyes were drawn to Ena, as always. She stared into the fire, a task which always seemed to soothe her, and Ty was soothed in turn watching her. He knew he must look like a fool, watching her incessantly as she stared at the fire, but he couldn't look away. Not now. Not when they were so close to—

Ty heard the noise first—the faint sound of a soft footstep on a beaten dirt path.

"Someone's coming," he announced in a whisper to the group, his eyes whipping towards the dark woods.

They all stood up, Ty's hand immediately going to the dagger on his belt. The footsteps were delicate, and sounded like they came from just one individual, but you never knew with witches.

It was a few minutes later that he saw her emerge from the dark wood, following the path that led to the Auster Coven's village.

She was as Ty remembered her, albeit a little older now. Her pale-blonde hair was mostly covered by the hood of the black cloak she wore, but the tip of her braid peeked out the bottom. Her face was—Iblis, it was so much like Ena's, with a gentle brow and rose-colored lips. But her eyes were different, slightly smaller and brown compared to Ena's big blues, and her skin wasn't nearly as pale.

And she was alone. Ty heard no other signs of approach—and silently thanked Iblis for it as he removed his hand from his dagger.

The sisters spotted each other, and Ty smiled despite himself as he watched them. Ena rushed towards her sister, the two of them falling into an embrace so natural it was like watching two vines entwine together, fusing as they grew.

"I missed you so much," he heard Ena say, her voice emotional and muffled in her sister's cloak.

"I missed you too," Greya responded, sounding relieved. Pulling away from her sister, Greya patted the leather bag slung across her body. "I brought what you needed," she added confidently.

"Did you commune with Gaia like I suggested?" Ena asked, her voice slightly choked.

"I did, and you're right. I believe that doing this is for the better, despite the risks. I'm with you, Ena."

The sisters smiled at each other, and Ena turned to look behind her, drawing Greya's attention to the rest of them.

Greya's eyes landed on him first, not in an unfriendly way, but definitely judging, as he approached them.

"You must be Ty," she said neutrally, looking him up and down. "You look different from what I remember."

"Nine years will do that to you," he said, meeting the witch's assessing gaze.

"It's nice to officially meet you," she said, extending her hand hesitantly.

"Likewise," he responded, shaking her petite hand in greeting.

She may have been hesitant—maybe because of his and Ena's history, maybe because he was a daemon, he didn't know—but her grip was strong and confident, like a matriarch's should be, and something in him settled a bit. He was glad Ena had her—this stable, loving force—in her life. She deserved it. She deserved so much.

"Where's Perse?" Ena asked as they broke their handshake.

Greya looked at her, clearing her throat slightly. "I may have...slipped him a sleeping potion with dinner."

Ena gasped, fighting a smile. "Greya, you didn't," she said, chastising her lightheartedly. Iblis, it was good to see her smile. Though an irrational pang of sadness struck him that he wasn't the cause of it anymore.

"I didn't want him to be involved in this," Greya explained defensively. "The fewer people that know, the better, at least until we can ease the Coven into the idea of this. It's the best way to protect him."

"Did you two ever..." Ena began, her tone tinged with sadness.

"Yes," Greya responded guiltily. "We were handfasted a few weeks ago," she confirmed. "I wanted to wait for you, I really, really did, but I didn't know when you were coming back, and Perse—"

"Stop," Ena said, holding up her hand. "It's alright. I understand completely. I'm so, so happy for you two," she said, reaching out to squeeze Greya's arm. "I'm just sorry I wasn't there. Do you forgive me?"

Her sister smiled at her, looking relieved. "Always," she said, reaching out to hold Ena's hands.

"Aren't you going to introduce me?" Turner asked, as he approached the three of them.

Greya turned to look at him, too, using that same assessing gaze.

"Greya, this is Turner. Turner, this is my sister Greya."

"Is he a…?" Greya asked, seeming surprised by his demeanor.

"Yep, daemonic through and through," Turner replied, extending his hand to shake hers in greeting. "It's nice to finally meet you. We've heard a lot about you."

Ty could see Greya relax slightly at Turner's overt friendliness.

"Nice to see you, Greya," Cris greeted as he joined the group too.

"Good to see you, too, Cris. I'm glad I'm not the only one Ena convinced of this," she said as she laughed familiarly at him. "How did you get Northe's permission to come?"

"I, uh…didn't," Cris said sheepishly, rubbing the back of his neck. Iblis, the man's timidity was grating. How could Ena have ever dated this fucker?

"I see," Greya replied, understanding clearly dawning on her of the consequences of that. "And you must be…" She looked over at Mel next, where they stood near the fire.

"I'm Mel," they said simply. "It's nice to see you in the now."

Greya's brows furrowed slightly, as everyone's usually did when they spoke to Mel.

"Mel is the seer from Occidens I told you about," Ena said as Greya nodded her head in understanding.

Silence fell over the group after the brief introductions, a tension now palpable as they all came to a collective realization.

It was time.

No more waiting. No more objects. No more research. They had everything they needed.

They could break the bond.

He turned to look at Ena, and she met his gaze unflinchingly. She seemed calmer than before—her reunion with her sister clearly having grounded her. She felt...powerful.

"Well, Ena," he said, breaking the beat of silence. "Are you ready?"

"I am," she replied, her gaze like steel. "Let's break the bond."

***

Ty watched in admiration as Ena took control.

"Turner, go get the amulet from my pack, please," she said as Greya reached into her bag and pulled out the chalice and athame she'd brought, handing them to Ena. "Mel and Cris, join me in the center of the grove as we form our sacred circle." Turning back to her sister, she spoke quietly. "You don't have to stay for this, Greya. Thank you so much for bringing the objects, but maybe it's best if you return, so you're less culpable."

Greya shook her head. "No, I'm here for this. I need to be here."

Ena nodded, a pleased smile on her face, and Ty felt another part of him settle. Maybe Ena really would be alright after all this. If Greya could accept this, then maybe the rest of her Coven would too.

Leaving her sister on the edge of the grove, Ena moved to the center of the clearing with Mel and Cris. The three of them stood in a circle, and Ty made his way in, centering himself in the middle, just as she'd described to him.

He faced Ena, their bodies close. He could feel her warmth as he towered over her, guarding her like the trees around them. She looked up at him, her ocean-blue eyes filled with reverence and certainty, trust and faith.

"Kneel," she said, her voice gentle yet commanding in a way that he had never heard before. He'd be lying if he said his cock didn't shift at the sound of her voice like that, and suddenly, every nerve in his body felt alive in her presence.

He lowered himself to the ground, submitting himself before her.

His dark goddess.

He felt it the instance the three witches around him began to reach into their Knowing, preparing for the spell. The stillness of their bodies was eerie as they communed with the signs around them.

Ty was so focused on her, watching her breathe as she prepared to begin the spell, that he made a mistake.

He didn't hear the person's approach until it was too late.

All of a sudden, the world around him began to move slowly—Ena opened her mouth to speak, but it was barely moving, like she was stuck in molasses.

Ty, finally sensing something was wrong, turned to look at the other witches. They, too, were so still they appeared to be frozen. Standing up, he looked to the edge of the grove to see Greya standing there, looking like she was carved from stone.

That's when he saw her.

The matriarch of the Auster Coven emerged from the dark woods, her wrinkled face screwed up in effort as she held her hands outstretched towards them.

The matriarch's Gift was *tempus*—the power to slow down time—and from the looks of it, the way she held all four witches at once, she was very powerful.

Ty's stomach plummeted. This was the very thing he'd feared. The thing he'd dreaded—and like a fool he thought they'd avoided it.

His heart began to race, and he looked around frantically until his eyes locked with Turner's. As daemons, they were the only ones unaffected by the matriarch's magic, and he didn't need to speak to know they were on the same page about what needed to happen next.

He couldn't let her stop this. They were so close—finally. Everything he'd worked for. Everything his mother had set in motion. Everything Ena had bled for.

He wouldn't let her take it all away, no matter who she was.

Without thinking, he moved, pulling his dagger from his belt as he stalked towards Heran.

"Stay back, daemon!" she shouted, her voice full of mettle and venom. "You will not triumph on this day."

"Release them," Ty said, menace in his voice. "I don't want to have to hurt you."

Maybe he would be able to intimidate her enough that she would drop her magic and let Ena speak to her. Maybe she could convince her. But if she'd already alerted the rest of the Coven...

"Never," she said, her voice sounding strained. Was the use of her Gift wearing on her already? "You can never hurt me. Gaia is with me, and she will not let you descend this world into chaos."

"This is Gaia's will, witch. Release them and let Ena explain," Ty said, his voice coming out angrier than intended. He felt his rage boiling inside him. He did not want to hurt her, but he couldn't let her ruin this. This was their only chance to *fix* everything.

"I don't know what you've done to twist my dear Ena's mind into believing you, but I swear to Gaia, if you—"

Ty moved closer, meaning to threaten her with his physical presence, maybe grab her and hold her arms down, when suddenly the old woman doubled over.

She cried out in pain, clutching her left arm as if it hurt, but Ty hadn't even touched her yet.

Then everything happened quickly.

The old woman released the other witches from her *tempus*, and Ty heard Ena begin speaking once more.

"Wha—?" She looked around, confused at Ty's apparent disappearance from their circle. Then her eyes landed on Heran at the same time Greya's voice rang out.

"Heran!"

Greya rushed towards the old woman as she collapsed. She looked pale as death, her face screwed up in agony.

"Ena, help!" Greya called, her voice choked with a sob.

Ena rushed toward her sister and the matriarch, falling to her knees beside them. "What happened?" she asked frantically as she ran her hands over Heran's face. "How did she get here? I was about to start the spell and then all of a sudden, Ty was over here."

"She used her Gift," Ty said, trying to explain while the old woman struggled to breathe. "She tried to stop us, and I told her to let you go, but then she collapsed."

"I think it's her heart," Greya said in panic. "She's been slowing down the last few months and I—we need to do something."

"Run back to the house and get some herbs. Do you have any hawthorn tincture?" Ena asked Greya. Her voice shook but she spoke clearly and decisively.

"Yes, I think so," Greya said. "But what about—"

"Ena," the old woman gasped, her face desperate as both Greya and Ena focused on her. "Do not...let...Iblis...triumph."

"I swear I serve Gaia, Heran. I swear," Ena replied.

"His...Power...destroys... Please, my child," Heran whispered frantically.

"Heran, please, hold on, and I'll explain," Ena begged, her voice childlike and afraid. "Greya, go—"

Ena's words cut off as Heran's eyes drifted closed and she lost consciousness.

"Heran?" Ena called, putting her hands on the old woman's face. "Heran!"

Her voice echoed around the dark clearing, her helplessness cutting Ty to the bone.

"She's not moving," Greya said. "Ena! She's not moving anymore."

Ena reached out to feel the old woman's pulse, grabbing her wrist and placing two fingers atop it. "I can't feel her pulse," she said quietly, her voice shaking.

"Are you sure?" Greya asked in disbelief. "Heran? Heran!" she called, wrenching her wrist away from Ena to feel for the pulse herself.

Ena looked up at Ty, desperation on her face. He watched helplessly, not knowing what to do. Not knowing if there was anything *to* do.

"Lay her down. We need to compress her chest," Ena said to Greya.

The woman complied instantly, laying Heran on the cold dirt.

Ena moved over to her, placing her hands in the center of the old woman's chest, lacing her fingers together. Ty had no idea what she was doing—he'd never seen anyone do this before. Was it a witch thing?

Rhythmically, Ena began compressing the old woman's chest, moving her body with the force of her motions. She did that several times before tilting the woman's head back, lowering her mouth over the old woman's and breathing into it.

Then she repeated the process. Again. And again.

The silence of it all was deafening—everyone frozen as if still trapped in the woman's Gift, watching, waiting for her to move, to breathe.

Eventually, Ena stopped, breathing heavily, her own body shaking with the effort.

"Why did you stop?" Greya asked, her voice a panicked sob.

But Ena didn't reply. Instead, she looked up at Ty, searching his eyes for absolution.

He shook his head solemnly at her. Did she know it was over? It seemed like it to him, but he didn't know how to tell her that.

How do you tell someone the woman that raised them is dead?

She looked away from him, the realization clearly dawning on her, too, as she turned back toward her sister.

"Greya," Ena said in a broken whisper. "She's gone."

Chapter Thirty-Seven

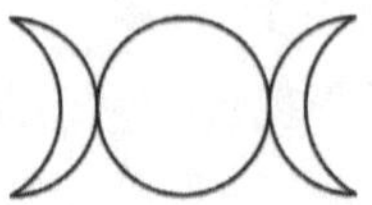

Ena

DISBELIEF HIT ENA LIKE a ton of bricks. Was this really happening? This felt like a dream.

Heran's body lay before her—unmoving on the ground. She looked so...still. Not the stern yet kind and full of life woman Ena had known her whole life. Here now was just a body—getting colder by the second in the frigid winter air.

Ena was shocked by how small she seemed. How frail she looked like this. This vessel looked like her, and yet it wasn't *her*, and it was so confusing.

Ena looked up at Greya. Tears were in her sister's eyes as she collapsed on top of Heran, sobbing. Her cries echoed around the Sacred Grove, and all Ena could think was: *what just happened? What is happening? I don't understand.*

One second, Ena had been starting the spell, and then Ty was gone and apparently Heran had come and used her Gift, and then her heart had stopped and there hadn't been time to get the hawthorn and then she did the compressions like Heran taught her and...

Please, my child.

Heran's final words to her echoed through her head, and now Greya was crying and Ena felt frozen in place. She forgot how to move and couldn't remember how to go on. Should she go on? What should she *do*? Shouldn't she be crying like Greya? Shouldn't she be doing *something*?

She felt a warm hand on her shoulder. Turning to look, her eyes met Ty's. They were light green with a dark ring around them—beautiful as always—and they anchored her to reality.

"Ena, we need to finish the spell. We need to finish it now before anyone else comes. I'm so sorry, Ena," he was saying, his voice filled with anguish, but she had trouble understanding his words.

"Ena—do you hear me?" he asked gently.

She could hear him, so she tried to speak.

"Yes," she said, finally mustering a word, but her voice sounded monotone and unfeeling. Was that her voice? Why was it coming out so strangely?

"Now is our chance. Do you think you can finish the spell?" he asked softly, but there was an urgency in his voice. "I don't know who else might be coming. I don't know if anyone else heard us. It's now or we need to leave, for your safety," Ty said.

Ena looked around the Sacred Grove. Cris, Mel, and Turner had come closer, their faces screwed up in pity. They stood, holding the ceremonial objects in their hands.

Ena's brain felt sluggish, like she was swimming through thick syrup. But slowly, she began to comprehend.

Finish the spell, yes. They had to finish the spell.

"Yes, yeah, I can. I need to finish the spell," she said, standing up and wiping wetness from her eyes. Had she been crying? She didn't remember crying. "But someone—" She looked down at her sister, who was distraught before her. "Someone needs to help Greya," she said, her voice cracking as she spoke.

"I'll sit with her," Turner said, coming immediately to Greya's side.

Greya looked up at her then, her eyes red-rimmed.

"Greya," Ena began. "I'm going to finish the spell, okay? I'm going to finish this, and then we can…and then we can figure out what's next, okay?"

At first, it seemed as if her sister didn't hear her, lost in her grief as she was, probably feeling just as overwhelmed as Ena, but then she gave a single jerky nod, like even that much movement was too much for her. She closed her eyes and leaned against Turner, who put his arm around her, holding her up and stroking her arm soothingly.

They needed to get Perse, Ena thought vaguely. Perse would help. But he was passed out from the sleeping potion, she remembered, so that would have to wait. Turner was all they had.

Ena turned away from her sister to find Ty next to her.

"Ena, look at me," he said, reaching out with his strong, warm hands and wiping away a tear with his thumb. "You are strong, and you can do this. Focus on me, on the spell, and nothing else right now. Do you hear me?"

"Yes," Ena said, feeling grounded by his words. He was right. If they were going to be successful, if they were going to end this, she needed to focus on the spell and let all other concerns dissipate. "Yes, I hear you, Ty."

She moved to the center of the Sacred Grove once more, her body and mind feeling numb.

Cris looked at her with a shocked and concerned expression, but Mel just looked sympathetic. Had they seen this coming? The thought struck Ena like a knife to the heart, and she didn't know if she should feel anger or pity if that were the case.

"Ena," Cris began. "I—"

"I'm fine," Ena said, centering herself, and letting it all go. Every single thing. "Let's just do this."

She reached down into her Knowing once more, losing herself to the familiar feeling of the woods around her, and she let it sweep her away. The branches swaying the breeze, the constant, steady rush of the River Wry, the densely packed earth beneath her feet, the fire that crackled and smoked nearby. There was balance to it all—purpose—but there was chaos, too, and it felt good to lose herself to it right now.

The water beat into the rocks, crushing endlessly, violently. The wind swirled and twirled in patterns unforeseen, each gust causing chaotic movements in the branches, making the weak ones snap. In the clouds above, Ena Knew there was energy building, nearly bursting as the water condensed, getting heavier and heavier as they approached the inevitable deluge. She felt the disequilibrium of the beetles in the nearby ash tree, eating and gnawing and devouring as they multiplied uncontrollably, disrupting the population of trees that only wanted to live.

There was chaos all around her, and it was this force, this part of her Knowing, that she reached for.

Nodding at Ty to once more enter their sacred circle, she watched as his beautiful, strong features came into focus as he knelt before her.

He was chaos incarnate. The harsh lines of his face were devastating to her, causing her heart to beat erratically. The dips and whorls of his *onata* along the sides of his head and neck were dark and untamed in the glow of the firelight.

She could feel his barely contained rage vibrating inside him, ready to spill out, and she drew on that too.

She took the athame from Cris, who held both it and the chalice, and examined it with intention. She wanted to Know it.

The knife's silver blade was waved and deathly sharp, and the handle felt cold and unforgiving in her hand. The metal was like stone—it had no intention but to maintain its state, but it was ancient and malleable, having changed forms many times over.

Next, she took the golden chalice from Cris too. It was one she recognized—the same one she'd used during her Summoning. The symbol of Gaia shone on the front, the gold metal it was etched into gleaming in the firelight, and Ena was filled with a fresh clarity—she Knew in her bones that this was Gaia's will.

She offered the blade to Ty handle first, and he took it. He held it above his wrist, hesitating for just a second before slicing deeply into his skin.

Ena held out the golden chalice, positioning it below his wound, and watched with fascination as his blood welled up and dripped willingly into it.

She couldn't help but contrast the vision of it with what she'd seen in her vision from Gaia—when the daemon woman's blood was forcibly taken as she cried out in pain. Because here was Ty, sacrificing all that he had to give for his people, for their future, and she felt her heart swell with pride and awe of him.

After several minutes, she removed the chalice, now half-full with his crimson offering. Turning to her right, she nodded to Mel, and the witch opened the wooden box containing the amulet, revealing it to the night air.

The dark purple of the uncut amethyst looked almost black in the moonless night, but the lighter white-purple at the edges seemed to glow, reflecting more light than was available. She gently traced her finger over each of the four symbols etched into the silver setting in turn—the ones representing Gaia, Iblis, the three Covens, and the binding rune. Ena felt the way she always did looking at it—filled with awe and inexplicably drawn to its power. Usually, she held back, but this time, she let that power pull her in.

Reaching out, she picked up the amulet, holding it delicately by its braided silver chain. She lowered it intentionally into the chalice filled with Ty's blood, submerging it as deeply as she could. Something about the way Ty's blood looked, deep red in the chalice, contrasting with the silver and purple of the amulet, the way the thick substance dripped and moved as she lifted the amulet back up, enthralled Ena, and she found she couldn't look away.

Handing the chalice back off to Cris, she slipped the amulet over her neck. It hung heavy atop her chest as Ty's blood dripped down her skin, and instantly, she felt its power vibrate through her, filling her with...*more*. All at once, she Knew its intentions, as if it were its own entity, rather than just a sum of its parts. It was blessed and powerful, and wanted to flow through her, making her the vessel through which it would enhance her spell. Gaia's magic, Iblis's magic, the three Covens' magic—it wanted to give her *all* of it. And she would let it.

Reaching out, she joined hands with Cris and Mel. She couldn't help it—her Knowing felt them, too—felt their unique combinations of wariness and righteousness, excitement and dread.

She nodded to them, indicating that it was time. They'd rehearsed the words, and together, they did the unimaginable—they summoned Iblis.

{*Diabolus vocare*} they chanted as one.

Instantly, she felt a dark void bloom within her. It was infinite, endless, and nothing, but at the same time, it was blinding in its intensity. Ena was filled with a bone-deep terror, feeling as if on the precipice of a reckoning, on the edge of losing complete control to the unknown. She wanted to cry, to scream in horror as she tried to pull away from whatever it was, but then just as swiftly, the terror was replaced.

There was peace. There was contentment. There was gentleness—and above all, there was purpose.

Her eyes flew open, landing on Mel and Cris. Their faces were stricken with awe just as hers was. She had no idea what was going on. Had something gone wrong with the spell? Was this Iblis? Because somehow, it felt like...

Mel nodded to her once in reassurance. This was okay. They had to continue the spell.

Ena nodded in return, locking eyes with Mel and Cris in turn. Both of their faces were filled with determination as all three of them reached into the entity they'd summoned and spoke again.

{*Tellus restore*}

Ena heard Ty gasp—like he was taking his very first breath—and her eyes fell to where he knelt before her.

His eyes, normally that beautiful light green she loved so dearly, were drenched in black. They appeared almost as dark as the void she'd felt within her—almost as if the void was now within him, flowing through *him*. He seemed frozen in fear and awe as his eyes stared into the pitch black.

What was he seeing? What was he feeling? He didn't seem to be in pain, but he—

Just as suddenly, his eyes changed back. The light green with the dark ring returned, but there was a sheen to them now.

It was tears. His eyes were filled with tears.

"Ty," she asked, suddenly concerned. She dropped Mel and Cris's hands, and moved to cup the sides of his face, drawing his gaze to hers. "Are you alright? Are you hurt?"

"No, I—" he spoke, his voice choked with emotion. "I can feel her," he said. "She's here. She's...everywhere."

"You can feel her? You can feel Gaia?" Ena asked, emotion overwhelming her now too at the look of utter rapture on Ty's face.

"Yes," he said, breaking into a smile. "Yes, I feel Gaia. You—" He paused, bringing his hand up on top of hers where it rested, looking deep into her eyes. "You did it, Ena."

Ena smiled at him as tears filled her eyes. Looking up, she saw similar looks of relief on Cris and Mel's faces.

"We did it," she said to them, her voice exhausted and relieved. "I can't believe we did it."

Ty stood up, turning to look at Turner, who still knelt next to Greya on the ground at the edge of the grove. The man was clutching his heart, with his head bowed, and Greya was looking at him worriedly, her face tearstained.

"Turner, are you alright?" Ty asked, moving towards his cousin.

Turner looked up as he approached, reaching up to take the hand Ty offered him. "Yeah, I—I think so," he said, his voice sounding overwhelmed and confused. "I think..." He gripped Ty's shirt in his hand, as if to steady himself with the feeling. "I feel her too."

"What does it feel like to you?" Ty asked, his brow furrowed.

"It's like this...understanding that wasn't there before. This sense of rightness and balance to everything, where before, it just seemed...chaotic. I mean, the chaos is still there, too, but there's something new now. It's like—"

"Seeing through different eyes," Ty finished for him.

"Exactly," Turner said, looking at his friend with that wide smile of his. "To be honest, though, I don't know if I like it."

Ty laughed—that infectious way he did when he was carefree and happy. "We'll have to get used to it, I guess."

The two men embraced each other, hugging like their lives depended on it, and it warmed Ena's heart to see.

When they broke apart, Turner looked to Ena, where she still stood next to Cris and Mel.

"Thank you," he said, his voice sincere and emotional. "To all of you. This is..."

"How it was always meant to be," Ena finished for him. "I Know that, and...something else too," she said, her brow furrowing in concentration. Was that right? Could she...

Reaching out with her Knowing towards Turner and Ty in that way that usually was met with nothing, she felt *them*. She could read their signs—the way they stood, the way they moved, the way they breathed, all of it told her of their intentions and their emotions, just like if they were a witch or a mortal. "I can feel you, with my Knowing," she said. "Can you too?" she asked Cris and Mel.

"I can," Cris answered, and Mel nodded in affirmation, too, the witch's small face relieved and peaceful, as if things were working out exactly as they'd seen.

"I guess now that the bond is broken, our magic works on one another again," Ty said. "That's...going to have some consequences."

He was right. What would this mean for relations between the Covens and the Underworld? Would it escalate tensions or ease them? Ena had no idea. Suddenly, she felt so overwhelmed by everything, the repercussions of all this, what had happened to Heran—whose body still lay on the ground at Greya's feet, now covered with a blanket from one of their packs.

Her body felt exhausted, and for the first time, she noticed how badly the cold air had gotten to her extremities. She moved to sit by the fire, but realized she still wore the amulet, which had dripped Ty's blood onto her clothing.

Pulling it over her head, the blood-soaked amethyst brushed her mouth slightly as it passed her lips, transferring a drop of half-dried blood onto her. She could smell it there—metallic and rich. She didn't know what came over her, but like some half-forgotten instinct, her tongue darted out and she licked it, pulling the drop from her lip into her mouth. Gaia, it tasted...

"So are we gonna talk about what happened?" Cris asked the group.

Ena jolted—suddenly pulled away from the ambrosial taste of the blood in her mouth as she redirected her focus to Cris.

Quickly placing the amulet back in the box, she looked at Turner as he responded. "What do you mean what happened? The spell worked, didn't it?" he asked.

"Yes, clearly, but how did it work? What the hell was that that we summoned?" Cris asked.

"I thought you summoned Iblis," Ty asked, his dark brow furrowed.

"I thought so too," Cris said. "Or at least, that we were supposed to, but that didn't feel like Iblis to me. It felt like—"

"Gaia," Ena said. "You're right. I thought so too when it happened. It reminded me of my Summoning." How could that be possible, though? The spellwords they'd used definitely derived from the runic word for chaos. "What did you feel, Ty? When the entity entered you?"

"It felt like Iblis to me, or at least what I remember from my Trial," he said.

She turned to Mel, who had been suspiciously silent throughout all this. "Mel," Ena began. "What did it feel like to you?"

"It was like you said, it felt like Gaia, or what I remember of Gaia from my Summoning," they replied, but they averted their eyes from the group, fiddling with their hands in front of them.

"What else do you know?" Ena asked. She Knew Mel was hiding something. It was obvious to her now when they were being intentionally vague about their visions. She knew Mel believed the future was unchangeable and liked to keep things close to their chest until they knew for certain what would happen so as not to upset people, and it was one thing if Mel hadn't warned her about Heran's death—especially if there was nothing she could've done anyway—but Ena still felt she had a right to know about something this big.

Mel sighed, collapsing onto the dirt next to Ena by the fire. "I don't know much," they began. "Just that...there are others."

"Others?" Ty asked.

One by one, everyone came over the fire, even Greya, who looked stunned and struck by all that had happened, but was present and listening once more.

"Yes," Mel said. "There are others who have noticed the...overlap between Gaia and Iblis before. And they worship something else entirely."

"What do they worship?" Ty asked, his face serious and unsettled.

"Omnis," Ena replied, remembering that vague reference she'd read in *The Evolution of Magic* all those weeks ago. "They worship Omnis."

CHAPTER THIRTY-EIGHT

Ty

FOR ONCE, THANK FUCKING Iblis, no one pried further into Mel's Knowledge. These revelations about some being called Omnis, and everything that had happened with Heran's death and the breaking of the bond, had left everyone reeling.

Ty watched as the group dispersed—Mel and Cris settling by the fire with Turner, and Ena kneeling beside her sister next to the covered body of the matriarch.

Ty stood frozen, though, not knowing where to go or what to do. He felt guilty for how things had gone down with the matriarch and wanted to comfort Ena, but he figured he should give her and her sister some space to grieve. He knew he needed to remain vigilant for other intruders, but it was so hard to focus on that.

Because they had actually done it—they had broken the bond—and all around him, there was so much *more* than before.

His mind raced with his newfound sense of Gaia, or whatever it was, inside him. This new feeling of purpose—of balance—within. His every breath, his every move and thought, could still cause chaos, yes—it existed all around him, just as it did before—but now, so did equilibrium. So did stasis. So did a feeling of calm and regularity that he wanted to reach for, but didn't quite know how to yet. He'd lived his whole life feeding into disruption. How could he now live for peace?

He was drawn from his reverie as he saw Ena stand up, saying her goodbyes to Greya who prepared to walk back to her house to wake her husband Perse.

How was she feeling about all this? That became Ty's only and omnipresent thought as he watched Ena walk away on her own, disappearing into the woods.

Where was she going? Should he follow her? Make sure she was okay? He knew she was mourning Heran and was likely as overwhelmed as everyone else by what had occurred during the ritual. Maybe she just wanted to be alone.

It felt like pulling sharp splinters from under his nails, but he forced himself to stay put and not pursue her. She deserved time to herself. And who was he, anyway, to go after her? They were nothing anymore. Not after this, not now that the spell was done. She would go back to her Coven, and hopefully find some way to be accepted back in, under her sister's guidance as the new matriarch, and he would... Where would he go?

For the first time since they'd left the Underworld, he let himself contemplate that. The Underworld was likely in shock right now. If all daemons' senses had shifted as drastically as his and Turner's had, they would be reeling. How long until they realized what had happened? Until they realized their magic now worked against witches? What would Cole do then?

Part of Ty wanted to return, to help guide his fellow daemons and explain, but he knew it wasn't safe for him, not after his escape and what he'd done. Cole would punish him, maybe kill him, at all costs now. He was the heir, yes, but only because he was the first son of the first son. Zak would replace him as heir if he were killed, and if Cole were to make it look like an accident, or something perpetrated by the witches, there wouldn't be too much of an uproar.

Maybe that would be for the best...

Fuck, why was he thinking like that? The Underworld was *his*. He should be coming up with a plan to return and overthrow Cole. He should be plotting his next move. His people needed him, were relying on him. But...why did that all feel so hollow now?

All he'd wanted for so long was to break the bond so daemons could reunite with mortals and witches, so they could choose something different than the shit order Cole insisted on. He'd never loved the burden of being the future king, but he knew no one else was going to fucking do it, so he *had* to. And he'd found purpose in that, especially during those years separated from Ena. But now... Somehow, it all felt empty without *his* witch.

How could he just say goodbye to her now? After everything they'd been through? After everything he'd felt? He'd never loved anyone but her, and he knew deep down he never would. And he knew that he'd failed to protect her, that in so many ways he didn't deserve her, but the idea of leaving her now... Iblis, his entire being rebelled at the thought.

Maybe it was the prospect of actually having to walk away, or maybe it was his newfound sense of Gaia—the completeness he felt knowing for the first time that he *could* find peace if he truly chose to—but suddenly, he was filled with a clarity he'd never had before.

The only reason he'd failed to protect her was because he'd followed Cole's orders, and he'd put the Underworld's needs above hers. He'd felt torn at the time, but he hadn't listened to his instinct. But now—now it was screaming at him.

And he would listen to it this time.

He needed to go find her. Right now.

He needed to tell her.

Ty took off into the woods, following her scent through the forest surrounding the Sacred Grove. But he didn't really need it to tell him where she was—he already knew where she'd go.

He followed the bend of the River Wry, the path coming back to him like it was just yesterday that he'd last been here. He remembered the hope he'd felt as an eighteen-year-old, coming to meet Ena for their dinner under the stars. The way he'd been consumed by her even then—by her mind and her body and just fucking *everything* about the way she was.

Quietly, he emerged from the forest onto the rocky beach. The sky above was filled with stars, the clouds having parted to display the moonless sky. Their multitude of tiny lights shone down on Ena as she crouched by the edge of the water—watching.

She turned to look at Ty as he approached, and he could see her face was troubled.

The sight of it made him angry—he wanted nothing more than to destroy whatever it was that was making her upset. Just absolutely obliterate it so he could see her smile, see her laugh. But he knew he was powerless to do that, and that made him feel so damn inadequate.

He swallowed as he approached her. "Hey," he said, his lame greeting belying the turmoil within.

"Hi," she said, standing up.

"Are you alright?" he asked gently. It was a stupid fucking question. Of course she wasn't alright.

"No," she said, looking away as her eyes filled with tears. "I'm not."

Ty rushed to her. He wanted to take her in his arms and hold her, comfort her. Would she let him? Did she want that too? He felt paralyzed by his uncertainty so he settled with something simpler.

Raising his hand, he pushed a strand of her dark hair back from her face, tucking it behind her ear before cupping her cheek like the precious thing she was. She leaned into his hand, closing her eyes as if savoring his touch, but it clearly made her more sad, because tears started to flow down her cheeks, dripping onto his palm.

"Ena," he whispered. "Don't cry," he said, knowing it was futile. She could cry if she needed to, he just hated to see it.

"Why are you here, Ty?" she asked, opening her damp eyes. "The spell's over now. We did it. Greya will be back soon with Perse, and you should be—"

"No," Ty said, his voice hard and angrier than he intended. "Don't say it."

"You should be going," Ena pleaded. "You need to go, before other witches come, before..." She paused, taking a deep breath as if to steel herself. "You have a duty now. You need to go back to the Underworld and free them from Cole's rule."

"And what about you? Where will you go? What will you do? You and I know that the rest of the Covens won't be as forgiving as your sister for what you and the others did. What if they don't accept you back in as you'd hoped?"

Ena looked away from him, and he didn't miss the way she refused to answer the question. And that settled it for him.

"Ena, look at me," he commanded.

She turned her eyes back to his, and he lost himself in the deep blue of hers. The peace of the sky on a clear summer day and the mystery of a calm ocean was before him in her eyes. Constant and beautiful. Deep and restorative.

"I've made a decision," Ty said, his voice calm and certain. "I'm not going back to the Underworld. I'm staying with you—here, if you want, or we can go into hiding if we need to. But I'm not leaving you. I'm not putting others above you ever again. I can't, so don't ask me to."

"What?" she asked, her eyes widening. "Ty, you can't be serious. What about the rest of the daemons in the Underworld? What about everything you've been working towards for them? You're the heir. You can't just abandon them. I won't ask you to do that."

"I know you're not asking me. I'm making a choice, Ena, and I choose you," he said, his voice moving into desperation as fear crept in. What if she didn't let him stay? "Ena, please, hear me out."

He grasped both her hands in his, holding them tightly, close to his chest, so she could feel how much he meant this.

"The truth is, I'm selfish, and you need to know that. Yes, I've been working to break the bond to give my people a choice, I do want that, but deep down, the only reason I ever wanted to break the bond was so that we would have a chance to be together. I know that might sound terrible, but it's the truth. None of this means anything without you. And I know I'm supposed to be king, but, fuck, I don't *want* to be."

He released one of her hands to run his own through his hair, attempting to soothe the agitation he felt now. He couldn't even articulate how pissed he was at them all—his father, his mother, his uncle, Iblis and Gaia or whoever the fuck they were—for forcing him into this life, and he let that fire in him burn for her to see.

"For the first time in my life, I see a different path for myself. One not dictated by my blood or my uncle or my duty, but by me. What *I* want. And *you* are what I want, Ena. I'm yours, and I can't stop being yours. I'm so in love with you, so please. Don't make me go. Let me stay. Let me be yours."

Tears started to fall down Ena's face anew until she was sobbing, and Ty's heart sank. What was wrong? Did she not love him back? Did she not want him to stay?

Fear kept him paralyzed, and he clenched his jaw to steel himself for her rejection.

"Ty, there's something I need to tell you," she said, her voice broken and hurting. Something about the vulnerability in her eyes scared him. "I'm...I think I'm pregnant."

Ty froze. Had he heard her right?

His brain was fractured; his mind was mush. He was somehow utterly incapable of processing this information.

In all of his wildest imaginings, he had not seen this coming.

"Ty..." she began cautiously, noting his silence. "Please say something. I know this is...that this might change things and—"

Finally, the meaning of what she'd said dawned on him, and his heart shattered into a million pieces, each one sharp and painful as he realized the consequences of it all. The pieces cut him, tortured him. There was fear and trepidation, anger and grief all at once, but underneath the pain, there was something else...a glow.

Something warm, something hopeful, grew inside him. It was so incredibly beautiful, like this tiny eternal flame—a bright light in the darkness.

Ena was going to have a baby. *His* baby.

And it was settled for him.

"Stop fucking talking," he said, silencing her anxious thoughts immediately as he hauled her into him. He wrapped his arms around her, hoping his body could communicate what he was still struggling to say out loud. He held her tightly, infinitely, as he stroked the back of her head, then kissed the top of it.

"Ena," he began, his own voice breaking with emotion now as he felt tears well in his eyes. "I swear to you there is nothing I won't do to protect you and our baby. I know I failed you before, but that will never happen again. Do you hear me? Never. I'm not going anywhere. I will be wherever you are and I will love you and our child, endlessly. I am yours, and now, I am theirs too."

He felt her break down in his arms, her body shaking with her sobs until she cried them all out. He couldn't even imagine how much she'd been dealing with on her own, with this knowledge, on top of everything else that had happened in the last few hours. Iblis, she was strong. He loved her even more for that.

Gradually, her sobs quieted down, and she looked up to face him. "You really mean that, Ty? You won't leave me alone?"

"I promise, Ena. Never again," he replied, his words a vow.

She smiled at him—a gentle, trusting expression of relief that warmed his heart to see, though her eyes were still filled with sadness. "You never failed me, you know," she said.

"I did, but only because I didn't have my priorities straight. I do now, and I'll never let anything distract me from them again," he spoke soothingly, pushing her hair off her damp face.

Iblis, how was she so fucking beautiful, even after she'd been crying? Her blue eyes and pale skin reflected the light of the stars, and he wanted nothing more but to kiss her perfect lips and let her know everything would be alright. He would make it alright.

"And besides, if I do anything you don't like, now that your magic works on daemons, I give you permission to use your *visanis* on me," he added, the corner of his mouth tipping up as he tried to break the sad tension.

She huffed a small laugh, and the corners of her mouth tilted up ever so slightly. There was his prize again. "But Ty…what are we going to do? Everything was already complicated enough, and now this. I have no idea how my Coven will react to a mixed child. Greya is matriarch but she can't convince everyone to accept me, and if they overrule her and it goes like it did for your mother, then I could be banished."

"Shh, viper, calm down. We'll figure it out together. I promise."

"No, Ty, you don't understand," Ena responded, refusing to be soothed. "It all makes sense now—why we saw the Canus Elk."

Ty felt his entire body turn to ice.

He'd nearly forgotten about the Canus Elk. The one they'd seen right before they arrived at the Underworld, the one that died giving birth.

"You don't think…?" Ty asked, his voice dripping with fear.

"I don't know," Ena said. "Not for sure, but it can't be a coincidence that we saw her just weeks before I, myself, got pregnant. And whatever it means, whatever it portends for the future for us and our baby…it can't be good."

She was right. Whatever that meant, whatever was coming for them...they had to take action to protect themselves. Whether it was Cole and his followers in the Underworld, or the Covens and the ways they might act against Ena and their child, one thing was clear—they needed to find somewhere safe to go, and he wasn't sure the Auster Coven was the place for that.

"You're right. I don't think we should stay here," he said to her, gripping her face in his hands and stroking her cheeks with his thumb. "At least not now, until we see how things settle. We'll talk to your sister, see what she thinks, and then we'll leave."

She nodded in his hands, her eyes aflame with the same fearful certainty as his. "Where do we go?" she asked, her voice still shaky, but she wasn't terrified. Facing the unknown didn't scare her as much as it used to.

"I might be able to provide some guidance on that."

The voice came from the edge of the forest, and they turned to see Mel approaching, their slight figure shrouded in darkness at the edge of the tree line. "Let's go talk with the new Auster matriarch and then I'll tell you what I've seen."

CHAPTER THIRTY-NINE

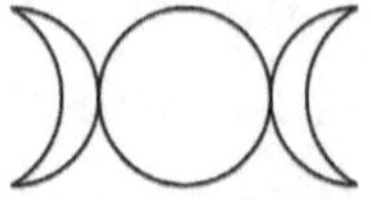

Ena

ENA, TY, AND MEL made their way back to the Sacred Grove. Ena was wobbly on her feet—all the emotions of the last several hours had taken a significant toll on her. She needed to rest, but she wouldn't be able to until they came up with a plan for what came next—for all of them.

Blessedly, Ty was there to steady her, his grip steadfast and warm around her hand. Her heart was still distraught and full of guilt about Heran, confused and overjoyed about the breaking of the bond, and simultaneously terrified and hopeful about the prospect of a child. It was almost too much to process, and she didn't know what to focus on.

So right now, she chose the child—*her* child, *Ty's* child—and how to make sure it was safe.

Gaia, that felt wild to even think. She'd never spent much time thinking about having children at all, let alone Ty's child, given their circumstances. And now, this was all happening so fast, she didn't know how to feel about it. It was only in the past couple days that she'd begun to suspect she was with child. She'd been feeling so rundown and food had been increasingly unappetizing, but it wasn't until she'd had a second to herself by the river to think that she'd realized without a doubt.

And she was so overjoyed that Ty had chosen to stay with her—she couldn't imagine handling this on her own—but still...the thought of a child was overwhelming to her. She couldn't even begin to contemplate what that would be like or if she would even like being a mother. What if she wasn't good at it? What if she couldn't keep it safe? What would her future even look like now?

These vicious thoughts swarmed inside her, and she hoped to Gaia that whatever Mel had to share might guide them. But mostly, she just needed to talk to Greya. She would know what to do.

The three of them arrived in the Sacred Grove to find Turner and Cris huddled around the fire with Greya, who had since returned, but without Perse.

"How did it go?" Ena asked, taking in her sister's deathly pale countenance. The loss of Heran was clearly hitting her hard.

"Perse's awake, but groggy. He's too drowsy to help with...the body, so I was thinking..." She paused, addressing the group with uncertainty. "I want to go back to the house so we can all talk. I explained a little of what is going on to Perse, but I want him to be there for this. And besides, I need someone to help carry her back," Greya explained, purposely avoiding looking at the body in question.

"Do you think that's safe?" Ty asked. "Us all going back to the village?"

"I think we should take the chance. Now that Heran is gone, there will be no one else in the house to disturb, and there's still a few hours before dawn, when everyone else will be emerging from their houses. We'll be more comfortable there anyway."

Ty gave a reluctant nod, but she could tell he felt wary about it. She, on the other hand, felt relieved.

They'd been traveling on the road for weeks. The thought of being warm indoors, even for an hour—let alone in her own village—sounded so incredibly amazing she almost teared up.

"Should we...?" Turner asked Ty quietly, gesturing towards Heran, where she lay shrouded on the ground.

"If that's okay with you and Greya?" Ty asked her.

Ena looked to her sister, who nodded at them.

"Yes, thank you," Greya said, her voice cracking a bit.

Together, Ty and Turner carefully lifted Heran's body, which had already begun to stiffen in the cold, and held it respectfully between them. Following Greya's lead, the six of them began to walk the familiar, well-worn path back towards her village.

Ena was struck with memories of the last time she'd walked this path—right before Ty, Turner, and Steig had taken her on the night of Samhain. She'd been so lost then. In many ways, she still felt that way.

The village was dead silent as they weaved through the houses. The gardens were all dormant this time of year, but still, Ena could make out the familiar spot in front of Thyla's parents' house where she, Ena, and

Greya had spent hours replanting garlic one fall after a chicken had escaped and torn up the original plantings.

Then, of course, there was the old stone barn, where Ena had often been sent to milk the goats. Though it had never been her favorite activity, she had loved the quiet comfort of the animals, and the peaceful stillness of her mornings spent there before the rest of the Coven would wake.

Seeing these familiar haunts, it hit her now—despite her uncertain future, she didn't want to return. She couldn't. Not truly.

Following Ty to the Underworld, despite all the bad that had happened there, had set her free in so many ways. And even though after she'd been attacked she'd desperately craved the safety of home, she realized now that she could never go back to the way things were. She had changed too much, and that safety she'd once felt here was gone. She could only go forward, and what her path looked like now...that was still painfully unclear.

But at least she had Ty with her once more. At least they could figure it out together.

The six of them silently approached the newest, largest house in the village—one Ena hadn't yet seen. It had been rebuilt on the very spot the old house had been, before it had burned to the ground thanks to Turner's Power, and Ena could still see the remnants of scorched earth on the outer edges of the garden by the new fence that encircled it. Ena realized that Perse and Greya must've been living here also since their handfasting. She'd always thought Greya had intended on moving into Perse's house, but maybe with Heran's health declining they'd decided to stay.

Guilt hit Ena anew that she had been absent for all of that. There'd been no indication of Heran's frailty when she'd last seen her in Occidens.

Please, my child.

Heran's final plea rang through her mind again.

Had she betrayed her by doing this without her permission? Mel maintained that the future was unavoidable, but even so, Ena was filled with so much regret for the way things had turned out.

Her vicious, self-blaming thoughts swarmed again as they walked up the path and Ena spotted Fergus, the black cat, padding down the path to greet them. She read his signs and Knew he was quite happy to have visitors this late, and particularly happy to smell Ena again. He entwined himself around her legs as she walked, purring quietly as they entered the large front door.

The home was warm and smelled of freshly cut wood. She instantly felt an overwhelming sense of déjà vu given that the layout was nearly identical to the old house—the house she'd grown up in with Greya and Heran.

Turning to her right, she made her way with the others into a small sitting room, where an extremely sleepy-looking Perse sat perched in a cushy chair by the fireplace.

"Ena!" the man exclaimed as she approached. He stood up slowly, steadying himself on the arm of the chair, and wrapped her in a warm hug. "We've been so worried about you. I'm so relieved you're alright."

Ena had forgotten how tall Perse was—even taller than Ty, but much lankier. She only came up to the lower part of his chest, but her arms easily wrapped around him as he hugged her tightly. "It's so good to see you, too, Perse," she said, squeezing the man who'd always been like a brother to her.

Ena pulled back to look into his sleepy hazel eyes that began to fill with sadness and suspicion as Turner and Ty walked in with Heran's body.

"Did Greya explain what happened?" Ena asked him, redirecting his attention towards her.

"Yes, a—a bit," he said, clearly confused and overwhelmed already by the little he'd heard, and she didn't blame him.

"Where should we put her?" Ty asked Greya, who had closed the door quietly behind them.

"You—you can put her in her bed. Upstairs, first door on the right. I think that will be for the best," Greya said, her voice grief-stricken, but decisive.

And Ena realized with a swell of pride that even in this small first decision, Greya was stepping into her new role. Because on top of all her grief, she would now be expected to step into Heran's shoes and lead the Coven through this tumultuous time.

In many ways, she felt like she was truly seeing her sister for the first time—not as the stalwart eldest sibling who'd been born to lead and always knew what to do, but the ever-changing woman, just like her, who was trying to find her path in this world. Greya had been thrust onto hers unexpectedly tonight, and Ena so badly wanted to stay and help her, but it was a journey

Greya would have to undertake alone, just as Ena had hers.

As Ty and Turner moved towards the stairs in the hallway, Greya ushered the rest of them into the sitting room, where Ena took a seat on the large new upholstered couch next to Mel and Cris.

"Greya," Ena said, drawing her sister's attention to her as she perched on the arm of Perse's chair. "What's your plan for Heran? What are you going to tell the rest of the Coven?"

Greya smoothed the front of her dress, which was wrinkled and covered in dirt from their time in the Sacred Grove. "I've been thinking," she began. "I'm not going to tell the rest of the Coven about what happened here tonight. They will be reeling enough from Heran's death. They don't need to know the truth of how it transpired—not yet," she began, clearly wrestling with the idea of spreading more lies. "I want to slowly start to introduce the information that's been kept from us—about the daemons and the amulet and the bond—before we tell them about our involvement in breaking it, or anything about what happened with Gaia and Iblis, because I don't even fully understand that myself yet," she said, rubbing the space between her eyes as she closed them briefly. "As far as the rest of the Coven will know, Heran went peacefully in her sleep."

Perse reached out, grabbing her hand, and she gripped his arm back, steadying herself on him.

"I think that's smart," Ena replied. "If they suspect foul play from daemons was in any way involved with

Heran's death, it'll be harder for them to accept them back into society."

"Exactly," Greya said.

The fire crackled and popped in the hearth, and Ena's body began to thaw a bit in the warm coziness of Greya's house.

"But," Greya continued, "I recognize that, pretty soon, the river will run its course, and word of daemons' and witches' magic working against one another will alert the Covens that there's been a change in the status quo. I'm hoping that laying the groundwork by explaining how daemons were forced into serving Iblis will keep things from escalating."

"And what do you think the daemons will do?" Cris asked Ena.

As if summoned, Ty and Turner reentered the room. Ena noted how tired Ty looked as he came to sit by her side, gently resting his arm over the back of the couch behind her.

"Cole, the leader of the Underworld, will likely come looking for Ena, Turner, and I," Ty answered once he'd settled. "Looking to punish us or interrogate us about what happened. The majority of daemons don't know about the amulet, so they're probably scrambling to understand what happened right now, but I'm sure he already suspects we had something to do with it," Ty explained.

"Where will the two of you go then?" Cris asked Ty and Turner. "Will you return and attempt to overthrow the king as you planned?"

Ena caught Ty's eye. She had no idea how the others would take this, but she chose to trust in them—the people who had helped them all this far. They deserved to know.

"About that," Ena began. "There's something else you all should know."

Ty lowered his arm around her shoulders, encircling her with his warm, solid presence. She saw Turner's eyebrow raise at their obvious change in relationship status, and a look of confusion fall over Greya's.

"I'm pretty sure I'm pregnant," she said.

Silence greeted her, the only sound the popping of the fire and the distant meow of Fergus.

Then her eyes went to her sister. Greya's face was a mixture of shock and concern. "Gaia, Ena, are you sure?" she asked.

"As sure as I can be until it grows more," she said. Part of her wanted to place her hand on her lower abdomen right then, to see if she could feel something—any-thing—about the life growing inside her, but she didn't. For some reason, the thought of doing that felt terrify-ing in and of itself.

Then Greya moved to her—so fast she barely had time to blink—before enveloping her in a hug. "What a blessing from Gaia," Greya said, as she squeezed Ena tightly.

Was it a blessing from Gaia? Part of her felt that way and was endlessly fascinated by the idea of a child—*her* child—but another part, a louder part, was so terri-fied and overwhelmed by the thought that she couldn't imagine how this was a *blessing*. It felt like a terrifying unknown that she didn't know how to face, and that thought brought another wave of guilt that she wasn't ready to deal with.

"Are you feeling alright?" Greya asked as she pulled back, looking Ena over more thoroughly.

"For the most part, yes. Just tired," she said, giving her sister a reassuring smile. She didn't want Greya to worry. She was doing that enough for the both of them. "There's more, though," Ena said, addressing the group once more. "A month or so ago, before Ty and I arrived at the Underworld, we saw a Canus Elk."

"Wow, really?" Cris asked, his pale eyebrows jumping up. "That's amazing."

"It would have been, except it was in childbirth, and I...I tried to save it, but it died. And the calf was stillborn."

Ena watched Mel's brow lower on their face. Their focus on the conversation clearly came and went, but this had gotten their attention.

"Ena," Greya said, reaching out to comfort her where she knelt at her feet. "Just because you saw them die does not mean you will too. Do you understand me? Yes, Canus Elks are auspicious and hold meaning, but that meaning is not always clear."

"I know," Ena replied, feeling slightly relieved to hear Greya say that. "But still, I don't want to take any chances. What if it's a warning? What if it means our child is in danger? Cole could be coming for me. He knows I was involved in whatever Ty was planning, and even if he's not, although I know you and Perse will support me no matter what, I can't say the same thing about the rest of the Covens. Either way, I can't stay here."

Greya closed her eyes, the reality of her situation sinking in, but when she opened them, she was all fierce loyalty. "You're right," she said. "You can't stay here. Not now, not until I have a chance to clear the way for you."

"Where will you go?" Cris asked. "You can't travel alone. It's not safe."

"She won't be alone," Ty said, replacing his arm around her shoulders now that Greya had released her. "I'll be with her."

"What do you mean?" Turner chimed in, his brow furrowed in confusion. "You're not going back to the Underworld?"

"No. I've decided that my place is with her, and not in the Underworld. Not anymore."

Turner grit his teeth slightly and looked away, and Ena could tell that he felt some type of way about that declaration from Ty, but he didn't say anything.

"As to where we'll go," Ty continued, ignoring Turner's negative reaction for now, "it seems our seer might have some insight about that."

Ena looked to Mel then. "So, are you ready to tell us what you've seen?"

Mel nodded at her. "I've seen where you go, where you're supposed to go—both of you—but I don't think he's gonna like it," they said, gesturing at Ty.

"What do you mean?" Ty asked, his brow deepening in wariness.

Mel sighed, as if steeling themselves for an inevitable reaction. "You remember the others I told you about, the group that worships Omnis?"

Ty and Ena nodded in unison.

"I've seen you with them, and with her. Your mother."

Ena's jaw nearly hit the floor.

"My mother is with the group that worships Omnis?" Ty asked quietly, his brow furrowed but his face otherwise unfeeling. The only indication that this troubled him was the sensation of his arm tightening around her.

"Yes," Mel replied simply.

"And you think we need to go to them too?" Ty asked.

"All I know is that I've seen you with them, so I would assume you do *need* to go there, but I'm not sure."

Ena supposed that made sense but she didn't like how uncertain Mel sounded.

"Where is there? Where are they?" Ty asked.

"Somewhere on the other side of the Chasm Mountains."

Ena stiffened. The other side of the Chasm Mountains? No witch that she knew of had ever been there. There were rumors about what was on the other side, and up until just a few months ago, she'd thought Ty was a rare mortal from there, but, of course, that had turned out to be a lie, so who's to say what were truths and what were falsities spread by daemons. And then, of course, there was that story Greya used to tell her when they were children...but she'd always assumed that was just a child's overactive imagination.

"Why would they need to go there?" Greya asked Mel.

The witch just responded with a noncommittal shrug.

"Well," Ena answered instead, her mind racing with possibilities. "If Ty's mother went there, they might accept a witch who has been in league with daemons, so it could be a safe place to deliver the baby." But would that be safer? To travel such a far distance and entrust themselves in the hands of people they had never met before?

"Why not just pose as mortals in a mortal village instead? If Ty grew his hair in a bit and covered some of those tattoos, he'd be less recognizable," Cris suggested, waving in Ty's general direction.

"That certainly would be easier," Ena said, her mind spinning with apprehension. But something in her gut—no, something in her Knowing—told her this was correct. This was Gaia's will. "But clearly we do go there. If Mel has seen us there, then it's inevitable, and there must be a reason."

She couldn't deny that everything had led them to this point—her having the vision from the amulet, a vision given to her by Gaia, had led them precisely *here*, to breaking the bond, and to the realization that Gaia and Iblis were far more intertwined than they'd previously thought. She just didn't know how or if that realization and these worshippers of Omnis were connected to the safety of their child, but she had no other options. She had to keep trusting her path. There was just one more thing she had to know...

Part of her didn't want to ask. She didn't even know if Mel would tell her. They were so secretive about the future, but she knew she would regret it if she didn't.

"And what about the child?" she asked, afraid already of the answer. "Have you seen anything about them?"

"I have seen a child, yes," Mel responded gently, her brown eyes filled with kindness.

"Have you seen anything else? Will the child and I be okay?" Ena pushed.

"I..." Mel said, closing their eyes as if searching their mind. "I am still trying to understand what I have seen, and that is the truth. I cannot tell you when I myself do not yet Know it all."

Ena sighed. She'd expected that answer. She was, unfortunately, growing used to Mel's cryptic slow drip of information from their visions. But she didn't blame them. If anything, she understood. Besides, she'd been getting good at facing the unknown—she could do this too.

"Ena—are you sure about this?" Greya asked. "I know it's what the seer has seen but I really don't like the idea of you and Ty traveling over the Chasm Mountains alone in the late winter—let alone while you're pregnant. What if something goes wrong with the baby?"

Turner cleared his throat. "They won't be alone," he said, repeating Ty's earlier words back to them. "I'll go with them."

Ena turned to look at him where he leaned against the wall, his face set in determination.

"I don't know anything about pregnancy or babies, but I can help," he continued, looking from her to Ty. Clearly, whatever issue he had with Ty not returning to the Underworld was not disrupting his intense loyalty to the man.

"We'll be grateful to have you, brother," Ty responded, giving him a nod.

Ena felt relieved to hear it, but Greya still wasn't convinced.

"No offense, but I don't exactly trust two daemons with my pregnant little sister, no matter how nice they might be."

"I know it's risky," Ena said to Greya, then looked over at Ty. "But something tells me it's right. That's where we need to go. And if we make it, Ty's mother is a witch. She'll at least know how to deliver a baby safely."

"Okay, then," Greya said, her voice filled with acceptance. "If you think this is your path—I trust you. I should've been doing that all along."

Ena looked at her sister and gave her a small smile.

It felt immeasurably good to have her sister and Perse back. To have Ty back. To have friends who understood and supported her. And while going over the Chasm Mountains felt terrifying—it gave her hope that she had all her friends and family on her side, at least in this moment.

"The sun is almost up," Perse pointed out, looking at the window behind her. "You all should be getting back to the Sacred Grove."

"Wait for me there," Greya said as they all began to stand in a rush. "I'll gather what travel supplies I can for you all."

Ena nodded, her stomach suddenly filled with butterflies.

Part of her couldn't believe they were about to do this—journey over the Chasm Mountains. Ty gave her hand a squeeze, as if sensing her apprehension and drawing her attention back to him.

Her eyes locked on his beautiful green ones, and she was filled with a feeling of *rightness*, just as she had been when she'd decided to go with Ty to the Underworld. She knew without a doubt that she'd face whatever unknown she had to to be with Ty and keep their child safe.

CHAPTER FORTY

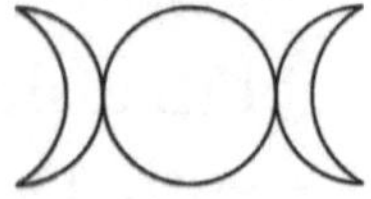

THE FIVE OF THEM walked quickly and quietly back through her village to the Sacred Grove. As they reentered the ring of trees, they began to ready their horses for their respective journeys. It went without saying that they needed to be on their way by sunup to minimize their chances of being seen by the rest of her Coven.

No one spoke, but there was a feeling of finality between them all. They'd been together for a while now with one common goal in mind, and now they were going their separate ways. Soon, Ena found herself standing next to Ty and Turner, ready to leave as soon as Greya arrived with the supplies, while Mel and Cris stood opposite them with their single horse.

Ena found herself filled with a sudden emotion. A sudden reluctance to say goodbye to these witches. They may have been from different Covens, but they'd believed her, and supported her through both the balance and the chaos.

"Will you be alright going back to Occidens?" she asked Mel, not quite knowing how to say goodbye after all they'd been through.

"I don't know," Mel replied, kicking some dirt with their boot. "But it's the only place I have to go. I think Syrelle will understand that I was following Gaia's will and did what needed to be done. Eventually."

Ena could sense the weariness in their voice. None of them had slept last night, and Ena knew the journey would be toughest on Mel, given the burdens of their Gift. She was glad they would have Cris with them, for part of the journey at least.

"And you?" Ena asked Cris. She'd been hesitant with him, especially after her pregnancy news and very obvious reconciliation with Ty, because she knew he was still healing from her rejection of him. But he had come to her aid when she'd asked—he'd trusted her, and that meant so, so much. So she hoped, given time, that they could be as close as they once were, because she knew he was a friend she wanted to keep for life. "Will you be in a lot of trouble with Northe?"

"Some," Cris sighed as he stroked the neck of his horse, who was stomping anxiously to leave. "My leaving was unapproved, but if I make up some excuse about going after a girl..." Cris said, turning a bit red in the face. "I think I'll be alright in the end."

"Good," she said, giving him a small smile.

"But I was thinking," Cris continued. "Do you think I should tell people too? About what I've learned? I know Greya said she was going to slowly introduce people to the information that's been kept from us, and Occidens already knows, apparently, so I thought maybe I should do that too. For Aquilo."

"I do," Ena said, pleased that he was willing to take that chance. "The more we can get Auster and Aquilo on the same page, the more we can be prepared for what might come with the daemons. But I'd be cautious about what you reveal and to whom," Ena warned. "We don't want to escalate tensions."

Cris nodded in agreement. "I think maybe I'll start with my brothers at least, and see how that goes. They can be stubborn as hell...but they're good witches. I think they'll understand."

Just then, Ena heard movement along the path in the woods, and Greya and Perse emerged, their shoulders laden with several more saddlebags filled to bursting.

After some logistical wrangling, they got the saddle-bags distributed between the four horses, and they stood ready to leave.

The sun was just beginning to lighten the sky, and Ena tried not to cry. She didn't know when she would see her sister and brother-in-law again, or Mel or Cris, and it almost felt too big to contemplate.

Greya, as if reading her mind, came over to grip her shoulders.

"We will see each other again, Ena," she said firmly. "This is not the end. You go and do what you need to do to keep my little niece or nephew safe, and I'll make sure the Coven is ready to welcome you when you return."

Ena pulled her sister in close and wrapped her arms around her. She smelled like clean laundry and baked goods. She was everything that was good and warm about her home, her Coven, and part of her never wanted to let her go, even though she had to. Even though it was best for her.

"I have something else for you," Greya said, pulling a small, green-tinted glass bottle from her pocket. "This is some water from the Sacred Pool, the last that I have for now. I read that if you pour it into a bowl, you can use it to communicate with me if you need to, just like you did before."

Ena gripped the bottle in her hand, clinging to it like a lifeline. The only thing tethering her to the shore, to keep her from being swept away from her sister forever.

"That's smart, Greya. Thank you. For everything," Ena began. "And I just want you to know...I'm so proud of you. I know you have some big shoes to fill, but something tells me you'll be the best matriarch our Coven has ever had."

Greya's eyes teared up as she pulled her in for another hug, the two of them leaning on each other, growing together, like they'd always done. And Ena was filled with a sudden confidence that, even though they had to grow separately now, they would always come back to one another. As sisters, they were a part of each other, and they always would be.

Greya released her reluctantly, and Perse came to her next, pulling her in for a hug too.

"Don't run off with daemons again without telling us, okay, kid?" he said lightheartedly. "Or maybe just bring us with you. I bet they have some wicked good parties down there," he added with a wide grin.

Ena laughed at that. If he only knew about the *alluci-nae*...

Greya looked to Ty and Turner next to her, giving them a nod of approval. "I'm trusting you both to keep my sister and her unborn child safe. I know there's been mistrust between our peoples in the past, but I sincerely hope that our generation can move past that, and I for one am going to do my part to lead it. I want you to know that."

"Thank you," Ty said, giving Greya a nod of respect.

Greya returned it, and gave Ena one last glance, eyes full of emotion, before turning to go.

But Ty stopped her.

"Wait—" he said, his voice coming out urgent, as if he'd been holding something back. "One more thing, before you go."

He stroked his beard in that way he did when he was nervous, and he seemed to be filled with a frenetic kind of energy all of a sudden.

"Now that you're the matriarch, I wonder...do you have the authority to perform handfastings?"

Ena's heart leaped in her chest, and her head whipped to Ty. Was he serious?

Greya arched her brow, looking from him to Ena. "Yes, as a matter of fact, I can," she answered, a small knowing smile gracing her face.

"Good. Because I want to prove to you, to all of you," Ty said, looking around the group, "that I will do my best to keep Ena from harm. But most of all, I want to prove that to you," he added quietly, looking down at Ena.

Ena stood in stunned silence.

"What do you think, viper?" Ty said, turning to her with a deep vulnerability in his eyes. "Will you handfast with me?"

Ena's heart stuttered in her chest. Never in her wildest dreams had she thought this would be possible. Just hours ago, she was prepared to say goodbye to him forever, and deal with their child alone.

She wanted to break down sobbing. Because did he know that everything she did was for him—to love him, and be with him? She had never dared to hope for such a thing—not after nine years of separation, and all the obstacles between them in the Underworld, but now she realized: nothing in this world would make her happier than to be his wife. Nothing would make her feel more whole and safe and loved than being handfasted to him. To be *his* forever.

Raising her hand to his beautiful face, she looked at him, deep into his eyes so he would know she meant it. "I love you, Ty," she said. "I've loved you for nine years. I'm already yours, and I always will be. Nothing would make me happier than to be your wife."

She saw a film of tears spread over Ty's eyes as he pulled her in for a kiss. His mouth was warm and soft and he smelled like home. He kissed her deeply, and thoroughly, and Ena wanted to melt into it and never stop. It had been far too long since he'd held her like this, since she'd felt his lips on hers, but she was suddenly reminded that they had an audience when Greya cleared her throat pointedly.

"One problem—I don't have any handfast bindings," Greya said apologetically. "I can run back to the house to get some, but I'm worried—"

"No need," Ty said, reluctantly letting go of Ena's face and reaching to pull something out of one of his bags.

It was the handfasting ropes. The ones he'd taken from Heran's house and used to bind her wrists when they'd kidnapped her.

"You didn't seriously keep those?!" she asked him, disbelief and amusement warring in her voice.

"Of course I did. They're good ropes," he said, snapping them tautly.

Greya smiled widely at them. "Well alright then. We don't have much time, so let's do this."

***

The seven of them moved into the center of the Sacred Grove—witches and daemons alike. Friends and family. Allies and rivals.

The trees were illuminated with a soft glowing light from the creeping sunrise, casting them in wintery golds.

Greya stood in front of the burning remains of the fire. She gestured for Ty and Ena to come before her, while the other witches formed a sacred circle around them, Turner following their lead.

Greya looked to them both, pride shining in her eyes. "Mother Gaia, Giver of life and Bringer of death, she who maintains the Turning of the seasons and celestial bodies, and balances the Light with the Dark, I call upon you to bless the union of these two beings."

Ena had been present for many handfastings before, but her sister had never been the one to speak these words. It had always been Heran, and a chill went through her at the thought. She wished with her entire heart that Heran could have been here for this moment, but she realized with a sad clarity that may never have happened. In all the sadness and confusion of her passing, it had led them exactly here. To this moment.

Ena felt guilty for it, but she felt a glimmer of gratitude for the path that had led them here, despite all the bad.

Taking the decorative rope in her hand, Greya delicately wrapped part of it around Ena's left wrist—the one that had been broken but had since healed—and continued the ceremony as she spoke the sacred words.

"May your love be like the air—powerful and ever-changing."

She wrapped part of the rope around Ty's wrist next.

"May your love be like the water—constant and deep."

Returning to Ena's wrist, she looped the rope again.

"May your love be like the fire—passionate and all-consuming."

Finally, she laid the rope over top of Ty's wrist one last time.

"May your love be like the earth—stable and true."

Greya's words rang out across the grove, and Ena could feel with her Knowing the birds and squirrels emerging from their homes for the day. She could feel the sun upon her face and Knew the breeze through the trees. It was as if Gaia, or...something, was present—listening, watching, Knowing—as Greya pronounced their union.

"Now the blessing of—oh, fuck," Greya said, slapping her forehead with her hand in almost comedic fashion. "I completely forgot about the blessing of the sacred object. Do you two have something?" she asked, looking between them.

Damn, Ena had forgotten too. Handfasting ceremonies also usually entailed blessing a sacred circular object—a bowl, a chalice, a wheel—something to represent the sacred circle and never-ending bond of a handfasting union. Both couples were meant to protect the object and utilize it on special occasions as a reminder of their bond. What could she—

"Oh, wait," she said. "Yes, I do have something!"

Reaching with her free hand into the small leather satchel attached to her belt where she kept her needle and thread and other small objects that required safekeeping while traveling, she pulled out the sapphire ring Ty had made for her.

When she'd ended things with him, part of her had wanted to get rid of it, but something had compelled her to keep it close. She'd both loved and hated having the reminder of him. It had hurt, but it was also tangible—a physical reminder that their love had been real and it had happened, even if she had had to let it go. And now, she was eternally grateful that she hadn't tossed it into the River Wry.

"You kept that with you the whole time?" Ty asked her, raising his brow in pleasant surprise. He was so smug, as if it brought him great pride to know she'd pined over him, and she had to fight the urge to roll her eyes.

"Of course. Now shut up and let her finish," Ena replied with a small smile, trying hard to keep the blush off her cheeks.

Greya took the ring from her and held it in both hands before them. "May this ring be a symbol of your union and your love, everlasting and cyclical. May you protect it as you protect one another, and rejoice in both its beauty and purpose as you rejoice in one another's."

Taking her own knife from her belt, Greya gently sliced the palm of each of their hands, dipping the ring into the blood on Ena's hand, followed by Ty's.

Ena watched as the blood flowed from Ty's wound, and a wave of dizziness overcame her so suddenly that she had to look away.

Gaia, what was wrong with her? She'd never reacted so strangely to the sight of blood before.

Shaking it off as it passed, she turned her attention back to Greya, who held the ring out before them once more.

"Hearts as one, bodies as one, blood as one. Blessed be," she said reverently.

Greya handed the ring back to Ena, who placed it on her left pointer finger for safekeeping.

The ceremony was complete, and Ena took a second to look around at the friends and family that lovingly surrounded them. Turner had tears in his eyes as he smiled like a gleeful child, and Perse had his hands clasped before him, a look of pride on his face. Cris gave her a small, timid smile, and even Mel looked to be enjoying themselves, or maybe it was just the brief vision-free moment they were having.

And lastly, she looked up at Ty.

His head was haloed by the sun, his strong features stark and beautiful in the light. His green eyes seemed to glow as he watched her and reached out, cupping the side of her face as he stroked his thumb across her cheek. "I love you, Ena," he said softly. "Through whatever unknowns may come."

Ena smiled at him with tears in her eyes—her heart filled with love and fear, hope and despair, for all that had happened, and all that was still coming.

"I love you too," she echoed. "Through whatever unknowns may come."

Epilogue

Cole

HE AWOKE IN THE dark, the pitch black of the room suffocating him.

He looked around, barely able to see his hand in front of his face—but he could *feel* something.

Was there someone in the room? Someone coming for him? The witches? His nephew? His...

No, that wasn't possible. Haden was dead. Haden was gone—he'd taken care of him long ago. His brother could never come for him now.

Still...something wasn't right. His sense of his Master, that pull to the chaos in his mind, that knowledge of how to please him, serve him—it had gone quiet.

Closing his eyes, he retreated into the depths of his mind, the way he often did when he sought Iblis's guidance, and he was pleased to feel him there, but...that urge to destroy, to disrupt, to spread chaos with his Power, it was muted somehow.

What in Iblis's name was going on?

He'd never felt this way before, it was as if...

Clutching at his chest, he rose, moving swiftly through the pitch black to grab his rune stones from the gilded gold table in the center of his chambers. He didn't need light to see them—he knew their placement like the back of his hand.

Scattering them across the table, he picked up the ones that had landed face up, feeling the runes etched into them one by one.

Diabolus

Vocarus

Tellus

Restoras

His body went cold. Those runes...that combination. He'd never seen them before. Especially *Tellus*—it had been defunct since Gaia's abandonment. It had never come face up in a reading before. And that last one...

His blood turned to ice. It couldn't be. How would that even be possible? They had done nothing—*nothing*—to regain Gaia's favor. She had abandoned daemons centuries ago, and they'd never once sought her forgiveness. Why would she...be restored to them?

Closing his eyes once more, he sought that connection to his Master, and there it was—there *she* was. This sense of...contentment, and peace. Balance. Everything the witches stood for, everything the witches *forced* onto them, onto the world. Everything they leveraged to maintain power and control over mortals—it was now here. Inside him.

The thought disgusted him.

Closing off his connection to Iblis, he threw the rune stones down and grabbed his darkrock lantern from the decorative oak table next to his bed. Fumbling around in the drawer, he pulled out his flint and striker, and lit the lantern, instantly bathing himself in its deep-blue flame.

Storming shirtless and shoeless from his chambers, he moved down the dark passageways of the Underworld toward the Great Antre.

An *imperi* walking the opposite way froze when he saw him. "M-my king, I was just coming to prepare your breakfast. Do you require something?"

Cole loathed it when they spoke to him. They knew he wanted them to be silent in his presence—their words not fit for Iblis's ears or his own—so why did they constantly push him?

Of course, he hadn't specifically asked this one not to speak to him, so punishing him would be frowned upon. But no matter. He would find an excuse to later.

"Fetch my brother and the other upper-level daemons for a Convening. Now!" he declared.

The *imperi* turned around and scurried down the hall towards Zak's quarters, but Cole stopped him as he called after him.

"Steig too," he added. He needed to know what his little tool knew about all this...because deep down, Cole was sure of it.

This was no coincidence. Just weeks after he discovered his nephew was plotting something with his witch-slave, this happens?

No, he was no fool. He knew without a doubt Ty had something to do with this—the boy had always been tainted by witches in the most despicable ways.

There was no doubt in his mind that he was responsible for this. And he would fix it, and then, as Iblis was his witness, he'd remove his heir from the line of succession—one way or another.

Rushing through the passageways, he arrived in the Great Antre and took his place on his throne at the head of the Convening table, a plan already forming.

He'd go after him. He'd been lenient when Ty fled, choosing to bide his time until the boy made his whereabouts known again. Without him in the Underworld, the threat was all but gone—or so he'd thought.

But his nephew was more of a threat than Cole had ever realized, and he would find a way to end him at all costs.

In record time, the other upper-level daemons who served him began to arrive.

Zak arrived first, his dark-blond hair ruffled from sleep. Cole would have to talk to him later about the disrespect of his disheveled appearance. Then Gunnar and Chans, his most loyal, obedient hellhounds, and the elders. They all whispered and chattered amongst themselves, and Cole let them.

He didn't need to take part in their tiny, tittering conversations—moving around like scared little mice. When he was ready, he would speak, and they would listen.

Last to arrive was Steig.

The man walked sullenly into the Great Antre, silent as the grave, as he so often was.

Cole tracked him with his eyes. He knew something about all this. Cole knew he did. Steig and his nephew had always been sickeningly close—their bond weak and demeaning in his eyes, given Steig's mid-level parentage.

And because Cole was confident that Steig had had prior knowledge of this travesty, there was only one fitting repercussion.

The man would have to prove his loyalty.

Once all his daemons were settled around the table before him, he spoke to them, their eyes rapt like the good little children they were.

"There has been a sickening development," he began. "Our connection to Iblis has been disrupted." He looked around the table, assessing each of them for signs of disloyalty. For signs of argument.

There were none.

"I am confident this is a power play by the witches, meant to destabilize my rule, and we will not let this stand."

There were murmurs of assent and agreement around the table as he looked to his brother on his right.

"Is it true, my king? Is what we sense correct? That...Gaia has returned to us?" Zak asked.

Cole paused, looking around the table at their sad little faces. "Yes. It is true," he answered simply.

A gasp or two echoed around the chamber.

"How is this possible?" Zak asked, his brow concerned, mirroring the others.

"That is what I intend to find out," Cole replied, his eyes drifting to Steig. "And why I have invited my son-in-law."

Everyone's heads turned to Steig. The man in question returned his gaze, and Cole narrowed in on it, looking for any hint of hesitation—of fear—but Steig gave nothing away.

"How can I assist you in this dark time, my king?" Steig asked, lowering his head in deference.

A show. It was all a fucking show.

"Don't give me that," Cole spit. "I know my nephew had something to do with this." He leaned forward on the table so the man could see him better. "You will tell me what you know, or you will be punished."

"I know nothing of what you speak, my king. You think Ty had something to do with this?"

"Don't fucking question me!" Cole yelled, his voice echoing around the cavern. He could feel his blood beginning to boil.

Against him. They were all against him. They were all trying to oust him in Ty's favor—because Haden always got everything, and now his son would too. Haden always took what was *his*—even her.

The table fell silent at his outburst, and Cole tried to calm himself. To quiet the raging sense of *wrongness* inside him that Gaia's presence had induced.

He was quieter when he spoke next, though he could hear his voice shaking involuntarily. "You will go after him, boy. You will bring him and his witch-slave to me. And if you refuse, or if you disobey me in any way, you will never see your children or my daughter again," he threatened, his eyes boring into Steig's with venom. "Your newfound upper-level status will not stop me from putting you in the collar you deserve."

Steig's eyes burned with a hatred, a fire, that Cole loved to see in him, because he so enjoyed snuffing it out. This piece of trash had never been worthy of his daughter—and Cole would never stop reminding him of that.

"Do I make myself clear?" Cole asked menacingly.

Part of him hoped Steig would try to disobey, if only so he could put him in his place. If only so he could unleash his wrath the way he'd always wanted. But he watched as Steig swallowed whatever he felt, whatever he had to say, before he responded.

"Yes, my king."

"Good," Cole said, enunciating the word so they all heard it clearly. "Gunnar and Chans will accompany you, to ensure you keep to your mission. And I know just where you should go first to look for them."

"Where's that, my king?" Gunnar asked, seeming pleased at this development. The man was always so thirsty to serve Iblis.

"Where this all started for my nephew—the Auster Coven."

END OF BOOK TWO

Bonus Chapters

Wondering what was going through Ty's mind during his spicy scene with Ena in the waterfall cave? Don't miss out on a special bonus version of Chapter 4 from Ty's POV!

Wondering what Ena was thinking when she realized she was with child? Check out the special bonus version of Chapter 38 from Ena's POV!

You can find both bonus chapters on my website at mmparks.com under Bonus Content.

***

Ena and Ty will return in the final book of the Omnis series, coming Summer 2026!

Follow M.M. Parks on social media or join her newsletter for book 3 updates.

ACKNOWLEDGEMENTS

Wow! Another book in the Omnis series is out in the world for all to read. I truly cannot believe it! This past year and a half since I began writing this series has been a whirlwind, with lots of big changes in my professional and personal life. Writing these books, and going on this journey with Ena and Ty, has helped me process so much of my own past and grief as I, too, journey an unknown path. I know without a doubt that I would not be where I am today without the love and support of you, my beautiful, witchy readers! Your kindness and enthusiasm for these books has buoyed me endlessly, and I thank you all so much for your faith in me and my books. I cannot wait to show you all what I have planned for our wonderful characters in the final book of the Omnis trilogy!

First of all, I want to thank my alpha and beta readers. You all were critical in shaping the final version of this book, and I value your thoughtful feedback so much! Jen, Louve CH, Morgan, Carolyn, and Michelle— thank you for taking the time to read my unedited work, you all are the best!

More specifically, I want to thank my sister. You are always there for me when I need you, whether to talk about extremely specific lore details, or big picture life or book things. I love you so much, and I don't know what I'd do without you. Ena and Greya would not be who they are without you and me!

I, again, want to thank my parents for their endless support of this new endeavor. Your belief in me has kept me going when I, myself, doubted if this all was possible! Thank you for always being in my corner.

I also want to thank my kids for putting up with me being on my phone probably a little too much as I try to keep up with social media and all the tasks that come with being an indie author. Your imagination inspires me daily. I love you both always and forever, and through my writing I hope to show you that your dreams can become reality, just like mine have.

Finally, I want to thank myself! Is that weird? I'm not sure but I'm going to do it anyway! I've had to learn to stand on my own these last few months for the first time in my adult life. Through it, like Ena, I've realized I'm a lot stronger than I knew. I want to thank MYSELF for never giving up on me, for always being there for me, for believing in myself, even on my darkest days, and for finally learning how to put myself first.

I hope you all believe in and love yourselves too. Don't be afraid to embrace the unknown, because even when you do, you're never alone, and sometimes the scariest path is the blessed one.

-M.M.

About the Author

M.M. Parks is a fantasy romance author living in Oregon, USA. Her work is inspired by her love for nature, romance, and culturally diverse fantasy worlds that explore other ways of knowing and being in the world. She has a PhD in Anthropology and loves growing paw paw trees on the hobby farm where she lives with her two children and dog.